TO BE
a
Hannah

Sequel of:
Laughing and Dancing Solo

JUDY BUCHHOLZ FRUEH

TATE PUBLISHING
AND ENTERPRISES, LLC

Published by Tate Publishing & Enterprises, LLC
127 E. Trade Center Terrace | Mustang, Oklahoma 73064 USA
1.888.361.9473 | www.tatepublishing.com

Tate Publishing is committed to excellence in the publishing industry. The company reflects the philosophy established by the founders, based on Psalm 68:11,
"The Lord gave the word and great was the company of those who published it."

Book design copyright © 2014 by Tate Publishing, LLC. All rights reserved.
Cover design by Jim Villaflores
Interior design by Mary Jean Archival

Published in the United States of America

ISBN: 978-1-63268-187-4
Family & Relationships / General
14.08.19

TO BE
a
Hannah

Novels by Judy Buchholz Frueh:

Book I: *Laughing and Dancing Solo*
Book II: *To Be a Hannah*

To David,
who walks this road with me daily, enriching
my life and making it incredibly fun.

Chapter 1

How had the parent-child relationship gotten so messed up?
Indefinitely estranged? Almost as if it had never happened. It
had all started out perfectly, where life begins—with a baby.

Jasmine capped her pen and turned the pages back to the
beginning of her journal. Her thoughts followed.

"Mrs. Kirmis?" Jasmine recognized the voice of their social worker.

"Yes, this is she." She grasped the phone tightly, pressing it to
her ear, not wanting to miss a single word of the message.

"We have a baby girl for you and your husband—almost
eleven months old, green eyes, golden ringlets, and a smile that
will warm you through a North Dakotan winter."

Holding her breath, Jasmine's heart leaped erratically. The cool
air-conditioned kitchen, a sanctuary from the late August heat
outside her window, suddenly seemed stuffy. The social worker
continued to give details of the child awaiting an adoptive home.

A baby girl! Another answer to prayer! A sister for four-year-old Jacob, who had entered their home a year ago. Their family would be complete.

Her phone snapped shut. Grasping her little boy's fingers, she excitedly proclaimed, "We are going to go see Papa." News this grand could not wait until Evert came home for supper.

"Now?" Jacob inquired, turning his eyes up to his mother and off the Play-Doh he'd been smoothing out on the table with a miniature rolling pin. "Is Daddy workin'?"

"Yes. Let's surprise him, shall we?" After hurriedly grabbing bottles of cold lemonade from the refrigerator to place in a small cooler, they headed out the door.

Evert, along with his two hired hands, was constructing a house on the outskirts of their small North Dakotan town of Prairie City, population just over seven hundred. Had the temperature been cooler, she and Jacob would have pedaled their bicycles.

After buckling her son into his booster seat, Jasmine flipped the air on high and backed out of the garage, her mind skimming ahead to the beautiful years ahead of them. A family of four! No more waiting; it was happening! How disappointed they had been when she couldn't conceive. Like Hannah in the Bible, she had begged God to be gracious onto her. And He had!

Within minutes, a framed structure topped with a plywood roof came into view. Piles of lumber, shingles, and foam insulation sheets dotted the site where a huge pile of dirt had been pushed back from the structure, presumably dug from the basement hole. One of the guys with his goggles in place was sawing a two-by-four on the makeshift table set out front. Evert was balanced on a ladder measuring a window opening.

Hearing the vehicle drive up, he turned. Recognizing the visitors, he smiled broadly and waved. His wife and son often checked up on him when his carpentry jobs were close to home.

Strong enough to release his own seat belt, Jacob sent it flying and tumbled out of the car to greet his dad. Spotting a hammer lying on the ground, he raced to it. "Can I help you, Daddy?" His dark head leaned back to peer up at his father.

Soaked in perspiration, Evert immediately descended the ladder to ruffle his son's hair. "You betcha. We need another man around here." Jacob awkwardly picked up the heavy hammer with both hands and swung it against a hard chunk of concrete trolled off the cement pad of the garage days earlier.

"Here, Jacob. You can have this scrap piece Mason cut off the board." Out of the nail apron tied at his waist, Evert produced a nail. "See if you can pound this into your wood." Purposefully, the boy accepted the challenge.

Jasmine loved watching her husband and son interact. No doubt, when Jacob had a few more years on him, he would spend summer days working beside his dad, learning the trade of a professional carpenter.

Lifting his cap to run his hand through his sweaty gravel-colored hair, Evert's eyes found Jasmine's. "You picked a pretty hot day to come poking around here."

"I thought you guys could use a cold drink." She pulled the cooler from the car. "Cold lemonade, anyone?"

"Yeah!" Mason bounded right over. "Hey, Rodney. Jasmine's got lemonade!" Another head appeared between the two-by-fours of the garage, a red bandana tied around the forehead to keep perspiration from dripping into his eyes.

"Whoopee! That means we can take a break, right, boss?" Rodney joshed Evert.

"Yup, when my lady appears, all work stops." Evert's lopsided smile showed the intrusion was welcomed. Mason and Rodney each snatched a bottle from the cooler Jasmine held open.

"Come on, little buddy," Rodney said, scooping up Jacob with his other arm. "Let's head for the shade under the roof." Holding onto his wood scrap with the projecting nail in one hand and the hammer in the other, the youngster allowed himself to be carried to cooler quarters. He was used to the men working for his dad.

Peering at his wife, Evert judged. "Now, if I didn't know you better, I'd say there was another reason for you coming out in this scorching heat, other than to save three men from dying from thirst." The lemonade was only a treat. A five-gallon dispenser of ice water was filled each morning for the workday.

Jasmine couldn't stop her smile from stretching like a rubber band, or the bubbles of laughter erupting from her throat. No hot day could smother the excitement exploding in her chest. Heck with the sultry temperatures. She was burning up with something better.

Twisting the lid off his bottle, Evert threw his head back and took a long swig. Wiping his mouth with the back of his hand, he again caught his wife's dancing eyes. "What gives?"

Her gaze held his. "Annie called."

Abruptly, her husband's plastic bottle froze in midair. "And?" he coaxed.

Jasmine couldn't hold back any longer. Raising her voice, she squealed, "We're getting a baby girl!"

Evert's face held stunned disbelief. "A baby girl? For real?" He grabbed her forearms.

"Yes, for real, silly. Nearly eleven months old. She could be in our home within a week or so!"

All traces of fatigue and heat exhaustion were wiped from his countenance. "Oh, wow…whoa! We're going to be parents again!" His voice had started out softly but had escalated with each pause. Wrapping his arms around his wife, he lifted her off her feet and swung her in a full circle.

Her face pressed into his sweat-drenched shirt, Jasmine breathed in his masculinity. It was a good smell, one of hard work, dedication, and strength. They had waited on the Lord, and He was filling all their dreams one by one. She kept a lined journal at her bedside to scribble in each day's summation. Today's announcement would take up a whole page.

His lips at her temple teased, "Let's celebrate tonight by eating at McDonald's in honor of our new baby girl and Jacob."

"Since Prairie City doesn't have a McDonald's, would you settle for macaroni and cheese?" She giggled in return.

He chuckled. "Ugh! Maybe we'd better have a beefsteak while there is only one short person to object." Loosening his embrace, he rested his forehead on hers. "Mrs. Kirmis, do you think you can handle caring for three kids."

"It's two, not three," she corrected.

"Three. Don't forget me." Bending slightly, his lips touched hers, sending a shiver through her insides. Deepening the kiss, the couple forgot where they were.

A shrill whistle broke through the heat waves shimmering in the heavy air. "Hey, boss, does this mean we can take the rest of the day off?" Rodney was grinning a toothy smirk.

Not bothered by being caught in a kiss, Evert raised his head and retorted, "Heck, no. I'm gonna be a daddy again! We're gonna have to work twice as hard!"

Sitting cross-legged on the floor, hemmed in by a circle of wallpaper books, Jasmine flipped through the samples of borders, attempting to choose one for their daughter's nursery. She'd painted each wall a different soft hue of the fall colors, accented by a fresh coat of buttery yellow paint covering the woodwork and closet doors. Wooly lambs, nursery rhyme characters, butterflies, and Popsicle designs careened into each other as she sifted through the pages of the demo books.

Although adoptive parents had the right to change a child's given name, Annie said they might want to consider keeping the baby's first name, as the tyke already seemed to recognize it as her own. Having been born at the flip of the calendar to October amidst the colorful change of the seasons, the birth mother had christened her infant Autumn.

Jasmine was instantly thrilled by the image it painted of the golden, rusty red leaves fluttering in their own backyard when the hot days of summer cooled, ushering in the harvest moon to act as a backdrop for the V-shaped flocks of geese winging their way south. Jasmine's heart had grown wings as well—wings of joy. First, Jacob, and now, Autumn. They had not specifically prayed for a girl, but in her heart, Jasmine was thrilled they'd have a boy and a girl now. If two children would ever be loved, it would be these. Joy was all-consuming. Evert had agreed their little girl would be Autumn Joy.

Jasmine had reread 1 Samuel in the Bible. Like Hannah, she too had been barren and pleaded with the Lord to give them children. But Hannah had added a promise to her request. If the Lord would grant her a baby, she would give the child back to Him. And she did. When Samuel was still a little shaver, Hannah took him to the Lord's house at Shiloh and gave him to Eli the priest. Each year, she would make the journey back to Shiloh to visit her son and give him the new clothes she had sewn for him.

Maybe Jasmine didn't have as much in common with Hannah as she first thought. Giving either Jacob or Autumn away to anyone was beyond Jasmine's comprehension. Maybe she was selfish, but a gift was a gift. There would be no giving away either of her children.

Last night, Evert had come home bearing a bouquet of bright yellow pansies, saying it represented their little girl with the hair of sun rays. He danced a polka across the linoleum floor with Jasmine before heading to the basement to reassemble and carry up the crib stored away after Jacob had transitioned to a twin-sized bed. He was as excited about this family addition as she was.

Continuing to page through more samples, a strip of multicolored leaves seemingly floating lightly in a breeze, flipped open. Maybe it wasn't very baby-like, but the wallpaper border breathed Autumn, Autumn Joy who would soon be sailing into this very room.

Jasmine felt overindulged to have Autumn Joy and Jacob Evert. Her quiver was full. "Thank you, God," she whispered.

Conversation and laughter filled the school's library, temporarily transformed into the setting for a baby shower. Pastel tablecloths covered the round Formica tables, a huge pink helium balloon floating above each one. A lunch of fruit kabobs, cheese-and-cracker platters, and a bowl of sherbet punch was laid out on the librarian's checkout desk. Piles of gifts, opened and still to be unwrapped, were set on each side of Jasmine as Jacob manfully helped her undo the pretty ribbons and paper.

Surrounded by her fellow staff members in the Elton Public School, a fifteen-mile drive from her home in Prairie City, Jasmine and her children were the focal points of attention. Coworkers Cynthia Burns and Andrea Feutz were hosting this after-school party in celebration of the newest member added to the Kirmis household. Jasmine would be starting the school term late this fall, having been granted a six-week leave of absence. Cynthia and she taught the two first grade classes while Andrea was an aid floating wherever she was needed in the elementary school.

Dividing her attention between the gifts at hand and her precious little girl being passed from lap to lap, Jasmine took pride in the heartwarming comments being made about Autumn. Yes, she was a pretty child, resembling Evert with his lighter complexion and hair, while Jacob's hair was dark like his mother. Her dainty bone structure and curly blonde hair were characteristic of a princess in the making. Now just shy of a year old, Autumn could pull herself up along furniture and walk a few wobbly steps hanging onto a chair seat or end table. *Oohs* and *ahhs* pattered through the room when one of the teachers set her on the floor, holding onto her wee fingers. Autumn showed off quite well, taking a couple steps forward before letting her bottom hit the floor. Then she clapped her hands together in surprise. Her audience applauded appreciatively. Jasmine's heart swelled.

"Mommy," Jacob redirected her, "this ribbon is too tight." She eased the restraining tie out of his way, giving him the opportunity to tear the paper off yet another package revealing a baby's photo album. In just the four short weeks since Autumn had made her debut into the Kirmis family, there was already enough photos taken to fill the book. The very first one was taken at the adoption office where Evert and Jasmine had first glimpsed their new daughter. Her temporary foster parent had been holding a tiny underweight version of the toddler that was delighting everyone today. Even though Autumn had never seen Jasmine or Evert before, she willingly came to them, smiling and gurgling, switching back and forth between the two new parents.

"Hey, Jazzy, are you going to be ready to come back to school in two weeks? You look pretty nestled into playing the mommy role." Cynthia quizzed, taking the photo album and replacing it with the next present needing to be opened.

"Evert's mom is going to do day care for us. Since Emily lives in Prairie City too, it will really be convenient. In fact, she has agreed to come to our house, so we don't have to haul the kids. We're hoping Autumn's adjustment to our family will be more secure having Grandma as the sitter." Lifting the lid off the box and sifting through the tissue paper, Jasmine held up a darling pink dress with a ruffled skirt. "Oh, it is going to be fun dressing up my little girl in these frilly outfits."

"Believe me, it is," Cynthia commented. "Katie is in kindergarten this fall. I don't know how much longer she'll let her mommy pick out her clothes."

"It seems impossible Katie is starting school already. It doesn't seem that long ago when you were the one packing up the diapers and bottles and begging us all to save coupons for formula and Pampers," Jasmine reminisced.

Setting a gift bag in Jacob's hands, her gaze skipped to her daughter, now squirming momentarily on June Max's knee; June was quickly losing the challenge of holding a toddler's attention. June, the school secretary, was the ear Jasmine often confided in. Tiny fingers grasped the folds of June's skirt and shimmied down her leg like a fireman's pole. Dropping to all fours, Autumn scooted to the discarded wrapping paper and ribbons at her mother's feet. The first handful of crushed gingham printed paper went into her mouth, a taped bow stuck to her fingers. Shaking her hand to rid herself of the unaccustomed embellishment, her emerald eyes were tantalized by its proximity.

A camera flash caught the moment as the fan club surrounding the mite appreciatively tittered. Bending over, Jasmine detached the bow from her doll's hand and stuck it to the top of the blond curly head instead. Another flash lit up her face. A grin displaying four front teeth was followed by a giggle. Love poured out of Jasmine's heart for this perfect child she had been given. Closing her eyes, she again inwardly thanked the birth mother who had given life to such a miracle, who had unknowingly answered her prayers beyond all aspirations.

Had Autumn come from her own flesh, she could not have been loved more than she already was.

Chapter 2

Together, Jasmine and Evert were introducing their daughter to the first day of kindergarten in Prairie City's public school—a small village school in comparison with the cities across the country. Her class had desks arranged for fourteen students.

With a pink camouflage schoolbag strapped to her back, her golden ponytail bobbing, Autumn blithely circled the classroom. Jasmine had wanted to hold her hand as they crossed the street and traipsed their way down the long hallway, but Autumn shook her fingers loose. There was no fear in her, no yearning to hide behind a parent's pants leg. Her mother fought the stings in the corners of her eyes, and her father watched his pride and joy solemnly; they knew life was about to change. No longer would they be the prime focal points of their youngster's day. It was hard to let go, to realize their baby was a school girl and teachers and friends would widen her circle of interests and activities.

Having readily picked up on learning from her big brother Jacob, Autumn was more than prepared for this initial entrance to school. She could count to thirty, read simple books, and neatly print all the letters of the alphabet. Her schoolbag had been packed for over a month with her new supplies.

Conversely, Jasmine had been mentally dreading this day, her mind filled with maternal memories of the past years: The dandelion bouquets she'd been presented, the handprints pressed into the fresh cement of the pad Evert had poured for the playhouse, the marks on the laundry room door visually displaying the year's growth on each birthday. There were the toddler tea parties on the tiny table in Autumn's bedroom, the picnics at Evert's construction sites, the monarchs caught with the butterfly net, and the mud pies made after a spring rain. A new bicycle in the garage replaced the tricycle, a full-sized bed set where the ivory crib had been, a booster seat instead of a car seat was strapped into the vehicle. The years had flown too quickly. Jasmine wanted to grab on to the moments and stretch them into years like the bubble gum Autumn pulled in long sticky strands from between her teeth.

Shaking her head to dispel the mental reenactments, Jasmine chided herself inwardly. She was definitely not the biblical Hannah. After all, she was only dropping her daughter off for a day of kindergarten, not a lifetime enlistment into the mission field or the military in a foreign country.

"You can go now, Mommy and Daddy. I have work to do." Autumn had found the desk where a tag boldly inscribed in perfect manuscript said her name. Bending down for a hug and a kiss, Jasmine swallowed the lump in her throat. It seemed she needed the little girl more than the imp needed her.

"Bye, sweetheart. I'll see you after school." Then Jasmine walked at a stiff clip beside Evert down the long corridor and out the main door. She climbed into her van, barely had the door shut before a wave of sniffles kept her company all the way to her teaching job in Elton.

Parenting. What a free fall!

Evidently, there was a whole lot of difference between being a teacher and a parent. Jasmine could have kicked herself. Why hadn't she foreseen the problems Autumn would have in school? She and Evert adored their children, teaching them to be self-reliant, showing them how to do simple chores, explaining nature's mysteries, instilling values and manners, sharing Bible stories, and teaching them how to pray—all the time believing they were preparing them to be individuals in a classroom of students.

Yes, Autumn excelled in her reading ability and could hold her own with the math principles taught at a kindergarten level, but her social skills lacked measurably. Her teacher, Ms. Stevens, had already summoned Jasmine and Evert in for a conference by the third week of school. It seemed Autumn was bossy, refused to follow directions, and wouldn't share classroom resources. Her fellow classmates were beginning to steer clear of her. She tired quickly of any paperwork and would stuff it in her desk and take out crayons or erasers to play with instead or wander the room when it was not appropriated.

Thinking back, Jasmine surmised that their day care setup was some of the problem. Having had her grandma to herself during her preschool years, Autumn no doubt didn't have to share toys. When she tired of an activity, Grandma would let her do something else. When she insisted on choosing her way, Grandma probably let her. As parents, they were at fault too.

In her professional role as Mrs. Kirmis, Jasmine had dealt with a parent who thought her child was exceptionally intelligent. She had a hard time convincing the distraught mother that her son needed special services to raise him to the academic level of his peers. "Why, he even can tell you who the president of the United States is!" the indignant mother had proclaimed.

"Yes," Jasmine agreed. "If you taught him the name of the president, I'm sure he can repeat it back, but there are other concepts that he needs help with."

As a teacher, Jasmine Kirmis knew she saw the children on her first grade class roll in a different dimension than their parents did. Her view not only showed the individual child, but also how each excelled compared to peers the same age.

No, Autumn did not sit long in one place; she hardly sat at all, always skipping from one spot to another. Her attention span was short. They knew what a handful she could be during the Sunday morning church service before it was time for her to leave for children's church. At home, the only other child she played with consistently was Jacob. When he tired of her bossiness, he simply walked away and did something on his own.

Furthermore, Ms. Stevens had noted that Autumn always wanted to hug the other children in greeting. Her classmates were tiring of her overtures.

Autumn's problems didn't go away, no matter how many times it was talked about at the supper table at home. She said the other kids were mean and wouldn't let her play. She said she wasn't *bossy*, but the other kids didn't know how to do things right. Jasmine sighed. Evert suggested Autumn let one of her friends choose a game to play, but Autumn said she would if they didn't always pick something babyish. Evert smiled.

As parents, they tried to be more heedful in ensuring their daughter carried through on chores at home. Having had her inadequacies brought to their attention, they were amazed at how many prompts it did actually take for Autumn to complete a task. When playing a board game or sport on the lawn, it was evident her temperament could only handle winning.

They too had noted how Autumn would hug mere acquaintances, even adults, when she first met them. Her familiarity with almost all strangers bothered them. Evert suggested she come along classmates with a one-armed hug around their backs, which wouldn't be quite so smothering. At times, she remembered his instructions. At other times, she was pushed away by a peer who didn't want to share her space.

The school year dwindled on, each day bringing a new impairment. When the Prairie City School principal, Rodger Borstead, called it was to inform them Autumn had accidentally broken a window during recess. The school was dropping the issue but still wanted them as parents to be aware of their daughter's behavior. Autumn gave a different synopsis of the episode. She and another student had been playing target practice with a rock. The center crosspiece of the window frame was the bull's eye. She had missed it. Although the principal had said the school's insurance would cover the repair, as parents, they still wanted Autumn to experience a consequence. After dumping her piggy bank out upon the comforter on her bed, Autumn selected pennies, nickels, and dimes to seal in a plastic baggy and deliver to Principal Borstead. It was a total of $2.31.

Prior to the class Valentine's party, Ms. Stevens was enraged when she caught Autumn opening up her Valentines and eating the candy hidden inside the envelopes. Over the phone, she asked Jasmine if she thought it would be too harsh to make Autumn sit out of the Valentine's party when it came. Inwardly, Jasmine was boiling. *Who ever heard of keeping a five-year-old from a party!* But her reply was more subdued. "Why not put her Valentine box in the closet until the party so Autumn doesn't have access to it?"

Another day, Autumn reported she'd gotten to visit Mr. Borstead. Her antennae raised, Jasmine asked why she'd received such an honor as visiting the principal. "'Cause he wanted to help me with my numbers paper."

Jacob, as a fourth grader, was more knowledgeable on school protocol, and he corrected his younger sister. "You had to go to the office because you wouldn't do your work."

Ms. Stevens had been Jacob's kindergarten teacher as well. Jasmine had esteemed her. Yet Jacob was a totally different child than Autumn. He was liked by his peers and teachers. Quieter in disposition, he cooperated in the classroom and wanted to excel in his studies. Stickers on his papers had been a big deal to him. Autumn could have cared less.

Knowing she was dreading the spring parent-teacher conference, Evert patted her arm before they entered the school. "Remember, you don't want to be one of those parents who drives a teacher nuts." Swallowing a sarcastic reply, she nodded and followed him to the door.

Autumn's academic report was just what they expected. She would be ready for first grade. But in the Social Development and Work Habits columns, check marks dotted the page, noting improvement was needed in numerous categories—works well in a group, exhibits self-control, follows classroom rules, cooperates well with others, stays on task, follows directions, adequate attention span. Jasmine bit her bottom lip as Ms. Stevens embellished on the negative traits. Lowering her voice almost to a whisper, the kindergarten teacher confided what she thought the parents would take as a great truth, "You know, she could probably use a good spanking once in awhile."

Jasmine's blood pressure soared. Evert's firm grasp on her elbow reminded her to plug a forthcoming outburst as he thanked Ms. Stevens for her time and escorted his wife hurriedly out of the room.

She sputtered all the way home. Never was she so glad to see the last day of the school year in May, not for herself and her first graders in Elton, but for her daughter in Prairie City.

The toddler years had been as vibrant as the colors of the leaves in the fall that Autumn was named for; however, one season makes way for the next.

Jasmine wondered if she was up for it.

Chapter 3

K ids' voices screamed in play, splashing water on each other at the edge of the beach. Along with Sheila and Jane, her two best friends in Prairie City, Jasmine lounged on a beach chair in the afternoon sun, smothered in sun screen, her eyes shaded by dark sunglasses. Sheila and Brent Philips owned the lake cabin on the hill behind them. As an annual event, they invited Jane and Jordan Runk and their children, Emma and Evan, along with the Kirmis family to join them at their lake cabin for the Fourth of July holiday. All being residents of Prairie City and parents of young children, they had a lot in common and welcomed each other's company.

When Evert and Jasmine had introduced Autumn to them in the first days of her placement in their home, the gals had been jubilant. Both the Philips and the Runks had girls close to the same age. Maria Philips was already walking then, and Emma Runk wasn't far behind. The trio would transition through Prairie Public School as the Three Musketeers. Jasmine took it as another sign of how God had chosen the perfect child for their family.

The guys were off fishing on a nearby lake where the walleye had been rumored to be biting, leaving the ladies to laze away the afternoon. They promised a fish fry for supper, and yet Brent had left some frozen hamburger to thaw in the sink. Must be an omen.

Cynthia Burns, Jasmine's coworker in Elton, was recovering from gal bladder surgery. To give her some quiet time and her daughter some entertainment for the holiday, the Kirmis's had brought Katie with them to the lake. Katie, being the oldest of the children assembled on the waterfront, showed uncharacteristic responsibility in supervising the youngsters. Jasmine wondered if it was because she was an only child. Organizing the kids, Katie had them forming sand castles in the wet sand. Denny Philips, a year older than Jacob, joined forces with his friend, vowing to build the tallest castle ever.

Now a gangly nine-year-old, Autumn's golden head bent over her sand masterpiece using a flip-flop to gouge out a moat around her castle. She was a creative child, molding a turret at each corner and a drawbridge to lower at the front gate. Watching her, Jasmine witnessed her turn to her right, where her friend Emma worked on her own structure. Tugging the sand pail out of Emma's hand, she ran to dip water out of the lake to fill her moat. Emma, startled by the theft, looked on then shrugged her shoulders and picked up a plastic shovel to continue her assemblage.

Why didn't Autumn get it? All the social injustices she racked up weren't forgotten by her peers. Sometimes, for fun, she and Evert would make up situations for Autumn and Jacob to act out in the privacy of their living room, hoping their daughter would learn some appropriate social graces. They'd ask Autumn then, "What should you do if someone unintentionally bumps your desk while you are writing? How about if you are playing kickball? The first baseman says you're out, but you don't think so. Another girl is sitting by Maria at the table in the cafeteria, the exact spot where you wanted to sit. What should you do?"

Birthday parties had been a huge drama catastrophe. Prairie City was a small school. To not be asked to a fellow little girl's birthday party was a devastating blast to Autumn's ego. One classmate told her she couldn't come to her party because she stole all the malted milk balls out of the treat bags at the last party.

"Life certainly has changed," remarked Jane from a neighboring lounger. "Remember the years when we had to be in the water with the kids at all times, always fearful they'd wade out too far and be swept away?" Her Evan, at six, was the youngest of the bunch.

"Vacation is a lot more restful now," Jasmine agreed, "but still, I miss not being needed as much."

Sheila, handing them each a fresh water bottle before stretching out on the beach towel laid out on the sand, added, "It's much easier coming to the lake cabin on weekends with the kids being older. When Maria and Mark were in the terrible-twos and turbulent-threes age span, it was easier to stay at home than add lake water to the list of safety zones to monitor."

"We have the teenage years to look forward to next," Jane playfully added. "They should be fun!"

"Yup, we'll get to shop for prom dresses, sit in the passenger seat while our kids drive, and wait up nights when they miss their curfews." Sheila giggled. "I guess if our parents weathered through it with us, we can do the same."

Jasmine hoped she would. There was something different about Autumn compared to Maria and Emma. Sheila and Jane had an easy camaraderie with their daughters. Maria and Emma were apt to plop themselves on their mothers' laps in the middle of a conversation or loop arms with them as they strolled along a pathway.

Autumn was much more standoffish, like she didn't want to be touched. Almost always, a stiffness would course through her when Jasmine would pull her into a close embrace and plant a kiss on her temple. Yet at the same time, she and Evert still had to remind Autumn it was not appropriate to hug people she was not close to. She was an enigma. Although they shared the same house, the same surname, and the same breakfast table, their genes were decidedly different.

Autumn's first grade teacher had tried to spare her parents from a play-by-play of their daughter's daily misdemeanors, but at their parent-teacher conference, she admitted Autumn seemed to have a hard time focusing. Maybe just for their own satisfaction as parents, she should be tested for attention deficit hyperactivity disorder. If the testing didn't indicate a deficient amount of a chemical in the brain preventing messages from passing from neuron to neuron as they should, then great! ADHD could be crossed off as a possible deterrent.

Taking her advice, Evert and Jasmine had taken Autumn to a pediatric neurologist. After doing a battery of tests, he deducted that the ADHD tendencies she exhibited were in the very low range, and he would not suggest a medication for it. Instead, they should work with her teachers on some behavioral modification plans. He also chuckled and said that one report he'd read suggested keeping children away from sweets, especially soft drinks, and load them up with tuna, fresh fruits, vegetables, and high protein foods.

Meals at the Kirmis dining room table were already notably healthy, making it hard to decipher if any diet changes Jasmine made were actually doing anything to alleviate Autumn's hyper behavior.

"That Katie sure is a sweet gal." Jane shielded her eyes against the glare of the afternoon sun, taking in the collection of kids on the waterfront. Katie was helping Evan pack sand into a bucket.

"Yes, Cynthia and Kevin can be proud of how she's turning out. She's starting high school in Elton this fall." Katie had babysat for Jasmine's children at a pretty young age, entertaining them at school when she and Cynthia were setting up their classrooms before the commencement of another year or working late on a project. Both Jacob and Autumn adored her. "There are no airs about her. She is simply just pure sweetheart through and through."

The afternoon languished away with pleasant conversation, a game of beach volleyball, and a water fight with the kids. By evening, everyone was winding down, their energy spent.

At dark, the families congregated on the deck of the cabin wrapped in beach towels or light blankets to fend off the cool breeze from the lake and the bite of occasional mosquitoes. This was the night show—the jubilant recognition of the country's birthday. Brent Philips prepared way in advance for the spectacular fireworks display he showered on everyone the final night of their camp out. Even now, he was at the water's edge assembling the sky rockets in a systematic order for lighting.

Jasmine cuddled into Evert's side on a deck couch. He squeezed her hand, bringing it up to plant a kiss on her knuckles. Jacob plunked down beside him, and Katie slid under the blanket next to Jasmine. The sky was already filled with a million stars putting on their own show.

"Let's see some action, Dad!" Maria Philips yelled into the darkness. A wave of chuckles skipped around the deck. As if in answer to his daughter's impatience, a burst of red and white flames shot from the beach sand into the heavens, sprinkling a sparkle of diamonds into the firmament. A murmur of awe followed. Then a perpetual cascade of fireworks, triggered every fifteen seconds, lit the sky with swirls and streaks.

"Beautiful, isn't it?" Evert intoned.

"A perfect ending to a weekend," Jasmine agreed.

Carrying a bottle of soda, Autumn swung open the screen door and gamely climbed over legs and around bodies to cross the deck. "You're missing the fireworks, honey. Come sit with us," Jasmine invited.

"Nah, I'm going up by Emma," she threw back at them. Jasmine noted Emma sitting between her parents on the top step of the deck. There didn't appear to be room for one more, but when Autumn pulled in, Jordan shifted himself two steps down to give her space. *Guess the assimilation game of what she would do if she wanted to sit by Maria in the crowded cafeteria had no carryover.* Jasmine winced.

"Let it go, hon," Evert whispered near her ear. "She'll mature. Give her time." He had a way of knowing what she was thinking even if she didn't voice it. She rested her head against his shoulder, continuing to enjoy the finger-painted spattering of the heavens. When the last lights died out, everyone was quiet, all lost in their own thoughts.

Abruptly, Denny jumped up, yelling, "Grab a flashlight, it is time to play Ditch!" Immediately, the kids scrambled to find flashlights to take part in a game of hide-and-seek made much more challenging by the darkness. The adults were left alone.

"Wow, I wish it worked that fast when I say, 'Bed time,'" Jordan Runk joked, shaking his head.

"Well, it works for me," his wife Jane sleepily responded, stifling a yawn. "I'm headed to our camper."

"I think I'll turn in, too." Jasmine agreed. "My sleeping bag is calling me." Evert and Jacob had set up the huge tent they used for such outings. Before long, the adults all turned in, allowing the kids to have this one last night together until they decided to crash.

Sunlight streamed into the tent window, heating up the nylon interior. In their sleep, the covers had been kicked aside as the coolness of the night was replaced by a warm humid morning. Katie, Jacob, and Autumn appeared to be dead asleep in dreamland, their mussed hair covering their pillows. Crawling out of the tent, Evert and Jasmine headed for a cup of coffee before tearing down the campsite, giving the weary youngsters a few more minutes of rest. They would be moving slow this morning. The other two couples joined them on the deck for one last caffeine rendezvous.

"Mark us on your calendars for next summer," Sheila Philips warmly reminded her friends, setting a platter of fruit on the picnic table.

"We look forward to this all year, even if that school of walleyes is elusive," assured Evert.

"I like grilled burgers," teased Sheila.

"And anyway," Jordan chimed in, "at least we don't have to clean any fish that way!"

After recapping their mugs a second time, they agreed to start the cleanup procedures.

Rousting the drowsy tenters was no easy task. Jasmine tried singing to them her off-key version of a good morning nursery tune she used when waking them up for school, but Jacob pulled his pillow over his head. Evert tickled Autumn's bare foot sticking out from her sleeping bag. Moaning, she drew it back under the folds of the bag. Only Katie sat up, sheepishly stretching. "Hey, there, sleepyhead." Jasmine tossed her clothes at her. "Did our ghosts play in the moonlight too late last night?"

"Yah, I think so." Katie gave a half smile. "When I was lying in the grass hiding behind the boat trailer, I was tempted to drift off to sleep and let those goofy kids stay up all night."

Chuckling as he started rolling up sleeping bags, Evert surmised, "It will be a quiet ride home today."

After more aggressive wake-up maneuvers, the three kids padded off to the bathrooms with their clothes in hand. By the time they came back, Evert and Jasmine had the tent and its contents packed in the back of the van.

Over the years, the three families had established a routine in putting the grounds back to normal. The Philips did the necessary chores inside the cabin to close it up until their next visit. While the Runks scoured the beach area of toys, inflatables, and loaded their boat back on its trailer, the Kirmises conquered the garage. Evert immediately grabbed a broom while Katie and Jasmine carried the extra lawn chairs and coolers outside to make the sweeping job easier. Jacob volunteered to crush the pop cans accumulated from the weekend, throwing them into a garbage bag as he did so. Bending over to scratch the Philips' calico kitten,

Autumn scooped it into her arms and carried it with her to one of the lawn chairs deposited on the garage pad.

"Come on, Autumn. Everyone helps," Jasmine encouraged sorting through a pile of flip-flops and tennis shoes. Autumn didn't move.

"Autumn!" Jasmine said more sharply.

Autumn wasn't a morning person. Her head jerked up. "I don't see why we have to clean their garage."

"We helped dirty it," Jacob pointed out, smashing another can with his foot.

Crabbily, his sister had an instant retort, "When we have people over, we don't make them clean up the mess. The Philips should take care of their own cabin."

Jasmine turned to stare at her. Sometimes, their daughter could be utterly rude. Why was it so hard for her to be the friend she wished to have?

Intervening, Evert swept his way over to her, stopped, and leaned the broom against her knee. "Here, try dancing with a broomstick for awhile. It won't even seem like work if you think of it as a dance." He snatched up another broom propped against a garage wall and pretended to do a romantic waltz. Autumn tried not to look amused, but a slight grin cracked her sulking face.

Reluctantly, she got up and at least did an imitation of moving the dirt around.

Chapter 4

S itting on a corner of Autumn's cluttered bed, Jasmine valiantly attempted to overlook the shrouded floor, knowing irritation would rankle her like fingernails on a chalkboard. She'd only be able to take it so long before flaring out at her daughter, lecturing with her 156th version of the how-to-keep-your-room-clean speech. Wisely, Evert had mentored his wife into letting their household pack rat arrange her nest as she saw fit, as long as her accumulated salvage stayed within the boundaries of her room. A relationship was more important than the color of a carpet buried underneath a layer of whatever the tide brought in. "A door," he reasoned, "wasn't so much for the privacy of the person inside the room, but for those outside who might be offended by the refuse." Meaning his *wife*. Inevitably, the stillness had been broken one evening by Autumn's earsplitting screech. Her door flew open then banged shut, rattling the dishes air drying in the sink. "A mouse! There's a mouse in my room!"

When her mom and dad shared an I'm-not-surprised look with each other from their recliners in the living room, their sizzling daughter's temperature climbed five degrees.

"Aren't you going to do something?" she demanded, her hands on her hips.

Calmly, Evert instructed, "Go get two mousetraps from the cupboard in the garage."

"You expect me to actually touch those filthy things?" she choked out.

"It's the best way to catch those nasty varmints." He turned the page in the newspaper.

Stomping to the backdoor, she disappeared into the garage. Returning with the offensive traps, her hands were encased in a pair of her father's oversized work gloves.

"I'll get the peanut butter for bait." Evert hoisted himself out of his chair, ready to lend assistance, wisely stomaching his amusement.

Tiny pieces of chewed up pink foil, once covering chocolate Easter eggs, led a trail to her forgotten basket from months earlier. "I think mice find your room inviting," her dad surmised. "You lay out quite a nice spread for them. Here's a chip bag, some stale pop, and some broken pretzels as well."

That night, their disgusted daughter refused to sleep in her room until the unwanted visitor was dead. Gratified by the carcass of the mouse caught in the trap the following morning, she went to work cleaning up her mess without even a parental suggestion.

And her bedroom stayed meticulously neat for two and a half days.

Unaware of her mother's discomfort, Autumn was pulling a dress on over her head; she'd purchased it while shopping with Sheila and Maria in Bismarck, a distant two-hour drive. Having brought it home, she now decided it needed to be taken in on the side seams. Her mom's sewing ability was sure to alleviate the problem.

Staring at the wallpaper border which still seemed to gently sift a tumble of fall leaves through the air, Jasmine was reminded of the day she had glued it to the wall in readiness for the daughter about to become theirs. The autumn pigmentation covering the walls and woodwork was soothing. As it had done back when she sat in the room dreaming of their baby girl, it now too warmed her with its watercolor wash of nature's fall hues. Their baby girl had become a long-legged fair-skinned young lady, her blond hair cascading about her shoulders, ready to enter junior high. What had worked to appease a one-year-old toddler was no longer in the manual. Adolescence had slipped in, and her mom had better be able to bend and flex with the waves.

Her fingernail slid along the bottom edge of the border, torn and picked at in many spots, invariably as Autumn lay in bed at night. Chunks of some of the intricate leaf patterns were actually missing, torn from their paper edging. Running her eyes along the painted walls, mars in the surfaces were noted as well. A puncture in the Sheetrock had been the result of a chair tipping over, and the scuff marks along the woodwork spoke of the use the room had received in the last dozen years. This fall, Autumn would turn thirteen, a teenager. It dawned on Jasmine then that this room was way overdue for an overhaul. Although Autumn had never complained about the room's décor, there came a day when a facelift was needed.

Facing her full-length mirror, Autumn twisted to the right and then to the left, endeavoring to get the full effect of the outfit. She pinched in the fabric at the waist then let it fall loose again. "I don't know. What do you think, Mom? Does it need some redoing?"

Her focus on the ruffled valances gathered along the window top, Jasmine emphatically declared, "I'll say. I don't even know where to begin." Decorating for a toddler who had no say in the matter was going to be far different than designing a room for a teen.

"Really?" Autumn looked confused, eyeing herself in the mirror.

"Why did we wait this long? It should have been done eons ago!" Jasmine was already rising to the challenge.

"It should have been? I only bought it last week!" In confusion, Autumn studied her reflection, wondering what she was missing.

Her eyes sliding to the adolescent, Jasmine laughed out loud. "No, not you. I meant the walls. They badly need a paint job. Your outfit on the other hand looks perfect on you."

Autumn's eyes did a quick loop of the room before coming back to peer at her reflection.

"You don't think it should be sewed a bit tighter at the waist?" She turned sideways, looked over her shoulder, pondering her image.

Standing behind her, Jasmine pulled the material tighter at the waist. "When we do this, it makes your butt stick out, although you don't have much rump to protrude."

Smirking, Autumn agreed, "Yeah, maybe you're right."

"So what do you think of this room? Is it time to give it an overhaul and bring it up-to-date with the grown-up young lady you've become?"

"Gosh, I'd never really thought about it." It was the girl's turn to slump onto the bed. Lying back, she gave it some consideration, her eyes skimming the interior.

"If you were designing the color scheme, what would you choose?" her mother prompted.

"Hmmmm." She sent her mom a sly glance. "I'd paint the ceiling black—"

"No way," Jasmine interrupted. "We're not going to have you living in a cave."

"You didn't let me finish. Then, over the top, I'd paint a glossy galaxy of white stars, every size possible. Oh, yeah. And the stars have to be done with florescent paint. That way, when I lay on my bed, I can see them at night. Wouldn't that be cool?"

"How about a dark blue instead of black?"

"I guess that would be okay. And then the walls, they should be striped."

"Striped?" Jasmine repeated dumbly. Maybe the redecorating idea hadn't been her best idea for an attempt at meeting her daughter on her own terms.

"If the ceiling is going to be blue, the stripes could be different shades of blue like azure, cerulean, navy, powder blue, and definitely some sapphire, plus a burgundy stripe every so often for accent." A contentment settled on Autumn's countenance as she gazed at the opposite wall, almost like the painting was already completed.

A full minute of silence ensued—Autumn dreaming of the utopian habitat she envisioned, and Jasmine racking her brain for a compromise. Did the aspirations of a child and parent ever intersect in such a way to navigate toward the same dream?

"How wide are these stripes?" Jasmine at last entertained.

"Oh, all different widths—tiny and wide and in between." Autumn's hands gestured visually to show what she meant.

"Four striped walls might a bit overwhelming. You might feel like you're in jail. How about one wall striped and a sunrise barely peeking out above your door frame, carrying the burgundy tint to the east wall?"

"Hmmm. That might be a nice effect."

Jasmine was amazed. They were actually in agreement. When was the last time that happened?

Autumn struggled to a sitting position. "Okay, I'll try wearing these duds the way they are. But if anyone makes a snide comment, I won't be seen in this dress again." Adding the new clothing to the pile flung over the back of her chair, she excused her mom. "That's all I needed, Mom."

The home improvement topic was dropped faster than the trap had shut on the invasive mouse. Jasmine wasn't sure if her daughter was excited about it or not or had been playing her along. As for herself, she would miss the autumn equinox the room radiated.

That is if she only viewed the top half.

⁓⁕⁓

Since third grade, the Three Musketeers had attended summer Bible camp together—a solid week away from home, doing fun kid stuff at Crystal Springs Lake on the eastern side of the state. All three looked forward to the annual event the first week in August, packing suitcases way in advance. It was a culminating highlight to the end of summer, one last getaway before school commenced.

When Autumn filled out her preregistration form, she, as always, wrote Maria's and Emma's names down on the line requesting bunk mates. Initially, all three of them had done this in their timidity of being first year campers. But now, four years later, as seasoned campers, it wasn't really necessary. In fact, Jasmine thought it would be best if Autumn would give the other girls some room. Tension had crept into the trio's relationship. There was something to be said about too much togetherness.

Because of their parents' close friendship, they had been playmates since they were toddlers. They also were in the same Sunday school class and in the same grade at school. The girls hadn't had much choice in choosing their own chums. They had been thrown together and mated like socks coming out of the dryer. It had been expected of them. Autumn was a hard friend to have with her moodiness and continual domineering personality. Emma and Maria did most of the giving. Jasmine surmised the girls may have complained to their parents about Autumn's behavior a time or two but were told to let it ride. Day in and day out, that could get wearing. Thus, before mailing off the preregistration packet, Jasmine herself crossed out Maria and Emma's names. Autumn would be furious if she knew, yet hanging out with some new companions might be the reprieve all three needed.

Sheila Philips was driving the three girls to camp. Jasmine had volunteered to pick them up at the end of the week. When Sheila's Suburban pulled into the Kirmis driveway, Autumn was ready for it. Her suitcase, sleeping bag, pillow, and miscellaneous handbags were all piled on the step. The other girls were already inside the vehicle. Autumn pulled open the side door and climbed in, leaving the loading of her baggage to Sheila and her mom. Snapping the rear door closed, Sheila exclaimed, "We're off! I see they're all sitting in the back. As their chauffeur, I'll have my thoughts to myself."

Her friend grinned. "I think you'll be able to hear them just fine from your frontal position." Reopening the side door, Jasmine teased the three junior high girls, "Are you ready for a week of no sleep?"

In unison, the trio let out a whoop. "I don't know why the camp even schedules a bedtime. We talk and giggle all night anyways." Maria nudged Emma.

"We do a lot more than talking and laughing. There are pillow wars to be fought, fingernails and toenails to be painted, hairdos to be fashioned." Emma added.

"Well, you girls have fun, but before you take off, I need a hug from my daughter."

Making a face, Autumn grimaced. "Bye, Mom."

"Not good enough. I need a hug and a kiss," Jasmine insisted, letting her eyes dance.

Reluctantly, Autumn climbed out, groaning. Wrapping her arms around the stoic statue in a tight bear hug, Jasmine rocked her gently. "I love you, honey. Miss you." Before releasing her daughter, she kissed her on the forehead.

"Bye," Autumn returned, alighting a second time and putting a slammed door between them. For the benefit of the other girls, Jasmine's smile stayed pinned in place, but her jovial spirits were already falling at her feet in lumps of broken hopes. Was the lovely girl who looked like a human with a head, two arms, and two legs, empty inside? When God created her, had He forgotten the most essential part—the heart?

Waving until the Suburban was out of sight, Jasmine picked up her dashed hopes lying crumbled on the pavement. That was the good thing about *hope*. It didn't give up. It tried again and again, and that is exactly what she intended to do.

Secretly, Jasmine had been planning the redecoration project of Autumn's bedroom ever since she had broached the subject over a month ago. She had picked up paint chips of blue hues to lay against each other in choosing the colors for the ceiling and stripes. While at the quilt shop in Elton, she had purchased yards of calico printed with a soft smattering of stars to tie-quilt a new comforter for her bed. Evert said he would use his router to mold a wooden decorative strip to replace the wallpaper border of leaves. The curtains were an enigma right now, but hopefully, as the room progressed, the perfect window dressing would come to mind.

But first things first—housecleaning. No way could she paint without getting rid of the trash and organizing the clothes, books, and miscellaneous articles again covering every visible surface. Breathing a sigh of determination, she went to it.

In plastic shopping bags alone, she dislodged thirty-three of them from underneath the bed, some empty, some still hiding a notebook, makeup brush, or a snack her daughter had purchased and then forgotten about. One held stinky shorts, a tank top, and damp towel from a swimming trip at the river. Picking up a black banana peel draped over Autumn's CD player, Jasmine surmised some uplifting music may keep her on a positive keel. After thumbing through the piles of cases on the side table, she selected one and pushed it into the machine. The melodies of Twila Paris relaxed her senses.

She put dirty clothes in the hamper and folded up clean garments. Stripping the bed, she marched the soiled sheets and pillow cases straight to the wash machine. Returning with a black garbage bag, she began ramming in anything Autumn wouldn't miss. Next, she moved smaller pieces of furniture and accessories into the hallway, giving her more room to maneuver. A drop cloth stored in the basement for just such jobs was spread over the carpet. Old blankets draped the furniture she had to leave in the room.

She was ready to tackle removing the wallpaper border. Finding some loose edges, she tugged on them, hoping to remove a long strip of the trim in one motion. No such luck, only a couple of inches at a time let loose and these in straggly ribbons. The old glue was doing its job, adhering stubbornly. Not having a steamer, Jasmine tried wetting a rag with hot water, holding it against the wallpaper until it had absorbed the moisture. Tidbit by tidbit, the paper came off. When she heard the backdoor open and close, followed by Evert's heavy footsteps, she was alarmed at how late it already was.

Poking his head around the door frame, Evert surveyed the room. "Hmmm, looks like my little wife is filming the next episode of *Extreme Makeovers*."

Sheepishly, Jasmine acknowledged her husband home from his workday. "I forgot all about supper! Where's Jacob?" At seventeen, Jacob had already spent a couple summers working with his father in his carpentry business.

"That's okay. I'll throw some burgers on the grill, but first, let me get a screw driver. If we take the frame and mattress out of here, it will be easier for you to paint. You must have also forgotten that our son has baseball practice tonight. He went straight over to Paul's house since he only had a half hour."

Not only did Evert remove the bed, but a dresser and book case as well. Then he gingerly popped off the baseboards circling the room.

Sitting on the back patio, biting into a juicy hamburger smothered with ketchup and pickles, Jasmine went over her week's itinerary with her husband. "I have five days to accomplish this, and then on the sixth day, I travel to camp to pick up the girls."

"Suppose the painting will take a couple of days." Evert passed the bowl of mixed fruit to her.

"More. The stars and stripes are going to be tedious."

"I suspect you're right. She didn't choose the simplest fashion statement for you." He pulled off a couple of grapes from a stem.

"Truthfully, I'm not sure if she cares about her room being redecorated at all. I can only try. What makes her so standoffish?" Jasmine turned to connect with his gray eyes.

"I don't know. Maybe it's a phase."

"Awfully long phase," she mumbled. "Anyway, there is an oval full-length mirror at Penny Pincher's in Elton. It has an ornate wooden frame and is self-standing on two legs. It has a feminine look to it.

"I take it you will be making a purchase from the notorious secondhand store," he teased, knowing how many treasures his wife had already fallen in love with in the past.

Smirking at her husband's badgering of her bargain mania, she admitted, "I already bought it. Delores agreed to hold it for me until Autumn left for camp. The frame needs some touch-ups, but I might paint it white like the stars, or maybe the burgundy accent color."

"Whatever you do, it will turn out amazing." He helped himself to a second hamburger.

"And then there is the quilt top to sew and tie. Heaven forbid I don't have enough hours to hand quilt a piece, but the print I bought will be fine. Maybe if I get it all stretched out, your mom would help me tie it."

"Why don't you do that first and get it laid out in the living room. Then she can work on the quilt while you're painting stars." His suggestion was a good one.

"Tonight, I want to finish up removing the wallpaper border. Then tomorrow, I'll make a run to Elton to pick up paint and the mirror. In the afternoon, I'll sew the top and bottom yardage together, put the cotton batting in between, and get it stretched on the quilt frame. That leaves four days to paint." Jasmine finalized the plan.

And that's exactly the way the week transpired, except the stars took two coats of the fluorescent paint to cover the midnight blue beneath them. Masking tape helped mark the edges of the differentiating stripes, but still, the paint had a way of oozing underneath, giving her multiple touch-ups. Sitting back to take in the effect, she then remembered a sunrise was to peek above the door melting into the dark blue heavens of the ceiling. Her paintbrushes swished again.

The jingle of the telephone interrupted her blending of the dawn hues. Grabbing the cordless phone from its charger with her left hand, she continued applying even strokes of the brush with her right hand. "Hello, Jasmine speaking."

"Hi, Jasmine. This is Steven Peterson." Jasmine recognized her school principal's voice without having to be informed. "Are you enjoying the last days of your summer vacation?"

The summer break was coming to a close quickly. In another week, she would have to start getting her first grade classroom set up for a new school year. "Ah, yes. My summer to-do list at least is getting shorter. But I won't complain, for you are already hard at it."

"The reason I am calling is about a new family from out of state who has moved into our district. There is quite a thick paper trail following the two older students registered in junior high. And then there is a six-year-old boy coming into your first grade class. His older siblings have a diagnosis of reactive attachment disorder which we as a staff haven't had to deal with thus far, knowingly anyway. There is a two-day seminar on the topic in Bismarck on the fifteenth and sixteenth of this month. I am sending a group of my middle school teachers down to attend hoping to get a handle on what we are dealing with. Then I thought, just as a safety net, it probably wouldn't hurt to have you and Cynthia Burns receive some education on this disorder as well."

"As a teacher, any information helping me meet the needs of my children is appreciated. I'd be game." Cocking her head to one side, she added a pink blend of the white and burgundy paints to the bristles of her brush.

"Okay, I'll add you to my list. I'll be in touch to give you the particulars. Have a good day."

Replacing the receiver in the kitchen charger, Jasmine jotted the workshop into the correct squares on the wall calendar.

On the final night before Autumn's return, the conspiring couple's heads didn't hit their pillows until 2:30 a.m. Jasmine was sewing the edging around the quilt top while Evert put the furniture back in the room. Together, they mounted the window brackets for the wine valances of layered scalloped voile over the white blinds. Making up the bed, which had the new quilt comforter touching a white dust ruffle, finished off the room. "Let's get the effect," Jasmine suggested, flipping off the light switch. Side by side, the two sat on the edge of the bed, viewing the canopy of twinkling florescent heavenly stars above them.

Dropping an arm around his wife's thin form, Evert whispered seductively in her ear, "Makes a man think of his courting days, when a pretty chick sat by his side in the porch swing."

Jasmine chuckled. "That would have been the BC era."

Lifting his head away from hers, he objected, "Huh? We're not that old!"

"Bc—before children," she clarified.

"Oh yeah. Back then, we didn't have to use artificial stars to create a mood."

Jabbing him lightly with her elbow, she joshed, "Come on, old man. Let's go to bed."

Even though every muscle of her body screamed for rest, her mind kept racing ahead, refusing to quiet enough to let sleep overtake her. She could hardly wait to show Autumn the surprise. Wouldn't she be amazed? She prayed her hard-to-define daughter would love the room and the effort her parents had exerted for her.

Camp dispersed at 4:00 p.m. on Sunday. After the morning church service and a light lunch, Jasmine was in their silver Impala on her way to pick up the girls. Evert had volunteered to accompany her, but he would have missed the men's annual golf tournament. Aware of how much he enjoyed the friendly rivalry, she discouraged him from going with her.

The drive gave her a couple of hours to think. Then again, maybe thinking wasn't so great. Rehashing her relationships with her children didn't change anything. Jacob, who had arrived on their doorstep a year before Autumn, was an easygoing fellow. Nothing seemed to rile him, except, occasionally, his sister. He accepted his adoptive parents as a given, never dwelling on what his life would have been like had he stayed with his birth parents. Although she doubted he'd choose carpentry as a lifetime career, he willingly followed Evert to work each day during his summer vacation, probably not realizing the expert construction worker he was becoming from the experience. He laughed and joked with the other employees, earning his way up. Copying his father, he would bestow a kiss on his mother's cheek each morning then, whistling a country western tune from the radio, grab his lunch box, and jog out to the pickup truck.

Autumn, on the other hand, seemed to carry a chip on her shoulder. Even at a mere eleven months, she already had seemed to have an inner knowledge that they weren't her original parents. Jasmine wondered what the wee one's life had entailed prior to her placement. The social worker's information had been sketchy at best, followed by the sealing of the files when they went to court six months later, finalizing the adoption. Someone had cared for her before she had been theirs. Had Autumn felt the change in the hugs and kisses she'd been lavished with before and after the move? Had her newborn heart bruised missing the voices and touches familiar to her? Even the feel of her blanket or a smell she had grown accustomed to were wiped away when she was placed in the freshly painted nursery of the Kirmis home. She,

Evert, and Jacob had loved her even before their eyes had seen the paleness of her skin, the angelic waves of her hair, the tiny dimples of her smile, or the dainty tiptoe steps she took sliding along the kitchen chairs.

But all the while, Jasmine had been selfishly indulging in the beautiful gift they had been given in the form of a darling daughter. Had she truly had empathy for the child who did not find one iota of her past life in her new home? She had been carried and sung to. She had been tenderly bathed and dressed. She had been fed and read to. She had been drenched in hugs and kisses.

But had she wanted them? Or rather, had she *endured* them? Autumn was never one to sit on a lap for any length of time or cuddle with a soft blanket; instead, she was always jumping loose, running for freedom—running away. How could she reach her daughter? Or did she even want to be caught?

As the distance to her campground destination shrunk, as dictated by the mile numbers on the roadside signs, she found a ripple of excitement starting to course through her veins. Even if Autumn's moodiness could irritate like a pebble in a shoe, Jasmine was realizing how much she had missed having her around. No one else was completely honest about the cooking. Evert would always have a compliment to give her after every meal, but Autumn's critiquing on the other hand could tell her if the dish needed more spices or less sugar or if it was baked too long, or even if she should rip the page out of the recipe book. Leave it to Autumn to be blunt. The same could be said for her mother's apparel. An in-house critic kept Jasmine from making a fashion mistake.

The sign protruding from the huge pile of rocks seemingly dropped from heaven by a providential hand announced the entrance to the camp. Swinging her Impala into the curve, she descended a hill into a valley of centrally located buildings surrounded by individual cabins wrapped along a clear crystal lake.

A bustle of activity encased the campground. Campers streamed in and out of every door. Vehicles backed up to cabins, and open trunk lids were being packed tightly. A tractor mower was already trimming the open meadow in the middle of the layout in readiness for the next flux of campers. From past years, Jasmine knew which cabin was named The Upper Room partly from its position high on the hill, but also in reference to the Biblical story of where Jesus and His disciples ate the Last Supper. This was Autumn's cabin.

Motoring slowly upon the winding camp trail, Jasmine had to brake often to allow pedestrians to cross the path. Passing the camp dining room, Emma and Maria spotted her before she did them. Waving profusely, they jogged up to her open window. "Hi, Jasmine. We're all packed up and waiting for you," Emma greeted.

"Yeah, we just needed to replenish our snack supply at the Snack Shack to ensure we'd survive until we got home." She giggled at her own announcement.

"Hi, girls," Jasmine returned. "Seeing all these kids here, you must have had a very full camp this week."

"I think the director said there was over two hundred of us." Maria pulled her hair back off her shoulders.

"Wow! That must be a new record!"

Another gal intervened to encircle each girl in a farewell hug.

"We'll meet you at the cabin, Jasmine," Emma promised.

"We'll be there in a jiffy," Maria chimed in.

Releasing her foot from the brake, Jasmine let her vehicle roll forward, keeping an eye out for her daughter. A cluster of girls with arms linked at the elbows passed in front of her, chattering loudly. Following the bend to the hill, the gymnasium loomed off to her side. Scanning the faces crisscrossing the grounds, Jasmine searched for a bobbing blond ponytail among the moving throngs.

Had she been looking to the right instead of the left, Jasmine would have missed it. For abruptly, the heavy metal gym door swung open. A thin figure with bleached wavy hair filled the opening. Taking three steps out, the green eyes swung and caught the silver Impala rounding the bend. It was Autumn. A beam of recognition highlighted Jasmine's face. Stopping the car and sliding the gear level into park, she was about to call out a welcome to her, but before the words could pass her lips, Autumn turned hurriedly on her heel and dashed back into the enclosure. The door echoed a loud *bang* as it shut.

Disappointment sagged within Jasmine like a porch roof needing a new pedestal before it caved to the ground. She'd driven over a hundred miles to retrieve her daughter. Instead of a welcoming grin or at least a friendly wave, she literally got a door slammed in her face. She felt like the worst mother on earth. Tears stung her eyelids.

A light tap of a horn behind her startled her. Glancing in the rearview mirror, Jasmine saw she was holding up traffic. Quickly slipping the lever into gear, she continued on up to the cabin and backed into a parking space like the van beside her had done. In the distance, she could see Emma, Maria, and another gal climbing the hill to the neighboring cabins.

She sat silently in her seat, all expectation and enjoyment sucked out of her. Maybe she was no different than her temperamental daughter. Her emotions seemed to skyrocket to amazing heights and then blast back to earth in a similar manner. As Maria and Emma advanced to the top of the hill, she knew she had to pull herself together.

Stepping out from the car door, she smoothed on a fake facade of normalcy.

"Pop the trunk, Jasmine, and we'll throw our things in. We stayed in the cabin next door to Autumn's." Emma reached her stack of belongings propped on the bench outside of her cabin and waited for Jasmine to give her access to the storage compartment.

"I'm sorry, Emma. I could have parked closer to you." She remembered now crossing out the names on the registration form. After pressing the button on her key chain, she inspected the area close at hand. "Where are Autumn's belongings?"

Maria glanced about with her. "I don't think she's hauled her stuff outside yet. It's probably still by her bunk."

Jasmine tugged open the screen door and stepped inside. Only a few rolled up sleeping bags and suitcases remained, except for the far bunk. A familiar sleeping bag lay in a twisted rope upon the mattress. Towels hung from the metal railings while clothes lay strewn in a haphazard circle on the cement floor. Who else but Autumn's? The monkey beach towel had been a birthday gift from her grandparents. By all appearances, Autumn had not started packing yet. Fortunately, Jasmine was picking up the girls, instead of Sheila or Jane.

Two other campers were in the cabin collecting their items. "Do you know where Autumn is?" she asked.

"The last time I saw her she was saying good-bye to all the staff members," one politely answered.

Sighing, Jasmine pulled the luggage bag out from under the bunk and started throwing shorts and tops into it. It didn't pay to fold anything. All of it would need the washing machine. The towels and swimsuits were still wet, but she smoothed them on top of the rest of the articles, knowing they wouldn't be in the case long. The floor was littered with candy wrappers and chip bags. Using a Doritos bag as a garbage container, she stuffed the remaining trash into it. Then straightening out the sleeping bag, she folded it in half and rolled it into a tight compact bundle, tying the strings securely to hold it in place. After lugging the baggage out to her car, she threw it in beside Emma and Maria's belongings. Autumn still had not put in an appearance.

"Want to go look for her?" Emma asked.

"I guess we'll have to." Jasmine was boiling on the inside, but she kept her tone light and even.

"She's probably down at the main dining hall. That's where most of the congregating takes place," Maria suggested.

"Why don't you girls hop in, and we'll drive down there. It'll save you some steps."

Within minutes, they were trooping into the dining hall to search out the missing member of the Prairie City trio. A scattering of campers remained inside, most waiting their turn at the window of the Snack Shack. Up front, by the extended kitchen counter used for serving meals buffet style, were a dozen or more college-aged staff members clearly identified by the red T-shirts—printed with *Staff* in bold white letters on their backs. Joking amongst themselves, they looked forward to a night with no campers to interfere with their conversations and activities. In the midst of the string of red shirts was Autumn. Ceremoniously, she hugged each counselor in a tight squeeze before asking each for their autograph and e-mail address. Patronizingly, the older youths readily complied to her wishes, giving her pats on the back and scribbling signatures on the notebook pad.

Deep down, Jasmine knew one of the reasons her daughter looked forward to Bible camp was the Christian staff members. They were more patient with her; they listened to her whining and offered plausible solutions to her string of piddly problems. She hadn't worn them out yet with her clingy attention-seeking personality. Although they too were probably relieved to see the end of a camp week come.

Hanging back, Jasmine knew she would not be able to steer her daughter from finishing this routine. "Hey, Autumn," Emma called out, "your mom is waiting for you." Emma wasn't even gifted with a fleeting glance. Shrugging, she walked off to talk to a tall girl dressed in a turquoise jogging suit.

Having tightly clasped the last staff member, Autumn appeared reluctant to end the exchange, continuing to make small talk, repeating memories from the week. Finally, one of the guys, who guessed correctly that it was her mother waiting off to the side, put one arm around Autumn's back and propelled her forward, depositing her at Jasmine's side. Addressing Jasmine, he said, "Thanks for letting Autumn come to camp this week. We've enjoyed having her." As Jasmine nodded, he turned to Autumn. "See you next year." He gave her a last squeeze before turning back to his comrades.

A darker version of the girl she'd sent off to camp stood before her, masked by peeling cheekbones and nose, severely bleached hair that was waving uncontrollably in the humidity, and dark eye shadows, signaling a lack of sleep. The vivacious young lady of a minute earlier slipped into her tired mode, letting her eyelids fall to half-mast and giving monosyllables in response to her mother's comments. "It appears you had a great time at camp, as always. Your skin really got burnt up by the sun. Ready to go?"

Dishearteningly, the girl followed her mother out of the dining hall and toward the car. Emma and Maria immediately disengaged themselves from their friend and followed too. Sliding into the driver's seat, Jasmine slipped the key into the ignition. "Oh, wait, Mom. I forgot to say good-bye to the lifeguards." Off she flew, heading for the beach area where some red T-shirts could be seen raking the sand.

Emma and Maria sighed for Jasmine. "This should take another fifteen minutes."

And it did.

Driving home, Jasmine thanked the Lord for giving her two extra passengers. Had the other girls not been in attendance, she might have let her frustration out and ruined the ride. As it was, she kept her smile painted on her face and plied the girls with questions about their week. It became evident that Autumn had hardly spent any of the week with her Prairie City classmates. Jasmine was glad they all had funny stories to tell, even if they didn't share the same memories.

As she dropped off Maria at her home, and then Emma, the anticipation of the surprise awaiting Autumn pulsed through Jasmine. Her grin became genuine as her mind raced ahead to the scene waiting for Autumn to discover it. Evert should be finished with the golf tournament by now too.

Having dragged her belongings into the laundry room, Autumn met her dad in the kitchen. He crunched her into a fatherly hug, teasing her about any new boys at camp. She was noncommittal, but a rip in her mask of exhaustion slipped just enough to show she liked his ribbing.

In a voice disguised with added hoarseness for effect, she mumbled something about crashing onto her bed. Jasmine had purposely closed her bedroom door before heading to camp. She waited in anticipation as Autumn filled a glass with ice water from the refrigerator and then padded out of the kitchen, waving weakly. Evert covertly winked at his wife. The usual twinkle in her eye was exploding in fireworks. Tiptoeing behind their sluggish daughter far enough to see her from the corner of the living room, they stopped, waiting for her to open the door hiding a week's worth of work.

With a turn of the knob, Autumn pushed the door inward, the room in shadows by the drawn blinds. She disappeared from sight. The stalking parents edged closer. Having flipped on the light switch, they waited for her squeal of delight to erupt—their signal to advance into the room. Nothing. Jasmine envisioned Autumn with a dropped jaw, staring in bafflement at the transformation of her room into a rhapsody in blue. Her lungs felt like balloons about to pop, but she forced herself to wait out their surprised daughter. Now her eyes would be zeroing in on the wall of stripes, amazed at the straight vertical lines standing at attention from the closet doors to the window. Then she'd notice the galaxy above her bed, and maybe even the star-sprinkled comforter on her bed. Not until she actually entered the room and turned around would she view the sun rising above her door, the full-length mirror, the new window dressings, and best of all, the illuminating stars twinkling overhead.

The door clicked shut. Even then, Jasmine's imagination saw Autumn rotating slowly in a 360-degree circle. The slice of light bleeding from underneath the door suddenly went out. She had evidently turned off her lights. Laying on her bed, she'd be delighting in the host of lights dancing on her ceiling. Jasmine and Evert waited…and waited. Evert finally gave up and headed out the back door to hook up the sprinkler on the vegetable garden. Jasmine leaned against the wall outside Autumn's bedroom. Ten minutes passed. Her back slid down the wall, depositing her butt on the carpeted floor.

While engaged in the week's long project, she had rehearsed the message of love she planned to give Autumn, when Autumn would gratefully grab the two of them in a long fierce family huddle for redoing her room just the way she dreamed it could be. Jasmine would tell her that she was the daughter dreamed of long before she became a reality. That God had fulfilled their wildest dreams in giving them a gift of a baby girl to add to their nest. How, as a mother, she looked forward to the years ahead where they would share many mother-daughter moments from the heart.

To no one in particular, Jasmine breathed, *You're welcome, Autumn.*

Chapter 5

Sitting between Cynthia Burns and Jeremy Fossen, the junior high social studies instructor, Jasmine scribbled notes furiously on a yellow legal pad, trying to keep up with the therapist up at the podium. The new family enrolled at Elton Public School had crossed into North Dakota from Montana, seeking one of the plentiful jobs made available by the oil boom. The three children, registered by their mother, had three different surnames, and the man she wrote down on the line for the "Guardian residing with" had a fourth name.

The speaker had Jasmine's full attention, not because of the possibility that her new first grader would exemplify some of the traits apparent in reactive attachment disorder, rather because the characteristics were all too familiar—the child's rejection of comfort by a parent or caregiver; the avoidance of touch, yet at the opposite end of the spectrum, the child's treatment of near strangers in overtures of inappropriate familiarity—embracing and even kissing them; impulsive actions, not thinking situations through before acting. "Such people are marked by social inadequacies. They do not attract friends, and when they do, they most often lose them." The speaker paused.

Fanning the crowd with his eyes, the speaker asked if any of the individuals in the room knew someone like he was describing. Jasmine practically had to sit on her hands to keep from waving a public declaration. He was describing Autumn in minute detail! The little gal who went to everyone, including them, before being placed in their home. Yet just a year later, didn't seem to prefer them as her parents and primary caregivers, over anyone else she came in contact with. Her lack of inhibitions with mere strangers was incongruous with her stiffening when her mom clasped her close. Ongoing social conflicts with peers were inundated with inappropriate remarks at untimely moments. She made the same mistakes repeatedly, as if not connecting a cause with an effect.

Cynthia nudged her with an elbow, alerting her to the motel waitress filling requests for a soft drink or cup of coffee. An abrupt shake of her head sent the waitress to the next table. Jasmine flipped over the sheet of paper, her pen continued to race. She checked the causes of reactive attachment disorder.

1. Bonding. The first months of a child's life are critical. Must not only be fed and diapers changed, but needs to be held and cuddled. Physical needs need to be met in a timely manner. A child learns to recognize and bond with his primary caregiver. Neglect can cause the child to distrust that he will be cared for.
2. Physical Abuse. If a child's needs are met, but pain accompanies the administration, the child will not attach to the adult.
3. Change of Caregiver. By eight months, a child recognizes his parent or parents. If separation occurs it can cause emotional and social distress.

Very little information had accompanied Autumn when she transferred to their home. Annie, their social worker, had said her biological mother had shown up at their office approximately a month before she was given to the Kirmises. She had been distraught and wanted to give up her baby because she was overwhelmed. When Annie suggested some of the services that social services offered to assist young parents, the birth mother had refused. She wasn't sure who the baby's father was and insisted on signing papers giving up the rights to her baby immediately.

Could there have been severe neglect after she was first born? Autumn had been considerably underweight compared to other babies at eleven months. Or had the change from her birth mother to a temporary foster home and then to her and Evert caused upheaval in their daughter's life? Yet Autumn's willingness to come right into their arms at the initial visit had surprised them. At the time, it had made their hearts soar, thinking the little golden girl wanted them. Could she have been suffering from reactive attachment disorder? If so, what did they do about it now?

Jasmine refocused on the speaker. "It is a long slow process to reestablish trust in a child's life. Young children need structure. They need to know they will be given three meals a day. They need to know that when they cry, someone will come to their assistance. They need a caring adult to sing lullabies and rock them when they're distressed.

"The older the child, the harder the fix. Therapy and patience go hand in hand. This disorder can accompany a young person right into adulthood in establishing healthy relationships."

Wow! So what should we do? It seemed as if a blanket of despair had been draped over her. There didn't seem to be a simple diagnosis, and even if there was, there was no simplistic solution. Did the knowledge of the unknown always help the outcome— or were some better left unearthed?

Jasmine could hardly wait to return home on the concluding day of the workshop to discuss the information with Evert.

Thoughtfully, he listened to her lengthy description of a disorder he had never known existed. Often reading from her notepad, Jasmine punctuated a character trait with, "Doesn't that sound like Autumn?"

Running a forefinger along the rim of his coffee cup, Evert mentally sorted through the data his wife had given him. Finally, he spoke. "Even though Autumn may share many of these traits, it doesn't mean she has reactive attachment disorder. I think we need to read up more on this matter. She does seem to have a lot of social issues which often makes her a very unhappy girl. I love her, and it breaks my heart to see her treated as a social outcast."

Jasmine was ready to refute his statement, but he held up his hands to let him finish.

"Yes, I know she brings most of it on herself. If she is going to struggle with obtaining friends, then I think you and I not only have to be understanding parents, but we also have to be her good friends."

The summer's dust had barely been wiped off the textbooks when Cynthia Burns perched on the corner of Jasmine's bulky wooden teacher's desk. A common stance for her, for there was much for the two first grade teachers to discuss on a daily basis. "How did your class do on the consonant blends? Should we repeat the lesson again today? The counselor is talking to our classes about citizenship. Whose room should we gather in, yours or mine? Will three thirty work for an IEP meeting for you? What do you think of the newly purchased reading series?"

Her jaw to one side, chewing on the inside of her lip, her eyebrows raised two degrees higher than normal, were signals her sidekick wasn't here for a first grade conversation. "Hey, what gives?" Jasmine lay down the paper punch she was using in preparation for an art project.

As if to disclose a deep dark secret, Cynthia leaned on one palm, lowered her chin, and fixed Jasmine with a hazel-eyed stare. "You realize what this year is, don't you?"

Having taught across the hall from Cynthia for a number of years, Jasmine was well acquainted with her mannerisms both at a professional and personal level. "Sure do. Katie is a senior. Congratulations! When our kids were young, we commiserated about those far-off teenage years when they'd first drive us crazy, then graduate, and finally, leave us pining in their empty bedrooms. Don't forget, Jacob is a junior. You beat me by one year!" Amusement shone on Jasmine's face. Cynthia had by all standards the *perfect* daughter, but everything was a big deal to Katie's mother.

She had poured all her energy into Katie, who had matured wonderfully—a good head on her shoulders, high grades, and a pleasant personality. Too bad Katie was an only child. Cynthia had enough energy to have spread across a half dozen children. She and her husband Kevin had a lot to be proud of in Kate.

"Yeah, but back then, we didn't have any idea what graduation entailed. Katie has an appointment next week for senior pictures with the photographer here in Elton. Back when you and I were finishing up high school, they took one pose of us stuffed in our favorite sweater, and we bought enough wallets for our fellow graduates and our aunts and uncles. Grandma and Grandpa got a size larger. Nowadays, kids take along fifteen different outfits for fifteen different locations of photo shoots." Her hands gestured as fast as her lips moved.

"Fortunately, Katie has already taken her ACT test for college entrance, but now she has to eliminate universities and pinpoint which college she wants to enroll in. Application deadlines are pending. We've toured four schools, but she is still wavering. She's not even sure what area she wants to go into. Maybe counseling, yet she has a bug for nursing as well. Note, *teaching* didn't make the top of her list."

Jasmine couldn't help let loose a chuckle. "Katie will do just fine. A more pertinent question is, how is her mother handling it all?"

"It's a given I will cry all through the graduation ceremony. However, I think I'm starting prematurely. This morning, I wept when she told me her class is voting first period on color selection for their gowns and mortarboards."

Reaching over to pat her friend's knee, Jasmine quipped, "Relax. This will be a fun year for both of you. And when the nine months are over, and she parades across the stage to receive her diploma, she will still be your Katie."

The warning bell rang for the start of the day. Cynthia hopped off the desk, smoothing out her skirt and winked at her partner, "Just wanted to warn you what you'll have to put up with this year."

"I'll take notes so when Jacob's a senior, he won't accuse me of being wacky, like Katie's mom." Sticking her tongue out and waving her fingers in her ears, Cynthia's form disappeared out the door.

The tone of the school year had been set. While the Burnses started enumerating lists for a graduation open house, the Kirmises monopolized the bleachers following Jacob's football team and Autumn's junior high volleyball tournaments.

Each evening, an hour was spent laboriously struggling over Autumn's daily math assignment. It wasn't so much that she wasn't mathematically inclined, it was more that her motivation was severely disinclined. The school's high academic standards to participate in sports was the one drawing card her parents had to keep Autumn's pencil to the paper. When Autumn had an unusually huffy night, Jasmine would throw up her hands in despair and walk away, leaving Evert to patiently bring his daughter back to the problem at hand, drawing diagrams of explanation on a piece of scrap paper or waiting as she erased her numbers again and again, all the time heatedly demanding her answer was correct.

Homework was an undercover agent's quest to discover. Although the teachers of Prairie Public School were required to post their weekly lesson plans online for parents to view, Jasmine and Evert never knew for sure if Autumn was completing them. If asked, she invariably had a plausible reply. "I got it done in school and handed it in. Mr. Barret decided to skip that lesson. We got to have a partner. We get to finish it during class tomorrow." Only if a dire transgression was committed did the school contact the parents prior to a scheduled parent-teacher conference.

Friendships also continued to be an agonizing battleground. Emma and Maria were still forced members of Autumn's social network, but outside of Sunday school and family get-togethers, rarely did the girls voluntarily seek out Autumn's camaraderie. If by chance, a new girl moved into the community, Autumn latched onto her quicker than ants attacking a sugar bowl, showing her around the school, inviting her to the house after hours, and tying up the home phone in constant chitchat. Once the newcomer became acquainted with the town and school atmosphere, she tended to pull away from Autumn's clutches, leaving Autumn angry and revengeful.

Such was the atmosphere when the calendar proclaimed her thirteenth birthday was a week away.

A teenager. How could Jasmine help her daughter smoothly transition into those years noted for independence seeking? When parents needed to loosen the reins, and yet guide their spirited fillies into the green grass of quieter pastures rather than the hard surface of the racetrack?

It was Autumn herself who came up with a party plan. Jasmine had scrapbooked photo albums for both of her children from the moment they became part of the Kirmis family. Paging through earlier albums, Autumn paused on two adjacent pages where she was shown in an oversized flowered hat, wearing a dress many sizes too big for her. A jeweled bracelet dangled from her tiny wrist. "Hey, Mom, remember when Grandma Ruth had a tea party for all the cousins? I must be only about three in this photo."

Jasmine had been shredding lettuce for a salad. Enticed by the memory, she accommodated her daughter's question. Leaning over to peer at the pictures, she noted it was indeed a tea party. Her mom had a huge dress up box in an upstairs bedroom for the grandchildren to dig through. All of them had come tripping down the steps adorned in old prom and bridesmaid dresses with lavish hats and jewelry. Grandma, not one to let a Kodak moment disappear, had immediately thrown a white lace tablecloth over the dining room table and found party snacks in the pantry. Using the glass cups from her punch bowl, she made the girls—and two boys—feel incredibly grown-up and important. *Oh, Mom, I miss you,* Jasmine breathed. How she would like to discuss Autumn's struggles with her own mom.

"That was fun." Autumn scrutinized the photos closely. "Do you think I'm too old to have an old-fashioned tea party again?"

The idea settled over Jasmine like the soft touch of fall leaves brushing her head and shoulders in a walk through the woods. It was perfect! Not too babyish for a budding teen, and yet not throwing her into activities she was not mature enough to grasp.

"Why not invite the girls in your class to a birthday tea party?" she exclaimed, completely taken with the idea.

"There's only six of us. Maybe we could ask the sixth graders as well," Autumn remarked, warming to the escapade.

And that's how it came to be. Dumping out the craft drawer, the two worked side by side creating invitations with the use of white paper doilies and colored wallpaper, cutting the paper into teacup shapes. Inside, they carefully printed the invite:

Ladies,
You are invited to an old-fashioned tea party
in recognition
of Autumn's 13th birthday.
Dig in your mom's and grandma's closets
to dress the part.
Date: October 3, 2:00–5:00
Place: Naomi's Diner in Elton
(Transportation provided.)

In place of gifts,
please bring an inexpensive personal item
found on a dressing table
for use in a parlor game.

At first, the Kirmis dining room was the obvious setting for the festive occasion, but after thoughtful deliberation, Naomi's Diner in Elton seemed more refined. Although it was fifteen miles from Prairie City, Jasmine and Naomi were acquaintances from when Naomi's children had passed through Mrs. Kirmis's schoolroom. Her diner had a cafe in the front and a dining room in the back used only for her buffet suppers. Since it was not used in the afternoons, Naomi generously allowed it to be turned into Autumn's birthday setting. They would have the morning hours to transform it into a feminine tearoom.

Jasmine couldn't recall when her daughter had willingly worked alongside of her with such enthusiasm. Evert's mom donated her collection of teapots to use as centerpieces holding mums and dried baby's breath from Jasmine's own flower garden. In addition, she had an assortment of antique china tea cups gleaned from backyard rummage sales. Autumn squealed in delight.

Fancy party-shaped sandwiches were filled with egg and ham salads. Strawberries dipped in white chocolate and miniature cupcakes embellished with cream cheese teardrops were laid out prettily on crystal glass plates. Since most teenagers hadn't acquired a taste for hot tea, chocolate lattes would be substituted. Ice cream parfaits served in tall fancy glassware with thin sugar cookies would complete the luncheon.

Autumn begged to wear Grandma Ruth's wedding dress buried in the hall closet between layers of tissue paper. At first, Jasmine absolutely refused, fearful her careless daughter would stain or tear the cream-colored gown with its tiny laced bodice and sleeves. Brooding on the matter, she relented. What good was the dress when no ever saw it? Autumn, with her tiny waist, would be gorgeous in it. Photos taken at the party would be a lifetime treasure.

Fourteen girls were chauffeured over the countryside by Evert and Jane Runk and deposited at the door of Naomi's Diner where Jasmine and Autumn awaited the guests. Evert begged off being a butler and headed for Elton's Lumber Yard instead, ordering supplies for his next building project.

Autumn was absolutely stunning in her grandmother's satin dress. It had taken only a few hand-basted tucks to ease in the looseness around the bust and waist. Jasmine hadn't realized how thin her mom must have been at the age of nineteen when she married dad.

Having curled her hair in loose ringlets held away from her face by jeweled combs, Autumn was indeed the princess Evert often used as her pet name.

The dining room had been cloaked in a cloud of white elegance with the help of lace tablecloths, netting, ribbons, and ornamental pearls. China teapots and cups nestled amongst the table décor added an inviting charm to the adolescent ladies emerging with delight into the heavenly wonderland.

Jasmine had clustered Naomi's artificial trees, glittering with white lights, into a backdrop for a photo booth. Giggling in their borrowed gowns of taffeta, silk, satin, chiffon, and chintz, adorned with crepe overlays, ruffles, and beads, each girl donned a feigned sophistication for an afternoon. Posing for a quick snapshot, their stylish hats tipped precariously as they fumbled with their finger gloves and clutch purses. When one would trip on her spike-heeled shoes, a wave of unladylike chortles would sweep through the room.

Calling each of the young ladies by their surname with a *miss* attached to the front, Jasmine designated their places at the circular tables. The girls performed their refined roles, promenading across the tiled restaurant floor and settling ladylike into the chairs.

Jane assisted Jasmine in serving the party lunch, smirking inwardly as the girls conversed in high society discourse.

"And how are your children doing?" Alicia asked politely, sipping her chocolate latte her pinky finger extended into the air.

Sage, sitting next to her, replied in her most ladylike voice, "Ah, quite well. Mason was ailing with a bit of an earache, but that seems to have left him." She daintily picked up a party sandwich, not sure whether to leave her gloves on or to remove them.

Joining the exchange, drowning in a lavender evening gown, Susan quipped, "Yes, don't those wee ones catch everything that flies by?" The other gals nodded in agreement.

By all appearances, the tea party was a hit. Bending their heads and huddling for a tete-a-tete, the girls kept up a running discussion on garden flowers, husbands, recipes, and the latest vogue fashions. Autumn's usual drama fit the make-believe atmosphere. Their appetites kept pace with their chatter, completely demolishing the supply of party sandwiches and sweets. Jane kept refilling teacups with the chocolaty latte.

Next on the program was the parade of party wear. Taking turns, the gals did a short stroll, circling the tables, modeling the outfit, and giving a short history of where the exquisite attire had been previously worn. Polite applause followed each budding teenager to her chair.

Autumn, having had prior knowledge of the afternoon's entertainment, knew exactly what she wanted to say when it was her turn to display her apparel. Walking like a professional model, her ringlets resting on her right shoulder, she paused, pivoted, and resumed her stroll, narrating her memorized recitation.

"Autumn Kirmis is modeling for us today, the floor-length cream colored bridal gown first worn by her grandmother Ruth sixty-one years ago as she floated down the church aisle into the arms of her beloved fiance, Ernest Buchholz. The laced bodice and the three-quarter-length fitted sleeves add a feminine softness to the shimmering satin overlaid with an additional single tier of the same material. Her matching pumps, supported by a two-inch heel, add height to her form, slimming her already slender physique. Add a ring of roses or a bouquet of white lilies, and you have the most picturesque bride ever to behold." With her conclusion, she bent her knees in a brief curtsy.

Jasmine's heart swelled at the beauty and lovely discourse her daughter presented. Someday, Autumn might very well wear this or a similar dress as Evert walks her down the aisle to a man God brings into her life. Ruefully, Jasmine added, *He will have to have the patience of Job.*

The fashion show was followed by a parlor game of Button Button and then the gift exchange. A basket was passed among the young ladies. Each was asked to select a folded piece of paper from its contents bearing a written number. Meanwhile, the wrapped gifts and decorative bags the girls had supplied were piled on a center table in full view. Autumn, being the person of honor, was asked to select and open one of the gifts. Pleased to be in the spotlight, she chose the largest pink foiled-covered box. After carefully lifting the lid, she brought out a tall shapely bottle of white citrus bubble bath.

"Thank you, Autumn. Would you please leave the bottle on display with the other gifts," Jasmine instructed. "Now, which of you drew out the number one?" A pause fell upon the room, as the girls' painted eyes rotated the circle of friends, until Maxine squealed, "Here it is!" She waved the square of paper in the air.

"Great! Maxine, you are the first player. You may now choose as your very own party gift—the bottle of bubble bath, or if you so desire, you may choose one of the unopened gifts. Come and make your selection," Jasmine prompted.

Slipping off her high heels to make the move less hazardous, Maxine pounced on a striped bag trimmed with fake feathers. She slipped her hand into the tissue paper drawing out a brush and comb set. Clasping it to her chest, she beamed, "Just what I need!"

"Okay, girls, we will continue with number two." Susan stood up ready to play the game. "Susan, you can choose from this menagerie of gifts or take the bubble bath or the brush and comb set that Maxine is holding," Jasmine said, explaining the rules of the game.

"You mean I could lose these?" Maxine teasingly pouted.

"Doesn't she get anything if I take her gift?" Susan never wanted to hurt anyone's feelings.

"Maxine would get another turn, either choosing a gift that is already open or one from the pile," Jasmine affirmed.

"In that case, I take the brush and comb." Susan triumphantly pulled it out of Maxine's hold.

The game continued as gifts were exposed—a makeup pouch, a handheld mirror, lip glosses, a manicure set, and a diary. Autumn was next. Prolonging the excitement, she purposely stopped in front of each gal already holding an item and examined the object in great length, exclaiming on how she could use it before returning it to the owner.

"Hurry up, Autumn," Maria ribbed. "I'm next, and I don't want you to take what I want."

Turning her green eyes on Maria, Autumn shook a finger in the air. "That wasn't very ladylike, Maria." Everyone burst into titters.

"I apologize for my rudeness," Maria jokingly humbled herself. "My husband will be expecting me home shortly, so I dare not dawdle with you lovely ladies too far into the afternoon. He likes his evening meal served promptly at six." Her ignominious explanation sent the girls hee-hawing again.

"Apology accepted." Autumn liked leading the crowd.

Approaching the table of the decorated packages still left, she picked one up, shook it, then set it down again. Finally, she decided on a uniquely decorated box of shimmering glitter tied shut with a simple length of white ribbon. Something exquisite must be hidden in such a treasure box casing. Autumn pulled tentatively on one of the ties. The bow gave way willingly. Everyone watched breathlessly as only junior high girls can do while Autumn lifted the enamored lid.

She peered inside then looked again. Shaking it upside down, a perplexed frown creased her face. "It's empty. Who would give an empty box?" Suddenly, the hilarity of seconds ago was erased, as if someone had hit the delete button on the keyboard, wiping away the friendly closeness of tea party ladies gossiping with friends.

Sarcasm dripped from Autumn's words. "What a stupid gift! It's just an empty box." A curtain of silence was drawn.

Susan guiltily explained, "I brought it. I thought it could be used on a dresser to hold jewelry, hair clips—you know, that sort of thing."

Stomping to her table, Autumn threw the unwanted box at her place setting. She plopped ungraciously into her chair. At the same second, the thwarted gift hit her teacup setting on the edge of the table, sending the chocolate drink plummeting into her lap. Initially, the dark liquid beaded up on the slippery satin material. The brown ugly mass grew in size, slowly soaking into the dress symbolic of purity, until it stained her slip and bare legs. Popping up like a jack-in-the-box, an ugly retort escaped from her throat. "Ugh! And now my dress is ruined!"

How could such a lovely afternoon spent nurturing the friendship of peers evaporate into a desert storm of driving sand hitting and biting everything its teeth came in contact with?

Jasmine felt the blood run out of her face, leaving it a sickly pasty white. How was she to graciously redeem the situation? Autumn was ruining her own birthday party—the party meant to groom her friendships. Jasmine slowly felt the burn of embarrassment creep up her neck and into her cheeks, painting her bleached complexion a scarlet red.

Riveted to the floor, one hand holding her camera, the other hanging onto the back of a folding chair, Jasmine was at a loss. What could she say to these girls to ease the situation? To continue the game seemed a facade, a useless interaction.

Jane witnessed the scene as well. Hurrying over to Autumn, she uttered some sympathetic words at the state of her dress. Dabbing at the blotch with some napkins, she soothingly brought Autumn to her feet. "Let's see if we can't rinse this out in the bathroom. If we do it right away, it might not even show." Ushering her out of the room, Jasmine dared to breathe a small breath. Now what?

"It's my turn next!" Maria bounced out of her chair, one hand clapped to the top of her head keeping her pillbox hat intact. She darted straight to the place vacated by Autumn. "I choose the box. It will be perfect for my bottles of nail polish. Thank you, Susan." Remarkably, the girls applauded, and the game went on. Displaying maturity, the girls had taken care of the situation themselves. Maybe Autumn's explosions were commonplace to them.

Autumn didn't return until after the last guest had made her choice and Jasmine was serving the parfaits and cookies. Avoiding eye contact with her daughter, she said something pleasant to each girl as she placed the refreshing dessert before her.

When the party was over, Autumn opted to ride back to Prairie City with Evert and his passengers. Her dad objected, viewing the messy dining room in need of restoration. Jasmine was cooking on low simmer inside. Evert hadn't observed the party fiasco. She wanted to discuss the matter with him before confronting their daughter. Jasmine sent a silent message to her husband; he shrugged and allowed Autumn to climb in with the other gals. Jasmine followed two hours later, after returning Naomi's Diner to its normal setting.

Parked in the driveway of their split-level home, Jasmine sat, emotionally spent. She stared out the window at their modest-sized house surrounded by a large lawn and billowing shade trees. The vegetable garden in the far corner had only pumpkins and carrots yet to glean. It was a nice place to raise a family. It was a small town. The population? Seven hundred friendly people. There was no crime to speak of. What could be more heavenly?

They were a family of four. With such an abundance of blessings, why did she feel utterly washed out, drained with the dishwater, never to be used again?

A knock on the glass window brought her face-to-face with her first blessing—her best friend, Evert. He reached for her hand to help her out. "Need a hug?" he asked. Walking into his warm comforting embrace, she spilled her tears of frustration into his shoulder. When she'd cried herself out, he engulfed her hand in his again and escorted her on a leisurely walk along the fringes of their village, talking to each other and their heavenly Father on how to parent their daughter Autumn. They were weak, but He was strong. They were perplexed, but He knew Autumn thoroughly.

> My frame was not hidden from you when I was made in the secret place. When I was woven together in the depths of the earth, your eyes saw my unformed body. All the days ordained for me were written in your book before one of them came to be.
>
> Psalm 139:15–16 (NIV)

Chapter 6

The school year tumbled forward in leaps and bounds, each day bringing the Burnses closer to Katie's graduation day. Cynthia continued to worry and stew about nonessential details. Katie poured over her textbooks, as if she was in danger of failing instead of having been selected as the salutatorian of her forty-nine member class. Kevin showed up at his job at John Deere Implement as the first rays of the sun peeked above the horizon and returned home after the sun's nocturnal dive. Planting season for the North Dakotan farmers was dawning, and he, being a much revered mechanic and technician in the area, was in full demand. Agricultural farm machines had grown not only colossal in size, but filled with computer monitors, GPS devices, and electronic equipment the ordinary farmer had difficulty troubleshooting. Kevin Burns's cell number was on their speed dial. For six to eight weeks, Kevin didn't have a life outside of John Deere. Once the planting season wrapped up, he could breathe—that is, until harvest moved in two months later. No, a May graduation was not convenient to his schedule.

And Jasmine got an earful from Cynthia. "He gobbles down the meal I've reheated in the microwave for him, aches and pains his way to his La-Z-Boy chair in front of the television, and promptly falls asleep. He wakes up hours after I've warmed up the bed for him, plops in beside me, and snores in my ear."

The graduation open house was rated, in Cynthia's esteem, right up there with the president's inaugural ceremony. Katie's monumental day would be treated with no less pomp and ceremony even if it killed Cynthia. Jasmine surmised it might.

Cynthia agonized over the menu, changing the cuisine weekly. Which salads could be prepared the day before, and which would wilt or melt if mixed too far in advance? Were all the graduation open houses in town serving ham? Maybe she should roast a turkey for sandwich meat, or better yet, cook barbecued beef. What quantities did she need?

Jasmine reminded her friend of the dozen or more invitations each of them received at the end of the school year. Being a small town, everyone knew the graduates, so invitations were passed out like campaign propaganda before an election. Guests couldn't eat a full meal at every open house they attended. It was a bit like trick or treating on Halloween. She needn't fill the child's plastic jack-o'-lantern pail full. A less lavish treat would suffice.

Although Cynthia agreed with her, she went right on planning for the feeding of the five thousand.

"I thought we'd have the festivities in our garage, but land sakes, we don't have enough chairs or tables," she lamented another day.

"Well, you should certainly be able to borrow from the school. Better yet, why don't you just host it in the fellowship hall at your church?" Jasmine wasn't sure why she kept making suggestions, since all of them were invariably falling on deaf ears.

"That would take care of the chair and table dilemma, but then I'd have to transport all the food and punch. I'm not sure which would be worse." Cynthia found something wrong at every turn.

Tired of the topic, Jasmine threw out, "Just put Kevin in charge of the tables and chairs and mark it off your list."

"Kevin! Are you crazy? I'll be lucky if he shows up for the graduation ceremony at all. He'll probably have to watch the video of Katie giving her salutatorian speech next winter when the fields are buried in snow."

As the scrapes and scratches in Autumn's social life continued to crash and burn, Evert joked that if she had been a Ford car instead of his daughter, he would have junked her for scrap iron by now. His wife didn't find any humor in the comparison. "Only trying to lighten the mood," he apologized, giving her his sorry puppy eyes.

"You didn't have to reason with Mrs. Resson. She was out for blood, or at least the cash to replace her daughter's gym bag which she clearly insinuated was ripped by Autumn during a brawl in the girls' locker room after gym class." Jasmine was in one of her no-nonsense moods herself.

"Maybe we should talk to the gym instructor and get an unbiased report," Evert suggested, tiptoeing around his wife.

"I already did. He apologized for the squabble, but being a male teacher, he couldn't very well monitor the girls' dressing room. So with my back against the wall, I agreed to send Mrs. Resson a check for twenty-five dollars and hope to hold the peace in this Cracker Jack box–sized town." Jasmine loved living in a small town—when her family wasn't the center of negative conversations.

The subject of reactive attachment disorder was revisited by the two of them repeatedly. They were in agreement that labeling their child with such a diagnosis would in itself be of no help to her. On the other hand, therapy might teach her some new skills in relating to peers. The first time they verbalized the suggestion to Autumn, she dismissed it as a piece of preschool sandbox wisdom.

"Back in elementary school, three of us girls would get called to the counselor's office for playdates. We'd play table games with the counselor and talk about how friends should get along. Didn't work. The other girls were all nicey nicey in her office, but as soon as we headed back to the room, they were just as mean as ever."

Following another call from the school principal, they tried again. Resistance throttled to the forefront. "What do you think I am? Psycho or something? Why are you always trying to push me into a psych ward?" She slammed an insulated glass on the table for emphasis; Diet Coke splattered over the countertop. Without Autumn's cooperation, a therapist was out.

The Bible story of Hannah and Samuel kept coming back to Jasmine to mull over. She wondered how Eli the priest would have handled the young boy Samuel had he been an Autumn instead.

Sitting in the fourth row of the piano recital between Evert and Jacob, Jasmine willed the struggling first grader to find the right note on the grand piano's keyboard. Do, do, mi, mi, so, so, *plunk*. Determined, the budding pianist started the piece over for the fourth time before the piano instructor reached over his shoulder and, with one finger, hit the missing melodious key—re. Smiling at his instructor's rose-painted fingernail, the lad astutely finished his memorized piece. Having slid off the polished piano bench, he stood. Crossing his arm across his waist, he bent his body in a final bow.

Appreciatively, the small audience clapped their approval for the fortitude he displayed. The procession of young musicians continued. Mrs. Voll introduced them in succession from the beginning players to the more experienced pianists. According to the printed program, Autumn would be second from the end.

When God sprinkled talents down on His children from above, Autumn must have been standing right underneath the pail marked Musical, receiving a direct hit, for everything about her breathed rhythm. From the bounce in her walk or the fast finagling of her feet in a dance step to the way she could clap on a surface imitating a full percussion section, music radiated from her. At times, it drove her parents nuts. She could be wiping the dishes and stacking the plastic glasses. Only suddenly, she'd have the whole shelf banging out a rhythm on the countertop. Dipping a spoonful of sugar into her cereal bowl, the spoon would dance against the glass side in a syncopated impromptu. They could be taking a quiet walk along a gravel road outside of Prairie City when her hands would start beating a cadence against her stomach muscles, moving unto her thighs, off an elbow, and finish on her cheeks. It was especially irritating when someone was trying to have a phone conversation and had a full percussion section drumming in the background.

All irritation was wiped away like a shammy on a bug-smeared windshield as she and Evert waited for Autumn's name to be called. Jasmine's heart throbbed erratically in a combination of pride and nervousness for her daughter.

Piano lessons had begun in the midst of first grade. As often is the case with new opportunities, the idea of playing the piano was initially received by their six-year-old whirlwind with rousing exhilaration. Attending a neighborhood auction sale, Evert and his daughter brought home a hundred-dollar bargain in the form of an old upright black piano on the back of his construction truck. Just to hear the succession of sounds, she would run her fingernail backward along the ivories of the full keyboard and imagine herself a concert pianist pounding on every key in a thunderous rendition of the theme song from the latest Walt Disney movie. Alas, when after laboring through a handful of lessons, and she could only play "Mary Had a Little Lamb" with one hand, she wanted to quit. For the first two years, Jasmine and her impatient imp sat side by side on the piano bench to complete the practice sessions.

And then miraculously, Autumn's musical ability took off. The pulsating rhythm found its way into her heart and vacillated out her fingertips. Simple melodies became enhanced with additional chords and trills of her own making. Her playing became smooth and effortless, a joy to listen to.

In fifth grade, they exchanged the antiquated upright for a brand-new instrument, in addition to a used saxophone for band lessons.

"Autumn Kirmis, a freshman, will now entertain us with the quick-tempoed Solfeggietto by Carl Philipp Emanuel Bach, followed by a modern arrangement of multiple tunes I think you will recognize. Autumn prefers the later, but I always insist she learn from the old masters first." Mrs. Voll smiled benevolently at the young lady who shared her love of music.

Inconsistent with her charged personality, Autumn gracefully alighted from her seat and stepped forward. Her flaxen hair, swept up loosely in a band at the back of her head, allowed two pipe curls to dangle, swishing her neck as she walked. The pale pink shift of rayon depicted an angelic countenance upon her. Jasmine wondered if she had a split personality, the portrait she presently displayed being a welcome contrast to her usual demeanor.

Relish the moment, the proud mother reminded herself. And she did.

With the charm of an accomplished concert pianist, Autumn situated herself in the center of the bench. Then deciding it was too close to the keyboard, raised herself enough to slide the seat backward a couple of inches. Satisfied with the placement, her right foot reached for the foot pedals as her hands sought the keyboard. The extension of space between her body and the instrument made her appear even more lithe and long-limbed than she was.

Next to Jasmine, Evert shifted, placing an arm around his wife's shoulders and dropping an expression of tenderness into her misting eyes. He knew her well.

From the touch of the first note, Jasmine was spellbound, watching her daughter's fingers flit across the keys in a rapid caress. Although the piece was lively, she was aware that nervousness was accelerating the tempo to a higher speed than Autumn had ever played it at home. Not until the final high C was hit did Jasmine realize she had held her breath the whole time.

A resounding thunder of applause swept the room, the listeners commending the excellent performance. With a small upward tilt of her lips, Autumn moved into her second number. Feeling more at ease, she inserted self-control, slowing the pace to the recommended delivery. The familiarity of the tunes brought delight to the attendees as they refrained from singing along, tapping a toe instead.

Closing her eyes, Jasmine relished being surrounded by people approving of Autumn's performance for a change. Instead of having to be on the defensive, grasping for ways to right the wrong or pleading with Autumn to be considerate of others, she could simply inhale the pleasure of being in her presence. Every so often, Evert would remind her they needed to be the friend to Autumn that she didn't have. If only it could always be this easy.

Putting her hands together, she clapped until they stung. She'd remind herself of the hope and strength this day brought her, to endure the bad that may yet lay ahead.

Not waiting for the usual morning conference conducted from the corner of Jasmine's desk, Cynthia spotted her partner on the way into the school from the parking lot, sipping from an insulated mug of tea. Waving at her friend, Cynthia called over the intervening vehicles. "Change of plans! Change of plans! You won't even be able to guess!" Her excitement was evident in the fast click of her sandals against the paved surface and the facelift she must have had performed over the weekend in the way her face glowed, ready to burst with the report.

"Really?" Jasmine waited for her to catch up to her. "Let me try."

"No, you can't guess, not in a million years." Cynthia held her hand up in a gesture to stop even an attempt. "The open house scheduled after the graduation ceremony is officially canceled!"

Jasmine paused. Something wasn't right here. The open house was canceled, but Cynthia was on a high hitting the top of the charts. It didn't jive. Reading the confusion on her friend's face, Cynthia laughed. "Gotcha! We are having a hog roast done right in our own backyard the night *before* graduation. That way, we won't have to share any of our guests with other graduates. Katie is thrilled!"

Not sure on how roasting a hog was going to alleviate any of the problems her friend had been fretting about routinely, Jasmine waited for more information. Obviously, the table-and-chairs dilemma must have been taken care of and the proportions of food calculated.

"Isn't it the best idea ever?' Walking briskly to the school's outside entrance shoulder to shoulder, Jasmine asked, "Am I still in charge of making the coleslaw and mints? Hopefully, I haven't been switched to pork duty."

Grasping the door handle, Cynthia swung the door open and waited for Jasmine to pass in front of her before letting the door clang behind them. "Oh, yes, that will help me immensely. But can you believe Kevin would come up with such a spectacular plan? I didn't think anything moved around in that head of his except wiring harnesses and gigabytes."

"Kevin?" Cynthia was right. Her husband, totally dedicated to his job, had suddenly turned into a party planner? "How did this all happen?"

"Art Ryder works with Kevin at John Deere in the sales department. He told Kevin he often helps his uncle with pork roasts over the summer months for family reunions and such. His uncle built this big contraption mounted on wheels, so it's portable. He gets his pigs from a hog farmer west of Norbert. Art will do the roasting. We just pay for the pig and supply him with bags of charcoal. Easy, huh?"

"Yes, it sounds great, but what happened to Kevin's tight work schedule?" Somehow, a full meal with a larger crowd didn't seem like a plausible solution.

"Jack Weber does the same technician troubleshooting Kevin does. His kids are all out of high school. He offered to cover for Kevin both days. If two farmers need him at the same time, one will just have to wait. And get this. Jack is a member of the Lions Club, a community service group. They have a bunch of picnic tables we can borrow."

"Didn't I tell you it would all work out?" Jasmine reminded Cynthia, turning a key in her own classroom door.

"Yes, you did. Guess I should have more faith."

"Maybe we should pray for those farmers. No breakdowns for graduation."

"I'll add it to my to-do list," Cynthia promised with a smirk.

But Jasmine didn't joke when it came to prayer.

"Today, we are graduating from high school. It seems like we have traveled a great distance since stepping on board this trip back in kindergarten. Each spring, having passed the yearly requirements, we were promoted one level higher. Surely, by now, having reached level twelve, we must be truly wise. We must know great truths and be ready to take on great tasks. Are you ready? Am I? We could visit great scholars and ask them our questions, and clearly, they'd give us very astute intelligent answers. But I think back to grade school to one of my favorite books, *Oh, the Places You'll Go,* written by one of my most esteemed authors, Dr. Seuss. It just might be I've found what I'm looking for. Would it be okay if I'd read you a story one last time before we move the tassel on our mortarboards to the other side and walk off this stage gripping our diplomas tightly?

Having flipped the book open, Katie Burns proceeded to read select pages to her classmates, allowing the rest of the packed auditorium to listen in. The familiarity of the rhyming rhythm was contagious; soon her fellow graduates were mouthing the words with her.

As seniors stepping out into the world, they were on their way up, about to make their dreams happen; only sometimes, they'd falter and fall. There would be confusion, and fear, and lots of waiting too—waiting for dreams to come true. And when they didn't, they might slide into a slump and stay there, or they could get up and show what they were made of by facing their problems and moving onward. She ended her salutatorian speech with a rhyme of her own.

> Our paths are diverse,
> We've chosen to travel—
> Each best suited
> For the person we are.
> No matter our destinies,
> Next door or afar—
> We've been given the tools
> To make them reality.
> Thank you to Elton Public Schools
> For sending us out
> Fully prepared for the route.

Her mother, sitting in the second row, front and center, cried from start to finish. And her dad sat steadfastly next to her, passing over his white hankie.

Chapter 7

"You come up with the dumbest rules. All my friends get to date. But me? Oh, no, I still have to sit in the nursery and have Mommy and Daddy hold my hand." Autumn was on a roll. Sarcasm dripped caustically from every word. "Jacob got to date when he was in high school. Of course, he is your favorite, and everything big brother does is fine."

The family was finishing up a lunch of taco salad and garlic bread, prepared at Autumn's request. Evert had been giving his wife and daughter details on the remodeling job he was presently working on at the Sutton's farm five miles out of town. It happened that Kristine Sutton was in Autumn's freshman class. Not exactly sure how the conversation had switched from oak cupboard doors to Kristine's dating book, Evert let his fiery daughter unload.

"Kristine has even gone out with a senior. They drove all the way to Norbert for the car races. If her parents let her choose her friends, then I think I should be able to decide which guys I want to hang out with." When she was angry, her eyelids lowered to slits, as if she couldn't handle the full view before her.

"Hmmmm." Evert appraised the challenge, wiping his plate clean with his last bite of garlic bread. "Has some young fellow asked you to go somewhere with him?"

"Well, no, but even if someone did, I'd have to say no 'cause you're keeping me locked in this house until I'm a junior." Her retort was sharp, stepping precariously into rudeness.

Sometimes, humor was the best recourse in dealing with her temperament. Squinting back at her, Evert laid his cards on the table. "That's good, because you have the biggest, meanest dad in the town of Prairie City. Why, I'm aiming to keep a loaded squirt gun right inside the door, and any guy who so much as looks at my princess will get it right between the eyes. And if that doesn't do it, I'll bring out my Super Soaker, and by the time I'm done with him, he'll look like a limp, soggy piece of cat fur drowning in the swimming pool. And mind you, that's only if he looks at you."

Rolling her eyes, Autumn let out a slow stream of air. "Don't you ever take me seriously?"

Entering the exchange, Jasmine propped her elbows on the table. "When I was a teenager, my parents set sixteen as the magical number to begin dating. Kids today seem like they are exposed to more at an earlier age. They see and talk about subjects that were largely taboo when I was growing up. But even if teenagers know about drugs, sex, and shacking up, that doesn't mean they are mature enough to make decisions for themselves in handling these issues."

"So it is a maturity issue?" Autumn was ready to pounce again.

"Yes and no," Evert intercepted the ball. "God has a purpose in each age we grow through. You are on the border between being a kid and becoming an adult. The way I look at it, you only have two years left to be a kid and the rest of your life to be an adult. Why not soak the kid age for all you've got? You can't back up once you become an adult. Responsibilities will weigh you down."

Not willing to continue the attack, Autumn crammed the remains of her taco salad into her mouth and emptied the milk glass. Leaving the table and the kitchen, she flung back, "I'm gonna call Maria and see if we had any homework."

"Weren't you in class?" her mom asked.

"Yeah, but I can't remember." And she was gone.

"Nice exit. Guess we're on kitchen cleanup duty." Jasmine handed Evert the rubber scraper.

"The only reason she can get away with it is because she's still a kid, but you and me, we've got responsibilities." Evert nodded knowingly at his wife. As Jasmine stood and started picking up the food containers to return to the refrigerator, he gave her butt a swat with the rubber scraper.

Arching her eyebrows, she threatened, "Watch it, buddy, or I'll get my Super Soaker."

Jasmine couldn't stop the advance of a new school year, yet she didn't applaud its approach either. Both Autumn and Jacob would be freshmen—Autumn at Prairie City Public High School and Jacob at North Dakota State University, four hours away, majoring in accounting. Her little boy had grown up and wouldn't be needing her at every intersection anymore. This is what parenting was all about, teaching the fledglings how to fly, and then backing away and letting them try their wings. He had been an easy son to raise—an amiable disposition, readily liked by peers and adults, spontaneous in giving a hand, gentle-spirited. He had taught them the ropes of parenting, making the experience an incredible journey of friendship between two parents and a child. A parent of such a child could easily become puffed up in pride, perceiving the difference she had made in a minor's life. A wise elderly father had once warned Jasmine, "If you think you are the ideal parent, have another child. You might discover it's not so much you, but rather, the makeup of the youngster, that decides his destiny."

As a family, they had moved Jacob into his dorm room, stood in line at the college book store as his first semester's textbooks slid across the cashier's scanner, hiked the paths he'd trek from his dormitory to the various class buildings. Ultimately, only the farewells had been left to say. There, he'd stood on the curb, as tall as his father in stature, one hand stuck in his jean pocket, a lopsided grin broadcasting he was more than ready for this step into manhood. And his mother, who thought she had it all together and was ready for this transition, bawled like a baby at leaving him behind. She'd understood Cynthia's behavior a lot better after giving her son that first good-bye hug. There would be more, but this one would always be imprinted in her mind as the hardest, or so she thought.

And then there was their second child, Autumn. Jacob had more than tolerated his younger sibling, often trying to lighten her mood with his dry jokes, yet to avoid her dramatic outbursts, or worse yet, to be drawn into them, he would often subtly slip away to do his own activities when she was beating her drum for a new tirade.

Joining the bleacher-sitting crowd, Evert and Jasmine spent many evenings cheering on the girls' volleyball team. Defeating to her self-esteem, Autumn also found her rump mandated to the bench of substitutes for the duration of the night by the coach. As a freshman, she was on the C squad and could only look longingly at the unforeseen day when her skills would improve enough for her to be promoted to the B and optimistically to the A squad. As a freshman, it was not surprising she was a member of the C squad. Most of the other freshman girls were there as well, except for a couple of superior athletes. But Autumn and one other girl saw virtually no playing time. How was a player supposed to improve if they weren't allowed on the floor? It was irritating for both Autumn and her parents.

Neither having a large enough pool of girls to draw from existing as separate units, Prairie City and Elton schools co-oped for sports. After-school practice sessions were shuffled between the two towns, players being bused back and forth. When practice was held in Prairie City, it was always delayed for thirty minutes waiting for the Elton bus to arrive with the coach and the rest of the team. This half-hour interval had become a fresh battleground for a spurt of new social attacks between Autumn and her fellow teammates.

"Mom, you don't understand. They snub me. They harass me about everything I do. I don't serve right, I can't block, I'm costing the team points. It is on and on and on. If I sit by them, they accuse me of trying to eavesdrop on their conversations."

Evert and Jasmine were at a loss. Small towns were a safe, wholesome place to raise kids. They liked their neighbors. Evert had done carpentry jobs for a large percentage of the town's residents and their local church. They wanted to protect their daughter and still be on speaking terms with the rest of the community. Autumn's tenacious personality threw up roadblocks, burned bridges, and constructed wide detours by those wishing to avoid her sharp tongue. As her parents, they too often traversed burning coals and fended off a lioness in attempts to get her to see the other side of a confrontation.

Yet, through it all, she was their little girl. Their gift from the Lord. Their Samuel. The answer to their prayers. They didn't want to see her bones picked clean by some skinny teenage vultures. Or pushed out of the freshman nest by cowbirds content to trespass where they didn't belong.

Where was the median? How could they pull Autumn out of the ditch and back onto the road with the rest of her freshman class?

The remodeling job at the Suttons had continued for a full month. In addition to building and installing new kitchen cupboards, Evert was constructing a mammoth wraparound porch on the old farmhouse. They had reached the finishing stages of cutting and mounting stair railings and decorative roof gables. If they kept at it, the project could be finished by quitting time at six.

The noise of the saw blade was abruptly cut short. "Hey, boss, the blade broke." Rodney's job was to cut the railing pieces to the right lengths.

"Must be a new one in the service truck," Evert called back, moving a ladder across the new porch boards to one of the house corners where the gables ended.

Scrounging through the boxes in the back of the pickup, Rodney rejoined, "Did you ever buy another blade after we threw out that dull one?"

Evert wasn't sure. He jogged down the steps to take a look himself. Carpenters didn't work without a saw. After a few minutes, he admitted defeat. "Start cleaning up the grounds. I'll run into town and get a couple. It looks like we might be short of railing material as well. I'll throw in another length to be on the safe side." Casting off the tool belt hugging his waist, he tore off in his truck, leaving a trail of dust swirls.

In minutes he'd reached the edges of their village. Hitting the main street through town, he slowed, not wishing to earn himself a speeding ticket in his haste. His eyes skimmed the brown tufted grass edges of the park as he motored past, his mind off somewhere else. Jasmine was usually home from school by five thirty. Checking his wristwatch, he figured school had already been dismissed for an hour. She always stayed after the final bell to prepare lessons for the next day.

A pink flutter on the far side of the park caught in his peripheral vision. A girl's relaxed form was lying full length across a picnic table, her back pressed into its flat top. An unzipped lightweight jacket lifted upward from her stomach in the slight autumn breeze.

A smile creased his tanned face. Like a golden waterfall, long hair fell over the edge of the table, swaying as it nearly brushed the dry weeds missed by the last mowing job of the season. In all of Prairie City, only his Autumn had such a full mane. For a while, when she was little, he'd called her Rapunzel. Over Christmas break that year, the two had watched the DVD musical *Tangled* four nights in a row. If was after the fourth viewing that he decided to go back to the nickname Princess!

He knew Autumn often cut through the park on her way to and from school. Evidently, volleyball practice had been canceled, and she couldn't resist soaking up some of the summer rays lingering into the fall. She didn't even lift her head when he tapped the horn in a light *toot*, unaware the greeting was for her. Evert propelled his truck onward. The interlude until quitting time was narrowing.

The electric garage door shut behind Jasmine's vehicle. The school day was over; however, the next portion of her day was just beginning. On her way to the kitchen, she stopped at the laundry room to drop off her heavy schoolbag and to shrug off her sweater hanging it on one of the many hooks lining the wall. Then she transferred the load of wet clothes waiting in the washing machine to the dryer.

Moving on down the hall to the kitchen, three flats of ripe tomatoes could be detected sitting on the counter, waiting to be skinned and cooked into salsa before being sealed in glass canning jars. This was the last garden produce awaiting processing, except for the pumpkins she planted for the sole purpose of giving a jack-o'-lantern to each of her first graders at Halloween.

After changing out of her school clothes, Jasmine pulled a package of pork chops out of the refrigerator and a skillet from below the stove. Getting supper in the oven was her first priority before tackling the tomatoes. Evert and Autumn would be home within the hour.

Evert arrived first, catching his wife elbow deep in a pot of tomatoes, squishing the skinned fruit between her fingers into smaller junks. "Ah, just what I like to see, my salsa queen." He dropped a kiss on top of her head and set his lunch box in the sink. "Smells good in here. What's for supper?" He opened the oven door a crack to have a look.

"Pork chops and rice. But first, I was hoping you'd help me get the onions chopped up. I always end up bawling from their stinging scent."

Even, with the use of the electric food processor, the air was charged with the pungent aroma of onions as he did as she asked. Jasmine had the dish towel pressed into her eyes while handing Evert a few jalapenos and garlic to chop with the remaining onions. "Where's a man's goggles when he needs them?" he asked, jokingly rubbing a bent arm over his eyes.

Autumn's steps could be heard approaching from the backdoor. They paused momentarily at the end of the kitchen counter. "Why don't you make it easier on yourselves and buy a case of salsa from the grocery store when it's on sale?" A hint of disdain edged her words.

"What?" her father mocked in reply. "And miss out on your mother's *excellente* hot salsa recipe? No way." Autumn's footsteps changed direction, heading for her bedroom.

"Okay, Evert, dump the rest into the kettle, and it can simmer while we eat." Having scraped the last onion and pepper bits into the hot tomatoes, he clapped the lid on the pot faster than tires screeching to a halt at a red light to prevent anymore of the onion scent from escaping into the air.

Jasmine couldn't help but chortle at the hilarity of the situation. Leaning back against the counter, she faced her chef partner. "Why do we go through this brutality every harvest season? Autumn has a point. Those onions are a killer. My eyes are still smarting."

"We made it!" He shoved the offending utensils under the cold water faucet, his nose dripping. "Have I earned a pork chop yet?" He ripped off a length of paper toweling and blew his nose long and hard for effect.

"Coming right up—wait, I have to check the clothes in the dryer." In her haste, she stepped over the pink jacket and gym bag Autumn had carelessly dumped in the hallway.

Returning to the kitchen, she lifted the steaming skillet of rice and pork from the oven. Raising her voice to alert their daughter, she called, "Supper's on, Autumn!"

Autumn slunk to her chair as her dad added a lettuce salad and dressings to the tabletop. After the blessing, small talk, mainly between the two adults, interspersed the enjoyment of the meal. "I finished at the Sutton's place today," Evert commented.

"Hey, all right!" Jasmine hailed. "Gravens will be glad to hear that." Ed Gravens was next on Evert's list. He wanted his single-car garage lengthened into three stalls.

"Of course, now I won't be able to monitor Kristine's string of suitors lined up on their new porch." Looking sideways at his silent daughter, he wondered if she'd attack his bait like a northern after a smelt. Jasmine caught his eye and ever so slightly shook her head in a negative motion, warning him not to arouse their prickly daughter needlessly.

Autumn said nothing, watching the thousand island dressing trickling off the lip of the bottle onto a lettuce leaf. She was in one of her silent, don't-talk-to-me moods.

"How was volleyball practice today?" her mom asked, trying to draw her out.

"Fine."

"Learn any new sets?" she attempted a second time.

"Nah. Larsen keeps us working on the old ones until we have them down." Autumn screwed the lid back onto the dressing bottle.

"Was Maria there today? Sheila said she was home sick yesterday, ear infection."

"She was back."

Listening to the exchange between his wife and daughter, an image of a gal lying on a picnic table crept into his thoughts. It bothered him.

"Did practice get out early?" he interjected casually, cutting the pork chop into bite-size pieces.

"Larsen let us out early? You gotta be kidding." Using her fork, she folded the lettuce leaves in half to spear them onto the prongs.

"Are you sure you were at practice today?" He hated catching his princess in a lie.

"Why wouldn't I be?" Vexation stiffened her spine. Her shoulders broadened as she sat up straighter.

"I don't know. That's why I'm asking. I saw you in the park, must have been sometime after four." He kept his tone light, hoping Autumn wouldn't erupt at being ensnared in a trap of her own making, or worse yet, shut down completely.

Ding! The cycle on the dryer ended. Jasmine jumped up to heed its call. Running into the neglected coat and bag in the hallway, she stooped to pick them up and take them with her to their proper places.

Shaking out the pink windbreaker to hang it from a hook, she was appalled to find the lightweight material had been ripped down the front on either side of the zipper in two long frayed tears. *What the world?* The jacket had been purchased new prior to school commencing. Forgetting about the dryer, Jasmine did an about-face and retraced her steps to where her two family members were frozen in a silent standoff.

Since neither was speaking, she ventured, "Ah, Autumn, what happened to your windbreaker?" She held it aloft, the rended front clearly visible.

"I, I don't know," she stammered.

Her dad leaned forward on the table, his forearms resting on each side of his half-eaten plate. "Come on, Autumn. We're on your side, remember?" His fingers touched her hand, but she withdrew it. Her eyes followed it to her lap.

A teardrop oozed its way out of the corner of her eye, slid to her cheekbone, hesitated a second, and plunged downward, following a zigzag path to her jawbone.

Gently, he asked again, "Did something occur prior to your practice session? Did you get into it with some of the players?"

The dam broke. Tears cascaded over each other, tumbling down her cheeks like a thunderstorm lashing against a riverbank, eroding its way into her parents' hearts. The wrecked jacket forgotten, Jasmine slid her chair next to Autumn's, placing an arm about her shoulders. Evert tugged his clean handkerchief from his back pocket. For a few minutes, their daughter could only weep, surrounded by the love she often rejected.

As the sobbing lessened and a hiccup escaped, Autumn mopped her face with the borrowed hankie. "I shouldn't have…I shouldn't have gotten angry, but I couldn't stop myself." Wiping her nose, she continued. "Sharice said my mom must have been a slut to give me up when I was a baby!" Her teeth clenched. "She doesn't have any idea who my mother was!"

A fierce protectiveness tightened within Evert's chest. Jasmine tucked wet tendrils of Autumn's hair behind her ears to clear her bedraggled face. They were aware Sharice was a junior and played on the A team.

"Whatever brought that topic up?" her dad probed for more details, conscious of the fact that Autumn wasn't usually innocent in disputes.

"She was trying to get my goat. Guess she did." Her downcast eyes never met her father's scrutiny.

The school had a no tolerance policy when it came to bullying. Maybe this matter needed to be taken further.

"Are you thinking about quitting volleyball?" her mother queried.

"Quit? That's what they want me to do! Why would I quit? I want to be in sports." Frustrating as it was to sit on the bench during matches, at least she could say she was on the team. To her, that made her somebody.

"Ah, so our little girl has a backbone," Jasmine commended. "Good! But remember, to be apart of a team, you have to be a team player. That means getting along with everyone, even if it means biting your lip once in a while or sticking your clenched fists in your pockets."

Evert took up the message. "What Sharice said was cruel, and I hope she apologizes to you. Did you hit her?"

Autumn nodded her head in slow jerks. "Anyway, I tried to, but some of the other girls held me away."

"Then an apology might be appropriate from your end as well." Jasmine rubbed her daughter's back with one hand. "You know, we sure are lucky to have you." She leaned her head against Autumn's temple.

Evert encircled them both with a hug. "We are blessed."

On his way to Elton the following morning, Evert formulated a plan within his head. His first stop would be at the Elton High School to catch Coach Larsen before the first bell. Then he'd stop off at Jasmine's room and decide with her if a formal complaint of bullying needed to be submitted. He knew they might be walking a tight wire drawn between small towns, especially with his wife being a teacher in the system. Yet, this was his daughter hurting. She was far from perfect, but she deserved to be treated civilly.

Coach Larsen was in his office, talking on the phone, when Evert filled his doorway. He motioned Evert to a chair, removing his clipboard from the seat. Seconds later, he put down his phone and reached out a hand to Evert. "Mr. Kirmis, I thought I might see you today."

"Really?" Evert grasped his handshake. "I'm not one to thrash coaches and plead for special treatment of my kids."

Larsen's mouth lifted. "I can't say I've seen you here before. Other than their last names, your son and daughter do not have a lot of similarities."

"Yes, Autumn is a bit sharp around the edges. It would be nice to take my sander and plane some of that off, but I guess it's a package deal. Can you fill me in on what happened yesterday?"

"Only what the other girls said, and that could be bias. I was on the bus with the Elton girls on our way to Prairie City when the ruckus took place. I just caught her running from the gym as I was coming down the hallway. I called out to her, but there was no way she was stopping. I asked the other girls what was going on. Seems Autumn had been riding Casey for a number of days about her mom not being married, yet always being seen with a different man. She called her some off-color names. Casey isn't one to fight back. However, some of the older girls did it for her and gave Autumn some of her own treatment. Guess she didn't like it very well."

Evert looked grim. The coach read him wrong. "Now, I am by no means condoning what they did. That's the story they gave me. You probably got a different version from Autumn."

"Yah, something about her birth mom being called a slut."

"I won't say that didn't happen, Evert, because it very well may have. Do you want us to call in the girls and question them one-on-one and get a facsimile of what really transpired?"

Evert let out a long breath. "No, I'll discuss it with my wife and daughter first. Anything that could be done about the unchaperoned half hour between the end of school and practice?"

"Technically, school gets out at 3:15 p.m. and practice begins thirty minutes after. The girls elect to come early and fool around in the gym while they're waiting for our bus to arrive. I realize it's an inconvenience not being able to start right after school, but that's one of the sacrifices made when we co-op between towns. I can only suggest for her to not show up until 3:45 p.m. Go home for a half hour or find some place to do homework."

Kneading the cap he held in his hands, Evert nodded. "Sorry to take up your time. Raising daughters is a hard day's wage."

Larsen laughed. "Don't tell me that. I have two coming up."

Taking a step toward the door, Evert paused and turned back. "Any chance Autumn could get more playing time? I realize she's not your most skilled player, but it is hard to improve if not given the chance to do so."

Larsen acknowledged the reasoning. "It's not so much that her skills don't measure up, it's more her attitude. She doesn't want to play as a team, setting it up, using the strategies we've practiced. She kind of becomes a one-man team and attempts to belt the ball over the net no matter where she is positioned."

As much as he would have liked to have refuted the coach and stood up for his daughter, he realized there was truth in what the man said. Shaking his hand a second time, he departed.

After touching base with his wife, Jasmine agreed to call the school counselor in Prairie City and pick her brain a bit to see how she could help in restoring relationships amongst the team members.

It was a tattered inauguration to Autumn's high school experience. They hoped they could some how sew the remnants together and move on. Yet the load rested primarily on their daughter's shoulders.

Chapter 8

"You are my rock, you are my rock!" In sync, the wall of standing students waved their arms to the ceiling, swaying to the rhythm of the bass drum and electric guitars. The four musicians ate up the microphones as they chanted the words repeatedly, sliding across the platform caught in the circular glow of the spotlight, their eyes closed in worship. Bending his mic stand backward, the lead singer knelt on one knee, singing a bass solo for two lines. Then he threw back his sweaty mop of dark hair and jumped to his feet, letting his pick rake the guitar strings vehemently. Two of his partners put their palms together, clapping out the beat of the music. Instantly, the crowd simulated the band, clapping their hands over their heads, vocalizing the repetition of words. Flashes of reds, blues, and greens oscillated throughout the darkened auditorium in carnival fashion. "You are my rock, you are my rock!"

Anyway, that's what Jasmine thought they were singing. With the speakers cranked up, and the singers' lips permanently attached to the microphones, it sounded more like noise to her. The lyrics could have been any phrase. Sneaking a glance at Evert beside her, she saw that he too was having difficulty appreciating the teenage concert. Her eyes twinkled in merriment. The hilarity of the situation washed over both of them simultaneously. A couple about to roll their birthdays to the fourth decade was definitely out of place in the mass of high schoolers embracing a Christian rock festival. Evert's shoulders shook in a small-scaled earthquake, which only heightened the roll of waves running a circuit in Jasmine's stomach. Placing a hand over her mouth, she resisted the urge to let out a loud guffaw, although with the volume's intensity ricocheting against the church's interior, it was doubtful anyone would have heard it. Leaning his mouth to her ear, Evert practically shouted his question. "Which song have you liked the best so far?" The witty query only pumped her chest faster. Knifing him in the ribs, she rolled her eyes in answer.

Wait till she pounced on Cynthia tomorrow at school! Cynthia had invited them to bring Autumn to the Christian youth concert her church in Elton was hosting on a Saturday night. The band had traveled from Fargo and was supposedly in great demand by youth organizations in the area. Watching Autumn weave back and forth with the rest of her age group, she didn't seem to have any inhibitions about the music. Jasmine had to remind herself that was why they had come.

Surveying the crowd, Jasmine noted the largest percentage of youth assembled seemed to be from Elton, many of who had passed through her classroom years back. A sprinkling of Prairie City kids dotted the crowd as well, mixed with a bunch she didn't recognize. Chaperones and parents hugged the back rows.

Half way through the concert, the musicians took a break, three sitting on tall stools placed at the back of the platform. Tilting water bottles, they quenched their dry throats. The fourth performer lifted his stool to the forefront within a few feet of the mob of kids still rocking on fire. Motioning to the throng, they settled down into their seats to listen to what he had to say.

"Hey, we serve an awesome God! Did you know that? Yes, we serve an awesome God! Everything we do up here is to God's glory, not our own. So let's give Him our applause."

Setting down their drinks and then standing up, the band members clapped, starting a chain reaction with the youth. Everyone was on their feet once again, applauding the Maker of the universe. An expectant hush descended on the room a second time. The speaker, reclaiming his stool top, waited for each person to give him attention. "We call our group Undeserved, for that is exactly what we are—undeserved. We don't deserve God's mercy. We don't deserve Christ's nails. We don't deserve His forgiveness, but we are so glad we've been given it! Hallelujah?" He twisted his torso to view his teammates behind him.

Immediately, his three buddies were on their feet, extending their arms heavenward, nodding in agreement. "Hallelujah!" A smattering of applause broke out again.

"Yeah! Christ died that we might have a room reserved for us in His mansion in heaven. And it's not going to be like getting a motel room here in Elton. We called all three of the motels here in town, and guess what? They all said they were full! We couldn't get in! What do you have going on in this tiny town that everyone wants to come here?" The young guy was likeable; the crowd easily chuckled with him.

"Heaven is not that way. The Bible says, 'Believe on the Lord Jesus Christ and you will be saved' (Acts 16: 31, NIV). That's it. Jesus plus nothing equals salvation. You make your reservation by asking Jesus to come live in your heart, and the heavenly desk clerk says, 'You're in! We have a room waiting for you.' Cool, huh? Real cool."

Holding a portable mic, the fellow stepped off the platform and into the center aisle. "Think of the best hotel you've ever stayed in—the state-of-the-art, all the dressings, including the price tag. The Holiday Inn, the Ramada, the Hilton—they are nothing compared to what is waiting for you in heaven. Golden terraces, angelic room service, triumphal music." Halfway down the aisle, he stopped, gazing at the adults listening attentively.

"I know what you're thinking." He laughed. "You're thinking to yourselves, 'I'm sure glad we won't have to listen to this music up there.' Am I right? You won't be able to turn off your hearing aids in heaven because all of us will hear just fine there."

Evert and Jasmine linked eyes and burst into an impromptu spiel of laughter along with the older generation of chaperones. "That's okay. We haven't gotten any premature booking dates requesting us to serenade for a night at the Heavenly Throne, but I do want you to realize that Psalm 100:1 says, 'Make a joyful *noise* onto the Lord, all ye lands!' (KJ). Hear that? Noise!" Another wave of laughter dominoed through the pews. "We are scriptural! How about that? And furthermore, I bet you wish we'd sing some of your old favorites—'How Great Though Art,' 'In the Garden,' 'When the Roll Is Called Up Yonder,' 'Amazing Grace,' or even 'Jesus Loves Me.' Back up to Psalm 98:1 with me, and it says, 'Sing to the Lord a *new* song' (NIV). Yes, it says new!"

Even though the band hadn't won the parents over with its blaring rock music, the leader had them right in his hand as he bantered over their taste in music.

"You know, I'm just ribbing you. I like the old hymns myself, and to prove it, we're going to sing 'Jesus Loves Me' right now."

Back to the platform he jogged. He leapt to his spot, grabbed his guitar, threw it in the air, and when he caught it, all four guys hit the first chord of the beloved children's hymn. The auditorium was filled with the melodious tones of teenagers and adults joining their voices as one. "Yes, Jesus loves me, the Bible tells me so." An instrumental improvisation was added to the end played ever so sweetly, dying away to silence with the last notes. No one even applauded at the end.

After five seconds of silence, the band members resumed their earlier style, tugging the youth back to their feet, swinging and screaming with the vibrations.

Following the concert, the youth congregated in the fellowship hall, conversing with the band members and eating pizza. Totally oblivious to her parents, Autumn loved socializing with these *new* friends. She was one of the group, accepted for a change. No one sidestepped her or gave her demeaning glares.

Even as the assemblage began to break up—youth leaders from other towns or churches herding their groups to the waiting vans—Autumn lingered on, getting to know the kids in the Elton youth group. She was packing a week of camp experience into one night. The group diminished to a dozen, which the youth pastor encouraged to assist in taking down the lunch tables and folding chairs. Autumn had latched on to a tall young man wearing a football jersey. He moved in the direction of the chair rack, but Autumn held him back from helping by her nonstop chatter. Evert and Jasmine could see their daughter was about to overstep her welcome if she didn't gracefully exit.

"Autumn, are you ready to go?" her dad politely called.

Glancing over her shoulder, she gave him a cool look. "In a minute."

Fifteen minutes later, the three walked to the parking lot. Autumn was unusually talkative with her parents, keeping a running commentary of the night's events. Listening to her chatter from the backseat, Evert reached over and squeezed his wife's fingers. The night had been a success.

Sunday found the Kirmis family back in their community church in Prairie City for the morning service. Having been up late the night before, it had taken more than mild coaxing to get Autumn out from under the mound of covers where she was dug in like a gopher for the winter. "I'm too tired. Go without me," she moaned.

When his usual cajoling didn't get the desired results, Evert used his unaccustomed sternness. "You have fifteen minutes to be ready and waiting at the backdoor."

Even in her sleepy state of mind, Autumn attempted to chart her own course. "And if I'm not?"

"You don't want to know," he retorted and moved off to his own room.

Inwardly, Jasmine was disappointed in her daughter's spiritual lukewarmness. Evert and Jasmine's marriage was grounded in their Christian faith. From the first day in their home, both Jacob and Autumn had been a part of the family prayers done at meals, as well as the bedtime prayers before they got tucked in for the night. Bible stories and songs were a nightly ritual. As they got older, Sunday school, vacation Bible school, and camps became a family routine. Yet, unless Autumn personalized her faith in Jesus Christ, inhaling Him wholeheartedly into her being, letting Him be her daily guide, it was synonymous with having a membership at the health club but never exercising.

Jasmine's mind traveled back to when Autumn had been merely five. As always, their family had been in attendance at the community church service in Prairie City. The pastor at the time had given a moving message on falling at the feet of Jesus. He had ended his sermon by inviting everyone who wanted to make that initial commitment to the Lord to come forward. The congregation had stood, singing the final hymn of the service, while the devoted pastor waited. An insistent tug on her sweater first went ignored. When it continued, becoming more of jolt than a tug, she turned about to see what was so important it couldn't wait until the church was over.

"Can I go up to Pastor Dan?" Autumn had whispered earnestly.

Hearing the question, Evert had sat down in the bench and put his daughter on his knee. Jasmine hadn't thought Autumn even listened during Pastor Dan's addresses, yet she must have caught his last request. Unsure whether she understood why he was asking people to come forward, Evert whispered back to her, "We'll talk about it at home."

"No, Daddy. I want to ask Jesus into my heart right now."

He wavered, not knowing if willingness or understanding were the criteria here.

"Daddy, I'll give you all the money in my piggy bank if you let me go." Her green eyes had looked pleadingly back at him and then up at her mother.

Evert had nodded, a mist fogging his sight. Autumn slipped past the legs of the elderly couple sitting next to them and walked a straight-legged fast jaunt to the pastor who welcomed her with open arms. Evert had wrapped an arm around Jasmine's middle; they were both internalizing the moment.

As the final verse of "Amazing Grace" faded away, Pastor Dan, overcome with emotion, choked out the words, "A child has heeded the call of Christ. Does no one else want Him?"

Autumn's Christian walk had begun with intense fervor at such a young age. However, in her last years, it had evaporated like the morning dew droplets on the wet blades of grass in the heat of the day. Had the scorching years of adolescence dried up her first love?

Midafternoon, Jasmine was occupied with a needle and thread, hand quilting a harvest wall hanging she had pieced together, stealing a few minutes here and there out of her busy days.

Nearby, Evert examined the blueprints for a horse stable he had been hired to construct, jotting down the materials he'd need at the work site to start the project. Hopefully, it would be a late fall, enabling him to erect the shell prior to a snowstorm being in the weather forecast.

Autumn wandered through the room, seemingly for no reason. Neither of her parents looked up, concentrating on the materials before them. Opening a storage cupboard, she rummaged through its contents, shut the door, and tried another.

Biting off a filament, Jasmine glanced her way. "What are you searching for?" She cut another length of quilting thread and weaved it through the needle's eye.

"Hot dog skewers, like we used over the Fourth of July out at the Philip's cabin for roasting marshmallows." Autumn moved onto the coat closet in the front foyer.

"Wouldn't they be with the camping gear in the garage?" Her needle moved in and out along the edge of the appliquéd pumpkin decorating the wall hanging.

"Makes sense, I guess. I'll check."

Finally registering what Autumn had asked for, she called out to her daughter's backside, which was racing to the backdoor. "What do you need hot dog skewers for?"

No answer. Minutes later, their daughter reappeared triumphant. "Ta-da!" she cried, holding up the sought out items like a prized trophy. "Found them."

Once his papers were stacked in a neat pile, Evert gave her his full attention, noting she was attired in blue jeans and a hooded sweatshirt. "Are you having a backyard bonfire with the dead leaves I raked up?"

"Fat chance. I'm headed down to the river beach outside of Elton. Some of the kids I met last night from their youth group are gathering for a campfire. I thought I'd join them." She had both of her parents' attention now.

"Oh?" her dad hedged. "Did they invite you?"

"It's not an invitation kind of get-together, Dad. Kids just hang out. Anyone can come. Do we have some hot dogs in the freezer, Mom?" Leaving the room, she headed for the kitchen.

Something didn't feel right about her offhand response. "And how are you getting there?" her dad's question followed her. She was still a year away from meeting the age requirement for a driver's license.

Digging through the frozen foods, she purposely didn't make eye contact. "I figured you'd drop me off."

After hefting himself up from his chair, her father trailed her footsteps to the kitchen and leaned his tall form against the door frame. Having found a package of wieners, Autumn stuffed them in a plastic grocery bag then knelt in front of the open refrigerator, pilfering condiments of ketchup and mustard.

"I don't think it's a good idea."

"Yes, it is. It gives me a chance to hang out with kids who actually like me, instead of the snobs in this town." The bottles followed the meat into the bag. "Mom, don't we have any buns?"

"Autumn, you had a good time last night. We're happy for you. That's why we took you. We wanted you to meet some new gals and guys, but let's not rush into this circle of friends. Give yourself some time, give them some room, and slowly expand your friendships," Evert spoke quietly.

Only too well were they aware of how she could smother a new relationship by becoming overly available and excessively talkative. Her dominating personality would move to the forefront, manipulating her peers and their activities.

Having put her sewing aside, Jasmine joined the duo, a tightness beginning to constrict her insides. Why did she feel as if they were always walking on eggshells when discussing a matter with their daughter?

"Dad, you think too much. They all adored me after the concert. They want me to be there."

As desperate as she was to be accepted to be a part of a group, Autumn's arrogance prevented her from stepping back and sizing up the situation.

"I hope they do," Jasmine agreed, looping her arm into her daughter's. "More than anything, your dad and I want you to have some wholesome kids to mix with. The concert was a good start. How can we strategically plan the next step so the kids will ask you to be a part of their group without you just barging in?"

Disentangling her arm from her mother's, Autumn's lips clamped into a tight line, her eyes rolled upward. "Are you going to take me or not?"

There was no give-and-take with her. It was either her way or no way.

Blowing a puff of air out as an introduction, Evert wearily replied to her ultimatum, "Autumn, I would be the first one in the car if I thought driving at top speed the fifteen miles to Elton was going to ensure your acceptance into this youth group for your remaining high school years. But because I want this for you so badly, I'm asking you to move slowly. Those kids will still be around next week or next month."

Autumn had heard all she cared to hear. Dropping the bag of groceries on the floor with a thud, she pushed past her father, tore down the hallway, and banged the rear door in her flight. Jasmine moved as if to follow her, but Evert intercepted, catching her arm. "Let her cool off. Maybe she'll come around." Gazing into his flecked eyes, Jasmine noted resignation. Somehow, when they had signed up to become parents, they hadn't consciously verbalized to each other or to themselves that along with the warm fuzzy anticipations of having a child in the home, there would be raging storms to calm, fires to douse, bridges to cross.

Eyeing the grocery bag left on the ceramic floor, Jasmine scooped it up to put its contents back in refrigeration.

"Jazz." Evert motioned to her with his head as he peered cautiously out the window into the backyard. The massive oak and maple trees shading the redwood deck in the summer had been stripped naked by the autumn breezes whistling a warning of cooler temperatures to come. Littering the lawn, the colored leaves had formed a mottled mat of rusty scarlet, hiding a green carpeted lawn beneath. Earlier in the weekend, Evert had begun raking the leaves away from the fence row, heaping up piles of fallen foliage. In the midst of the autumn scene sat the half-filled wheelbarrow, waiting for its owner to continue his job.

Now, sprawled on top of the leaves in the barrel was Autumn, her head resting on the handles, her bent legs dangling over the side. Her ponytail had come undone, leaving a mass of gold to blend in with the finger-painted scene of fall. Jasmine's heart warmed. Saved in a photo album were pictures of their toddlers romping in heaps of leaves, their faces exuberant with delight.

Although the picture before her would be a touching treasure, she didn't dare upset the applecart any more than it had already been spilled by running for her camera. Filing the Norman Rockwell scene away in her mind, Jasmine put it to memory. Later tonight, the moment would be captured in her journal, a written record of a visual masterpiece, a reminder of the beautiful daughter they had indeed been blessed to receive.

She resumed her quilting, and the late afternoon shadows crept up unnoticed as Evert snored softly in his recliner.

Rousing himself, he looked over at his wife who was curled up at the end of the couch, still stitching on her quilted square. "What do you say? Let's go for ice cream." In agreement, she stretched, setting her sewing aside. The pizza parlor in Prairie City was no bigger than a single-stall garage, yet it catered to the public, serving everybody's favorite—chocolate sundaes.

"I'll see if Autumn wants to come along." He checked her bedroom, but it was vacant.

"I'd guess she's still outside. I never heard her come in. She may not want to indulge in an ice cream treat with the enemy," Jasmine reminded her husband.

"Ah, but I'm buying." He winked back at her.

The wheelbarrow sat mournfully alone, as did the yard. "She might have gone for a walk." Jasmine walked into the garage to join Evert, who was climbing into the car. "Her bike is gone. Could be off on a bike ride with—" She stopped. A thought came to her. "No, she wouldn't take off for Elton on her bicycle..." That was crazy. It was fifteen miles, and it would be dark in another hour.

Evert paused at her supposition. "Yes, she would. She's stubborn enough to defy us." Bypassing the corner pizza joint, they headed out of town toward Elton, seeking a cyclist in the rapidly fading sunset. Seven and half miles later, the stooped silhouette of a rider and bicycle dragged off the highway into the rough stubble of the ditch took shape. Jasmine seesawed between cheering and crying—cheering that they had found her, yet crying because Autumn would go to this extreme to seek the company of peers. She was so needy. A gaping hole torn in her middle desperately needed filling. And if it wasn't filled with positive wholesome friends, she would allow anyone to step in and give her what she was desperately pursuing.

After coming to a halt on the shoulder of the road, the two parents stared out at their daughter, the wind tearing at her clothing and hair. Oil-stained fingers struggled with the task of rolling the chain back onto the gears.

Pressing the electric button on her window and letting it descend halfway, Jasmine tentatively called out, not sure what their reception would be, "Need a hand?"

Life visibly drained from the exhausted biker as she dropped her denim bottom on the prickly ground, deflated. "Yeah. This is the third time the chain came off."

Her dad was the man for the job. Joining her in the ditch, he quickly had the chain back in place. "Looks like it needs some adjustment. I'll tighten it at home." He held out an open hand to her. She accepted and he pulled her to her feet.

"Let's make a deal. We throw this bicycle in the trunk and head home. And on Wednesday evening, I'll make sure you're in Elton for their weekly youth meeting, and it won't be by way of a two-wheeler."

Wearily, she nodded her head, her blond hair blowing into twisted snarls. Together, they wheeled the bicycle up the ditch.

The vehicle made a U-turn on the desolate highway as the sun bid its occupants a good night, fading below the hazy horizon line.

A family, for the moment, traveling in the same direction.

Chapter 9

Drumming his nails on the kitchen countertop, Evert watched as Jasmine lifted the plug on the dirty dish water, letting it swirl into a tornado before plummeting down the drain. It always seemed they were trying to stay one step ahead of Autumn to prevent her from drowning in her own self-afflicted deluge.

In the last months, Autumn had been definitely a happier gal, not because of any significant change in her school life, rather because she had a midweek outing to set her sights on—a buoy to latch on to, floating calmly in a turbulent ocean of offensive remarks, diminishing friendships, missed opportunities, and lonely after-school hours endured largely at home.

Their daughter's philosophy became, "If I can just make it till Wednesday night." And then when she did, the youth activity in Elton swung her to such a high pinnacle that waking up on Thursday morning was something she could handle. Only two more days until the weekend. Occasionally, the youth group would plan a group activity on Friday or Saturday night, which was an extra cherry on her banana split attitude. Sporadically, the youth would help with the Sunday morning service by leading the musical praise time or dramatizing a skit conducive to the pastor's sermon. Autumn had even done a piano solo of old hymns. On such Sundays, the Kirmis family would worship in Elton rather than Prairie City. There was no coaxing Autumn out of bed on these mornings.

If given the chance, Autumn would have found an excuse to be in Elton every day of the week, but her parents gently pulled on the reins, wanting this newborn relationship to be reciprocated by the other youth attending the Wednesday meetings. Even though she never missed a group event thus far, she had not been asked by anyone to hang out in the way teenagers do. The balance teetered a bit too lopsided for Evert and Jasmine's comfort.

Hitting the counter with one final knuckle wrap, Evert quizzed his wife. "What's your gut feeling? Is open enrollment the answer, or is it going to smear her muddy waters all the way to Elton?"

Secretly, the two had been throwing back and forth the idea of open enrolling Autumn in the Elton public school for her upcoming sophomore year of high school. North Dakota law mandated an application of request be submitted to the admitting school by the end of February of the preceding school year. Upon review and acceptance of the application, a student would begin the fall term in the new school.

Two drawbacks accompanied an approval. The first was transportation. A school was not required to provide bus service out of their district. This was an easy ravine for the Kirmises to ford. Since Jasmine taught in the elementary building in Elton, Autumn could simply ride to and from school with her. They were, however, not sure Autumn would endorse the second challenge—sports. She would not be able to play varsity volleyball the first quarter.

"I wish we didn't have to decide months before the school year begins. A lot could happen between now and then." Jasmine dried her hands on a towel and hung it on the oven handle.

"Yah, I'm with you." Evert tried to view the situation from all angles. He was almost sure Autumn would jump at the chance of switching schools without even considering volleyball. Although her skills had developed over the season, so had everyone else's, keeping her permanently on the bench. Volleyball was more of a status symbol to her, something to list on her graduation profile.

He feared more that the same battleground encompassing Prairie City would eventually be duplicated in Elton.

"Look at this way." Jasmine attempted to broaden his viewpoint from still another perspective, like an artist with a brush painting a mural instead of a manicurist coloring a single fingernail. "A lot of people here in Prairie City are *tired* of our daughter. Her idiosyncrasies have gnawed on everyone—her peers, her teachers, the school counselor, her teammates. Even if open enrollment is not the glorious answer we'd like it to be, maybe it will give everyone, including Autumn, nine months of rest, nine months of relief, a change of pace, a renewing of interest. It's hard to keep rearranging the bag of tricks when dealing with the same magicians. It would give Autumn additional time to mature. And even if she falls into the same rutty pattern in Elton, and everything goes south, at least if we decide to bring her back to Prairie City a year later, the home troops will be refreshed. Autumn might wake up to the fact that in order to get along with people, she has to make some adjustments in her mannerisms." Her voice faded into silence with the enormity of what they faced, yet virtually had no control over.

Evert picked up the imaginary brush, adding a rosy tint. "And just maybe our fears are for nothing. Elton could be the perfect solution. She'll find her connection there. She doesn't need twenty-five close friends, a mere handful would do, even one or two." Rubbing the back of his neck, frustration gnawed at him. "Ah, what do I know? I'm just a carpenter, not a psychologist."

Her arms around his neck, Jasmine contradicted his claim. "Hmmm, the most well-known figure in history was a carpenter.

I'd say you are following in the footsteps of good stock." Folding her against his chest, he reckoned, "Well, at least I've got you fooled."

Broaching the subject with Autumn, they were not surprised she jubilantly internalized their suggestion, casting off the volleyball obstacle like flicking a piece of lint off her sweater. Cautioning her to be mute on the subject until it found its own peephole to leak through, they moved forward with the paperwork. Once the application was accepted by the Elton school, they were committed to this course of action, no matter what transacted between now and the end of August.

Meanwhile, Autumn whipped to school the following day, lighting fires furiously by announcing to her classmates she was done with their conceited, judgmental treatment of her and would soon be out of there. Bridges burned at her backside as they applauded her exodus.

The remaining months of the school year were an inferno of troubles. Autumn was charred in the fuel of her own making. If her weary parents managed to get her up in the morning and dropped off at the school door, the principal inevitably called to report a misdemeanor within the school building or to report her ditching the afternoon classes completely. Jasmine's cell phone was a constant buzz. By the final week, she wasn't even upset with her daughter's report card bearing three Ds and a flag in algebra for the last semester. Jasmine was just glad it was over. There was no way life could deteriorate any further, could it?

Summer crept in and out, a race the tortoise would easily have won again. The heavy stress cloud of trying to get Autumn to perform appropriately academically and socially had temporarily lifted, but most days, she acted like a dead rat, dragging herself in and out of her room for meals, suntanning on the back deck or lying in the bathtub for hours covered with billows of bubbles. There were no projects started and completed, no assistance volunteered in yard care or housework. Jasmine seriously wondered if she was battling depression, but she met immediate resistance if she implied a doctor's appointment might be helpful.

Evert finally coaxed their daughter into tagging along with him to his job sites for parts of days. Jacob had not come home for the summer. Having finished his first year of college, he'd been offered a job in Fargo that fit in with his accounting degree.

Depending on what point the construction was at, Autumn picked her jobs. She liked helping her dad shingle a roof or fit pieces of siding onto an exterior wall. Cementing jobs were frowned upon, and demolition work was strictly off-limits.

The only day she truly came to life was on Wednesday, when the carrot of the pending youth meeting dangling in her forethoughts transformed her into a motivated roadrunner. She would have the foods for the evening meal chopped, mixed, and baked by the middle of the afternoon, not wanting the family to linger a single minute longer than necessary over the supper table. Before Evert had the last spoonful of chocolate truffle dessert to his lips, she'd whisk his plate off the table and into the dishwasher.

Under her cajoling, they began attending the church in Elton on Sunday mornings, an easy concession for them as parents to make for their only daughter.

Other than occasional babysitting jobs of younger neighborhood children, Autumn removed herself from the presence of any of Prairie City's younger generation—even Maria Philips and Emma Runk, except for the week of Bible camp. When the pending Fourth of July weekend at the Philips's cabin surfaced, she raised such a fuss about attending that Jasmine embarrassingly came up with a lame excuse to Sheila and Brent on why they couldn't fit the annual event into their schedule. She was sure they saw through her flimsy pretense clearer than a freshly washed window.

The transition to Elton High School slid in smoothly; it was like skating on ice. Autumn chattered all the way home each day and continued right through the supper hour. "And guess what? Ms. Franklin says I have more aptitude for math than I give myself credit. Somehow, it is easier in her class." Autumn was taking geometry, but at the switch of the semesters, she wanted to register for algebra as well, to make up for the semester she had failed the previous spring. "Oh, and in Mr. Judson's class, I have to give an extemporaneous speech. Mine is scheduled for Thursday."

"What's your topic?" her dad asked, pleased at the daily reports they were receiving.

"Dad! Extemporaneous means impromptu. We have to pull a slip of paper out of a hat, think for five minutes, and then voila!"

"You should be good at that." He winked.

Giving him an exasperated eye roll, she burst out laughing. "I think you're right!"

If there was any nicks in paradise, it was in Jasmine's schedule. For almost two decades, she had chauffeured herself the fifteen miles to work, savoring the solitude by listening to music and praying. Arriving a good hour before any of her students traipsed into the room and plied for her attention with tales of their own, she could do the final preparations for the day.

Autumn had never been a morning person. Living mere blocks from the school in Prairie City, she previously arose soon after her mom departed for the day, freeing up the bathroom and kitchen for her use alone. Autumn's tendency to dawdle resulted in Jasmine having fewer minutes in her classroom before the start of the day. Irritation grated under her skin, like a pebble in a shoe. Reminding herself of the holocaust of Autumn's freshman year, she soothed her ruffled feathers and prayed for patience as she waited in the running vehicle parked in the driveway.

Even if this heavenly interlude was temporary, it was a sweet, soothing ointment to their bruised spirits, a rest where once there had only been chaos. Surprisingly, their daughter, who was usually lax when it came to helping around the home, started lending a hand. When Maria stopped over one afternoon to deliver some products from a fund-raiser, Autumn was more than civil, and the two girls ended up chatting for over an hour before Maria said she'd better continue with her deliveries.

Life had regained its quality. Yet subconsciously, Jasmine held her breath, fearful of when it would again unravel. The first frayed edge came in November blowing in with the north wind plummeting temperatures to the freezing mark.

The music department was formulating plans for the musical production, *The Music Man*. Initially, Autumn wasn't interested in trying out as a cast member; her eye was on the piano accompanist, priding herself in her expertise on the keyboard. Auditions for the pianist and background instrumentalists were scheduled for Tuesday after school. The cast auditions would be held on Wednesday.

On the drive to school, Autumn reminded her mother of her schedule following school.

"Did you bring along a piece of sheet music to play for Mr. and Mrs. Baumquist?" Jasmine questioned. The married couple were the head of the entire music department from kindergarten through twelfth grade.

"No, they said not to bring anything. They'd have what we need. Won't it be cool if I'm chosen to be the accompanist?" She hummed a few bars of "Seventy-six Trombones," tapping her hands on the dash. "I think I'll get it 'cause there aren't many good piano players in the high school."

"Just do your best and what happens, happens."

Pulling into the drop off curve at the high school, Jasmine then braked and came to a stop.

"Wish me luck, Mom." Out the door she went, throwing her backpack over a shoulder.

"Break a leg!" her mom rejoined. Autumn turned and gave her a grin before slamming the door. As she drove away from the curve, heading for the elementary parking lot, Jasmine had to again murmur a prayer of thanksgiving for the transformation of her daughter. And then a second one for the audition. It was genuinely fun to get the daily reports of her day, to have the twenty minutes each morning and afternoon to share together.

Minutes later, Cynthia slid into the chair next to her at the weekly staff meeting. "Missed you in church the last few Sundays," Jasmine whispered.

Sipping from her coffee mug, Cynthia nodded in confession. "I have no excuses. Just that since Katie is off in college, I don't particularly care to go by myself."

"Get Kevin to come." Jasmine opened her weekly planner ready to jot in upcoming school dates Principal Peterson always had for his staff.

"Yah, right. Either he's snoring loud enough to make the blankets rise, or he's already been called out and is tinkering on some farm machine."

Jasmine felt for her friend. She and Evert bonded in the importance of faith in their marriage. It would be tough not to have a spouse's affirmation.

Steven Peterson brought the chorus of dialogue crackling from all fractions of the conference room to a close when he focused their attention on the agenda at hand.

Slumped on the cement encasement ringing the flower bed adjacent to the school door waited a frozen teenager hugging her book bag in her lap. Like the brown marigold sticks withered in the gray soil, Autumn was a dejected pooch; her head was bowed inside the hood of her waist-length jacket, braced against the cold.

At the sight, her mother's eyelids closed, her heart drooped, already knowing the outcome of the auditions.

After throwing the backpack in the rear seat, Autumn climbed into the front, letting her straw-colored hair fall back to hit the headrest. She didn't utter a word.

Jasmine allowed a few miles to escape under the vehicle's tires before sending out an olive branch. "A lot of candidates for the auditions?"

Breathing heavily, Autumn was slow at answering. "Not for piano, only three."

"I'm sorry." Her heart broke for her little girl.

Exhibiting a morsel of life, Autumn raised her head and turned slightly toward her mom. "Janice Hirshcorn got it, and Melody Stafford got the backup."

"Did you hear them play?" Jasmine stepped lightly.

"Yeah, we were all in the same room. We had to play the song "Ya Got Trouble." It was hard. I was lousy." Staring out the side window, she added, "I betcha Janice and Melody knew what we'd have to play and practiced ahead of time." Disdain dripped from her words.

"Are you being fair? What grade are they in?"

"Janice is a senior, and Melody's a junior. It's probably because they're from Elton and I'm not."

Checking her rearview mirror, Jasmine ventured gently, "Since they're older, couldn't it be they've taken more years of lessons and may have more experience than you? Especially in doing accompaniment work."

Reluctantly, the glum girl admitted, "Maybe, it's just that I wanted it so bad, Mom. I wanted to be someone. For once in my life, I wanted to be noticed for something I can do well." Her hands clenched in her lap.

"Maybe God knew you weren't quite ready for this. You have two more years of musicals to look forward to. This isn't the end." When Autumn didn't respond, Jasmine plunged on. "Tomorrow is the cast auditions, right?"

Without making eye contact, Autumn dipped her forehead.

"Having seen a handful of performances of *The Music Man* in the past, I know it involves a huge cast. Besides the main parts, a drove of townspeople is going to be needed. They don't have lengthy speaking parts, but they're on stage a lot and sing along on quite a few of the songs. It would still be fun and wouldn't carry the weight of responsibility placed on the pianist. Messing up someone's solo part would be rather disastrous."

Autumn began warming to her mother's suggestions. "I'd rather have the female lead, Marian Parov. She's the librarian and piano player."

Her sophomore was still seeking the limelight. "She sings some solo parts. You haven't done that before," her mom cautioned, fully aware Autumn was setting herself up for another rejection letter.

And she did. After the auditions were completed, the cast member list was pinned to the bulletin board outside the band room's door. Autumn Kirmis was listed twice—once under Townspeople and secondly under Advertisement.

She was not to be subdued this time. Declining the parts, she told Mrs. Baumquist the assigned castings were below her potential. Her parents were helpless in the situation.

Some of her former exuberance for Elton High School frayed at the edges. The seam ripped a bit more when one of the Elton volleyball teammates told her the team had been better off without her. Threadbare spots marred the pattern of anticipation that had been exceedingly attractive.

Initially, Autumn missed Wednesday night youth group gatherings in Elton once every few weeks. Then it became once or twice a month. She even returned to church friends in Prairie City a time or two. The glitter had certainly rubbed off the Christmas bulb.

Nonetheless, when Evert and Jasmine compared Autumn's sophomore year with her previous term, they scored it an A. Maybe there was some tarnish on the locker door, but at least it still opened. She passed all her classes with a C or above, even alegbra. Although she had given up sports, she had joined

FCCLA (Family, Career, and Community Leaders of America), and played her saxophone in the pep band at home athletic events. Yes, she had alienated some peers and gotten on the hot plate with a couple of teachers, yet she was able to call the majority of her classmates *friends* in a loose sense of the word.

Thus, when Autumn declared in no uncertain terms that she was returning to Prairie City High School for her junior year, they were flabbergasted.

Confused, Jasmine sputtered, "Why?"

"I want to graduate from Prairie City the same as Dad. Besides, I've felt kind of like a traitor all year, turning my back on my former friends." A knot took up residency in Jasmine's abdomen.

Having gifted everyone with a sabbatical year, Autumn's reception back onto her home turf began peacefully enough.

Mother and daughter found the two embossed cards propped on the breakfast table Friday morning.

"Hey, what's this?" Autumn's curiosity was immediately piqued by the mysterious envelope, her name scribbled in her dad's handwriting. "Is he sending us on a treasure hunt?"

Jasmine picked up her card and slid a fingernail along the outside edge. "Only one way to find out."

Racing her mom, Autumn quickly ripped hers open and pulled out the elegant card. Reading it out loud, she intoned the message.

> To my only daughter,
> Dress up in your prettiest outfit,
> curl your hair, and color your nails.
> Be ready at six sharp tonight.
> Your carriage will be waiting.
>
> Love, Dad

Jasmine's invitation was similar. Laughing out loud, Autumn was delighted by the impetuous chivalry she hadn't thought her dad capable of. "This should be a blast! Maybe Dad is renting a white tuxedo for the night!" Finding her own fantasy preposterous, her chortles bounced off the kitchen walls.

In on the secret, Jasmine still found her husband's attempt at gallantry moving.

There was no dawdling after school hours that afternoon. Autumn raced for the shower, plugging in her curling irons to warm up. Inwardly, Jasmine knew this was going to be a night to treasure, a highlight to capture in her journal.

Occupied in their bedrooms, the gals didn't even hear Evert return home from work at five. After backing Jasmine's Chevy Impala out of the garage, he gave it a quick rinse job with the garden hose. Then he retreated to the basement to clean off the day's sweat and sawdust on himself.

Dressed in a sports coat over a buttoned shirt and dress pants, he waited for his ladies at the front door. Seeing his neatly combed hair minus the usual dent from his baseball cap, Jasmine's mind wandered back to the evening he had stood on her father's doorstep waiting for her the night of the junior prom. Aging had only made him more handsome as the gray at his temples blended into his naturally light hair. Wrinkles of crow's feet crinkled in smiles at the sight of his esteemed women.

Autumn's transformation from jeans and a T-shirt to a shimmering gray blouse with a scooped neck decorated by fabric pinched into gray roses was breathtaking. Her lovely blond hair was a mass of curls lying on her shoulders. A darker gray skirt and high-heeled pumps made her appear even taller than the slender willow she already was. Her father smiled approvingly before taking in his wife, attired in the soft rose dress she had bought for Jacob's graduation.

Extending a bent elbow to each of them, he escorted them out of the palace, down the cobblestone path to the waiting carriage—

Jasmine's car. It was a fairy tale night, being whisked away to Norbert, an hour's distance, by a handsome chauffeur who had reservations at the Homesteaders Restaurant. Easy conservation ensued. Autumn was at her best, delighting her parents with a pleasant exchange of topics. They chatted through a combination of rib eye steak and grilled salmon. It wasn't until the caramel apple pie a la mode was set before them that Evert intentionally steered the discussion.

"Jasmine, God has blessed me with your presence and love for twenty years now. I love you more now than the day I asked you to marry me. Thank you for saying yes to a nervous, broke, scrawny young man those many years ago. You have made my life worth living." Jasmine's eyes blurred at this unforeseen confession. Squeezing his hand, her tender look told him the same.

"You know, Autumn, you are the dream daughter your mom and I prayed for. God picked you out of all the beautiful babies on earth and gave you to us. We have been ecstatic ever since. We're pretty sure that someday, another young man is going to come into our lives and steal you away from us. He's not aware we are chain-linked together, that you're our little girl forever. But we might have to humor him and let him meet you at the church."

"Oh, Daddy." Embarrassed by his seriousness, Autumn's eyes sought somewhere else to alight.

"When your mom and I walked down the marital aisle, we were both virgins. We had saved ourselves for each other, a gift of purity to be given away only after exchanging our vows promising to love each other for as long as we both shall live." He nodded to Jasmine to take over the conversation.

Grasping Autumn's hand, Jasmine continued, "It is not easy in today's age to honor God's word when most people are not. But God knew when He created love that it would be the most meaningful within the bounds of a marriage. It wouldn't be cheap or for a season. It would be a commitment lasting forever between two people who loved God and each other. It would be utterly beautiful in His sight."

Evert interceded, "We would like that for you too, for you to remain sexually pure until the handsome prince of your dreams appears and asks for our little girl's hand."

Autumn's eyes flitted from her dad's to her mom's and away again. She was uncomfortable talking about something so personal and yet awed by the magnitude of it all.

"Having reached the tender age between a child and a young woman, your mom and I would like to give you a gift to wear that you will in turn present to your husband on your wedding day." Reaching into an inside pocket of his jacket, her father brought out a small box wrapped in the shiny paper of a jewelry store.

Autumn sucked in her breath, holding it in her lungs until the pain became unbearable. Her eyelids dropped shut as the importance of her parents' teaching soaked into her heart. Her wind came out in a rush. Slowly, she opened the miniature package. Pushing up the velvet lid, her imagination already held the image of the ring hidden beneath it. There it was—a thin gold band, a milky white opal set in an intricate pattern of leaves, October's birthstone.

Carefully, Evert's thick fingers grasped the diminutive ring, dislodging it from its slot. He picked up Autumn's right hand and slipped the jeweled band onto her finger. All eyes focused on the sparkling gem.

Softly, her mother intoned, "This is a ring of purity, a promise to your someday prince in shining armor that you are waiting for him and will not have sexual relations with any other man."

Autumn nodded. With all her heart, she wanted to be able to pass this symbol of purity onto her husband. Throwing an arm around each of her parents' necks, their heads met over the square table. "Thanks."

"This has been quite an evening," Jasmine smiled, sitting back in her chair again, acknowledging the special moment with her daughter. Magically, Evert placed an identical box on her place setting.

Raising a surprised eyebrow, she asked, "What's this?"

"Oh, just something for my girlfriend." Evert winked, sitting back to enjoy his wife's astonishment.

Peeling back the paper and then opening the box, a second ring twinkled back at her. A mother's ring with two tiny stones— an opal and a pearl—one for Autumn and one for Jacob. Her eyes shone as she stared back at her lifetime lover. Emotion trickled through her words. "You have a way of moving my heart. Thank you."

Sometimes, moments are meant to be held and cherished—to be remembered when life falls apart.

Chapter 10

L ife with Autumn was similar to riding a roller coaster
without an attendant to stop the ride when the allotted time
was up. The high-low swings left Jasmine fearful of the next tidal
wave, having barely survived the one before it.

Her junior year had begun on the carousel, slow and easy,
renewing some of her previously severed relationships. Maria and
Emma asked her to accompany them on a door-to-door service
project collecting canned goods for the food pantry. Evert spent
weekends teaching his daughter how to drive and, when she
secured the highly coveted license, brought the old 1998 Ford
Escort Jacob had used in high school out of storage from behind
the back shed, allowing her to use it at his discretion. She shifted
back permanently to the youth group of the community church in
Prairie City, even though it was not as active as the one in Elton.

The music department put on a theatrical Christmas supper
served on the stepped platforms of the band room. Autumn, who
had become an accomplished pianist, played the dinner music
harmoniously, flowing from one holiday arrangement into the
next. Evert captured the entire performance on video. Jasmine
was incredibly proud of her, recalling those first painful years of

lessons. After the meal, the diners were entertained by various vocal and instrumental solos, trios, and quartets heralding in the Christmas season.

Katie Burns and her fiance, Stephen Pierce, were married over the holiday. Katie asked Autumn to do the prelude music, which enabled her to do an encore of many of the numbers she had prepared for the theatrical supper. The wedding was tastefully simple, decorated only with white poinsettias and pine branches. Cynthia did not exhibit the frenzied agitation apparent at Katie's graduation. She said it was because the farmers' fields were covered with snow, forcing Kevin to have regular hours. Having surprised herself and her parents bypassing her first inclinations to take up counseling or nursing, Katie instead earned a degree in horticulture and had already secured a job in the town where she and Stephen would be living, a forty-mile distance from Prairie City.

Christmas was Jasmine's favorite holiday. She loved the multitude of ways it was expressed—in the glittering lights, the old-fashioned carols, the stately pine trees dressed in tinsel, the coming together of family. But most of all, it was the reminder of God coming to man in the form of a baby escorted by the angels from an extravagant palace to a humble feed bunk. The warmth of such love kept her humming through all the yuletide preparations and festivities.

It was fortunate she could feel the heat of the star radiating over the stable, for a cold harsh North Dakota winter would follow, when she'd wonder if she'd ever see the brilliance of the heavens again.

No matter how tired she was at day's end, slipping under the covers beat, Jasmine would awaken numerous times during the night. The luminous digital clock signaled the hour. Usually a sip of water from her glass on the bedside table and a repositioning of her body would be enough to allow her to doze off again.

But then there were those dark early mornings when her mind ran on a hamster wheel, refusing to shut down. On such occasions, she'd been known to quietly climb from her bed as not to disturb Evert, descend the stairs to the main floor of their split-level home, and take up a task needing to be completed. At dawn, her husband would shake his head to find she had balanced the checkbooks, varnished the woodwork for a remodeling project, or washed out the kitchen cupboards.

This was one of those insomniac mornings. Mentally checking off the day's list of duties, she realized she'd forgotten to set out the bottles of colored sand required for a first grade art project. Ah, and Evert's lunch. She should have taken a stick of summer sausage out of the freezer to thaw or she'd be slicing a brick for his sandwiches.

Carefully, she set the thick quilts aside, letting her bare toes find the carpet. Padding to the door and down the five steps, she was extra quiet as she passed Autumn's bedroom door, standing slightly ajar. Only Autumn slept on the main floor. Her room had first been dubbed the sewing room, but at her arrival, both bedrooms upstairs were occupied, leaving the sewing room for Autumn's nursery.

Jasmine flipped on the switch above the stove to give her a minimum amount of light. The indoor-outdoor thermometer propped on the window ledge read 5 degrees Fahrenheit. Frost framed the edges of the glass.

Locating the sausage in the freezer above the refrigerator was easy. The sand was in one of the cupboards in the laundry room. Traipsing past her daughter's door a second time, she paused, as she often did, to hear the sound of Autumn's slow even breathing. And then as she often did, she urged the door open a bit further, giving her eyes access to the ceiling where she could witness the twinkling of the starry hosts above her bed. Reminiscing the summer four years ago when she had surprised Autumn with the redecorated room, her lips drooped into a frown, aware her daughter had never uttered one word of gratitude. Jasmine wouldn't have even known her work had been appreciated had she not overheard Autumn on the phone weeks later telling a friend about her *cool* pad.

Even holding her breath, Jasmine could not hear the familiar soft nasal exhale of her daughter's slumber. Taking a step into the room, she paused and listened. Nothing. The bed was silhouetted in lumpy shapes of no resemblance to someone in repose. Almost tripping on the CD player on the floor, Jasmine caught herself, her arm in reflex motion extending toward the bed. Her hand touched a stuffed book bag. Feeling on each side of the bag, her hand moved up to the pillow. Coat hangers, fingernail polish bottles, clothes, a gigantic stuffed bear met her touch, but no sleeping body. Leaning in farther, her hand found the knob on the bedside lamp and twisted it.

Jasmine's eyelids blinked rapidly, adjusting to the sudden brightness wiping away the coal blackness. With a swing of her head, it was obvious that although Autumn's bed and floor were piled high with belongings, the owner was absent. Her cell phone, still plugged into the wall, balanced precariously on top of a clump of half-eaten grapes. Retreating to the living room, Jasmine hit the wall switch, flooding the room with light. No Autumn. Fear crawled up her spine and into her lungs. A blanket of frenzied apprehension slowly threatened to smother her. She found herself tearing from room to room, turning on lights. Down the stairs to the family room, across the floor to the storage room, back to the stairway, pausing at the basement bath. Anyone driving past would have questioned the Kirmis house being perforated with squares of light at 3:00 a.m.

Taking the steps two at a time, she landed in the foyer, swung a ninety-degree angle to the left and jogged to the laundry room where the outdoor jackets were kept. Scanning the hooks, her gaze came to rest on the vacant spot where Autumn's hooded Columbian coat usually hung. A gasp of alarm escaped from her chest as she yanked on the door to their two-stall garage. Prior to Autumn earning the right to drive, Jasmine's Impala and Evert's work pickup truck had always occupied the space. With the entrance of old man winter, Evert had courteously given up his half of the garage to Autumn's Ford car. One empty stall jumped out at Jasmine.

Since Christmas, Autumn had become more secretive, not sharing the trivia of her day, rather keeping to herself, spending hours in her room engaged in long conversations on her cell phone. If asked who she was talking to, she'd be vague and say the first name of a classmate that came to her. As no train wrecks had transpired, Evert and Jasmine were hesitant to upset the tranquility.

Letting out a siren's warning as she retraced her steps to the upper floor, Jasmine screamed, "Evert, Evert! Autumn's gone!" He met her in the hallway outside their bedroom, confusion etched in his drowsy posture. "Evert, Autumn has taken off somewhere in her car!"

"What?" Brushing past her, he proceeded to descend the stairway in his normal gait, not pronouncing judgment on the crisis his wife was panicking about until he surveyed the evidence. After checking the empty garage and bedroom, he picked up Autumn's cell phone, which she'd neglectfully left behind. A touch to the recent Messages button brought a list flashing on the screen. "She's been texting a Gerald Saxton. He asked her to meet him at the truck stop. Let's hope they're still there." He took the phone with him.

Jasmine's hand visibly shook as she attempted to snap her jeans and thread her head through the neck opening of the sweatshirt. *Please, Lord*, she silently prayed, *don't let her have taken off with this guy.*

Minutes later, Evert steered his pickup into the snow-covered parking lot of the twenty-four-hour truck stop bordering the state highway. Five semitrucks were lined up behind the building,

127

presumably allowing their operators to catch up on sleep. Autumn's older model vehicle was parked next to a four-wheel-drive pickup truck sporting a southern state's license plate at the curb. The recent oil boom in North Dakota had brought in a surge of people from every state in the Union looking for work. It was an economic upswing for the rural state, putting unemployment at an all-time low. Unfortunately, with the good had come the bad. An unprecedented shortage of housing, schools, and employees for lesser-paying jobs had descended on the state overnight. Prices for existing lodging, food, and wages had skyrocketed while the wear and tear on roads and crime kept pace.

Bucking the north wind, Jasmine shivered inside of her coat, unsure if it was from the cold or the fear pulsating within her. "Let me handle this," Evert ordered, entering the gas station ahead of her. Jasmine was only too willing to be a mouse.

A lady tending the till greeted them. Evert nodded curtly, not giving her more than a glance as he took in the only other occupants of the station. With their jackets piled on the table behind their booth, Autumn sat in a padded seat, her back to them, unaware of their presence. Across the table from her was a coarse-skinned man, maybe in his late thirties, his skin leathered from working in the outdoors. His dark oily hair was pulled back in a low ponytail. The short sleeves of his T-shirt fitted tightly against the muscles of his upper arms. Weaving over and down his arms were the most grotesque black snakes Jasmine had ever seen in tattoos. Virtually masking his skin, the multiple lines of the serpent slithered around his biceps to appear again at the elbow, slinking to his wrist, the deadly eyes peering out of the dark veins crisscrossing the backs of his hands. His fingers became the venomous fangs of the reptile ready to close in a death grip on whatever his hands picked up. For now, it was an oversized Styrofoam coffee cup.

Jasmine's eyes widened in horror, caught off guard by the evil the man's tattoos embodied.

In contrast, Autumn's blond hair had been freshly curled with an iron, a low-cut top meant to be layered over something else molded her breasts. Not expecting company, she had not bothered to turn about when the ding of the door had hailed their entrance. The man too had no idea he was about to meet the baby cub's parents.

In animated comics, Jasmine had seen screen characters literally shake in fright. She was no figment of someone's drawing pen, but her right knee was shaking so fiercely she was glad it was camouflaged under her loose cut jeans. How would they ever get their daughter out of the enticing grip of this seasoned man? She was far out of her league. Prayers hit the ceiling of the gas station.

Although the man had glanced their way when they had entered, he had no reason to believe he was the object of their middle-of-the-night excursion. Amused by Autumn's silly chatter, he baited her, not oblivious to her lack of experience. Taking one hand off his coffee mug, a thick finger reached across the table top to hook two of hers.

Jasmine wished her cell phone was in her coat pocket, rather than in her jeans, set on speed dial for the local Prairie City cop. She doubted that Evert, even with his six-foot frame, was a match for this rough muscular guy.

A fake tight smile attached to his lower face, Evert approached the table. Jasmine had always admired his composure in tense situations, yet she was convinced it wasn't going to work this time.

"Cold night. If that's your rig out front, these Dakota winters must just about freeze out your best intentions for moving up here to the north."

The man raised his eyes to discern if the words were directed at him. Seeing they were, he withdrew his hand from Autumn's. One thing for sure about this state was the friendliness given to total strangers. "You're a hardy bunch up here, all right," he agreed. "Where I come from, the only thing frozen comes from a freezer."

At the sound of the familiar voice, Autumn's head jerked to the side, her previously coy expression evaporated, her eyes bugging out at the sight of her father. Wisely, she pursed her lips and remained quiet, playing with her fingers in her lap.

"If I'm not mistaken, you're Gerald Saxton. Are you living here in Prairie City?"

Evert's question rubbed on the side of being inappropriately personal. The stranger's reply stiffened. "Who wants to know?"

"Seeing you're keeping company with my teenage daughter, I would." Evert kept his tone light, his face unreadable. Jasmine's heart thudded against her rib cage, realizing she was no backup for her husband.

An ugly semblance of a grin split the man's face, belying the steely coldness in his eyes. "No harm done here." He raised his hands, palms outward. "Just having a friendly conversation with what I believed was a dispatcher for one of the oil companies drilling in the Bakken formation. I must have been misinformed." His laugh was harsh and short. He lay a serpent arm back on the table, its deadly eyes ostensibly fastened on Autumn's innocence. "Look's like your bedtime is calling, little girl."

With a huff, Autumn tore from her seat, grabbed her coat, and without putting it on, tore out into the bitter cold night. Jasmine and Evert followed her.

"Better hang on tight to that one. She's a beauty." The man's raucous words hit them in the back as they let the door swing shut behind them.

Autumn was already grinding on her starter when they climbed into Evert's pickup. Her taillights reflected back at them through the dark streets of the town. Jasmine breathed in relief, yet aware only half of the nightmare had been relinquished. The other half was driving too fast on the icy pavement ahead of them.

With one slam of her car door, Autumn was on the steps headed into the house from the garage. She was angry and humiliated.

Having parked outside, her parents came in the front door, catching her before she was able to duck out of sight in her room and lock the door.

"Get out of my way. I'm going to bed." She fumed at her father, her words barely able to penetrate from between her clenched teeth.

His form blocked her entrance. "You missed that curfew hours ago. Now we are going to talk. What the heck do you think you were doing?"

Her eyes became mere slits in her distorted face. "Do you know how you humiliated me? You made me sound like a baby in front of that man!"

His voice raised in volume. "A junior in high school does not belong in the presence of a forty-year-old man in the middle of the night, or for that matter, any time."

"He isn't forty. He's thirty-four!" she shouted back, then clasped her hands to her mouth, realizing her parents wouldn't be anymore impressed with his actual age. No opal ring sparkled on her finger.

Jasmine closed her eyes at the absurdity of the situation. Their young daughter had perched on the edge of a lifetime consequence tonight had they not intervened. "Autumn, think. This man wasn't a high school friend from Elton or Prairie City. He is a grown man, who may have had his way with lots of women. You could have been raped."

Brushing off her mother's tendency to always think the worst, Autumn groaned. "I can take care of myself."

"Well, young lady, you are going to have to prove yourself. You broke a ton of rules tonight." Her father, usually the softer of the two parents, was grim. "Your cell phone stays in my possession for the next month."

"You can't do that!" Autumn wailed. "It's mine!"

"I pay the monthly bill," he reminded her. Holding out his hand, he continued, "The car keys please."

Glaring at him as if she couldn't believe he'd strip her of her two most important possessions, a shriek escaped from her lips. Slamming the keys into his hand, she rudely sneered, "Can I go to bed now?"

Stepping aside, he allowed her to push past him. Before slamming the door for a grand finale in defiance, she lashed out once more. "And just so you know, it wouldn't have been rape!" The echo of the door reverberated through the dwelling—the very home where Jasmine had once believed a perfect family lived.

Chapter 11

Jasmine felt as if she was wishing her life away. At the rate she was going, she would be nursing home material before turning forty-five. It was no longer the end of the present school term she yearned for, rather, the graduation exercise finalizing Autumn's high school degree.

Autumn's junior year continued on a downward slide after the episode with Gerald Saxton. Autumn's biting comment about wanting to be sexually active grated raw against Jasmine's values and faith.

Years back, when their daughters had been in the preadolescence age, Jane Runk, Sheila Philips, and Jasmine had had a lengthy discussion about teenagers using birth control during a Fourth of July gathering at the cabin. According to biblical standards, sexual intimacy was an expression of love reserved for a man and a woman after being united in marriage. This is what Jasmine and Evert had taught Jacob and Autumn upon reaching the age of understanding. Sometimes to be silly, the sibling duo had teasingly acted out a singsong rap to imitate their parents. "First we graduate from high school. Then we go to college. Get a spouse to marry us and then we make *you* grandparents." Using gestures to accentuate the words, they'd pointed their index finger at their parents, giving the *you* extra emphasis.

"At least they've got the message," Evert had whispered, chuckling at their chant.

Jane had argued that kids do not always embrace what they've been taught, so as parents, they had to help protect them from their own inner drives. Pregnancy during the junior high and high school years would not only be devastating to the teenagers, suddenly finding themselves expectant parents, but also to the children born to them. They weren't mature enough, nor financially set, to raise a child. "Common sense says we take precautionary steps to prevent an accident before it happens," Jane emphatically insisted.

Shelia had been more hesitant to provide a social safety net. "If we teach them that being sexually active outside of marriage is in violation of our Christian faith and then turn around and hand out condoms, aren't we being ambiguous?"

"Maybe so, but I for one don't want to be a grandmother babysitting for my daughter the night of the junior-senior prom," Jane had retorted.

Mentally sifting through their comments, Jasmine contemplated what reaction she and Evert would have followed back during their courtship had she been on an oral contraceptive. Emotions and physical desires were no different two decades ago than what they were today. The choice was the same. Not wanting to go against God's word, nor face their parents with a telltale message, they had stuck to their decision to remain pure until the marriage bed. It had been tough. Totally by the grace of God, they had triumphed.

But had she been on birth control, would they have given in to the passion of the moment? Who would have known? Other than God?

Autumn was no longer in the preadolescence age. She had all the makings of a woman. And it scared her mom to death.

Jasmine couldn't bring herself to approach the birth control topic with her daughter. Instead, she added it to her prayer list. *Please, Lord, bring Autumn through her high school years without becoming a teenage mom.*

Nowhere are the differences among the seasons of the year more appreciated and noticeable as they are in North Dakota. The huge snow piles of winter were no match for the heat of the sun when it rose a notch higher in the sky, its warmth meaning business. Puddles formed into muddy rivulets, eating away at winter's monuments. The red mercury line in the thermometer rose steadily, leaving the freezing mark behind. It encouraged the residents to venture into the outdoors for longer hours, languishing in the promised approach of spring.

On one such evening, Evert and Jasmine found themselves skirting the puddles as they too enjoyed a brisk walk about the town.

As soon as the ground dried enough for a construction site, Evert would begin building a new two-story home for a family in Elton. All winter, he had finished interior projects shelled up last fall before the bite of winter had set in.

"I see there's a two-day show in Fargo in the middle of May— the eighth and the ninth—on new equipment available for the construction business. I'd like to update some of my tools and machines. It would be a good opportunity for me to see what's out there. There's also new computer programs where potential buyers can view what their completed buildings would look like inside and out." Evert reiterated the workshop's itinerary according to a pamphlet he had acquired.

Sidestepping some muddy slush, Jasmine inquired, "You've sold me on its importance. Are you going?" As a teacher, she was used to in-service. There was always something new to learn in education as well.

"It would have been better had it been scheduled in January or February when no one wants to work outdoors, but I'd be giving up two days of work if I do." He waved to an acquaintance across the street, who was using a spade to reroute his melting snow to the curb.

"Is that a yes or a no answer?" she mused, already loving the return to their habitual evening walks.

"Well, I was kind of hoping maybe you'd want to accompany me. Could get in some shopping at the mall." His eyes twinkled down at her.

"Is that supposed to be an added enticement? You don't think circular saws, routers, and jigs would be enough to make me jump at the chance of a getaway for two in the big metropolitan city of Fargo?" she teased.

"Okay then, would you like to look at a new lift for installing windows or a cement power screed for pouring basements and driveways?" He knew his wife better than that.

"You're tempting me now!" Slowly, the amusement faded from her face. "I wish I could, Evert, but that's just two weeks before school is out. There is too much to accomplish with end-of-the-year reports, testing, projects to finish, and not to mention Autumn. We can't leave her alone." Purposely, she stomped her foot in a shallow water hole on the street, spraying the runoff into the air.

"Mom could look in on her." Evert ventured, knowing it wasn't even a possible option. Autumn would run over her. She was a far cry from the preschooler Grandma used to babysit.

"But you go, Evert. It sounds like a worthy reason for you to put your carpentry skills on hold."

"No, I can find out most of the information online. It wouldn't be fun without you, but I understand."

A loop of the town brought them back to their doorstep. Autumn was sprawled out on the living room sofa mesmerized by *American Idol*. Evert grabbed a magazine from the coffee table, rolled it into a tube, and planted himself in front of the TV. With closed eyes, he did his best karaoke imitation into his make-believe mic of the song the guy was singing on the screen.

"Dad, you're out," Autumn croaked, finding his performance hilarious. "Give it up, Dad. You'll never get past the judges."

Playfully, he swatted her on the butt. "They just don't know real talent when they hear it."

Bouncing up into a sitting position, Autumn questioned, "Did you get her to agree to go with you?"

"Hmmm. What are you talking about?" Her mom was busily straightening up the room. The pamphlet on the construction show Evert had mentioned was lying on the floor. Presumably, Autumn had scanned it.

"The lovers' dream getaway Dad wants to take you on in a couple of weeks." Autumn appeared to be thrilled with the idea. Sizing her up, Jasmine wondered if she was already making plans herself.

"It doesn't work," Evert explained. "It is too close to the end of school. Your mom and I will go some place really romantic when the timing is right." He winked at his two gals.

"Mother!" Autumn wailed. "What's the matter with you? Those first graders can get along without you for a couple of days. You need to go."

"The administration frowns on staff members using personal days the last weeks of school." She put Evert's magazine in the periodical rack by his easy chair.

"Hump! You are such a drag, Mom." Hoisting herself off the couch, she then disappeared behind the closed door of her bedroom.

"Do you get the feeling she wanted to get rid of us?" Evert ventured, raising an eyebrow at his wife.

"Yup. This old drag has messed up a scheme in the making." She slid the pamphlet into the drawer of the end table.

Hooking an arm around her waist, he drew her against him. He whispered into her ear, "I like older women." She giggled at his words.

Chapter 12

Cynthia's classroom door already stood wide open when Jasmine inserted the key into her own door across the hall. Before heading over to deliver a morning greeting, she flooded her room with light to welcome any early bird first grader.

Following her preschool ritual, Cynthia was writing the date on her front marker board in huge manuscript letters—Thursday, May 8. After the pledge to the flag and announcements given over the intercom, each day began by discussing the date. Jasmine did the same with her students.

"Hi, partner. You beat me in this morning," Jasmine greeted, noting Cynthia already had placed a first grade reader on each student's desk.

"Yeah, and that's not easy to do, even though I live here in Elton and you have to travel from Prairie City." She put the cap back on the marker and placed it in the marker tray.

"Just two more weeks, and we'll be kissing the urchins good-bye for the summer." Jasmine was upbeat.

"Actually, the reason I'm early today is because I couldn't sleep last night."

"Oh, did Kevin get called out on another farm job?"

"No, he was sawing logs when I left the house. For as sound of sleeper as he is, I don't know how he always manages to hear his cell phone when he's on call." Cynthia moved the book on the front desk to the side and set her backside onto the desktop. "We had some news yesterday."

Jasmine's ears perked up. "Hope it was good news."

"Yes, I imagine most mothers would see it that way. Katie and Stephen are expecting their first child." Her delivery was matter-of-fact, the way one would give the weather forecast.

Letting out a squeal, Jasmine rushed over to give her friend a hug. "Well, congratulations, Grandma! You must be thrilled!"

"I suppose I am—deep inside. It hasn't had a chance to seep to the edges yet," Cynthia hedged.

"What in the world is that supposed to mean? It would be more like you to take the day off to go shopping for a cartful of baby gifts." Jasmine's bubbly response didn't seem to be doing anything for the morose look painted on Cynthia's face.

"Don't you think I'm kind of young to be a grandma? I'm not sure I like the sound of Grandma Cynthia, or even worse yet, Granny Cynthia. Somehow, it whisks up the image of a gray-haired old lady, hair pinned back in a bun, knitting in a rocking chair."

Jasmine's chin dropped. She couldn't believe this. If anyone had been ecstatic about anything her daughter did, it had always been Cynthia. And why shouldn't she? Katie had been a model daughter, even stepping in tune to the Kirmis's rap song, Jasmine ruefully amended. First, we graduate from high school. Then we go to college. Get a spouse to marry us and then we make you grandparents.

"Is something wrong, Cynthia? Is the baby okay? Is Katie ready to become a mom?"

Waving her hand as if swatting at a fly, Cynthia returned, "No, no, nothing is wrong. Everything is perfect—the baby, the mommy. Guess it's just me, probably going through a midlife crisis. Give me a few days, and I'll be pushing that shopping cart like a maniac furniture mover racing to get to the new house before the owners."

"Sure you will, and I'll join you." Jasmine embraced her friend once more before walking to the door. Sticking her head through the opening for a last one-liner, she called, "Have a good day, Grandma." With a thumps-up, she disappeared.

"Story time, children. Come up to the carpeted area, and I will read you a Berenstain Bears book today." The students clamored to obey, squatting cross-legged on the floor, their expectant eyes on their teacher. Story time was a favorite midafternoon activity.

Mrs. Kirmis sat in the canvas director's chair, which was positioned in the middle of the carpet, with the class in a semicircle at her feet. Holding the book in such a way they could see the colorful cover, she read the title and author to them, pointing to each word in succession. *The Berenstain Bears and the Trouble with Friends* by Stan and Jan Berenstain. Do you ever have trouble with a friend?"

A rumble of agreement rolled around the circle, five hands shot into the air.

"Yes," Mrs. Kirmis agreed, "we like having friends, and yet sometimes, we get into spats."

"Let's see what kind of trouble the Berenstain Bears were having with their friends." Flipping to the first page of the story, Mrs. Kirmis took a deep breath to begin.

Flitting movement in the corridor outside her open door caused her to hesitate. Mr. Peterson, the principal, entered the classroom. "Mrs. Kirmis, would you mind if I read the book to your class? I like the Berenstain Bear books too." He advanced into the room with forced cheerfulness. "I'd like to see if they get into the same kind of trouble as kids in our school do."

Her eyebrows compressed slightly at his uncharacteristic behavior; a nervous tone had invaded his speech. "Why don't you grab your purse and take the rest of the day off? I can handle it here." Taking the book out of her grasp, he shooed her from the chair. Stunned at being replaced in such an unprecedented manner, she smiled faintly, perplexed as to whether he was serious or putting on a show for the youngsters.

It was then she saw the two additional men hovering in the hallway—Officer Al Forman, the town cop, and Pastor Harke from the church the Kirmises had attended sporadically here in Elton last school year.

The blast of a double-barreled shotgun ripping open her chest would not have been any more numbing than the instantaneous weight squeezing the very breath from her being. Her surroundings blurred, wiping away the children gathered at her feet, Mr. Peterson's voice droning out syllables of words, and the words formed a story. Her eyes swelled, staring at the human forms and what they represented. A man of the clergy and the town's chief of police sharing the same door frame in the midst of an ordinary school day spelled out a message of doom.

Frozen in space, she knew.

She knew.

The burnt edges of death were infiltrating her senses, emitting a putrid scent of singed residue in her presence. The only question left unanswered was the *who*. Her stomach compacted into the hard cement of a sidewalk, or worse yet, a tombstone. In the seconds she hesitated, a parade of pictures swept through her consciousness—Evert's mom, Jacob, Autumn…Evert.

It was Evert. No one had verbalized the message, but they didn't have to.

She knew.

At her indecision, Pastor Harke stepped forward, reaching over the heads of the children to take an elbow, beckoning her forward. He whispered something about her purse. Mechanically she walked to her desk and opened the bottom drawer, drawing it out. Then quickly, he ushered her out of the room, down the hall, and into the waiting patrol car at the curb.

Their words were quiet, expelling a minimum of fragmented information, but her mind was spinning wildly out of control, unable to organize the message clips chronologically—an accident, ambulance called, head injury, fastening rafters, high fall. She asked no questions, barely able to hold herself together during the short ride across town.

Officer Forman braked at the emergency entrance of the small town hospital. Pastor Harke assisted her out of the vehicle then tossed his car keys back to the police officer.

Jasmine didn't wait for an escort, pushed the glass door aside, and dashed into the reception area. Her mouth opened, yet she couldn't even formulate what to ask. One of the nurses immersed in paperwork at the counter recognized Jasmine as her son's teacher. At once, she lay down her pen, acknowledged Pastor Harke, who was lagging three steps behind, with a slight dip of her head, and came forward to put a gentle hand at the small of Jasmine's back.

"Let me take you to your husband. He'll be happy to have you at his side." Her voice was soothing, her touch tender. The rock formations cemented in Jasmine's insides shifted slightly. Maybe she'd been wrong, writing the final chapter when much of life was left to be lived. Evert had scolded her about jumping to morbid conclusions given only a smidgeon of information. Here she'd done it again.

Pinning a shaky smile to her lips, she'd show him she could handle a little bit of blood or a broken bone. Nursing wasn't her profession, but she could make a darn good assistant. Warm up some chicken noodle soup, keep a cold cloth on the forehead, check a pulse, take a temperature. Piece of cake.

The door to his room was shut. The nurse did not knock or ask permission to enter. She simply twisted the knob, letting it fall open on its own momentum, like a sun at dusk slowly dragging the day to its end.

Evert's closed eyes were turned toward Jasmine, his mouth slightly open, as if he had been watching for her, waiting to tell her something on his heart. But the white sheet over his chest did not rise and fall with his breath. It was deathly still.

After running the few intervening steps to his bed, she collapsed on top of his broad chest, burrowing her head into the space under his chin that had always been saved for her. Only now, no heartbeat thudded in her ear. No arms came around to hold her to him. Tears flowed unrelentingly, soaking the bed sheet and his shirt beneath, carrying away all yearning to live from the depth of her soul. She ached to crawl in beside him, to be carried to eternity by the angels who had safeguarded his journey. "Take me too," she pleaded, groaning into his neck.

A woman's hand began rubbing a circular pattern into her back, her shoulders, her upper arms. Over and over, the caress massaged her withered body as she wept for what was no longer hers.

Pastor Harke's deep voice shrouded the room in holy expectancy.

> The Lord is my shepherd; I shall not want.
> He maketh me to lie down in green pastures:
> he leadeth me beside still waters.

How many times had she recited these words? Green pastures and still waters had frequented her life.

> He restoreth my soul: he leadeth me in the paths of righteousness for his name's sake.
> Yea, though I walk through the valley of the shadow of death, I will fear no evil: for thou art with me; thy rod and thy staff they comfort me.

The shadow of death was darker than she'd ever perceived. Blinded by its veil, she could only grope. She could not traverse the valley alone. "For thou art with me." *Yes, Lord, I need you. I need your rod and staff.* Her fingers curled about the material of Evert's shirt, gripping it tightly.

> Thou preparest a table before me in the presence of mine enemies: thou anointest my head with oil; my cup runneth over.

Her cup did "runneth over." Often, she and Evert had mused over how they had fallen in love at such a young age. How had they ever had the wisdom to be worthy and lasting mates "until death do us part?" Surely, in her innocence, the Lord had blessed her with the gift of Evert. And then when she couldn't conceive, He blessed her not once, but twice more.

> Surely goodness and mercy shall follow me all the days of my life: and I will dwell in the house of the Lord for ever.
>
> Psalm 23 (KJV)

"In my Father's house are many mansions: if it were not so, I would have told you. I go to prepare a place for you" (John 14:2, KJV). Evert had reached the mansion. She could not hold him back. She couldn't begrudge him from getting to the prized land first.

Struggling to sit up, she rubbed her wet face with both hands. "What time is it?"

"Three. You can take as much time as you need." The nurse performed her job well.

"I have to go. Autumn will be out of school in a half hour. I need to go to her. I don't want her to find out from someone else." Lovingly, she bent over once more, kissing each of Evert's eyelids and then his forehead. Life was incredibly fragile. This morning, he had kissed her good-bye. She just hadn't known it was his final farewell.

Exiting the hospital, Jasmine asked Pastor Harke, "Will you drop me off at the school so I can get my car?" Previously, he had made arrangements for Officer Forman to bring his own vehicle to the hospital.

"I will drive you to Prairie City myself. My wife, Lois, is meeting us at the school's parking lot to get your car keys. She'll follow us." The Jasmine of yesterday, would have protested, insisting she could do it on her own. But today's Jasmine desperately needed to lean on the *rod* and *staff* God provided.

During the twenty-minute ride to Prairie City, Jasmine shakily took out her cell phone and touched Jacob's name in her contact list. With the social networking crisscrossing the country in seconds, he could easily have gotten the message from an onlooker before she had a chance to tell him his father had died.

A ring jingled in her ear, once, twice, three times. If he was in class, it would go to voice mail. She couldn't leave such a weighted message in a mechanical answering machine.

"Hello," his voice came across the waves unexpectedly.

"Jacob," her voice cracked, her throat filled. The sobs broke loose, overflowing the temporary dam she'd erected. Throwing her dark hair back against the headrest, she held the phone uselessly in her left hand, racked by another avalanche.

Gently taking it out of her grasp, Pastor Harke passed on the message to her son the best he could under the circumstances. Hitting the End button, he informed Jasmine, "He'll be here as soon as he can."

Telling Autumn would be the next chasm to ford.

Lois Harke drove directly to Evert's mother's home to inform her and to transport her to the Kirmis house. People said it was harder to lose a child than a spouse because of the predisposed natural order of life. Jasmine didn't know never having laid a child in a grave, but if it was the truth, Emily would also need a stout *rod* to guide her through the grief, for right now, Jasmine didn't have the strength to carry another burden.

The junior class lockers were directly across the corridor from the glass enclosed main office. Jasmine agreed to wait by

Autumn's locker while the pastor asked the secretary to summon Autumn out of class.

Her mind sought the words to say to soften the impact, but was there any kind way to tell a daughter her father was dead? That he wouldn't be there for her graduation? Or to walk her down the aisle to her true love? Or to be a grandpa to her children?

It didn't matter. A perplexed expression sat upon Autumn's face as she dutifully tapped the steps to the office. Seeing her mom loitering by her locker made her inhale a breath of impatience. *What was she doing here?* Then seeing the washed-out complexion, the eyes shining with moisture, Autumn's legs moved into a trot. Grabbing her mother by both arms, she shook her and yelled, "What's wrong?"

All Jasmine could get out was, "Your dad—" She hugged her daughter around the waist, pulling her into herself.

Leaning back to look her mom in the face, Autumn asked, "Mom, is Dad okay? What's happened?" An alarm clanged in her questions.

Shaking her head no, Jasmine wasn't able to prevent the tears from cascading again. Autumn's face dropped in horror. "Tell me, Mom. Tell me!" she screamed. "Is he hurt or is he dead?"

Convulsions of sobs racked through her chest as she mouthed the painful word back to her daughter—dead.

Staring at her mom in disbelief, she watched Pastor Harke approach to put an arm of support around her mother. Abruptly turning to her locker, Autumn knotted her hands into two fists and pounded on the metal door, screeching at the grievous wrong done to her. "No, no, no!" she shouted with each connection of her clenched fist on the unforgiving metal.

Through the glass wall of the office, the secretary and superintendent hopped to attention, ready to intervene in the hallway frenzy. Pastor Harke held up a hand toward them, stopping any additional pandemonium.

Finally losing the fight against the locker, her knuckles bruised, Autumn leaned her head on its cold surface, joining her mother in tears. Jasmine wrapped an arm around her middle, their sorrow blending as one.

The dismissal bell was just minutes away from resounding. It was imperative they cleared the hallway before being surrounded by a mob of high schoolers. Slowly, Jasmine dragged them both away from the locker door. Setting her sight on the Exit sign extending from the ceiling—an achievable goal—the mother numbly led her daughter toward it in a pell-mell path, both aware their lives had been changed forever, and not for the better.

Neighbors and church members descended on their home. Sheila and Jane took over the immediate running of the household, answering the phone, turning away unsolicited callers. Cynthia drove over from Elton as soon as the word reached her, promising to write lesson plans for a substitute teacher to use for the final two weeks of the school term. Jacob's arrival was followed by Evert's two sisters from Montana, who thought it best to take Grandma Emily back to her own home across town, where she might be persuaded to get some rest.

When the house emptied late into the evening, Jasmine and her children gathered in her bedroom. Autumn sprawled on the coverlet on Evert's side of the bed. Jacob took the recliner Evert had sat in each morning to read his daily devotional. They rehashed every piece of information they had received, most of which had come from Rodney and Mason, being they had been working with Evert on the two-story house in Elton. After the fall from the roof, Rodney had performed CPR until the first responders from the ambulance squad took over. But the blow he had taken to the back of his head had been fatal.

"Man, I just can't believe it. He was taken so quickly. No good-byes. No nothing." Jacob wiped at his eyes with the back of his hand. "I should have taken up building construction in college. That would have made him happy. We could have gone into business together."

"Jacob, your father was content with your decision to be an accountant. He didn't expect you to stay at home under his wing for the rest of your life." As a parent, Jasmine was pulling herself together for her kids. There would be time later for more tears. Years more.

Whimpering at her side, Autumn lamented, "I've already lost one daddy, and now, a second one." She blew her nose loudly.

"All us are only one breath away from heaven. That's why your dad always said we needed to be ready, to live in such away that we'd have no regrets. It's going to be tough without him, but if we band together, we'll make it."

Throwing herself back on the pillow, Autumn stewed, "I don't think I want to make it."

Although she couldn't voice it, Jasmine had the same inner turmoil. As the night deepened, their eyes sore from much weeping, they drifted off into a fitful sleep. Dreams tearing up the few hours remaining until dawn, when it would all start over again—life without Evert.

Chapter 13

Amid the hot August heat, the illusion of sun bubbles floated in the humid air, smearing a mist of sweat on the three members of the Kirmis family endeavoring to hold it together through a summer end farewell.

"Here's your cooler of water and soft drinks. I added a pan of peach cobbler, your favorite."

"Thanks, Mom, you're the best." Jacob took the small case and set it on the front passenger seat. His suitcases were loaded, his box of books, his dad's golf clubs, and a smattering of odds and ends to fill the trunk.

Three months had escaped since Evert's death, whisking Jacob back to his childhood home. He'd canceled out on the apprentice banking job where he had worked the prior two summers in Fargo. Even with the knowledge he had gained working alongside his father during his high school years, he could not take on his dad's construction contracts. Licensed carpenters would pick up the projects. Yet he did have enough skill to do small jobs—building a deck onto the neighbor's house, constructing a lawn shed for his grandma, repairing the picnic shelters in the town's park, and installing a handicap ramp on the side of the church. The town had kept him busy, and he had liked using his hands again, feeling the dryness of sawdust and the pride of a job well done.

His mom and sister had needed him, and he had needed these months as well to connect with the remembrance of the man who had chosen to be his dad. His father's presence was felt continually, his memory a daily embrace, as he measured and cut the boards the way the patient man had taught him. Only his dad's laughter had been missing as, piece by piece, a structure was fitted together.

Family and friends had carried the three through the week of the funeral, but then as each had left to carry on their own lives, the finality of Evert's absence had descended. Autumn had retreated to her bedroom, angry and moody, boycotting any attempts by her brother and mom to join their nightly walks to the edge of town or their talks on the back patio. She slammed doors and played music at a blasting level not even her closed door could contain.

Jasmine tried to be the super mom, listening to Jacob's memory recitals and his remorse at not returning home to help his dad during the summers in between his college years.

She was sympathetic to Autumn's grief, never herself having suffered the loss of a parent during her teenage years. Reaching out to coax her daughter into their circle of intimacy had been met with rejection. Normalcy was her prescription to getting them back on an even keel. Three meals a day, keeping up on the yard and garden work, answering the endless stream of condolences in their mailbox, daily exercise.

The hardest part she had to contend with herself—the legalities of a death, the paperwork, the death certificates, the financial accounts. Evert had been the bookkeeper of the family. She had no idea how she'd wade through the income taxes at the start of the next year. She left the problem there in the future, to contend with later. The weight of the present was oppressive enough.

Trying to be strong for her children left her with no time to grieve for herself. Only at night, alone in her bedroom, would she on occasion bury her face in his pillow and sob silently for what she had lost.

Jacob had been a godsend for Autumn. It was his insistent urgings that finally got her out of the house to pad after him, if even for only a few hours a day. She'd watch him work, hand him tools, hold a board, or mostly talk his ear off. When she tired of playing carpenter, she would retreat back to her bedroom, shutting out her friends and mother. At first, Maria and Emma stopped over, but Autumn would clam up like a turtle at their efforts to make small talk.

Now the summer had drawn to a close. School was starting— Jacob's last year of college at NDSU, Autumn's senior year in high school, and Jasmine, back to her first grade class in Elton. Each were forced to venture out of the nest alone, without each other, and without Evert. The first step was sending Jacob off to Fargo.

He wrapped an arm around his mom and sister simultaneously. Jasmine could feel the hard muscles he'd developed over the summer. "I love you guys," he said, planting a kiss on each of their cheeks. "Be good to each other. Dad would want us to move forward."

"You're right, honey. You get that last year of schooling in, and we'll be at your graduation come spring, cheering from the grandstand." Her voice quavered, but she caught herself and lifted his baseball cap to tousle his hair. "I couldn't have asked for a better son. Your dad would be proud of all you did this summer."

Swiping at a tear, Jacob nudged his sister. "I'll be at your graduation as well, so hit those books." When she didn't respond, he tickled her side, but she stepped away, looking sullen.

"I'll call you in four hours to let you know I made it." Aware if he lingered too long, they'd all be bawling, he jumped into his Dodge Charger, twisting the brim of his cap to the side just to bring a chuckle at his final exit. With a wave, he backed out of the driveway, pretending to catch the kisses his mom threw to him.

Jasmine and Autumn stood alone in the driveway, watching his taillights long after they had turned a corner and vanished in the heat waves. Somehow, a chasm had been dug between the two of them; Jasmine had no idea how or why. It would have to be she who found a way to span its deep-set gap, for her daughter seemed to relish solitary martyrdom. Although Jasmine would have liked to have sped upstairs to the comforts of her bed and have a good cry, she barricaded the grief deep down inside of her and tried her hand at a bit of humor. "So it looks like we're going to be roommates for the year. How should we split up the duties? Draw lots, flip a coin, or arm wrestle?" She dropped a friendly arm on top of Autumn's shoulders, pulling her toward her.

Pure disdain colored the girl's face; she wriggled free of any physical contact with her mom. "Sick," was her sole response. Purposefully, she tramped up the front steps to the house, letting the door swing shut behind her. Five seconds later, a resounding thud echoed inside, with the slam of her bedroom door.

"I think I'll have that pity party after all." Jasmine sighed and trudged wearily up the steps, hooking the screen door behind her.

Fearful of the first day of school, Jasmine had mentally braced herself for a battle over getting Autumn to school. But surprisingly, her daughter offered no resistance at all. She got up and dressed without being coaxed and was eating a bowl of Cheerios when Jasmine left for Elton. Autumn joined no extracurricular activities and dutifully came home from school each afternoon.

It all seemed too easy, like maybe after Jasmine left for her job, Autumn crawled back into the sack and slept the day away. But that wasn't the case. Her grades began to appear on the computer's PowerSchool program for parents to check. They weren't As, but they weren't failing either. If she spoke, it was in monosyllables, and then only if she had to.

Her bedroom was her sanctuary. Occasionally, she left it to watch television in the living room, but only if Jasmine didn't share the same room. If Jasmine walked in, she quickly grabbed up her possessions and headed out.

It was no different in school. Before Evert's accident, she had difficulty getting along with peers, opening her mouth at inappropriate moments, insisting on her own way, being sharp and dogmatic—generally, causing her fellow students to sidestep her. Now, it was if she didn't exist. She said nothing, did nothing other than the minimum amount of homework required, and kept to herself.

And saddest of all was the dormant piano sitting on the wall connecting the dining room to the living room. It begged for the touch of someone's fingers running across its keyboard bringing Beethoven or Schumann to life. Abandoned, it only felt the brush of a dust cloth along its sleek surface.

The school counselor called, asking permission to counsel with Autumn. "Please do. She has herself sealed tighter than a tin can, and I can't break the seal," Jasmine admitted, relieved to have assistance.

Three weeks passed, and the counselor connected again. "I couldn't get Autumn to open up to me either. She needs professional help, or I'm afraid she is going to crack." Inwardly, Jasmine had the same fear, yet she had hoped that given time, Autumn would come around without pressure.

After school, she made an appointment with Pastor Harke from the church in Elton. Even though he hadn't conducted the funeral, his noninvasive presence had been appreciated. Autumn had especially felt at ease with him from the year she had gone to youth group in Elton.

"Jasmine, I'm going to write down the name and number of a friend of mine in Bismarck. He is a Christian counselor with his primary focus on teenagers. He has had good results with some tough kids." Jotting the information on a Post-it note, he asked, "And how are you doing with your grief?" His kind eyes and gentle tone broke down her self-erected shell of protection.

Fumbling for a tissue in her purse, her words burst out. "I haven't had time to grieve. I've wanted to be strong for my kids, and Autumn has kept me in a continual tailspin."

"I thought as much. Yet it is important for you to care for yourself as well. The hospital here in Elton has a grieving support program. It meets once a week. When you are ready, I hope you will join. Autumn would benefit also." Pastor Harke shook her hand as they departed. "My door is always open."

Carefully, Jasmine planned the proper opening for broaching the sore subject of grief counseling with Autumn. Cooking, other than a sandwich or soup warmed up in the microwave, had virtually ground to a halt after Jacob left for college. When she did go through the motions of preparing a full meal, Autumn typically turned up her nose and grunted something about not being hungry.

Today, she was trying again. Most of her Saturday was being spent in the kitchen. Pork chops and sauerkraut bubbled in the Crock-Pot; a loaf of bread browned in the bread maker. Potatoes and homegrown cream-style corn baked in the oven. A chocolate cake cooled on the counter. It had been Evert's favorite meal. Surely, the aroma itself would bring about a warm receptive beginning.

Having had the delicious smells wafting under her bedroom door for hours, Autumn didn't need much persuasion to join her mom at the kitchen table. Pretty lavender place mats and a small bouquet of pink and wine-colored mums clipped from the fall flowers in the rock garden transformed the ordinary table into a special setting. Hot dishes waited to be savored.

Letting her gaze travel over her mother's workmanship, Autumn commented dryly, "Hardly a fitting time for a party."

"Just thought a touch of color might lift our spirits. I'll ask the blessing for our meal." She reached for Autumn's hand in prayer, but Autumn pretended not to notice and closed her eyes, keeping her hands tightly folded in her lap. Jasmine swallowed her disappointment and spoke a short prayer of petition and thankfulness.

Apprehension hung in the air, like fog on the horizon. Why couldn't the love they both harbored for Evert, and hopefully, for each other, be more than enough warmth to burn the tenseness away, to clear the air, allowing them to talk as one about the future?

Tired of the trivial chitchat their communication couldn't surmount, Jasmine craved to break open the topic of counseling immediately, but common sense held her back. It wasn't until they were licking chocolate ice cream and cake from their forks that she tiptoed in.

"Thanks for sharing this meal with me, Autumn. I wonder how many times in my life I cooked these very same entrees for your dad. He sure loved a meal with meat and potatoes."

Autumn mumbled a few words.

Jasmine pushed forward. "Grieving has to be the hardest thing we are ever asked to do in life. To say good-bye to someone we love." She reached out and pulled a tufted mum from the vase inhaling its fragrance. Mums were a hearty plant that could endure through the first frosts of the fall season. Adversity brought out their poignant beauty, bravely blooming among the other foliage which had withered and browned, having succumbed to nature's harshness.

Silence. Autumn's eyes bored a hole in her empty plate.

"Sorting out our knotted up feelings in the erratic emotional state we're in is mighty tough."

A big sigh of breath exhaled. The layer of fog thickened.

"Your dad was my prince charming. It is hard to think of continuing on in life without him, but neither of us has a choice."

Sliding her plate back, Autumn drummed two fingers on the table edge, as if she had heard this all before.

Worried the teenager was going to slip away to her room, destroying her carefully laid plans, Jasmine plunged on. "In order to move on, it's important for us to talk about what is going on inside of us. Sometimes, it is hard to do that with the people we love the most." Wishing Autumn would give a positive gesture or at least eye contact, she held the words formulated in her mind in suspension. When no acknowledgment was offered, she ever so slowly tipped the invisible vessel, letting the suggestion slip out one syllable after another until it had been laid on the table between them. "A Christian counselor might be able to help if we gave him a chance—"

"Stop it!" As feared, Autumn came unglued at the very mention of another counselor. She had spoken few words during the month since Jacob's departure, yet it seemed she had stored up a warehouse of them for this onslaught. "Mom, my whole life you've been trying to get me to a shrink! There is nothing wrong with me! I just want to be left alone! Aren't I allowed some solitude after you killed my dad?"

At first, Jasmine didn't think she had heard the angry words correctly, so she skipped right over them. "We all grieve in different ways. Sometimes, it is in silence. At other times, it is in anger, but talking about it can help. If not with a professional, then what about with Pastor Harke or even me? I've lost the same person you've lost."

"You?" Autumn exploded again. "Why would I ever want to talk to the woman who murdered my father?" Abruptly, she stood up, bumping the table in her haste. "I hate you! All I'm trying to do is get through this last year of high school and be out of here!" Her face was distorted in repulsion, as if the very sight of her mother was abominable.

Alarmed, Jasmine's head jerked up, slashed by the sharpness of the piercing daggers. "What are you talking about? Your dad died in an accident. A simple accident. We don't have control over accidents." Stiffly, she rose from the table positioned between them to face this unexpected onslaught.

Rage screamed from within the beautiful teenager slinging words at her mother like lit sticks of dynamite. "There wouldn't have been any accident if it hadn't been for you! Dad asked you to go to the construction show in Fargo that day, but no, your job meant more to you than spending some time with him, just the two of you! He stayed home and went to work. He would never have fallen from the roof had you gone with him!" Her eyes became two ponds shimmering above the snapping white teeth.

The pain Jasmine had felt when Pastor Harke and Officer Forman had appeared at her school door diminished into a mere scratch, a pinch, in comparison to the gut-wrenching accusations her daughter was hurling at her from across the table. The prairie fire within Jasmine, literally incinerated her heart, torching it into a million flakes of ash, threatening to steal her last breath as well.

"You said you loved Dad! Then why wouldn't you go with him? You killed him! You took my daddy away from me, and I will never forgive you!" Saliva wet the corners of Autumn's mouth.

So shocked by the unfathomed indictment, Jasmine simply stared speechless at the young girl who had spewed forth the vicious venom at the very person who loved her the most. Had Autumn been nursing this horrible belief ever since May? A moan of deep anguish rose from her throat.

Autumn, still wound tight, wasn't done. "You don't even care that he's gone! When was the last time you cried? Instead, you're being the merry little house wife, cooking pork chops and chocolate cake or dashing off to your first grade darlings." A purplish tint shadowed her features, her once-lovely face replaced by a gruesome snarl and slitted eyes. With a shove, her chair tipped on its side, and she dashed out the backdoor, slamming it with every bit of strength she had, making the light fixture suspended over the remains of Evert's favorite meal shake in the aftermath.

Covering her ears with her hands, Jasmine bent over in pain, wondering why their home continually echoed with the crashing of doors against doorjambs. Waiting fearfully for the sound of a garage door opening and a car starting up, she screeched out a prayer. "Please, Lord, don't let her take off in her car in anger. I can't lose her too." Framed momentarily in the kitchen window, she caught a glimpse of Autumn leaning low over the handlebars of her bicycle, gaining momentum as her legs pumped hard on the pedals, headed down their driveway.

"Thank you, Lord. Thank you." She'd let her go. They both needed to cool down, to think reasonably, to pray.

Jasmine's mind tried to rewind to the day when Evert had brought up the workshop. After discussing the inconvenient scheduling of the construction show, they had both dropped the idea and never brought it back to the table. Did its date actually coincide with his accident? Was Autumn right? There'd been a pamphlet on it. What had happened to it? More than likely thrown in the wastebasket. She remembered Autumn questioning her dad about it after the two of them had come back from their evening walk. Autumn had been watching TV.

Circling the living room for clues, Jasmine's eyes fell on the end table. Yes, she remembered now. She had wanted to get the paper out of sight as quickly as possible, for Autumn had been doing some undisclosed scheming. One quick pull on the handle, and the drawer's contents were exposed; the pamphlet lay in plain sight. In large black letters across the front, the dates were posted—May 8 and 9. Evert had died on May 8.

Aghast, a hand slapped over her mouth, her body slipping in slow motion into the soft cushions of the couch. Everything within her reasoned that life couldn't be lived on *what ifs*. It was merely a coincidence. But it was a coincidence too blatant to dismiss.

What if she had taken a day off from school? What if they had gone to Fargo instead of to work? What if? What if? The words were doing exactly what Autumn had intended for them to do—casting blame on herself for Evert's absence. Was she responsible for his death?

Chapter 14

S hakily, Jasmine entered the lobby of the Elton hospital. This was her first return since the day Evert had died. Her heart pounded not only from the reminder, but also due to her decision to give the grief support group a chance. It met every Monday evening in the conference room off the reception area. She was arriving exactly on the hour, not wanting to be forced to engage in small talk with anyone holding the chair next to her. Strategically planning her entrance, she'd surmised she would slip into the back row unnoticed and merely listen undetected to the proceedings. This most certainly could be her first and last session.

After the catastrophic attempt two weeks earlier to enlist Autumn, Jasmine had resolved to seek assistance for herself. She had lain in bed that Saturday night, wide-awake until 2:00 a.m. before hearing the sounds of Autumn fumbling with the backdoor. Three years ago, when Autumn had taken off on her bicycle unannounced, she and Evert had gone after her. And last year, when she had sneaked out to the truck stop in the middle of the night, Jasmine had panicked.

Prayer had been her only remedy after the newest explosion. Calmly lying in her bed, watching the display of lights on the ceiling from an occasional car passing on the street, she had been content to wait out Autumn's return without fretting. Had Autumn backed out of the garage recklessly and torn off down the street on two wheels, Jasmine would have been terrified. But she had been on her bicycle, angrier than a pit bull on the attack. Physical exertion would help release her pent up anger. Following her trail in hopes of reasoning with her had been out of the question. If Autumn returned, it would be on her own.

And she had come home.

Neither of them had uttered a single word of that fateful night, fearful a rehash even more forceful than the first would ensue. It was if the searing words had been blotted out, removed by a gum eraser.

Gone, but not forgotten. Along with her deep grief, Jasmine now dealt with guilt.

Timidly entering the room, her lips turned faintly upward in a fake semblance of sociability, Jasmine saw her stratagem had been foiled. There was no back row. Padded folding chairs were arranged in a large circle, a dozen or more already occupied. Hesitant in indecision, she tarried. Sitting in a seat with everyone staring, waiting for her to speak was outside her comfort zone. Observation was safe; dissertation, definitely not.

Rummaging in her jacket pocket as if looking for something, she turned back toward the door to escape. An amiable voice intercepted her. "Hello. I'm Anita, one of the facilitators for the evening. I am so glad you came." Shorter in stature than Jasmine and pleasantly rounded, the lady gave the newcomer her full attention.

Kindness exuded from her blue eyes, which were framed by the addition of tiny soft wrinkles when she smiled. Taking Jasmine's hand in her own, she squeezed it gently. "I know it is hard to take the initial step, especially on your own. I bet you feel like bolting right now."

Jasmine let a nervous chuckle be her answer. Before leaving for school that morning, she had left a note for Autumn informing her of her intention, secretly hoping Autumn would cave in and accompany her.

"I was the same way when I started. The group has been a true blessing for me. Can I escort you to a chair?"

Nodding in compliance, Jasmine's heartbeat slowed slightly. Once seated, she didn't have long to wait before the meeting commenced. A middle-aged man with dark hair and a neatly trimmed beard greeted the participants. He too had a kind, inviting nature about him, his eyes resting on each person individually as they traveled the circumference of the circle.

"Welcome to each of you. I am Chet Martin, and to my right is Anita Townsend. We are cofacilitators for this support group on grief. It is nice to see some new folks here and to have familiar faces return. We all walk down a pathway of grief. How we do it is as varied as there are people in this room. It is a process. There is no timetable saying when we must finish the journey.

"Before we begin our discussion, let me lay out the format we use for those of you who have joined us for the first time tonight. Grief is a natural reaction to loss. We may have lost a fulfilling job or lost our place of residency due to relocation or a disaster. Maybe our loss is in the form of rejection, such as in divorce or getting fired. In this group, we focus on the grief caused by the loss of a loved one or even a beloved pet through death.

"Each week, either Anita or myself will introduce a topic for discussion related to our walk through grief. Then we invite any of you to voluntarily tell us what is going on in your immediate life. What are the stumbling blocks in your path? What triumphs have you experienced as of late? This group meets in order to support each other. We pass no judgments on you, for there is no right or wrong way to grieve, as long as you are not choosing to use any self-debilitating methods such as eating binges, drugs and alcohol, perverted sex or pornography, or contemplating suicide. These, in the end, will only add to your struggles."

Jasmine shifted in her seat. So far, she was comfortable with the proceedings. Glancing around, she noticed the majority of the participants were women. The youngest was a gal appearing to be in her twenties. Two white-haired elderly men sat side by side, listening intently.

"Our topic today is anger. Like any of the topics we discuss, some of you may never experience this attribute in your walk with grief. Bear with us. Others may be battling it right now.

"Who or what feeds our anger? Possibly, we are angry at the person who left us. Maybe they did something foolish in our estimation—drank too much, refused to go to the doctor, drove too fast, didn't take advice. The death could have been avoided. Maybe we are angry at someone else who we believe caused the death—a drunk driver, a demanding boss, an adulterous spouse. Maybe we are angry at ourselves for letting our last words to the person be unkind or for not giving more of ourselves when we still had the time to do it."

Jasmine felt a twinge of guilt biting at her.

"Or maybe we are mad at God. Why didn't He intervene? We prayed for our sick loved one. Why didn't He use His miraculous healing? Why didn't He stop the intruder, the disease, the oncoming car, the bullet, the death? Why? Why? Why?"

The young woman across the circle twisted the ring on her finger. Another lady wiped away a wayward tear.

"Anger is an emotion, like jealousy, hurt, despair, hopelessness. If we let our thoughts dwell on our anger long enough, bitterness will eat us up. It will consume us. Some of us have kept an ongoing discourse running inside of our heads for so long, we hate to even be left alone with our negative thoughts continually feeding our anger. It is absolutely paramount that we work through our anger.

"Easily said, but how do we do it? There is no quick, slick trick. Grieving has a way of stretching everything out into a miserable elastic band, so taut it could break and hit us in the face. Let me give you a few suggestions. No doubt, you have many more you have discovered for yourself.

"Exercise. Are you a jogger or a walker? Do you work out at the gym or hoe in the garden? Do you go for a bike ride or vacuum your house?

"Talk out loud about ill feelings. Verbalizing our grief can actually lighten our load. Some people prefer to journal. Write down what bothers you. That too is a form of release."

Jasmine was already writing her thoughts. She had done it for years, only now it had become more intense. Pages upon pages of her bedside notebook held her neat script.

"Finally, do activities that give you personal joy or contentment. Do you like to bake? Bake up a storm! Just don't eat it all yourself. Give some away." A soft ripple of laughter circled the group. "Do you like to fish? Grab a pole. Do you like mechanics? Tear apart an old car. Do you like to redecorate? Paint a room. Hang out with friends.

"Whatever your preferred approach, work through your anger. Don't let it devour you. And eventually, somewhere down that winding path of grief, it might lead you to forgiveness. Forgiving your spouse. Forgiving your friend, your boss, your loved one. Forgiving the neglectful driver, the deadly disease, the finger behind the trigger. Forgiving yourself."

Leaning back in his chair, Chet Martin paused. Each person chewed on his message fitting it into his or her own engaged walk through grief.

Sometimes, Jasmine admitted, she was angry with Autumn. Why did her daughter have to be so hard to live with? Yes, she was a teenager who had lost her father, but she had been a difficult child before the accident. Why was she seldom able to see someone else's pain? Everything was about her. Then, too, Jasmine was angry with herself. Autumn's accusations had struck a knife into her heart, twisting it into an aching hole. She had refused to accompany Evert to Fargo for the construction show. He obviously would not have been on the roof had they been in Fargo. Was she to blame? If she was, it was a mistake she could never correct.

Interrupting her spinning thoughts, Mr. Martin brought the group back together. "Now comes the part of our evening where we introduce ourselves, giving our first names and the relationship we had to the person we grieve. If you do not feel comfortable doing this, simply pass. Let's start with the person on my left." His gaze fell on a lady approximately the same age as Jasmine. She appeared to be incredibly tired, as if her sadness had washed all energy from her.

Evidently, this was not the lady's first session, for she knew the routine. "Hi, I'm Karen. I grieve for my mother."

An older woman next to her took up the introductions. "I'm Gladys. I grieve for my spouse."

Each, in turn, gave their name and loss.

"I'm John. I grieve for my wife."

"I'm Mattie. I grieve for my daughter."

"I'm Val. I grieve for a girlfriend." None passed. They all sought healing.

One of the elderly men's voice broke as he talked. "I'm George. I...I miss my sweetheart."

"I'm Harold. I too lost my wife."

"Hi, I'm Carla. I miss my college roommate." This was the youngest woman in the circle.

Jasmine was next. She had thought this would be hard, but it wasn't. Everyone had a story. Everyone had a heartache.

Besides the phone calls with Jacob, Cynthia Burns was the person she most readily dumped on. And Cynthia always listened sympathetically to Jasmine as long as she wanted to talk. Yet Cynthia didn't really know how it felt to lose a spouse. Sometimes, Jasmine thought she was burdening her friend too much by rewinding the same tale week after week, month after month. After all, there was nothing for Cynthia to say in reply. Evert wasn't coming back. The last chapter had been written and read.

It was different with this group. They were in this together. Losing a loved one was insistently on their minds. They didn't have to refrain from rehashing the same event, the same last words, the same guilty probings.

"Hi, I'm Jasmine. I am grieving my husband."

One after the other, the voices opened their wounds. Anita and Chet were last. "Hi, I'm Anita. I grieve for my husband and son who I lost five years ago." Her ready acknowledgment hit Jasmine off guard. Grieving *two* loved ones. Jasmine swallowed hard.

"And I, as you all know, am Chet. I grieve my teenage daughter who was killed by a drunk driver seven years ago this month."

Anita took over the meeting at this point. "I always like us to start with the baby steps you have taken this past week. Those teeny pushes against the comfort zone we have erected around ourselves. What can you pat yourself on the back for? Who would like to start?"

"I will." Gladys had a lopsided grin on her face, which was wreathed by her lovely white hair. "I have been coming to these meetings for three months now. You suggested I reach out to people more. On Sunday, after church, I asked another widow lady if she'd like to come over for lunch." A smattering of clapping sounds followed her remarks by the folks who had been there before. Grinning wider, she admitted, "I wasn't ready to go out in public to eat, so we had a salad at my house. Nothin' fancy."

"Good for you," Anita congratulated her. "How did you feel about it?"

"I don't know." She twisted a handkerchief in her lap. "I suppose, pretty good. We played dominoes for most of the afternoon."

"Sometimes, we have to be the instigators of friendships," Chet intervened.

"Who else has something to report?" Anita waited for a response.

Harold raised a gnarled hand. "Yup, me too. Instead of sitting in my house all day, I moved out to the front porch. More action there." Harold appeared to be in his eighties. *How lonely he must be*, Jasmine thought.

The responses continued. Nothing earthshaking was reported, baby steps like Anita had suggested. "Grieving is a slow process," Chet continued to remind the group.

After a lengthy exchange, Anita switched gears. "Okay, what do we need to work on this week?"

Mattie raised a hand. She was in her thirties, a pretty lady with pensive eyes. "I've been thinking about what Chet said about anger. I think anger is part of my trouble. I am angry at my husband. We both lost this baby, but he doesn't seem to need support like I do. Sometimes, I accuse him of not having loved our tiny Nevaeh. Then I'd like to snatch back my angry words because I know they hurt him." Her voice broke at the end.

"Remember what Chet said about us each being different? We each grieve in our own way. There is no right or wrong way. How we grieve or how long we grieve is not a measurement stick for how much we love." Anita's words were coated with gentleness. Others too gave Mattie affirmation.

The two hours disappeared quickly. Jasmine was unaware of the lapsed hours until Chet brought the meeting to a close, inviting everyone to return the following Monday. On the way out of the building, several people greeted Jasmine.

Driving the dark highway back to Prairie City, she realized she had staggered forward one small baby step as well. She had found enough bravery within her to seek help.

Not surprisingly, the house was dark when she hit the remote to open the garage door. Evert's work pickup truck was a black silhouette still setting outside. She needed to advertise it, yet Jacob had used it for his carpentry jobs over the summer. Too many decisions to make.

Lulled by the motorized noise of the door reclosing, she climbed the two garage steps to the house door. Deep in thought, she almost missed the gallon paint can setting on the stoop, the dried runs down its side designating its black color. Autumn must have been busy with a school project and found the used paint amongst the garage shelves of half-used gallons. Absently, Jasmine picked up the two-inch paintbrush laying across the lid. Frowning at Autumn's carelessness, she saw the brush had not been washed out and was already stiffening. An empty ice cream pail hung from the water spigot by the door that opened into the backyard. Two cranks on the knob brought water rushing into the pail. Once a sufficient amount had poured in, she dropped the brush into the clear liquid, letting it soak overnight.

Noiselessly, she crept past Autumn's bedroom on her way upstairs. "Good night, sweetheart. Sweet dreams."

Chapter 15

Peering out her schoolroom window, Jasmine was hypnotized by the large snowflakes sifting through the frosty air, painting an old-fashioned Christmas card for her enjoyment. Perpetually, the final days of fall were crudely stark, marked by naked trees stretching awkwardly to the sky, stubby brown grasses lining the roads, the lush summer foliage replaced by the dead, brittle grays of a killing frost. Deep inside of her, Jasmine felt lonely and empty, as if the plunging thermometer was freezing the life out of her also, sucking the color from her days. Leaning into the window, the cold glass pressed against her forehead.

Cynthia had been absent from school today, thus there'd been no across the hall banter between the two first grade teachers. Having taught together for years, they knew each other like a missing glove. A little parley prior to the morning bell, a few sentences snatched while supervising their cherubs en route to the gym, the lunchroom, or the library, a fifteen-minute lunch break with other staff members to exchange the day's hot points, and a final wrap-up after school. But today had definitely been on the bleak side.

Nature must have known she needed a change of season. The shimmering white snow transformed the mundane playground into a glistening fairyland, the vacant slides and swings sculptured into swirls of meringue and frosted icing. With a whisk of an oil brush, old man winter had overlaid the depressing drabness with sparkling brightness.

Gradually, she had been letting the minutes after school stretch in length to correct papers, plan lessons, and to organize her classroom once the activity of the day had quieted. Autumn had been hired to work the after-school shift from four to seven behind the till at the truck stop. After her escapade with Gerald Saxton, Jasmine had been hesitant about giving her permission, yet it took Autumn out of her bedroom for a few hours each evening.

Consequently, there wasn't much to go home for right now. Actually, with Autumn holing up in her room, their split-level house hadn't felt too homey for months. Instead of a mother and daughter sharing girl talk, trying new recipes, or styling one another's hair, they lived like two strangers next door to each other. She was tired of being optimistic about the future getting better, for searching for a bright spot in tragedy, for trying to make conversation with a blonde mannequin. Her haven had become void of any human warmth—no friendly chatter, no human touch. At least at school, there were always a few teachers still in the building, plus the janitor who cleaned her room each afternoon—people who actually enjoyed having a conversation with her, who thought she was worthy of their recognition, who didn't accuse her of doing away with her husband.

Leaning her head against the cold glass, her eyes closed. *Lord, hold me. I need to feel the warmth of your arms pressing me against you. Give me the strength to carry on. I am so weary.* And as an afterthought, she added, *And say hi to Evert for me. I miss him.*

Softly, a two-tone chime stole into the quietness, angelic in its tone. The snowy yuletide scene displayed before her brought visions of angels greeting the shepherds on a holy night outside of

Bethlehem. A savior was born. A warmth crept into her heart, a love from above meeting her on the holy ground of an elementary classroom, not with the bleating of sheep, rather with the patter of children's footsteps temporarily stilled. "Fear not: for, behold, I bring you good tidings of great joy, which shall be to all people" (Luke 2:10, KJV).

The good news, the Christmas message, it was for her too. *Fear not.* The Lord was in control then, bringing enlightenment into a dark world. He would do the same for her.

Ta tum.

A second chime pulled her thoughts back to her desk still cluttered with files and papers. Her cell phone winked. Ah, a text message from Cynthia.

"The stork has arrived! Baby boy. Six pounds, two ounces. Light hair. Katie is fine. Nana Cindy."

"Whoopee!" Jasmine belted into the air. "More good news!"

The school's janitor poked his head around the door frame. "You talkin' to me?"

Laughing out loud, Jasmine replied, "Sure, I'm talking to anyone who will listen. Cynthia is a grandmother to a baby boy."

"That's why there was a substitute in her room today. Guess that's a good reason to be absent." He grinned back at her before continuing down the hall with his wet mop.

Quickly texting a reply, her fingers flew. "Congratulations, Grandma! Give my luv to Katie & Stephen."

Seconds later, the words flashed on her screen. "Hold the grandma bit. I am now Nana Cindy."

Shaking her head, Jasmine clipped back, "Doesn't nana mean granny?"

"Maybe, but it sounds better."

Deciding to end the day on a pleasant note, Jasmine jaunted out into the winter wonderland, letting the delicate snowflakes wet her cheeks and hair. A bright star had appeared on her horizon, and she'd enjoy it as long as it was beaming.

Two inches of snow had accumulated on the highway, but the snowplow was diligently at work, sweeping the first flurry of the winter season off the roadway. From a far distance, the lit up lights of the overhead truck stop sign could be seen even through the snowfall. Turning into Prairie City, Jasmine checked to see if Autumn's Ford Escort was parked at the station. Like a white mound of mashed potatoes, it sat behind the building out of the way of road traffic. Her shift wouldn't end for another hour.

Jasmine's good spirits continued to hum within her. After dropping her coat on a hook in the laundry room, she bent to swoop up a dryer full of clothes she had tossed in before leaving for school. Neatly, she folded the assortment of shirts and slacks, stacking them into two piles—one for her and one for Autumn.

On the way to the kitchen, she stopped at her daughter's closed door to deliver her pile of laundry. Balancing the load, she twisted the knob and pushed open the door with her foot. Just enough daylight still filtered in through the window to cause the disheveled room to jump out at her, yet she was determined not to let Autumn's housekeeping habits steal her newly acquired upbeat spirit, however fragile it might be. Carefully, she lifted a foot, using a toe to nudge a bag of makeup and a circular hand mirror out of the way before stepping down. Strewn clothes, dirty and clean, were a maze to hopscotch through.

Noticing a dark spot on a white T-shirt, she stooped snatching it up to deposit in the corner hamper. "Hmmm. All of these clothes have splotches on them." Frowning, she set the laundry pile on top of the littered dresser then squatted down to closer examine the articles of clothing. Black smudges appeared on many of them, even the comforter draped over the bed. Baffled, she tilted her head back and raised her sights to the ceiling. No starry firmament delighted her. No twinkling heavens. It was if the fluorescent stars had become hidden under dark foreboding clouds, leaving only a hint of white specs dotting the ceiling here and there, in no set pattern. "What the world?" Curiosity prompted her to mount the mattress, one hand extended to the wall for balance. Her fingers traced the ridges of the black paint smeared in every direction over the dark blue background color and the stars she had painted so painstakingly as a birthday surprise. The back of her hand covered the shocked drop of her jaw. Autumn had done her best to wipe out the starry sky and had let the black paint rain on her bed, her clothes, and snitches of carpet bleeding out from under the congested floor.

Heat rose in her chest; it worked its way up her neck and into the set of her jaw. What was wrong with her? If Autumn didn't like the stars, she should have said so, and they could have used the leftover blue paint to neatly extinguish them without ruining her clothes and furnishings. This newest paint job appeared to have been done in a fit of anger. It was having the same effect on her mother. "Lord, what is her problem?" she screamed at the ceiling.

She's grieving.

Gulping in a huge breath of air, Jasmine tightly squeezed her eyes into two lines. Yes, her daughter was grieving. Over the weeks, Chet from the support group continually repeated the old cliché, "Everyone grieves differently and on an individual timetable." Jasmine had a choice—she could stew and create a big scene when Autumn got home from the truck stop, yelling and ranting about the expense and work it would take to rectify the defacement, or she could ignore it. Like a pinched balloon, she exhaled slowly, allowing the hot air to suck out the oppressive anger with it. She just wished she could understand her daughter more, that Autumn would let them work through their grief together, instead of each being alone on a deserted island.

Her decision formulated, she jumped off the bed, picked up the stack of clean laundry from the dresser, and resolutely left the room, pulling the door shut behind her.

When Autumn returned from work an hour later, she was met by a stack of freshly laundered clothes sitting outside her bedroom door.

Chapter 16

"Can you move the strand a bit higher?" Jasmine stood back to view the freshly cut tree as Jacob, atop a six-foot ladder, looped the strands of lights aloft in the branches. A heavy Scotch fir fragrance hung in the air, intermixed with the tantalizing ham aroma rising from the German knoephla soup bubbling in the Crock-Pot. "There's kind of an empty gap in the middle."

Good-naturedly, Jacob poked the clear lights into the space indicated. "I always aim to please. If you give me the angel, I'll fasten it on the top while I'm still up on this ladder."

Sitting cross-legged on the couch, a box of ornaments in her lap, Autumn spoke up, "The angel is supposed to be the last decoration to go on the tree."

Taking the antique cherub from Jasmine's outstretched hand, Jacob teasingly replied, "You've watched too many of those sentimental Christmas movies on Hallmark. In the Bible story, an angel always preceded a big event—an angel dropped the bomb on Mary and Joseph about them becoming parents before Jesus was born, the angels scared those slumbering shepherds before they headed off to Bethlehem. And here in the Kirmis household, the angel from the branches high is going to watch you put the rest of the ornaments in the right place."

Making a face, Autumn answered dryly, "Yeah, right."

"You don't believe me?" Jacob feigned offense. He descended the ladder and set it aside. "Okay, ladies. It's your turn."

Jasmine selected a bedraggled wooly sheep out of Autumn's box. Dangling it from its wire hook for all to see, she reminisced, "Jacob, do you remember making this in first grade?"

"He looks like he has seen better days." Sprawled out in the La-Z-Boy, Jacob tucked his arms behind his head to observe the process.

"Here's my clown." Autumn pulled a Styrofoam creature with curled pipe-cleaner hair from the collection. "We made these in art class. I can't believe all the stuff you keep, Mom." For once, her tone didn't hold disdain as she continued to rummage through the box for more treasures from the past.

For three whole weeks, Jacob would share their company over the university's holiday break. Although this first Christmas celebration was going to be hard without Evert, Jasmine had yearned for her son's return, to bring a smidgen of normalcy back to their lives. She had thought about decorating the house before his arrival, but the truth was, she couldn't bring herself to do it. Autumn wouldn't have contributed a hand, and by herself, she couldn't drum up the energy. Anyway, the preparations were now giving them some good family time.

Earlier in the day, they had driven to a tree farm south of Prairie City. The Kirmis tradition had always been to chop down their own tree. Jacob had gotten his father's pickup truck running and found his ax among the tools in the garage. His stocking cap pulled down over his ears, his green scarf wrapped about his neck, he embodied one of Santa's elves. Autumn had tried to opt out of the excursion, but her brother wouldn't hear of it. First, grabbing her around the knees and then flinging her over his shoulder, he resolutely carried her to the laundry room to don her outdoor clothes.

Halfheartedly, she fought him off, secretly relishing the attention her brother was heaping upon her. Once out in the snowy grove, they had tramped through every row of white-laced trees until all three could agree on the perfect tree. They were a merry bunch, dragging it back to the pickup, singing an off key version of "O Christmas Tree."

Jasmine knew Jacob was giving one hundred percent and then some to help them through this first Christmas season. He was struggling inside also, but his gift to his mom and sister was going to be to brighten their holiday, even if it was for only a few weeks.

Hidden under layers of remorse within Jasmine's heart were the words of hatred Autumn had used to lash out at her. She never breathed a word of them to Jacob during their long weekly phone conversations. Her reasoning was ambiguous. Would he too cast a blaming finger her way if he realized the date of the construction show and his father's death aligned? She didn't really think so, yet she was afraid to receive a definite response. Moreover, she didn't want to burden him with the state of affairs at home. He was grieving and, at the same time, had his studies to concentrate on. She couldn't expect him to take on a fatherly image for his sister, nor become a crutch for her to lean upon. She was just thankful his presence could draw Autumn from her room. It was almost as if they were a family.

Once the last shimmering glass bulb and string of tinsel were hung upon the boughs, Autumn dimmed the room in shadows to get the full effect. "Ahh." Jasmine approved. "It is beautiful." The glimmering fir tree, robust in size, moved the three of them.

Breaking the quietness before it melted into despair, Jacob cleared his throat. "What does a man have to do to get a taste of that soup you've been tempting us with all day?"

Chuckling, his mom readily invited, "Come and get a bowl and a couple of crescents. I don't have any Christmas cookies to entice you with yet."

"I like the word *yet*. It means there is still hope in seeing the kitchen counters filled with every cookie in the cookbook." Jacob jumped to his feet, beating his mom and sister to the kitchen.

"Dad was the real cookie monster," Autumn reminded them. "He could whip up five different kinds and never use the oven."

"That's because he used almond bark and melted marshmallows in most of his selections." Her mom's lips smiled, softly wishing she could scold him about the pile of dirty dishes he'd leave stacked in the sink, or the remnants of ingredients dotting the floor.

"Let's eat our meal in the living room where we can watch the twinkling lights." Autumn ladled out a bowl of steaming knoephla soup.

"Good idea." A buttered crescent disappeared into Jacob's mouth. He grabbed up three more. "And then I'm going to challenge the two of you to a game of Scrabble."

"Ughhh," Autumn wailed. "You know Mom always wins."

"She will now be dealing with an almost college graduate," he reminded his sister.

"It won't help," she flipped back. "You're screwed."

An hour later, his sister pronounced the verdict as she added up their scores. "Some things never change, brother dear. Not only did Mom beat you, but I as well."

"At least I took third. Should be a trophy for that." Whisking a throw pillow from the couch at his sister, he instigated a pillow fight, fully aware his sister would accept the challenge.

Jasmine was storing up each jovial remark and playful act for the long cold winter ahead.

Christmas Eve dawned clear and white. Another snow flurry had moved through during the night, touching up the gray spots previously blown open. It was as it should be. Dakota Christmases mandated snow. It was one of the benefits of living in the north country, where songs like "Winter Wonderland" and "Jingle Bells" actually made sense.

Grandma Emily had invited her daughter-in-law and grandchildren to her home on Sunday to celebrate an early Christmas. All weekend, she had puttered in the kitchen, stirring up all their favorites and Evert's as well. Although losing her son was not in the natural order life orchestrated, she was doing her best to give his family the traditions they cherished. Rolled triangles of the Norwegian lefse spread with melted butter and sugar were for Autumn. Cooked cranberry sauce from the real berries were for Jasmine. And Jacob said everything else on the abundantly laden table was for him since he loved them all.

Grandma's gifts had been thoughtfully devised, reminders of the son, husband, and father they all were missing. Photo albums created on an online website depicted Evert as a baby all the way through last Christmas—Jasmine's wedding pictures, Evert holding Jacob at his adoption, Autumn pinching her daddy's cheeks, Evert and Jacob dressed in florescent orange beside two deer hanging from a garage rafter, Evert holding onto Autumn's bicycle, Evert and Jasmine holding hands while out for a walk. Page after page met the eager onlookers, their lives laid out in pictorial antidotes in chronological order. Most of the afternoon was spent paging through the years, stopping often to retell an incident, to laugh hilariously, or to blink back a tear. It was almost as if Evert had spent Christmas with them after all.

"Thank you, Emily." Jasmine folded her mother-in-law into her arms. "You have always given unselfishly of your love."

After one more round of ham sandwiches and cookies, they all piled into Grandma's car to transport her to the train station in a neighboring town. The rest of her holiday would be spent with her two daughters and their families in Montana.

"What do you mean you're not coming with us to the Christmas Eve program at the church?" A break in Jacob's easygoing nature had cracked as he nursed a mug of coffee after snowblowing the driveway.

Still in her pajamas, Autumn sat on top of the kitchen counter, slowly stirring a cup of hot chocolate.

"I told you, I have to work."

This was the first, Jasmine had heard of her daughter's schedule at the truck stop. "You have to work on Christmas Eve?" Alarmed by the fact, they would not be watching the dramatization of the nativity story together, she stopped peeling the potato in her hand.

"Not everyone gets the holiday off. Some people have to work, you know." Autumn eyes swam in her cocoa as if mesmerized by the marshmallow liquefying on its edges.

Living in the small town, Jasmine naturally was acquainted with the station's owner, Tom Neir. He was a kindly man, efficient in his business, yet always had a minute to converse with her when she filled up her Impala with fuel. Somehow, she couldn't see him putting Autumn on the work schedule for Christmas Eve when he was aware this was their first Christmas without Evert.

"No one else can take your shift?" Jacob was alert, his eyes glued on his sister's downturned face.

"Why would I ask someone to fill my spot? Everyone wants Christmas off. I have to take my turn." Abruptly, she jumped down from her perch, dumping the contents of her cup down the drain.

It did make sense. "But you get off at seven. You'll only be a few minutes late for the service." Jasmine was relieved it would work out after all.

"No, not tonight. The shift goes until midnight. That way, less employees have to have their holiday interrupted. I get tomorrow off." When neither her brother or mom commented, she moved off toward the hallway. "Guess I'll take my shower."

Sitting in the church pew in the darkened church sanctuary lit only by the glow of candles lining the aisle, Jasmine's spirits were quaking. To have her family reduced from four to two was picking away at her heart. Jacob, sensing his mom's disparity, reached for her hand and held it. Closing her eyes, she again whispered a prayer of thanksgiving for the son God had given her. She hated to think of the New Year dawning, calling him back to his studies at the university.

Friends pushed in on all sides of Jacob and Jasmine as they made their way to the door. "Merry Christmas," rang out repeatedly. Stopping in the foyer, the pastor greeted them heartily. "We're trying something different this year. The annual caroling party is sandwiched in between Christmas and New Year's to give an opportunity for out-of-town family to take part. We hope you folks will attend."

As she slipped on her gloves, Jasmine concurred, "We're looking forward to it."

Grabbed from behind, Jacob twisted his head to view his attacker. It was Denny Philips, one of his high school buddies. "Hey, Jake. How's the college dude?"

"How's yourself?" Jacob returned the greeting. "Can't miss a Prairie City Christmas."

"If that ain't the truth. I talked to Paul. We're going to do some snowmobiling and ice fishing this week. Want to hang with us?" Denny and Paul had gone through grade school and high school with Jacob, spending more hours gopher hunting, muskrat trapping, and fishing than they'd spent in the classroom.

Hesitating, Jacob laid his watchful eyes on his mom. Not surprisingly, his first thoughts were not about himself. She answered for him. "You better believe he is in on it. And I'll provide the fixings afterward."

"Hey, all right! We'll hold you to it. I'll give you a call." Denny punched Jacob's shoulder in parting.

"Merry Christmas, Jasmine." Sheila gave her friend a one-armed hug around the waist.

"To you too. I see Denny is home. Isn't it nice to have the kids underfoot?"

"Hmmm." Bending her head to lay it against Jasmine's dark waves, she reminisced, "Evert loved Christmas."

Jasmine's eyes misted. She appreciated it when friends and acquaintances mentioned her husband by name. As the lapse of months since his death stretched, people grew more hesitant in bringing him up in conversation, as if mentioning him by name would remind Jasmine of her loss. Didn't they realize he was heavy on her thoughts every minute of every day?

"I miss Evert's star," Sheila confided.

His star? Shocked at her neglect, Jasmine's eyes widened. "Oh, how could have I been so forgetful?" Evert had fused together a gigantic five-point iron star and then welded a special bracket extending above the garage roof upon which to fasten it. Situated at the east edge of town, the star shining above their home had been dubbed by the town's folk as the star of the east.

"You've had so much on your mind." Sheila waved the oversight away. "I'm praying you through this first holiday season."

An errant tear threatened to fall over the embankment. "That must be why it is going so well." Their heads touched in another embrace.

"Don't forget the New Year's Eve party at our place," her friend gently reminded.

"I won't." Although she would have chosen to stay home and not be a part of the world of couples, this was one misstep warned against at the grief support meetings—don't turn down overtures from friends. You need them.

A light snowfall dusted their heads and shoulders as they hurried through the cold to the parking lot. "How shall we spend the rest of the evening?" Jacob cranked on the starter.

"I'd prefer to share it with both of my children. How about we pack up some hot cider and cookies and join Autumn at the truck stop?"

Shifting into gear, Jacob acknowledged, "I'm with you. But I have to do something first."

"What?" Lights twinkled from the windows and rooftops on nearly every house on the street.

"You'll see."

Once home, Jasmine bustled to the kitchen to warm up the apple cider stored in the pantry. While it was heating, she arranged an assortment of homemade Christmas cookies on a glass platter. These had been the product of a baking escapade Jacob had suggested the day after the tree cutting. He had taken over his dad's favorite recipes leaving the flour, sugar, and egg ingredients to his mom and sister.

Satisfied with the result, she scampered down the steps to the family room to retrieve a bag full of games.

Her son hadn't followed her into the house. Instead, he had headed for his dad's workshop. A thud against the house piqued her curiosity, however the steaming cider insisted on her undivided attention. The huge metal thermos Evert had filled on many chilly mornings before heading off to work still sat on a pantry shelf. Speaking out loud to him, she explained, "Not coffee, hon. Autumn prefers cider." She hummed a carol while carefully pouring the hot drink into the insulated vessel.

Jacob's entry was announced by the banging of the back door. "What do you want me to carry?"

She handed him the thermos and bag of games while she followed, balancing the cookie platter.

It wasn't until Jacob had backed out of the driveway that she viewed his handiwork. The star of the east, high above the garage roof, now beckoned the wise men of Prairie City. "Your dad would be pleased." She leaned over and deposited a kiss on his red cheek.

So was she.

Invaders of the truck stop, the mother-son duo loaded with the festive goodies were met by a hard-to-read frown from Autumn, who was presently filling the overhead cigarette racks.

"As ambassadors of peace on earth, goodwill to women, we are bringing some Christmas cheer to you poor working gals," Jasmine greeted, depositing her plate of cookies on one of the tables set in an enclosed booth.

"Ho, ho, ho!" Jacob entered the door behind her. "If it isn't my sweet little Autumn. Have you been a good girl this year?" Raising his eyebrows, he gave her a questioning look.

Ginger Freetag, the second employee sharing the shift, chortled cheerily. "So Santa sent two of his elves here, did he?"

"You betcha." Jacob looked every bit of an elf in his stocking cap and mischievous grin. "In his very own words, Santa firmly instructed us, 'Don't you dare forget those hardworking ladies at the truck stop in Prairie City. They helped my reindeer one stormy Christmas when we ran out of gas. Yesiree. They filled my team plump full with hamburgers and fries.'"

Missing the humor, Autumn dryly instructed, "Close the door, Santa. You're letting in the cold air."

"Excuse me." He swept out an arm and bent forward in a low bow, almost dropping his cargo.

Robust in girth, Ginger gave another hearty laugh. "Santa, you'd better set down your wares before you drop them." She took the thermos out of his grip and added it to the table top. "Looks like you're setting up here for the night."

"Yes, we thought we'd keep Autumn company since she already missed the Christmas Eve service." Jasmine shrugged off her coat.

"I told her she should run over to the church and I could handle things for an hour, but she wouldn't hear of it. Probably thought I'd get mugged by a Christmas grinch." She batted her eyelashes jovially at Autumn. "Anyway, it was nice she volunteered to work the late shift."

Volunteered? Jasmine suddenly felt selfish for wanting the three of them to attend the Christmas service as a family. Yet, on the other hand, she was perplexed her daughter wouldn't want to do so. "That's why we came. Any chance we can tempt the two of you into a game of Rummikub when the road traffic quiets down?"

"Quiets down? I'd say it is already dead. People are home celebrating, eating homemade delicacies of mama's and granny's doin', instead of something encased in a cellophane wrapper. We'll finish organizing the shelves here. You get that game set up." Busily, Ginger sliced open a cardboard box packed full of smaller items.

Jasmine caught Autumn's disgruntled frown but chose to ignore it. It would be easy to be a Scrooge this first Christmas, wallowing in self-pity. But why? There'd be plenty of dark winter days ahead when the choices may not be so plentiful. Bah! Humbug? She certainly wouldn't want to do it on Christ's birthday.

Dumping the box of tiles on the countertop, she wondered out loud. "Do you think the day Jesus descended to earth as a baby is marked on some celestial calendar and given any special recognition in heaven each year?"

Jacob flipped the tiles number side down. "Maybe. Then again, every day is probably so good up there, it's not possible to differentiate a holiday from an ordinary day."

"Yeah," Ginger chimed in, her back to them as she stacked additional cracker boxes into place. "Those angel choirs, no doubt, sing the 'Hallelujah Chorus' every day." She pushed her hefty form off her knees and swished the dust from her hands. "Sweetie," she directed at Autumn, "I'd say we're about done. Let's join the family fun."

Reluctantly, Autumn moved out from behind the till and meandered over to the booth. She and Ginger sat across from her mom and brother. Right at her elbow, she propped her cell phone in ready reach.

"Expecting a call from the bearded man?" Jacob jived. "He' s too busy tonight. Might as well concentrate on not getting your socks beat off you 'cause I'm hot!"

In reply, he got a view of her tongue. As the game progressed, her attitude loosened up, becoming as competitive as her brother. Occasionally, the bell above the door would tinkle and she'd jump up to wait on a customer. Mostly, as Ginger had predicted, the night was slow, the cold temperatures freezing a fuzzy frame of frost in each window.

Caught up in the board game, the hours evaporated. Cracking open the cider, Jacob filled Styrofoam cups while they all overtaxed the cookie plate.

Shortly before the midnight hour struck, all four of them pitched in to tidy up the place, sweeping and wet mopping the floor, washing off the tables. Ginger locked the front door. There hadn't been a single customer in the last hour.

"I must say, this has been a unique Christmas," Jasmine reflected. "In my entire life, I've never spent Christmas Eve in a gas station."

"I have, but never one this fun," Ginger conceded.

"In my estimation, it wasn't so bad," Jacob added. "What do you say, Sis?" He stuck his arm through her bent elbow.

Expecting a bored reaction, they were all pleasantly surprised when Autumn offered a thought-provoking comment. "Mary and Joseph had a similar Christmas the year Jesus was born, stuck out in a smelly stable. You'd think, for the first Christmas, God would have come up with something a bit more classy."

Pausing in motion to stare at her daughter, Jasmine couldn't help but be impressed by Autumn's observation. "Yes," she agreed. "Christmas can happen wherever we are—at home, at church, on the road, or in Prairie City's truck stop."

"And in heaven," Jacob concluded, thinking of his dad.

A bitter cold wind nipped at their cheeks as they jogged to separate vehicles. Turning out of the parking lot, the star in the east beckoned them home.

Chapter 17

Two weeks into the third quarter of school, Jasmine was preparing for parent-teacher conferences to discuss the previous nine weeks of progress with her students' parents. Such conferences were scheduled strategically throughout the school year to keep parents and teachers on the same page in helping children be successful in their education. However, the appointed days made for long, extended hours after the normal school day setting, keeping Jasmine from her own doorstep until late into the evening.

Elton Public School scheduled their conferences for a Monday in mid-January. On Tuesday, she'd wear the hat of a parent attending Autumn's conference at Prairie City High School.

Autumn came out of her bedroom Monday morning just as Jasmine was collecting her schoolbag and purse to head out the door. Autumn had been working more and more midnight shifts at the truck stop, which grated on Jasmine's preferred school night curfew. They hadn't had a meal together since Jacob had headed back to college right after the first of the year. Most of the communication between mother and daughter was done by scribbled notes on the table or a short text. Jasmine couldn't understand why Tom Neir would put high school kids on his work schedule for the late shift.

When confronted, Autumn had a ready explanation. "One of the employees quit. This is only temporary until Tom can find some reliable help."

"You can't do justice to your schoolwork when you don't have enough sleep," Jasmine objected.

"Oh, Mom, I have plenty of time to study when the station gets slow."

Jasmine often felt she was parenting from a tightrope stretched across the town. One miss word or facial expression, and Autumn would be out of here.

This particular morning, Autumn actually initiated the short interlude of verbal exchange.

"Don't you have conferences tonight?"

"Yup, I won't be home before ten." Breaking a banana off the bunch in the fruit basket to tuck into her bag, Jasmine asked, "Will you be at the station?"

"Actually, I have the night off." Autumn rotated the basket, selecting an orange.

"Really?" Jasmine thought it a bit peculiar her daughter's night off coincided with her own full schedule.

"You'll miss your grief support meeting." Autumn commented, using her fingernail to pierce the skin of the orange.

"Yes, I thought of that too. I look forward to Monday nights, but it will hold until next week. I gotta go. Have a good day at school." She waited for a parting response from her daughter, who was engrossed in pulling chunks of orange peel off her fruit. When she didn't even bother to give eye contact, Jasmine started walking down the hall to the back door, calling over her shoulder, "Love you."

But there was no answering acknowledgment.

Sitting in the chairs set out in the corridor, accessible to waiting parents, Jasmine and Cynthia shot the breeze. "How many conferences do you have left?" Cynthia asked, checking her wristwatch.

"Three. How about you?"

"Four, plus Billy's folks didn't show up at their designated time slot. Maybe they'll drop in yet."

Stretching her arms above her head, Jasmine sighed. "This really gets to be a long day. I left home at seven this morning, and now we're moving in on eight thirty in the evening." She crossed her legs and leaned her head against the brick wall behind her. "Any tough ones?"

"Nah, I thought Mr. and Mrs. Owens were going to blow some steam over their little munchkin getting hit with an ice chunk at recess, but they never said a word."

"One look at you, and they waved the white flag, surrendering before a shot was fired," Jasmine ribbed. "Gotta be tough to be a teacher of first graders!

"Hey, how is Katie doing in her new role as mother? Justin must be four months by now." Jasmine had missed seeing him when Katie was home for the holidays.

"He is one strong little boy. When I stand him up in my lap, those chubby legs lock. He practically holds his body upright. I think he has the physique of an upcoming wrestler."

"Is Katie back at work?"

"No, being in horticulture, it will be another month before she has to start planting seeds for this spring's greenhouse production. Her maternity leave fit nicely into the off-season. It will be difficult for her to return to her career with Justin in the picture."

"Yes, I remember those days only too well. I cried all the way to school the first morning I dropped Jacob off at day care."

"First day, my foot. You bawled for a whole month!" Cynthia exclaimed.

Jasmine grinned. "And now I'm bawling over a senior in high school. This motherhood business is emotional stuff. How are you doing as nana?"

Hesitating, as if to form her thoughts appropriately, Cynthia scrunched up her face. "The baby stage is not really my cup of tea. I think it will be better when Justin can walk, and we can have some intelligent discussions."

"Oh, yeah? What do you plan to discuss?" Jasmine raised her eyebrows, waiting for an answer.

"Maybe the topic of grandparenting being overrated." Seeing the alarm sketched in her friend's face, Cynthia quickly negated, "Only kidding. Someday, I'll actually be old enough to fit this role."

Before Jasmine could make a rejoinder, a set of parents appeared at her door. Everything Jasmine had ever heard about being a grandparent sounded like loads easier than being a parent. Maybe she and Cynthia should swap roles for a season.

After school the following day, Jasmine stripped off her professional title of Mrs. Kirmis and donned her parental label, alias Autumn's mom, as she stepped into the Prairie City High School gymnasium. In some ways, this role was much more daunting. As a teacher, she was the authority, the person who supposedly was trained to have the answers. As a parent, she was floundering, endeavoring to model correct values and morals, but wringing her hands in despair when her daughter chose to ignore her teachings and strike out on her own path. Ever since Autumn's first conference back in kindergarten, Jasmine had dreaded what the current news might be. Fastening on a semblance of a smile, a facade she had become adept at since Evert's passing, she moved toward the frontal table where the secretary was passing out the individual student report cards.

Shaking off her nervous trepidation, Jasmine tried to concentrate on the positive. Autumn was attending classes regularly.

According to the computer report on PowerSchool, her home-work was completed, maybe not exactly to her full ability, but at least passing. Principal Borstead had not summoned Jasmine to his office for any inappropriate behavior. It wasn't as if Autumn was driving her car in the wrong direction on a one-way.

"Good afternoon, Jasmine," Sally, the secretary, greeted her cheerily. "Here is Autumn's second quarter evaluation. Instead of making you run the hallway maze this year, trying to locate each teacher's classroom, all the instructor's have their own table scattered throughout the gym. You can visit with as many of them as you like. Please limit your discussion to ten minutes to give other parents a turn."

The paper slip was barely in Jasmine's outstretched hand before Sally was repeating the instructions to the couple behind her. Feeling caught, she moved aside to give herself a moment to digest the letters on the paper—three Cs, two Ds. Autumn had slipped a little. There was no way Jasmine expected an above average report on her. Autumn had always struggled as a student, and this year, with the death of her father, Cs and Ds might be as good as they could get.

Scanning the layout of tables, she saw some teachers already occupied by a parent. Her preference was to escape, to disregard any comments denoting Autumn's negligence in her studies; however, the professional educator inside of her prevailed. Students preformed best who had the backing and interest of a parent behind them.

Mr. Putman, the high school mathematics teacher, was open. Jasmine inhaled a full breath, forcing her left foot to follow her right foot as she cut a course to his table. At the sight of her, he stood, extending a hand for her to shake. "Mrs. Kirmis, it is always a pleasure to see you. Are you keeping those first graders in line in Elton?"

She smiled faintly. "Their energy is always a challenge."

He chuckled. "Over here in the high school, we sometimes have the opposite problem. Motivation grinds to a halt. Let's see what I have to show you for Autumn." In a few seconds, he had Autumn's grades up on the screen of his laptop computer. "I'm sure you have been keeping abreast of her Algebra 2 grades on PowerSchool, so I'm not showing you anything you don't already know. Her second quarter average was a 71 percent, a mere two points above failing giving her a 73 percent composite for the first semester. She is teetering a bit too close to the edge."

"Math has never been her strong point." Jasmine agreed with his numbers.

"Back when she was a freshman, she had difficulty with Algebra 1. I believe she failed the second semester." He punched buttons and soon had her math history on the monitor.

"Yes, but as a sophomore, she retook the second semester and was able to pass it. Simultaneously, she was enrolled in geometry. That was the year she was open enrolled over in Elton." Jasmine wasn't blaming Mr. Putman for Autumn's mathematics incompetency; she was merely stating the facts.

He picked up where she'd left off. "Then during her junior year, she opted not to take a math class." He noted the absence of a mathematics grade.

"Yes, she probably was suffering from an overdose of theorems and hypothesizes." Jasmine smirked.

Mr. Putman smiled back but then put on a serious expression. "It has put her in a hotbox with graduation looming ahead. North Dakota standards require three maths. She needs this last semester to graduate."

"I take it she hasn't put forth much effort," Jasmine sighed.

"Her assignments are completed daily but poorly. Sometimes, I think she is going through the motions in order to say she's done." He could see the sadness in the parent's eyes, the wilting of her shoulders. "Hey, this has been a tough year for both of you. I am more than willing to help her before school, after school or during the half hour of intervention. However, she has to want the help."

"Thank you." Jasmine's eyes dropped to her lap. "I'll talk to her."

Not meaning to compound the hurt already piercing her, Mr. Putman echoed her reply, "I'll talk to her too."

Clutching her purse, she rose from her chair, feeling like a cornered mouse panicking for a way out.

Forget the other subjects and teachers, she was out of here. Letting her eyes glue themselves to the grade sheet as if in deep thought, Jasmine propelled herself straight for the door, not looking to either side. She had almost achieved her goal when a friendly voice called out, "Jasmine, I'm free. Could you give me a minute?"

The summons brought her flight to a halt. Ms. Herr, the English instructor, had refilled her coffee mug from the cart near the entrance and was weaving her way through the mass of tables. Jasmine managed a tight inclination of her head; her fake smile had died minutes ago.

Settling into her seat, Ms. Herr conversationally addressed Mrs. Kirmis. "How are you doing today?"

Believe me, she didn't want to know. She would have staggered had Jasmine dumped her load of insecurities upon her. Fearing her voice would crack, Jasmine remained mute.

"Autumn has always been a fluent reader and writer. I'd often find her in the library searching for another good book. English has been an easy subject for her." Ms. Herr started with a compliment. Teachers were taught to put parents at ease by initiating a conference on a favorable note.

Jasmine's eyes moved down the list of subjects on the report card—English, C. Average. There shouldn't be anything too negative to recount. She forced herself to relax and concentrate on the teacher's words.

"Yes, Autumn earned a C this past quarter. We both are aware she is capable of more, but under the circumstances, a decline in her workmanship is understandable. We can live with a C. However, we are two weeks into the third quarter. Autumn has not turned in anything thus far. I am teaching them how to do research, to organize, and to write a term paper on any topic they choose. By now, each student should have their topic finalized and completed twenty-five note cards of information. Although I have asked Autumn for hers repeatedly, she always has an excuse. A lot of the research we have done in the computer lab during class, so she really doesn't have a valid reason not to be progressing."

"I'm sorry. I wasn't aware of this." Jasmine mumbled.

"English is a required class." She had heard this same lament from Mr. Putman. "I don't know how many credits Autumn has accumulated in her four years of high school. She may be close to the total number required for graduation, lessening the impact of failing an elective course. But she has to have this English class to graduate."

The weight on Jasmine's shoulders was becoming oppressive. She'd often wondered how women in Ethiopia could carry weighted baskets on their heads. Her neck was shrinking into her spine, a turtle withdrawing from the harshness of reality. How was she supposed to bolster her daughter's work ethics when they were barely on speaking terms? What were the odds Autumn was even concerned about earning her high school diploma?

Yet Jasmine did recall her screaming something about graduation being her ticket out of their house. Nice carrot to dangle in front of her: You do your work, you graduate, and you don't have to wake up to your mother each morning. That was some motivational learning.

Autumn had the midnight shift at the truck stop again. The discussion would have to wait.

Even though her gas tank indicator light wasn't blinking at her, Jasmine chose to fill up with fuel before school hoping to catch

Tom Neir at the station. She wasn't to be disappointed. Before she could stick the nozzle into the opening, Tom was at her elbow, taking over. "Wait inside where it's warm, and I'll do this." Jasmine was only too glad to comply. Self-service gas pumps were not high on her list of favorites, especially on a winter morning in January.

Inside, she was met with Ginger's bleak remarks updating her on the latest road report. "You be careful on that ice this morning. Trucker from Montana said it is sheer glass all the way from the border." Driving on ice was another of Jasmine's hang ups— knuckles white from gripping the steering wheel; traffic moving at a snail's pace; and someone in a four-wheel-drive pickup truck, or worse yet, a semitruck and trailer eating up her bumper, itching to pass. She'd be a nervous wreck before she got to school. Story of her life. A wreck.

Frigid air swept into the building, ruffling the rack of Prairie City T-shirts on display when Tom entered. Jasmine paid her bill before seeking out the owner in his office at the rear of the store. With a pair of reading glasses perched on the end of his nose, he looked up from a pile of sales slips when she stepped in. "Thank you again for filling my car for me."

"Glad to do it. I'm rather sorry that in this modern age, everything has gone self-serve. Takes away the personal contact between a businessman and his customer."

Hesitating slightly before continuing on, Jasmine bit her bottom lip. "I also appreciate you giving Autumn an after-school job. It gives her a few hours to think about something other than her dad." She broke eye contact with him, fumbling with her purse and gloves.

Slipping off the glasses, he replied, "Hey, it's my pleasure. She's doing a decent job. I need the high school kids to help fill in the hours between my full-time employees, so it is good for me too."

Not sure how to get to the point, she stammered. "I, I, I'm a bit apprehensive though about Autumn working such late hours.

With schoolwork and all…the weekends are okay…" Her voice died away.

"No problem, Jasmine. If you prefer she doesn't work on school nights, I can schedule her only for weekends." He rose to grab the January schedule off the wall where it was tacked.

"That's not it at all," she protested. "I like her being out of the house for a few hours each day, but I think midnight is taxing her ability to function in school the next day."

Tom laid the paper on his desk at an angle they could both examine. "I didn't think I ever put her on for the late shift. I actually prefer one of the adults for the closing. I take that back. She worked Christmas Eve, but she literally wouldn't take a *no* that night. I thought you'd want her home."

Sliding her eyes across and down the month's schedule, it was obvious Autumn's shift was four to seven on school nights. Jasmine slumped on the inside. Autumn was lying to her.

The truth was obvious to Tom as well. "I'm sorry, Jasmine. This is a tough year for you and Autumn. I have seen some young guys here, particularly one that shows up about the time Autumn leaves. I don't know the kid. He's not from Prairie City." He placed a hand on her shoulder. "Parenting is a tough ball game. She'll get through this."

"I hope the same can be said for me." Jasmine lips made a lame attempt at turning up at the corners.

He squeezed her shoulder. "I'll give the guy a hard time and see if I can run him off."

Doing better at a semblance of a grin, Jasmine replied, "Except you're not too scary. Thanks for listening."

"You have a good day, and slow it down on that ice out there."

It was days like this she coveted Evert's doting. If the weather had been threatening or if temperatures had wavered above the freezing mark, changing the snow to rain, coating the roads and trees with an inch of ice over night, he would chauffeur her to school and be there again at the end of the day to give her a lift home. Even the snowblower Jacob had helped her master over Christmas had been totally Evert's domain. Never did she worry about how she was going to back out the garage after a heavy snowfall. Up hours before her morning departure, he had the cement pad whipped clean of any drifts blocking their exit.

The stop sign barring her access to the highway connecting Prairie City and Elton was her first hurdle. Pumping the brakes well in advance of the intersection, she slowly maneuvered her car to a halt. A tanker truck hauling fuel passed by in front of her at a cautious speed. Twirling the steering wheel half of a revolution to the right, she concurrently pressed the accelerator tenuously to move her forward onto the highway. Her back wheels spun out on the slippery surface before the rubber tires gripped enough to propel her ahead. Her heart thudded against her chest, both hands gripping the steering wheel. Within the first mile, she already came upon the fishtailing tracks of a vehicle before it slid into the ditch. Its windows were vacant; she surmised a passing vehicle had picked up the driver.

Her back stiffened as she kept her eyes rooted to the roadway in front of the hood ornament. In the distance, she saw a semitruck approaching, its wheels churning up a cloud of snow blowing directly into her lane. Slowing down even more than the diminutive speed she was proceeding at, she mentally readied herself for its blast. With a *whoosh*, her windshield was swathed in a curtain of white, completely shutting out all visibility. Holding the wheel rigidly to abstain from accidentally crossing the dotted yellow line into oncoming traffic, she prayed her way through the blindness.

The air cleared again, her car properly traveling on the right side of the roadway. A sigh of relief exploded from her cheeks. She pushed the accelerator down a quarter of an inch, the speedometer needle barely advancing. She hoped desperately the ice would be burned off by the afternoon when she would reverse her direction homeward.

Two headlights from an oncoming car appeared on the horizon. They slowly advanced over the glazed highway toward Jasmine's Impala, like two cowboys in a western movie having a show down on Main Street. The approaching car was hugging the centerline too closely for Jasmine's comfort. She inched her vehicle to the edge of the road where the snowplow had left a ridge.

A middle-aged lady, with a grim face as nervous as Jasmine's, sat taut behind the wheel. Neither gave a courtesy wave as their vehicles moved past each other.

Steering to the left to align herself with the middle of her lane, Jasmine felt her car refusing to meet her demand, sucking her further to the side closest to the ditch. Suddenly, the car seemed to speed up on its on accord, swinging her in a full 360-degree circle. Although everything was happening so quickly, she still had time to contemplate her situation. Jamming on the brakes could produce the needed momentum to send her car into a roll. Twisting the front wheels in a dead turn to the right or left could do the same. Her only hope was to ride out the spin. Ironically, the fear that had held her frozen in her seat in a statue-like stance all the way from Prairie City melted away like a Popsicle on a scorching summer day. Her fingers wrapped around the steering wheel in a deadbolt grip, not wanting to be bounced about like a rag doll, even within the confines of her seat belt.

As the car started a second spin, the back end hit the ditch, sliding straight backward. One last abrupt bump from behind lodged the back wheels in the deeper snow depths with the front hood pointing at the highway in a ninety-degree angle. "Thank you, Lord," she breathed. The car was upright sitting on all four wheels. Taking a few deep breaths to steady herself, she very cautiously pressed the gas pedal, hoping she could simply drive out of her predicament. In answer, the back wheels spun a sickening tune, deepening their depressions into the packed snow. She was irrevocably stuck.

A sense of doom sifted over her stiff back and taut muscles, crystallizing into a massive ice chunk in her chest. What should she do now? Who should she call? It seemed becoming a widow had put her at everyone's mercy. In frustration, she let her forehead fall forward, hitting the top of the steering wheel, unable to check the moisture leaking out.

Helpless. She was utterly helpless against the elements of nature, a mere dry blade of grass sticking its head above the snow.

She was a failure as a parent. How was she supposed to get a teenage daughter to get excited about her schoolwork? Or to be honest in her speech? Or to desire a relationship with her mom? Life had become a Mt. Everest, demanding she buck up, dig in her toes, and climb it or be doomed. It would be immeasurably easier to let go, to slide to the bottom and admit defeat. What was there to win anyway?

The Bible story of Hannah and her son Samuel resurfaced. Hannah had given Samuel to the Lord, but she wasn't asked to hand over her husband in the deal.

Moaning, Jasmine forced herself to corral her thoughts before they slid into a dark oblivion. Autumn may not be her flesh and blood, yet she was still hers. Jasmine was not giving up on her blonde-haired green-eyed daughter. It may mean implementing some tough love, making their family battleground even bloodier; however, if it gave Autumn a brighter future, it was worth it.

A tap at her window brought her head up in a jerk, like a soldier saluting his superior. A bearded face peered through the glass at her from the warmth of a fur-lined aviator's type hat. The wind tugged at his insulated jacket but wasn't given entry. A stranded motorist did not fear a stranger along the windswept prairies in the coldest months of the year. Anyone who stopped to lend a hand to prevent a fellow travel from freezing to death was christened a Good Samaritan.

Depressing the button for the electric window, she listened to his instructions. Hollering against the noise of the wind, he made himself heard. "I don't think you're in too far. I've got a chain in the back of my truck. Sit tight, and I'll get it." Without making any small talk, the man lumbered back to the four-wheel-drive pickup truck parked on the side of the road near Jasmine's front end. Nimbly, he lifted an iron-linked chain from the box, attaching the hook to the ball hitch below his bumper. He stretched the chain to the Impala then lay on the frozen ground to find something to attach the second end to under her frame. Righting himself, he came to her window once more.

"I'll pull slowly until the chain is tight. Then work with me. Have your car in gear ready to accelerate." She nodded. He turned, lowering his head into the bitter northern gale, and trudged to his truck.

The chain, link by link, straightened into a rescue rope for the embedded passenger car. Jasmine touched the floor pedal and felt her tires move from a spin onto road contact. When free of the ditch, she steered her vehicle behind the truck at the side of the road. The man exited his cab a final time, unhooked the two ends of the chain, dropped it over his end gate onto the bed of his box. Lifting a hand in farewell, he jogged back to his door and disappeared inside. In moments, his red taillights moved away from her into the lane of traffic. Not expecting anything in return, he did his good deed and moved on.

"Thank you, kind sir," Jasmine threw the words at her windshield as she cautiously followed his trail. The man hadn't wanted to be paid or even thanked for his rescue. Jasmine realized that whenever she was at her lowest point, God made His presence known. It was if He wanted to make sure she realized He was in control no matter the place she found herself, whether the situation was tying her in knots or whether she was married or single.

Lesson taken.

⌘

The unexpected encounter with the roadway benefactor had bolstered Jasmine's spirits immensely. The impending confrontation with Autumn no longer loomed as a viscous, all-consuming monster like it had last night, attacking her when she was tired and emotionally riding a seesaw. She would be firm without letting Autumn drag her into a shouting match, understanding without allowing her to use grief as a scapegoat, tender without reducing her to guilt to thwart her authority.

Meeting her daughter at the station at seven was inconceivable. It was very likely Autumn would make a scene if her defiance was laundered in public. Jasmine decided to text her a brief message after school. "See you at supper at 7:10. I'm frying fish."

Anticipating a contrary text, she wasn't to be disappointed. Autumn typed back, "Can't. I work till midnight."

Be firm, Jasmine reminded herself. "No you don't. Be here." She pressed the Send button. Now she could only wait to see if Autumn would adhere to her request. Assuming she would, she put two small potatoes in the oven to bake, tossed a salad, and set the table. Twenty minutes prior to the designated hour, she heated a small amount of oil in a skillet and slipped the egg-and-flour-coated fillets into the pan. A car door banged just as she was flipping the perfectly browned fish onto a serving plate.

A look that would melt ice hung on Autumn's face as she entered, her schoolbag hanging from one shoulder. Choosing to ignore it, Jasmine greeted her warmly, "Just in time. I'll have the food on the table in a jiffy."

"I'm not that hungry." Autumn's eyes took in the fried fillets cooked the way she preferred them. Her bag hit the floor with a thud. She twisted one leg underneath her buttocks, lowering herself into a chair. Heat from the oven warmed her as her mom stabbed the hot potatoes off the top rack and then retrieved two salad bowls from the refrigerator.

A brief prayer was offered for the food before they dug in.

"How's school today?" Jasmine offered, pouring thousand island dressing over the lettuce.

"Same." Autumn was noncommittal, as usual.

Jasmine chattered on about some cute antidotes amongst her first graders. Then related the story she had shared with her fellow staff members of the roadside angel pulling her out of the ditch.

"That's cool." Jasmine was encouraged by the positive remark.

"It was way cool. I was about to lose it, and here he came, tapping on the window."

"Could have been a real angel," Autumn suggested, "since you believe in that sort of thing."

"An angel in disguise. You know, I like that. Whoever he was, I was deeply appreciative. I had a twenty in my purse I would have gladly given him, but he just waved and was gone."

"Double cool."

"Do you want some ice cream?"

"Yeah, one scoop."

Jasmine moved to the refrigerator to retrieve the pail from the freezer, two bowls from the cupboard, and a scooper. Reclaiming her seat, she dished up the dessert. "Have you seen your grades from last quarter?" Jasmine concentrated on the hard ice cream.

"Yeah. Figured you'd let me have it."

"Three Cs and 2 Ds aren't the end of the world," Jasmine objected mildly, handing a dish to her daughter. Inwardly, she wondered when her standards had dropped so low to qualify a D as satisfactory.

"So what's the problem then?" Autumn sucked on a spoonful of the cold treat.

"The problem is what you are doing, or possibly not doing, in the new quarter."

"What's that supposed to mean?" Autumn never looked at her mother.

"Mr. Putman and Ms. Herr are both concerned about the Math and English credits mandatory for graduation. If you don't poop it up a notch, you will be in danger of failing." She kept her voice feathery, endeavoring to keep any tone of accusation from surfacing.

"So I'll try harder." Autumn acted unconcerned.

"You need a topic for your term paper, not to mention a slug of note cards from your research for Ms. Herr." Jasmine got up to return the ice cream pail to the freezer.

"I gave her one today."

"One card or a topic?"

"A topic." The boredom displayed on her face inferred she didn't give a rip.

"Can I ask what it is?" Jasmine slipped back into her place.

"Tattoos." For the first time, Autumn glanced up hoping to be rewarded by a look of revulsion from her mother. Jasmine had vented at various times over a disgusting tattoo displayed on someone's body parts. She could handle a tiny heart, a winged butterfly, or a simple dove, but massive grotesque images obliterating an entire arm or back, she found disgusting.

Jasmine's stomach did a dive, but it didn't jar her facial expression. With causal aloofness, she suggested, "You'd best do some research tonight to get caught up."

Autumn grumbled something unintelligible, pushing back on two legs of her chair.

"Mr. Putman has offered to tutor you when it is convenient for both of you."

The chair's front legs hit the floor with an exclamation mark.

"By the way, I expect to see you about this time each evening. Curfew on school nights is ten." Jasmine began clearing the dishes away.

"Are you out of your mind?" Autumn was finally nerved out of the skin of listlessness she had fabricated for her mother.

"I don't think so," Jasmine replied, returning the condiments to their proper places.

"I'm a senior. That should be worth some fringe benefits." Sarcasm was edging in.

"Benefits have to be earned. You be vigilant in your classes, complete the required assignments in a satisfactory manner, and we can talk again."

"And if I don't obey your endless list of demands?"

"Your car keys will be confiscated."

Autumn let out a frustrated scream. "You'd think there would be some relaxing of the rules for someone going through grieving."

"Your dad would not want you to use his death as an excuse to damage your own chances at having a productive future. He loved you. He'd want you to persevere." Tenderness poured from Jasmine's eyes. "I sometimes feel the same as you do. Getting up and going to school can be a momentous act. As much as we think the world should stop revolving until we're ready to jump back into life, it isn't going to happen. Even though we'd like to shout that life isn't fair, it won't help. We have to keep moving forward. I'm sorry, Autumn. I too wish I could jump off this perpetual Ferris wheel for a few months."

Slowly turning her back on Autumn, Jasmine resumed the task of cleaning up the kitchen. Hot water filling the sink created noise, giving both of them a few moments to collect their thoughts. Doing ordinary tasks could help disengage Autumn from digging in her arsenal for more weapons to use in an offensive artillery attack. Jasmine squeezed in a generous portion of dish soap.

First scrubbing each dish and utensil, she then rinsed them before setting them in the rack. When she stepped over to the stove to retrieve the frying pan, Autumn's chair was still holding her weight, her elbows propped on the tabletop. Without any preliminary buildup, Autumn flatly stated, "I went to your grief support meeting on Monday night."

Known to throw in a lit firecracker to get a reaction, Jasmine held the skillet suspended in air, scrutinizing her daughter's expression. Her sagging posture coupled with a washed-out window to an aching soul indicated that, at least temporarily, the sparring match was on hold.

Jasmine submerged the greasy pan in the dishwater before leaning against the counter ledge facing Autumn. "What did you think?"

Raising her eyebrows and giving a disinterested shrug, she commented, "Kind of a bunch of wimps."

Jasmine's facial muscles softened, a hint of amusement creasing her lips. "In what way?"

Not meeting her mom's gaze, she muttered, "They all whined about something—being lonely, don't know nothing about fixing a furnace, uncomfortable out in public, no one comes to visit. It was more like a gripe session."

In some ways, Autumn was right. Sometimes, when the discussion opened up to the week's hurdles, there was a vast number of grumblings. "It kind of sounds like me," Jasmine admitted. "While I am comfortable teaching a class or running the household or planning a social event, my self-esteem falters when I'm bombarded with the jobs your dad oversaw. I struggle with the snow removal and taking care of the car. The tax forms needing to be filled out are going to be a nightmare to waddle through. I miss your dad, and Jacob too, being here with you and me doing normal everyday stuff." She wanted to reach across the intervening space to touch her daughter and hold her in a tight hug. However, Autumn didn't welcome physical contact, and Jasmine didn't want to break the fragile emergence of communication sprouting. "And I miss hearing the lovely sound of piano music permeating our home, floating from room to room."

Autumn glanced up momentarily. Jasmine added, "I think I fit in. I'm a whiner." She grinned at her daughter. "Anything that spoke to you?"

"Ah, I don't know. Guess if it helps them, it's a good thing," Autumn conceded.

"Will you go again?"

"Nah, I don't think so. There really wasn't anyone my age."

"We could go together."

Shaking her head, Autumn declined. "Then they'd just label me as your daughter, not my own person."

"How about if you go then, and I'll drop out." Inwardly, Jasmine knew Autumn would greatly benefit from sorting out her feelings with the support of the group.

"No, Mom, it's more your thing." Stretching as she stood up, she voiced, "Guess I've got some homework to do." Her veil of blond hair hid her face as she strutted to her room.

"Give me a holler if you need some help." Jasmine watched her teenager disappear down the hallway.

A tinge of hope flickered within her mother's heart. Just maybe, there was still a chance for the two of them to share a resemblance of friendship.

Chapter 18

Perspiration beaded on Jasmine's upper lip, her blouse sticking to her sore, aching back after having carted a deluge of totes and bulging bags up the staircase. Autumn's ponytail bobbed in front of her, her long-legged gait showing no manifestation of fatigue as she steadily mounted the college dorm steps of Seim Hall to her floor. With a throng of freshman converging on North Dakota State University all at once, the elevators had been jammed. Autumn suggested they use the stairs rather than waiting their turn.

Wearily, Jasmine let the heavy tote fall to the floor just inside Autumn's door, plopping herself on top of it like a shriveled up hotdog left warming on the grill too long. The one side of the room was already visibly occupied, the bed neatly made up with a T-shirt quilt, photos mounted on the bulletin board, school supplies stacked on the bookshelf. "Looks like Jeneen beat us," Jasmine puffed. Autumn had previously met her roommate during the freshman orientation days a few weeks earlier.

After ambulating a circular lap through the room, detouring into the bath shared by the adjacent room, and coming out again,

Autumn stopped at her lofty heap of luggage. "Small, but I guess doable," she concluded.

Warily, Jasmine pondered how Autumn was going to get along with a roommate, having always had a room to herself. If Jeneen was a neat freak, she was up for an adjustment. Contemplating the stack of personal items Autumn had packed in her car and Jasmine's Impala, it didn't seem possible it was all going to find a home in her half of the dorm room. "Want me to help you unpack?" she offered.

"No, I think I'd rather do it myself. Then I'll know where everything is."

"Maybe I should take some of this home with me. You won't need your winter clothes for awhile," Jasmine suggested without blatantly stating, "You have too much stuff." When Jacob had set off for college four years ago, he had only needed his backseat. Must be the difference between guys and girls.

Back in May, when he was home for Autumn's graduation, Jacob had gone car shopping with his sister, at their mom's expense, finding her a used Toyota to replace the unreliable Ford Escort they both had driven during high school. Autumn had been elated and had promptly motored up and down Main Street for the remainder of the day, draining the gas tank. It was a rude awakening when Jasmine said the fuel bill, licensing, and insurance would be her daughter's responsibility. Her paycheck from the truck stop for the entire summer was swallowed up by the expense of owning her own wheels.

"Hi," a friendly voice hailed from the doorway. "You must be Autumn's mom. I'm Jeneen Andrews." Lithe in form, the dark-haired gal sent a little wave across the room to Autumn.

"It's nice to meet my daughter's roommate. Looks like you're all set," Jasmine congenially returned the greeting.

"Yes, I got here early. I wanted to do some exploring of the campus. Hate to get lost on my first day of classes and be pinned a freshman." She broke into high-pitched giggles at her own expense.

Jasmine liked the gal immediately. There were no pretentious airs masking her simplistic personality. Her laughter was contagious. Jasmine and Autumn joined in.

"I ended up at the Memorial Union where we were told everyone hangs out. Not me. I didn't see a single person I knew, so I came back here hoping you had magically arrived!" Her gesture indicated she held an imaginary wand.

"After a few days, you'll both be familiar with the layout and be able to give guided tours," Jasmine assured them.

"Well, Autumn, what can I do to be of the most help to you?" Jasmine inquired again, sizing up the pile, thumping the peach crate containing pints of her homemade salsa recipe.

"Ah, Mom, you've done enough. You have a four-hour drive home. You'd better be on your way. I'll walk you to the car."

Jasmine felt as if she was being dismissed, her UPS services no longer required. She had daydreamed about this red-letter occasion—her daughter's first day at the university. How they'd talk nonstop, squeezing in everything they wanted to say, have a parting lunch together picking at the food, dragging their last meal out as long as possible to postpone the dreaded departure, when the tears would flow down their cheeks at the thought of the intervening distance lying between Fargo and Prairie City.

Wishful thinking.

Autumn's senior year of high school had not mystically transformed into happily ever after in the wake of their January dialogue over the supper table. To her credit, Autumn checked in each evening at the conclusion of her 7:00 p.m. shift, and if she left the house again, she met her school night curfew.

Weekends were another story. From working at the truck stop, she seemed to have garnered a new set of friends who were not from Prairie City—a rougher bunch, older and more reckless. Late one night, two sets of car lights shone in the living room window. Two guys were bringing Autumn and her car home. Once they had her braced against the step railing, they took off. Opening the door, Autumn literally fell into her mother's arms stonedrunk, her speech garbled, thanking her mom for letting her spend the night at her place. Autumn woke up in a wet bed in the morning having peed all over herself. Jasmine did not volunteer to clean up the mess.

Graduation came and went, Autumn donning a gown and the mortarboard she had been gifted with. Although her accumulated English grade for the last semester shook out at a C, the rest of her classes digressed to Ds. Her Algebra 2 percentage was below the cutoff for passing, but Mr. Putman had endowed her with a D minus, which fulfilled the last required standard for graduation.

Jasmine wasn't sure whether Autumn inwardly speculated she wasn't going to make the cut. For all her bravado and diminished schoolwork preparation, she acted as if she didn't have a care in the world, but, just maybe, she was worried the administration didn't hand out diplomas like they did water bottles with the school's insignia printed on them.

A month before the graduation ceremony, Jasmine began jotting down a list of friends to invite to an open house in Autumn's honor. Last fall, Autumn had clutched an armload of outfits while headed for her sitting with an Elton photographer. The CD of photos was gorgeous, having caught Autumn with her hair of gold in an array of fall-colored country settings. Jasmine planned to have copies made to enclose with the invitations. When Autumn chanced upon her mother's handwritten slip, she went ballistic. Fuming in a full-tongued lashing, she made it clearly known there would be no graduation party. "Everybody finishes high school. Why turn it into a carnival?" she demanded.

And so they hadn't. From the first strains of "Pomp and Circumstance," Jasmine was an emotional wreck, soaking up tissues from the stockpile in her purse. Along with Jacob and Grandma Emily, she clapped until her hands stung listening to

Autumn's name being called and then witnessing her graceful promenade across the platform to receive her diploma. The distraught motherly concerns Jasmine had kept locked away in her heart to privately mull over in the deep hours of the night were being diffused like a park fountain gracefully spewing its contents for the beauty of the onlookers. Closing her eyes, she inwardly whispered to Evert. *We've made the high school milestone. It will get easier now, I'm sure. How I wish you were here to mark this moment with me.*

"Come on, Mom. You need to hit the road." Autumn attempted to hurry her mother on her way.

Jasmine resignedly lifted herself off the tote. "Nice meeting you, Jeneen. Maybe you can come to Prairie City some weekend with Autumn."

"Hey, that would be great," Jeneen readily agreed.

As a premonition of the future, Jasmine asked, "Would it be all right if I got your cell phone number?"

"Sure." Jeneen repeated the number twice while Jasmine typed the information into her phone.

"Thanks. I hope you have a tremendous year here in Fargo."

Turning her eyes on her daughter, she reminded her, "Chances are, you'll run into Maria on campus. Maybe you two could carpool home on occasion." Maria Runk had also chosen NDSU for her continuing education. Jasmine had tried to steer Autumn toward a two-year trade school, thinking something hands-on might click more for her. But as usual, she and Autumn butted heads over the issue. Secretly, Jasmine surmised her daughter had chosen NDSU in order to follow in Jacob's footsteps, plus in her limited viewfinder estimation, a four-year college graduate was more prestigious than becoming an ordinary beautician or day care attendant.

Having caught the elevator between occupancies, it was a quick ride to the ground floor. Autumn stood in the parking lot, anxious for her mom to be on her way. Her long legs, small waist, and rope of yellow hair tied up at the crown of her head, was a knockout picture. Here where Autumn's previous reputation was wiped away, Jasmine knew she would attract a lot of male attention. A glint of sunshine bounced off the opal ring on her third finger. An all new world was opening up for her daughter. One in which her parent did not make the rules nor enforce them. Autumn was on her own.

And so was Jasmine. With a quick hug, Autumn disappeared into the dorm's entrance, leaving her mom alone to maneuver out of the busy lot and back to the freeway for her trek home.

And Jasmine was alone. After graduation from NDSU, Jacob had secured a job in Minneapolis at a sister bank to the one he'd worked at during his summers in Fargo. He'd been concerned about how his mom would take the news, for had she objected, he would have applied for positions closer to home. But she had put on her big girl smile and congratulated him on the move.

Grandma Emily had moved as well. Her two daughters from Montana had spent two weeks of the summer in Prairie City downsizing her belongings with a small household auction sale and then packing up her remaining furniture in a U-Haul trailer, taking her to an apartment closer to them.

It had been a summer of good-byes. Today had been the last one. There would be no one waiting on her front step when she pulled into the driveway after dark, no lights spilling out onto the front lawn—a telltale sign of occupancy—and no sounds vibrating from its inner walls.

She would be a widow, living by herself in a secluded village in North Dakota. She had gone from a family of four to being totally alone. How had it happened?

Her thoughts were not great company as she followed the gray highways home.

Four hours later, she flipped on the hallway light, spreading illumination from the backdoor to the kitchen. Tomorrow was the first day of in-service for her twentieth year of teaching in

Elton. Although the thought did not produce any throbbing excitement within her, she hoped it would come. She would need the little people who surrounded her knees at school to give her some worth, to prompt her to get out of bed each morning at the ringing of the alarm clock.

Rrriinng, rrriinng. Jolted out of her lethargic mood, Jasmine reached for the receiver of the landline telephone fastened to the kitchen wall. "Hello."

"Hi, Mom. I wanted to make sure you made it home okay." It was Jacob's voice.

"How are you doing?" he asked.

"Fine, just fine," she replied.

And at the recognition of his voice, she was fine *now*, for she did have a family, just not in Prairie City at the moment.

Chapter 19

Autumn felt an exhilarating freedom pulsing through her veins as she spied on Jasmine from inside the dorm's main entrance, watching the Impala exit the parking lot, taking her mother away from Fargo, away from her. Yes! Emancipation at last!

Skipping a step, she headed for the stairway then noticed two guys waiting for the elevator. Changing direction, she sidled up to them. Both veiled in dark tans and shades, she initiated conversation, "Going up?"

At the sound of her voice, the taller of the duo spun on his heel, giving her a quick scan from top to bottom. His buddy whistled softly through closed teeth. "I'd say there is only one direction this elevator goes from the ground floor."

The look of admiration didn't go unnoticed by Autumn. She flipped the dangling hair from her ponytail to lay in front of her shoulder. "Care if I join you?"

The whir of the doors signaled their opening. A group of girls got off. "Be our guest." The second fellow motioned with his hand for her to go first.

Each held up an adjoining wall of the small compartment after the doors closed. "So where do you all hail from?" Autumn again was the first to speak.

"We are the best that the industrialized city of Wahpeton in southeastern North Dakota has to offer." The second guy snickered at his friend's retort. "How about you?"

"I'm from a little bitty hick town in the center of the state, Prairie City. If you haven't heard of it, you haven't missed much."

"Actually, I have heard of it. You had a dynamite basketball team a few years back."

Before Autumn could send off a quirky comeback, the door slid open at her floor. Two more gals moved into the enclosure as she got off. "See you around," she said. The guys were already ogling the new occupants, oblivious of the swaying hip performance she was wasting on them.

Two girls were parked on her mattress when she got back to her dorm room. Jeneen was sitting on her desk chair, one arm slung over the back, visiting with the fellow freshman students. "Meet our neighbors, Autumn." Pointing to the pretty girl with auburn hair as long as Autumn's, she introduced, "This is Steph Meterson and Malinda Grier." Malinda appeared to be a shorter, stockier gal. "They were high school classmates in Dickinson." Jeneen seemed delighted with this tidbit of information. For her part, Autumn felt sorry for the pair. Horror of all horrors, there was absolutely no one in her own high school class she would have wanted to share a dorm room with.

After covering the usual starting topics, Steph got down to the real reason they had stopped in. "Being we have an adjoining room, the four of us share the bathroom."

"Yeah," Malinda chimed in, "and it only has one shower." She grimaced.

"Don't mind her." Steph chuckled. "She's an only child. She needs to see how the real world lives, with multiple siblings vying for the washroom."

"I left three sisters at home," Jeneen agreed. "I can relate. Some of our biggest arguments erupted when a closed bathroom door lay between us."

"Lots of pounding and shouting. Irrational demands and threats made." Steph's eyes jigged. "You're in for an education, woman!"

Malinda groaned, yet allowed a smirk to crease her lips.

"We just need a schedule," Autumn took control. "Who prefers morning showers and who prefers nighttime?"

At the end of the discussion, Jeneen, being a pacifist, took the least wanted slot—nighttime. Steph and Malinda both had 8:00 a.m. classes, so they would work it out between themselves. Autumn could sleep in the longest, her first class starting at 9:00 a.m.

"How about all of us finding a fast-food joint for some victuals? The dining hall won't be open until breakfast tomorrow, and I'm still on summer grazing. I'm used to eating often." Malinda invited, crawling off the bed.

Autumn's gaze settled on the mountain of trunks and bags, not only monopolizing her side of the room but, in addition, trespassing into Jeneen's territory.

Following Autumn's contemplation, Steph whistled. "Ooh, gal, you have some hard labor ahead of you"

Winking at her roommate, Jeneen surmised, "Might have been a good idea to have taken your mom up on her offer to help."

"No way." Autumn straightened her shoulders. "You don't know how organized my mom can be."

"That could be a good character trait," Steph conceded, her toe tapping the bottom tote.

"She'd have my socks alphabetized by color," Autumn satirically predicted.

A wallop of hee-hawing burst from her new friends.

"Really," Autumn tried to convince them of her sincerity. "My mom's a first grade teacher. How else do you think she gets them to learn their alphabet?" Giving the pile one more glance, she grabbed her wallet. "Lead on. I have a whole year to unpack this stuff. Why waste the first night?"

Vivaciously, the four freshman girls trooped out to the hallway, swinging the door shut behind them. College life had begun.

Her high school teachers had preached endlessly on how difficult classes were at the university level. "Professors aren't going to hold your hand. You do the work or you're out. And furthermore, their requirements are going to be stiff compared to what you get in high school." In her head, Autumn could picture Ms. Herr using the podium to hold up her weight, pointing her index finger at boys in the backseats that didn't like to write.

What a bunch of garbage, Autumn thought. *Fatalistic jerks.*

If a couple of weeks of classes were sufficient evidence to consummate a judgment call, she was overwhelmingly pleased to discover the contrary. She had registered for fourteen credits this inaugural semester of her freshman year. A full-time student was encouraged to take fifteen to eighteen credit hours. At orientation, when she was stuck on thirteen credits, her adviser had advocated finding an additional two- to three-credit class to make the investment worth while. Scanning the list of offered classes, she'd come upon piano. With her background, she figured it would be a breeze. And anyhow, it brought a spark to her mom's eyes.

What her high school teachers hadn't told her about was all the free time comprising a college day. Who would have guessed one only had to sit in class three hours a week to earn three credits? In high school, she had to attend class every day and only be allotted one credit toward her graduation requirement. Monday, Wednesday, and Friday were her heaviest days, but even then, the most she spent in the classroom was four hours per day. On Tuesday and Thursday, it dwindled to two.

"So you got any ideas for your essay?" Jeneen inquired, keeping abreast with her as they left Minard Hall after their college composition class.

"It won't take much. Five hundred words is nothing." A few seconds later, she asked her own question. "Doesn't the curriculum here seem incredibly easy? It's like we're having a review of high school. My math and history classes are the same way. Biology might toughen up quickly."

Jeneen thought about the summation. "We've only had two weeks. Probably don't want to scare us out."

"In Algebra 1, I was actually bored, and let me tell you, math is not my strong point. The professor said he doesn't even grade us on our assignments, just on the Friday tests. So why even do the work, or better yet, why not only go to class on Friday?" Autumn was talking to herself more than her roommate.

"Maybe so, but I prefer it that way. I wouldn't want to be drowning this early in the semester. I'll take the credits and the review we're being given. More than likely, it will get tougher." Jeneen would travel the safe road. She wasn't one to risk her future.

Changing the subject, Autumn's disposition brightened, "Did I tell you about the hunk I met in my physical education class?" She had enrolled in bowling, another easy credit in her estimation. "Blond curly hair lightened even more so by the summer sun, broad shoulders, a real crackup."

"Would that be the same Casanova who drives a Harley motorcycle around campus?" Jeneen teased. It hadn't taken long in her roommate's presence to realize what Autumn's thoughts were fixated on most of her waking hours.

"No, that was Ivan. I don't think he's even enrolled here. This guy's name is Nick Herman. He invited me to a frat party this weekend."

"Hmmm, upperclassman?" Jeneen was wary.

"Junior. Amazing he'd have anything to do with a piddly freshman like me."

"Are you going?"

"Yeah, I think so. You want to come too? It sounds like a free-for-all type of party. No one knows for sure who is supposed to be there. I think it will be fun."

"Thanks, but I'm headed home." Jeneen's tone wasn't exactly remorseful.

"Oh, my phone's vibrating." Autumn planted her feet on the sidewalk while digging in her tight jean pocket. Reading the name of the caller across the top of the screen, she groaned. "My mother calls me every single day. What's with her?"

"Mine does too. Guess they like us." Jeneen giggled.

Autumn clicked the phone off and shoved it back in her pocket.

"Do you ever take her call?" Jeneen was curious.

"Twice. She wants a detailed report on how my classes are going, who I've met, if I found room for all my stuff." Autumn threw her head back in exasperation. "She needs another bird in her empty nest."

The girls moved on headed for the dining hall. "It must be hard to lose a life partner," Jeneen ventured.

With a huff, Autumn showed no mercy. "Let me tell you, it is a heck of a lot harder to lose a father." With that final remark, she closed the subject.

Like a badger digging a new burrow, Autumn dug through her stack of totes, trying to locate the one hiding her jewelry. Contents spilled out onto the floor; lids scattered helter-skelter. Maybe she'd packed it in the small suitcase. Having tugged it out from underneath the garbage bags filled with blankets, she zipped it open and flipped the lid back. Yes! Rummaging through the chain necklaces, she found the multiple gold strings decorated with odd flat shapes dangling from the middle. Carefully, she lowered it over her head as not to catch the curls already pinned into place at the back of her head, then gazed at herself in the full-length mirror.

A rusty-colored top shimmered back at her, the scooped neck and the short shorts appeared flirtatiously daring. Her golden hair billowed out in a wide circle as she gyrated in place. Rolling her lips into a pursed kiss, she blew her reflection a smooch. *Watch out boys, here comes Autumn Kirmis.*

She parked her Toyota a block away from the house bearing the address Nick had given her. The streets on all sides were crammed with vehicles. Squares of light and music booming a heavy bass beat poured from every window of the old two-story house, an overflow of people congregating in the skimpy yard out front. Picking her way down the broken sidewalk, Autumn realized her high-heeled sandals although trendsetters, were definitely not long-distance walking shoes.

Nick Herman was already high into the party mood. A beer in both hands, he toured the rooms, pausing to shoot the breeze with one cluster after another, appraising the women already lounging on the couches and chairs or on someone's arm, keeping an eye out for the green-eyed freshman babe still wet behind her ears, wondering if she actually had the guts to show up. If she needed an initiation into the amorous side of university society, he was only too willing to volunteer for the job. He wasn't a fourth year junior for nothing. Life was too short to get all serious about book learning.

A raucous whistle of admiration directed his sights across the crowded living room to the foyer. His view was temporarily blocked by a line of fraternity guys boisterously singing Louis Armstrong's "Hello, Dolly" to a new entree. "Well, hello, Dolly, It's so nice to have you back where you belong." Elbowing each other, they kept up the charade. "You're lookin' swell, Dolly, I can tell, Dolly," One inebriated guy leaned too far to the right in swaying to the music. He'd have fallen had the fellow next to him not grabbed his arm and pulled him back upright. "You're still glowin', you're still crowin'."

The assemblage parted enough for Nick to glimpse the blonde beauty he'd been awaiting, an uncertain expression waxing on her face. His first beer can empty. He tossed it in the general direction of a garbage can in the corner of the room. It missed. Weaving his way through the throng, he kept his eyes on the slender long-legged belle, hoping she'd catch his stare. She did, with obvious relief erasing her bewilderment at the serenaded reception.

Her perfume reached him before he could extend an arm, wrap it around her waist, and draw her to him, a fish line pulling in a mermaid. "Hey, you made it. You look amazing." He eyed her appreciatively, letting his look rest a second too long on the skin exposed by her low-necked blouse. "How about a beer? You do drink, don't you?"

"Does any high school graduate not?" She sized him up as well, liking the strong arm he kept tightly about her. There was nothing to fear in this crazy house with a man at her side to protect her.

"Hey, well-spoken. Let's get you a Hamm's." He propelled her to the dining room table where a large keg had been set up on an antique oak table stretched to hold four boards. Behind the keg, coolers of beer and hard liquor had been set out. Autumn could see where an abrasive bottom had left a new jagged scratch on the fine piece of furniture. Her mom would have been furious if it were her table.

Nick dug out a cold wet can, popped the pull tab, and handed it to her. He watched her closely to see what she'd do with it. Autumn felt his eyes upon her. Nonchalantly, she put the can to her lips, threw her head back, and took a long swig. It wasn't like she hadn't drunk before. Heck, she'd even been drunk. She didn't want him to classify her as a pansy, the silly naïve freshman from Hickville. Nick swiped two more cans from a cooler than steered her to the back porch, where the occupants were fewer. The sun had dipped below the horizon, draping the yard in a hazy gray curtain. The two chitchatted about nothing of importance or very personal. He was merely checking out the chemistry. Hoping his was working on her.

Topics tumbled over one another, spoken about briefly and then dismissed. What kind of season were the NDSU Bison predicted to have? Were they headed to the nationals in football again? What advantages did apartment life have over the dorm? How expensive were manicures and pedicures in Fargo? Had she ever been at a party raided by the police?

"Are you engaged or something?" he asked, gesturing with his beer can at the ring on her hand.

Having forgotten it was even there, Autumn brought her hand up for his examination. Like an extension of her hand, she'd worn the ring daily since her parents had given it to her three years ago, except for the night she'd met Gerald Saxton at the truck stop.

"No, of course not. It's an opal, my birthstone." Its real value, she kept concealed.

"Oh," he wrote it off as some schoolgirl nonsense.

Darkness settled in, leaving two pockets of illumination on the porch floor where the windows spilled out the indoors. "I'll get you a refill." Nick left her sitting on top of the railing, her back resting against a post. A couple in the corner chaise lounge were passionately making out. The public display made her feel uncomfortable, so she shifted her body as not to appear gawking.

Nick first sought out a bathroom. Another beer should loosen her up. She was a bird in the hand ready to perform.

Balancing two Solo cups filled to the brim with frothing beer, he sidestepped a couple dancing, barely missing being jarred by a swinging elbow. With his cups intact, he made it back to the lady of the night on the porch.

"Here. You look thirsty." His fingers grazed hers as she accepted the cup, sending a warm tingle up her spine. Having already consumed a can, she wasn't sure how much she could hold before doing something stupid. She took a few swallows to be social then set the cup beside her on the railing.

As the evening wasted, a change in the music became evident, slower, softer, more compelling.

With a tug, he pulled her shapely form off the railing and into his arms, one still holding his cup. "Let's dance," he whispered into the silkiness of her hair.

His arms about her, his breath at her temple were magical. Irresistibly, she melted into him, letting her body sway with the measured cadence of the music, his solid chest against hers. Her body shivered in anticipation, and he met it by holding her tighter. Linking her hands behind his neck, she bent her neck to the side accepted the trail of kisses starting at her ear and moving downward. His loose hand massaged her back and side. She didn't know if she was drunk on his kisses or the beer, but whatever it was, she was falling fast and hard.

For his part, Nick could feel the girl abandoning herself to his caress. He was about to do it again—lay a freshman. His fingers crept below the silky material of her blouse touching the hot skin beneath, purposefully ascending to new territory.

Autumn's head fell back, her hair billowing down her back. She locked her fingers at the base of his neck, her index finger hitting the hard opal of the ring on her right hand. The jolt of the ring was almost more piercing than the fire he was lighting within her body. Her head cleared slightly. What was he doing? What was she letting him do?

"I think I need some air," she loosened her hold on him, expecting him to do the same with her.

As if he hadn't even heard her, he continued to press his wet kisses against her throat.

"Nick, let me go." Unlocking her fingers and then bringing them down to push against his chest, she realized the strength he had in his iron hold.

When he didn't release her, a panic welled up inside of her bringing out a primitive survival instinct. She struggled against him, stomping on his toes with her high heeled sandals.

Walking a thin line between sobriety and drunkenness, Nick didn't take lightly his prize virgin vixen turning on him. Using both arms to overpower her, he momentarily forgot about the Solo cup of beer he still held in his left hand. Accidentally spilling the tepid liquid, it poured down the back of her neck like warm pee. A high-pitched shriek escaped from her lips, along with renewed efforts to free herself from Nick's clutches, alerting the coeds sharing the porch.

First, laughter from the onlookers met her screams, until the intensity of her struggles alerted them to intervene. Two guys dragged Nick away from her. Completely embarrassed by the scene they'd created, Autumn stumbled down the porch steps, wanting to lose herself in the black of the night. Her high heel caught on the bottom step, sending her sprawling into the dewy grass, bringing a chorus snorting from the porch. Fighting back the tears threatening to blind her, she tugged off both sandals and rolled to her feet.

"Run back to your mama, you little flirt." It was Nick's voice, laden with taunting contempt, a cover-up for his own bruised masculine pride.

With a bird-like flight pattern, Autumn rounded the house, concealed by the dark shadows of the midnight hour. Her bare feet, sore from the pebbles and dried thorny weeds laying a prickly escape path, were ignored as she fled the long block to her car. Shakily, she slid the key into the ignition, cranked it and the steering wheel in one fluid motion, to flee from Nick Herman's pawning attack.

Not until she was in the confines of the locked doors of the dormitory did she attempt to slow her pounding heart. *How could I have been so stupid?* she chided herself, washed in humiliation. How would she ever meet the eyes of the college students in attendance at the party crisscrossing the campus? Maybe they were all too drunk to even recollect the image of her wrestling with the overly aggressive jerk and then falling flat on her face in her rush to rid herself of his clutches.

Toppling into bed, she didn't even bother to undress. The alcohol had numbed her senses, allowing her to slide effortlessly into a deep slumber. Her last waking thought was being keenly thankful that Jeneen wasn't here to witness her blundering induction into the university's social network.

And that her mother was not here waiting up for her.

Edges of sunshine slipped unnoticed onto her dorm room walls from behind the closed blinds, frames of gold blissfully broadcasting to the lethargic tenant that nature had outdone itself in creating a lovely Sunday morning there for the taking.

A headache was pounding behind her eyelids, only compounded by the cheery sun rays penetrating uninvited. Groaning, she tugged a blanket over her head, like a turtle pulling inside of its shell.

Stuffiness soon overtook her, sweat smoothing a sheen over her skin. She kicked the blanket clear, dropping an arm over her eyes. Her other arm groped for the digital clock propped on the bolster of the bed, bringing the ticking timepiece to her line of vision—11:23 a.m.

Church time.

Not that it meant anything to her, but she knew her mom would be sitting in the worship service in Prairie City. Growing up, there had never been any discussion about where the family would be on Sunday morning. Jacob and she were both impeccably aware there was no argument on whether to attend church or not. The Kirmis family would be there.

That is, until her dad died. Now she didn't even need one hand to count the number of services she'd been in attendance. She no longer trusted a loving God sitting up in the clouds somewhere, treating her like a pawn instead of a cherished child. He had taken too much from her. It was bad enough not having her birth parents to raise her, to know she had been loved from conception. But they had dumped her into a new family, a couple wishing for a baby, taking whatever came their way. She just got lucky and beat the next orphan in the lineup.

And now her adoptive dad was snuffed out too.

One well-meaning sympathizer had fabricated the idea God was short of carpenters in heaven to construct the many rooms in his mansion for the rest of his children coming soon.

Hogwash! If He was such a mighty God, He didn't need mortal man to build the heavenly apartment building; one celestial command, one *whoosh*, and it would have been done.

It was she, Autumn Joy Kirmis, who needed her father, and he was gone.

In primary Sunday school classes, her gray-haired teacher had told fantastic stories of guardian angels watching over each child on earth. If that was so, then where had her dad's angel been the day he fell off the roof? Taking a lunch break in paradise?

Autumn wanted to bury her head under her pillow for the rest of the day; however her bladder protested. While stumbling to the bathroom, she felt her stomach lurch. In a rush, she vaulted for the toilet seat, but her guts retched before she could cover the short distance, drenching her wrinkled clothes and stringy hair in vomit. Standing in the filth of her own making, her head fell forward, wet tears spewed forth as she bawled like a baby, not understanding why the world had to be so incredibly harsh.

After her initiation into the campus nightlife, Autumn decided she could handle a few hours of boredom. The following Monday, she dutifully headed off for her morning classes, having skipped more than attended. Today held a blank script. Might as well fill it with a dull teacher.

After being caught masquerading in a role beyond her comfort zone and experience, she now shrunk from the appreciative glances guys bestowed on her. She wondered if they knew. Did they whisper when she passed? Was everyone sneering at the show she had put on? She didn't have long to find out.

Steph and Malinda waved her over to their knot of girls in the dining center, their fingers greasy from the french fries they were inhaling. Each slid over a fraction to make room for another chair in the circle. After cutting her burger into halves, Autumn picked up one half and bit into it.

"Hey, Autumn, see you made Facebook." Steph snickered. "Gotta hand it to you. You are one brave chick."

Autumn's jaws froze. She hadn't breathed a word of her weekend escapade to anyone. Her peers found her stunned expression comical.

"Thought you could keep a secret, huh?" Malinda goaded. "You should know by now that doesn't work in this modern age." A round of laughter followed.

"I liked the photo of you shaking some sense into that blond gorilla. His eyes are rolled back as if you were a sumo wrestler about to throw him over the ropes." Guffaws followed.

"Yeah, your tiny muscles bulging like Popeye," put in Jill, another gal from the dorm, showing off a bicep.

"Stop, stop," Jeneen wailed, having quickly swallowed her juice before it sprayed from her mouth. She hiccuped in merriment.

"The one of your heel grinding into his sandal is even better," Steph ribbed. "We'd better hang with you if we want a bodyguard."

Autumn couldn't believe what she was hearing. It was obvious that whoever took the pictures that night had probably been snockered as well. The photos didn't reveal the true story.

The shell she had erected the past two days as a shield to ricochet off the snide remarks and demeaning stares had a pip hole. The higher the girls' hilarity escalated, the more chunks of the cracked casing began to shake loose; her self-esteem molded itself back together. By the end of the lunch hour, Autumn had stretched back to her normal height of five foot seven. She even started believing some of the bigger than life stories they fabricated.

The gospel according to Facebook. Who was she to refute it?

Chapter 20

Trying to assure herself she was not alone was a whole lot different than believing it. There were nights when the walls literally shouted their silence at her, their bewitching eyeballs pursuing her from room to room, floor to floor. Call it nonsense, but Jasmine took to wearing hard sole shoes in the house, just to hear the echo of her own footsteps.

Although Evert had died a year and a half ago, Jasmine felt as if the grieving process had been rewound, forcing her to embark from the beginning. She grieved for Grandmother Emily living in an apartment in Montana. No longer could she run across town and drop in for a fresh cinnamon roll and a piece of advice from her kindhearted mother-in-law. She grieved for her son, Jacob, who had grown to be a man taking care of himself. He'd watch over her and lend a hand if needed, but from afar. She grieved the loss of Autumn, who had left her mom far before her move to the university in Fargo. At least when Autumn had sealed herself behind the door of her childhood bedroom, there had still been life in the family dwelling. Now, it was only Jasmine's own heart pulsating in the premises.

And most of all, she grieved for the loss of her best friend, her lover, her helpmate. Everything she and Evert had ever done was now left only for her. One cup of coffee percolated each morning. The end-of-day walk was a jaunt by herself with no one to share the day's events. There was no arm flung over her while she slumbered in the bed wide enough for two, no hand to grasp while the table grace was recited, and no one to kiss welcome home. Sunday mornings, she sat unescorted in the church pew, unwilling to join the bench of widows far older than herself. The name on her mail no longer read Mr. and Mrs. Kirmis, on legal forms, she checked "Widowed." Even her medical insurance changed from "Family" to "Single, plus dependent."

And she grieved for the choice she had made the day of the accident. Why hadn't she said yes to Evert's suggestion to attend the construction show in Fargo? So what if it had been scheduled close to the end of the school year? She could have accompanied him and still completed her school reports if done by burning the lightbulb late into the night. Had she been selfish? If so, she was paying high stakes for it now.

Closing her eyes, she let her head fall back onto her pillow. An inner ache reminded her she wasn't being fair as she wallowed in self-pity. It was easy to embrace the bleak, the cold, the despondent, the mournful cry of her soul. However, God's word promised something entirely different.

> Be strong and courageous. Do not be afraid or terrified because of them, for the Lord your God goes with you; he will never leave you nor forsake you.
>
> Deuteronomy 31:6 (NIV)

Shifting her train of thought, she let the Lord remind her of the numerous ways He was going with her by strategically placing people in her path to uphold her. Never had she been left without His hand of guidance forging arrangements behind the scenes. What about the stranger who had pulled her car out of the ditch or her CPA working extra hours assisting her to attain the necessary numbers to complete the year's income tax filing? How about the school's janitor who changed her flat tire without even being asked? Or the neighbor who got her snowblower running the second winter after the gas had settled over the summer? Or the presence of Jacob those first critical months when they were all adjusting to life without Evert? Or Cynthia being her daily sounding board in school? Or the high school teachers' informative concern for Autumn? Or the grief support group? Or ? Or?

Forgive me, Lord, for always letting myself slide backward, instead of hanging onto you for strength. And take care of Autumn too. Discreetly bring godly people into her future, pointing her back to you.

Like old masking tape slowly losing its adhesive bond, Jasmine could feel herself pulling away from her two best friends in Prairie City, Sheila Philips and Jane Runk. Partially, it was her own unsubstantiated conjecture, feeling she no longer fit in with even-numbered married couples, her being the lame odd duck without a drake. Although they continued to invite her to neighborhood gatherings or an occasional dinner or theater out-of-town, she found herself inventing excuses, as if her calendar as a widow was exhaustively jammed. Instead, she sat home in her empty rooms, counting the ceiling tiles overhead.

No, it was more than the forced change in marital status that bothered her. Their daughters, Emma and Maria, had excelled in high school, while Autumn created havoc. The Three Musketeer trio formed during their childhood years had disintegrated into dust, swept away by the winds of adolescence and the forks in the road during the changeable teenage years.

When having lunch with Sheila and Jane, the conversation invariably veered to their daughters. Maria was taking up physical therapy while Emma had her mind set on counseling. Emma was doing volunteer work at the children's hospital in her off hours at an out-of-state university. Maria was overloading class hours her very first semester, endeavoring to get through her basics as quickly as she could. Jasmine was purposely vague about Autumn's intentions, for truthfully, she didn't even know what they were. Possibly, Autumn didn't either.

With trepidation, Jasmine listened to Sheila's cordial voice on the phone. "I'm taking off for Fargo on Friday to spend the weekend with Maria. She thinks she needs to do some clothes shopping for the colder weather." Sheila's voice lilted pleasantly. "I thought it would be fun if you would join me for a mothers and daughters' weekend."

It did sound like fun. How Jasmine wished she could give a ready reply of acceptance, and have an outing with her daughter; however, Autumn held the deciding vote. After promising to get back to Sheila, Jasmine tried Autumn's cell phone number. Not surprisingly, a voice came online, telling her to enjoy the music while her party was being reached. Subsequently, Autumn's cheery recorded voice sounded in her ear, "I'm sorry, but I'm not available to take your call. More than likely, I'm in class or studying. If you leave your name and number, I will be sure to get back to you at my earliest convenience. Have a smashing good day."

Why should today's attempt at contacting Autumn be any different from the dozens of times she had tried in the last month? Whether she called or sent a text message or an e-mail, there was no response. Autumn's phone was irreversibly glued to her; therefore, wherever she happened to be on or off campus, she got the message. And with caller ID, she knew exactly who was calling. Her mother wasn't on her list of callbacks, unless her daughter had overspent. Then Jasmine would get a text message. "Running low. Please drop some money in my account." There was never a thank-you.

Sighing, Jasmine typed out a text message. "Sheila & I are coming to Fargo to visit you girls this Friday. Hope your weekend is open. Love U, Mom."

In less than a minute, she had a response. "Don't come. I'm going home with a friend."

During one of her daily chats with Cynthia, Jasmine had bared her soul, confiding in her friend.

"Jasmine, leave her be. She didn't have the best communication skills when she lived at home, so this really isn't anything new. You can bug her every single day, but she can delete you with a touch of her finger. Like a bird, she wants to fly. You can't hold onto her. You've taught her your values, now you have to let her go. How she uses that knowledge is up to her. She knows where you are, and when she is ready, I reckon she will fly back to the nest and her mama."

Whether Cynthia's advice was right or not, she honored it.

Because there was absolutely nothing else she could do.

If anything fulfilling was budding in Jasmine's current season in life, it was the gift of time. For years, a deep-rooted yearning had stirred within her to pick up a pen and write. She had always written down her thoughts in a journal, starting way back when she was still a young girl. The habit had carried into her marriage, notating on paper all the moments of a day that made life worth living. Her memoirs were a family history.

And after the fateful day Evert had died, her diary had almost become a substitution for the close relationship they had shared. What she had once poured into his ear, she now poured into her documented notes. Her thoughts and dreams, once bounced off of Evert, were now scribed onto pages in a neat cursive penmanship befitting a teacher, for her to reread when she sought to be reminded of the inspirations she'd once had for life.

Yet her yearnings had been profoundly more entrenched than keeping a log of daily events. She wanted to write a novel, not simply a sentimental story to entertain a reader, but a novel with a message that would make a difference in people's lives.

The character formulating in her mind was coming together piece by piece. He was a lonely little boy with no place he could definitely pinpoint as his home. Even though he lived with caretakers, attended school, played with peers on the playground, he led a solitary existence inside of a shell of his own manufacture. Some days, Jasmine pictured her imaginary imp as a brunette. Other days, he was a redhead. Every so often, he had hair of gold, like Autumn.

Although she had the same number of evening hours at the end of the school day as she had had before, she no longer had school activities for Autumn or Jacob to attend, nor carpentry jobs to estimate with Evert. The laundry and cooking had decreased to a pittance. Her social obligations were shrunken like a prune, and her clean house stayed clean. That is, after she systematically purged Autumn's bedroom and painted the ceiling a solid white to cover the storm clouds smeared over the starry heavens.

With subdued anticipation, she dedicated the evening hours to making her fictional character come to life one page after another.

In Ecclesiastes, she read, "There is a time for everything, and a season for every activity under heaven" (Ecclesiates 3:1, NIV). Maybe this was the season that God ordained for her to write. For had she not experienced the desolation of loneliness herself, how could she ever have captured for the reader the frailty of the forlorn scruffy youngster beginning to take up residence in her empty house?

Chapter 21

Autumn was shocked by the score the professor had given her on her latest Friday quiz. She'd been absolutely sure she had solved the quadratic equations correctly, or was she getting mixed up in the terminology? Coefficients, formulas, functions—who gave a rip? What did algebra have to do with real life anyway? Disgusted, she wadded the test paper into a ball, tossing it into the wastebasket as she filed out of the classroom.

"Miss Kirmis."

At the sound of her name, she turned back to see who was addressing her. Professor Carry stood at his desk, peering solemnly at her.

"One's performance on tests is directly related to one's attendance in class, coupled with the completion of daily work." Having delivered the message in a deadpan tone, he dismissed her by looking down again at the papers in front of him.

Burning a bright red, Autumn lowered her head, moving at a fast clip through the hallway.

Unbelievable, he even knew her name! He never bothered to take roll, how in the heck did he discern who was there and who wasn't? And then yet connect a name with each person? Maybe he was more with it than she had given him credit.

From high school, Autumn knew it was almost impossible to catch up in math if one missed out on fundamental knowledge. Everything built on top of previous lessons. She could seek help from a tutor, or even Jeneen. Even dropping the class was no longer a prerogative, the deadline had passed. But in reality, she really didn't care.

Then why was she fuming inside? The man made her look small, stupid, as if she couldn't connect the dots on how to be successful in school. Imitating his austere expression, she pinched her lips and repeated his words in a low voice, "One's performance on tests is directly related to one's attendance in class, coupled with the completion of daily work."

Anger seethed dangerously close to the surface. Her jaw set in a straight line, she rounded the corner, blindly running smack into Trent Warson, Steph Meterson's boyfriend.

"Whoa, little lady." He took her arm, letting the impact of her startling collision bounce off his chest. "You okay?"

Catching her breath, she smiled crookedly up at him. "Sorry, Trent. I blanked you out."

"No harm done. It's not every day I get smashed into by a pretty girl. I won't even file charges." His easygoing nature made it easy to see why Steph was smitten by him.

The balloon of anger had fizzled with the jolt.

A second guy clearing his throat, transferred her attention to him. He was about six feet tall, lanky, dark eyes. She liked what she saw.

Taking the hint, Trent apologized a second time. "Pardon me, Autumn. This is my buddy, Luke Boyle, from Minnesota. He just drove up today to spend the weekend with me, staying at my apartment." Tossing a side comment to Luke, he added, "Autumn lives next door to Steph in the dorm."

"Hi." Autumn shifted into flirtation mode. "So how does Trent entertain a guest?" A teasing grin was attached to the question.

"Ah, we're going to the Bison football game tonight, and tomorrow, we're going to kick a few tires." There was a slow laziness about his voice, in the way he dragged out the words.

Her eyebrows hiked up. "Do you kick tires for kicks?"

Both guys caught her pun. "Back where I come from," Trent admitted, "we'd do most anything for entertainment."

Sticking his fingers in the side pockets of his jeans, Luke clarified, "I'm hunting for a different pickup truck. I'm going to search out a few dealers down here and see how they compare with trucks back home."

"Where do you hang your hat in Minnesota?" She purposely coiled a strand of her golden hair around a finger.

Shifting his feet, Luke replied, "Oh, about a stone's throw from Minneapolis."

"Hmmm, a city man."

"Yeah, I grew up playing video games at the arcade and going to the park to throw a baseball. That's why I have Trent to teach me about rural life."

"Gotcha." Autumn couldn't think of anything to say to prolong the conversation. He probably already thought she was playing Twenty Questions.

"We'll catch ya later, Autumn. We're meeting Steph at the student union." Trent started moving off. "Hope I don't ram into you for a second hit." A lopsided grin followed his banter.

Allowing his eyes to linger for a second longer, Luke put a finger to the brim of his baseball cap. "I wouldn't mind running into you again at all."

Autumn admired his backside until the duo was lost in the mass of students moving through the crosswalks.

The rage she had nursed minutes earlier against Professor Carry had vanished. Nick Herman had taught her far more in one night than what any professor could instill in her in a whole semester. Mercy, she wouldn't let a negative experience with

Nick swear her off all men. She'd be more careful and learn from her mistake.

The weekend was here, and there was new blood in town. Bison football hadn't been on her agenda, but it was now.

With a bottle of Coke, a bag of sunflower seeds, and a game program clutched to her side, Autumn, closely followed by Jeneen, patrolled the walkway dividing the upper tiered seating from those below, who were situated closer to the sidelines. Purposely, Autumn had putzed with her hair and makeup, delaying their arrival at the Fargo Dome to coincide with the end of the first quarter. Presumably, Steph and Trent would be parked in their seats by then, and she could *happen* to sit in the same section. Jeneen would have preferred to run out to the West Acres Mall to do some shopping, but she readily complied when her roommate suggested the game. Miss Congeniality didn't suspect she was an accomplice in a greater game.

Autumn's green eyes scanned the crowd, moving from one section to another. Almost ready to admit defeat, her sight clapped onto Steph's pink sweatshirt amid the yellow and green sea of school colors. Only Steph would be brave enough to invade Bison territory dressed in pink.

Keeping her attention on her feet, Autumn climbed the steps until she and Jeneen were a handful of rows below the one occupied by their friends. "Could we slide in please?" she asked the balding man in the aisle seat who was intent on the action below on the field.

Not taking his eyes off the action, he stood to let them pass. A shrill whistle from above caught Jeneen's attention. "Hey, Autumn, there's Steph and Trent."

Feigning surprise, Autumn raised her head. Steph was pointing to two empty seats positioned in front of them. After thanking the man, the girls proceeded upward.

"What luck finding you in this mob," Jeneen squealed, obligingly sinking into a seat.

Autumn too smiled her appreciation, her gaze skipping down the row past Trent to land on Luke, his elbows propped on his knees. "We meet again, Miss Autumn." His paced speech seemed to caress her name.

"Must be fate," she said lightly then turned her attention to the football game. Even with a team as notorious as the NDSU Bison, Autumn could not focus on the tarmac. Was Luke intent on the game watching every play, or was he intent on her? She dared not twist her head about in hopes of sneaking a peek. Mechanically, she applauded and cheered when the fans on all sides of her did. When the Bison scored a touchdown, she was on her feet, her fist beating the air.

At the sound of the final horn signaling the end of the game, a roar escalated from the Bison fans. Their team was one game closer to the playoffs. Naturally, Autumn was excited, the game had finally drawn to a close.

Sweeping her hair up to draw her jacket under its cape, she felt her jacket being lifted. Her chin turned. In gentlemanly fashion, Luke was holding open her trendy waist-length leather jacket for her to slip into. Her heart knocked against her rib cage.

"Thanks," she murmured.

"Why don't you girls hang out with us?" Steph offered. "I'm outnumbered. We're going to give Luke a tour of Fargo and point out the best car dealers for him to check out tomorrow."

"Yeah," Trent seconded the proposal. "I work at the stables for a while on Saturday, so it's best if I give Luke the layout tonight."

"Thanks, but no thanks," Jeneen replied. "No offense, but I think I'll get started on some of my assigned reading for next week."

"You in?" Luke peered at Autumn.

"Why not? It will give me a chance to get better acquainted with this city as well. I've been kind of a timid driver."

After dropping Jeneen off at the dorm, Autumn climbed into the backseat of Trent's sports car opposite Luke. Trent peeled out of the driveway, heading for a canvas of the city. He explained the layout of streets and avenues, the one-way headed south, another taking the traffic back north. They cruised the two interstate highways intersecting at Fargo and took the bridge across the Red River that separated Fargo from Moorhead. He sped through the parking lot of the West Acres Mall and navigated the narrow streets of Old Broadway hosting quaint specialty shops.

"Now, let's get down to the important joints—car dealers!" Trent narrated a running log as he tore up and down the streets from one dealership to another, Luke jotting the business names and addresses on the back of the Bison football program. Autumn was having the ride of her life, reveling in the independence she now had as a university student.

When a noisy yawn escaped from Trent, he announced, "It is now the hour when the only working employee of this foursome needs to turn in and get some rest before slopping out horse stables in the morning. I am therefore kicking two female passengers out of this limousine." His car had come to a stop in front of Seim Hall. Playfully, Steph hit him on his arm.

"Hey, Trent, I enjoyed the tour immensely. Thanks for the invite." Autumn pushed open her door and stepped out onto the sidewalk. Luke did the same, giving Trent and Steph a minute alone to say their good nights. Luke walked Autumn up to the entrance.

"Any chance you'd like to kick a few tires with me in the morning?" He seemed a bit shy about asking her.

Autumn liked that; he wasn't a womanizer. "Providing you don't start kicking when the sun comes up."

"Would eleven be long enough for you to get your beauty rest? Although I don't think sleep could make you any prettier." Their eyes held for a brief instant.

"I think that would be sufficient." Her saucy grin made him smile too.

⤜⤛

Although the November breeze held a brisk nip, the sky was lathered in sunshine, an omen for a pleasant outing.

The coughing muffler on Luke's beat-up truck heralded his coming a block before he pulled up. "See why I'm in the mood for trading?" he bemoaned his own noisy entrance. "Even hard-of-hearing old grandmas stick their heads out from their porches when I drive by."

"If the racket is your truck's only hang-up, why don't you just replace the muffler?" Her eyes playfully questioned.

"Point taken. Did I mention the high mileage on the odometer or the leaky radiator? How about the clunk in the rear end, the squeaky brakes, the rip in the upholstered seat, or the crack in the windshield? Try your electric window. It doesn't work."

Laughing at his continuous ramble, Autumn held up a hand like a highway patrolman stopping traffic. "I get it, I get it." Then she impishly added a defection of her own, "Don't forget the peeling paint job."

Luke was not to be outdone. "Fortunately, it's not August 'cause the air-conditioning gave out two summers ago."

By then, Autumn was doubled up, holding her stomach and waving an imaginary flag of surrender. Yup, the pickup was a pile of junk.

When Autumn later recounted the day's adventures to Jeneen, she summed up their first date concisely, "It was a total blast!" She'd sat behind the wheel of nearly every make and model of pickup trucks on the lots, from the newest editions of the year to the older trade-ins Luke said were in his price range.

Sitting in a booth with a taco pizza smothered in extra mushrooms and olives between them, they'd talked for hours. Autumn gleaned from Luke's intermittent remarks that he was employed in a gas station changing oils, replacing brake pads, and rotating tires. On an exciting day, he might replace a fan belt. "Nothing too glamorous about my job," he admitted.

"Ever consider going on to school?" Autumn questioned.

"Some. But my old man doesn't have any extra cash. I could have gotten a loan, but I was afraid if I didn't stick it out, the money would be wasted, and I'd still have to make good on what I borrowed."

Autumn decided not to share the fact her mom was financing her first year. "Do you live with your folks?"

"My parents are divorced. Dad was pretty hard on my mom. She left when I was in elementary school."

"That's a bummer," Autumn sympathized. "It could be worse though. I don't even remember my parents. They dumped me when I was a baby, ended up getting thrown into an adoptive home."

"That might be a better deal. Adoptive parents choose their kids. They'd hardly do that if they didn't want you," Luke reasoned.

Abstractly, Autumn rotated the oval ring on her finger, her thoughts discomforting.

"Nice ring. Any special significance?" he noted her preoccupation with the piece of jewelry.

Realizing what she had been unconsciously manipulating, she nodded her head. "It's from my dad."

"Must have a definite bond with him."

"Except when I was a junior in high school, he died in an accident."

He stared at her. "I'm sorry. Just you and your mom now?"

"And an older brother. He's adopted too." Autumn toyed with the napkin stained with tomato sauce from the pizza. "Mom and I have a rather estranged relationship. The accident was her fault."

"If it was an accident, she must not have meant to do it intentionally."

"Ya well, let's not go there. Let's just say, I am very happy to be on my own, sharing a taco pizza with a guy who drives a four-wheel-drive truck." Her attempt at changing the mood worked, redirecting the conversation into lighter avenues.

Before parting ways, he promised to come by on Sunday before leaving town. He and Trent had some catching up to do first.

Autumn literally floated on clouds taking the stairs up to her floor, already replaying the hours she'd shared with Luke.

Quietly opening the door to her darkened room, she could hear Jeneen's soft nasalized breathing. Feeling about on her cluttered bed to find her nighty, she was eventually triumphant. She groped for the bathroom door, nearly losing her balance stumbling over her makeup case and mirror left on the floor earlier. With a toe, she moved the offending objects under her bed.

With a snap, the bathroom light flooded the small enclosure, forcing her to squint until her pupils adjusted. Lying on the sink counter was a note written in Jeneen's penmanship. "How about joining me for the ten-thirty church service in the morning?" A pen lay beside the paper waiting for a response. Autumn picked it up and scratched an answer back. "Thanks. How about another time?"

Yup, no doubt about it; her mom would love Jeneen. It was even possible Jeneen was an answer to one of her mother's prayers.

Luke's text message didn't come until early evening, asking her to meet him outside the dorm. His beat-up truck was already idling at the curb. She jumped in and immediately slid across the bench seat to his side. All afternoon, she had hoped he'd cut a generous portion of the day out for her. Then she'd chided herself, knowing he had come to hang out with Trent.

"I gotta be on my way. I have four hours of blacktop to eat up before I'm home." Gazing into her green eyes, he could hardly believe his good fortune. "Couldn't leave without saying good-bye though."

She pouted prettily. "Barely got to see you today."

"Yah. What about next Friday? You gonna be here?" The lilac smell of her shampoo filled the cab.

"Certainly could rework my schedule if you're thinking of making a return trip," she sweetly said, picking at the pocket seam of his jacket.

"Then I'll be back." Tapping the steering wheel, he was torn between getting on the road or being with her. He yanked his door open. "Come on, I'll walk you back to the door."

Their elbows brushed during the short jaunt. Facing her, he said his farewell, "Then I'll see you Friday. It will be late as I work until six."

She nodded, inwardly wishing he'd do more. When he awkwardly turned to leave, she put a restraining hand on his arm and impulsively stood on tiptoe to press a kiss into his bristled cheek.

"What was that for?" he asked.

"Just thanking you for the weekend," Autumn replied coyly.

"Trent said I'd better not try any moves on you or you'd bust me." An uncertain smile played on his lips.

"I only do that to womanizers, not to a gentleman like you." Her wrists hooked behind her back.

"In that case…" Luke gently put a hand to her back, pulling her to him. Ever so tenderly, he lowered his mouth to hers. "Good night," he whispered as he disengaged himself and beat a path to his truck.

Watching him, Autumn wondered if it was possible to fall in love in the short span of a weekend.

On Wednesday, a single red rose was delivered to the dormitory for her. The miniature card stuck in the folds of tissue paper read, "Missing you." She was totally smitten. No man had ever sent her fresh flowers before. *Luke Boyle, I am going to marry you someday.*

True to his word, Luke traveled the miles between Minneapolis and Fargo the remaining two weekends prior to Thanksgiving. If the days were cold and blustery, he and Autumn hung out with Steph and Trent at the apartment, playing games and watching movies. Luke supplied the cases of beer while the girls used their domestic skills to layer meats and cheeses in submarine sandwiches.

Nestled in the circle of his arms the final Saturday afternoon, Autumn could feel herself sinking into despondency. Rubbing his chin against the side of her face, Luke prodded, "What's the matter with my little wolverine? You're not the quiet type."

"Just thinking. I'm not sure if I can survive two long weeks without seeing you." Neither she nor Jacob had been back to Prairie City since August. Her brother was swinging through from Minneapolis on Wednesday to pick her up, and together, they'd make the Thanksgiving journey home.

"Hey, you said you're close to your brother. Your mom is missing you too. It will be good for you to reconnect with family." Luke's fingers locked with hers.

His words bounced off of her. "Maybe you and I could have our own Thanksgiving holiday." She looked in his eyes, wanting to see a glitter of possibility.

"I have to work the following Friday," he reminded her. "There's always another vehicle wanting an oil change."

Autumn repositioned her body to sit up taller. "Why couldn't I go home with you for the four-day break?"

Luke hedged, choosing a point past her head to set his focus on. "There won't be any turkey eaten at my house. It's just another day for my dad. You go home. With texting and calling, it will almost be like the real deal."

Autumn's face sunk in rejection.

"How about if you and I spend tonight alone? We'll go to a fancy restaurant, just the two of us, maybe take in a movie, and count the reasons we're so crazy about each other." His arms enveloped her in a tight bear hug.

His silly comment brought a lift to her disposition. "I'd like that."

Autumn had plaited her horse's mane into a french braid starting at the crown of her head. A feathering of bangs and free hairs by her ears softened the effect. She changed out of her jeans and sweatshirt, choosing an outfit more feminine and worthy of an evening alone with Luke.

"Rapunzel, Rapunzel, let down thy golden hair," Luke greeted her as she hopped into his old pickup. He still hadn't made a decision on upgrading. His road trips to Fargo were slicing a chunk out of his paychecks.

"That's exactly what my dad called me when I was a kid," she informed him, cuddling up to his side for warmth.

"Nothing against your dad, but somehow, I don't want my pet name for you to bring up images of him. Rapunzel is out."

"What's wrong with Autumn?"

"I'm selfish. I want my own endearment. What's your middle name?"

"Joy, Autumn Joy. Guess my arrival brought joy to my parents," she supplied.

"Then it shall be AJ."

"You're changing my name for me huh? AJ." She liked the sound of it. "Okay, I'm cool with AJ."

He kissed her on the forehead. "It's just you and me tonight."

Sitting thigh to thigh in the Chinese dining room, the two reveled in the physical effect each had on the other. Though the room was crowded with other people eating out, they were lost in a world of their own. A variety of Chinese foods from the buffet line was heaped on their plates. "Here," Autumn instructed, "try my wonton." Gingerly, she held it between two fingers as Luke bit into the end of it.

"Not bad, but I think you'll like the egg rolls even better." He held his up for her to taste. There was something sensual about feeding each other.

When their stomachs were pleasantly full, they cracked open the fortune cookies the waiter had brought with the bill. "Listen to this," Autumn read. "Move forward before the opportunity is gone." Her eyes lit up. "Do you think it is referring to our relationship?"

"Nahh." Luke shook his head. "More aptly, it refers to one of those trucks we test drove a few weeks ago." Two fingers pinched his side. "Ouch! Give me some room, woman," he joshed.

"What does your cookie say?" Curiosity plagued her.

"Here it is." He cleared his throat. "Stay away from women with yellow manes."

"It doesn't say that!" She grabbed it out of his hand; however, he snatched it back, but in the fray, the tiny slip of paper ripped in half. Holding it away from him, Autumn read, "Poverty is…"

"…no disgrace," he finished the quote from his half,

"Whew!" He wiped his forehead with a napkin. "This girlfriend I have is going to send me straight to the poorhouse. At least I'll be able to rest in peace, knowing there is no disgrace in being busted!"

"You poor dear." She gave him no sympathy.

"So what do you say we head out to the cinema at the mall and see if we can hit a late show?"

"Are you sure we should? Movies are kind of spendy," she asked with an innocent expression on her face.

"As long as we don't eat any popcorn and soda, A.J., I should be able to swing it."

Twenty minutes later, they were hunkered down in a back row of the movie theater, acting like two grade school kids naughtily harassing and tickling each other. When the title of the movie splashed across the screen, they settled down, content to be sharing adjacent seats.

Partway through the flick, Autumn's head dropped to his shoulder, her braid falling into his lap. Luke draped an arm about her shoulders and brushed her arm and cheeks with the frayed end of her braid, creating havoc within her chest. The stars on the screen were forgotten as they became hypnotized by the stars in each others eyes. Sharing kisses, they sank deeper in their seats.

Once more, Luke picked up her braid, which was like the one Rapunzel had worn. After tentatively unwrapping the tie holding the hair in place at the end, he began to lazily but deliberately unravel the three strands forming the thick braid. As he moved up the braid, his legs became covered with the loose flaxen waves of hair shimmering in the glow emitted from the picture screen. A sea of gold. She felt his fingertips reaching the top of her head, massaging her skull and loosening the last of the braid. She closed her eyes, enjoying the sensation of being touched with such tenderness.

Putting his lips to her ear, he whispered, "A.J., let's get out of here."

She nodded in assent. He took her hand. Blindly, she let him guide her out of the dark theater. Once outside, their arms laced through each others, and they trotted with quick steps across the cold parking lot to his truck, whose sanctuary was beginning to seem like home sweet home.

Without a word, he drove the roaring rickety old truck out of town, leaving the lights of the city behind them, seeking a deserted gravel road where the only illumination was from the natural lanterns shining out of the firmament. Leaving the heater on high, he parked on an approach into a farmer's field. Then turning to the golden girl of his dreams, he took her shapely form into his arms with such intensity it took her breath away. His kisses left wet trails down her cheeks and neck, her heart pounding till she thought it would burst. Never had she felt like this before. His thumb and index finger found the zipper on her jacket and then the buttons on her blouse underneath.

Unbeknownst to Luke, she resolutely twisted the opal ring over her knuckle, let it drop with a faint thud onto the floor mat, and willingly let him have his way with her.

And in that moment of lust-filled passion, she gave away the treasure her dad and mom had begged her to save for her prince in shining armor on her wedding day—the gift of her purity.

She lost it on the ripped seat of a rusty old pickup truck, a vehicle its owner found blatantly inferior. He willingly stole what she freely gave.

Hours later, when the fuel gauge indicated empty, the two teenagers awoke to the piercing coldness of the cab, the windows frosted over, and scrambled to cover their naked bodies with the clothes they had earlier discarded.

Realizing then the exorbitant price she had paid to make this night into a memory, some of the ecstasy lost its shine; the treasure became used and tarnished.

Mentally, she grasped for an excuse. *But daddy, he is the one.*

Chapter 22

"You are a living saint, Jeneen," declared Malinda, being careful to hold her head in a statue-like pose as Jeneen painstakingly trimmed her bangs with a hair scissors. Strains of a Christmas melody played softly from a CD player on the desk.

Sprawled on Jeneen's quilt top, Steph seconded the declaration, disgustedly surveying the massive clutter obliterating the floor, desk, and bed on Autumn's side of the dorm room. "Jeneen, how do *you* stomach looking at such a mess?"

"Oh, it's not so bad. Autumn just has a little trouble with organization." Jeneen waved the scissors in the air as she talked. "She'll get to it one of these days."

"Get to it?" Steph sarcastically repeated. "Those are the same totes she made her mom haul up the steps back in August, and they're still full at Christmas break!"

Malinda huffed at the disaster. "My mom used to complain about my room at home. She should see this."

Again, Jeneen backed her roommate, "Autumn's a nice person. I like her." With a beautician's eye, she critiqued her work, studying Malinda's bangs intently. "I think I'm done. See what you think." She passed Malinda her hand mirror.

"Perfect. Like I said, Jeneen, you are a saint in every way. Thanks!"

A bump on the outside of the door indicated someone entering. Using her bookbag as a tool, Autumn pushed the door open. She dropped the bag on top of her desk, her winter coat and gloves followed. Malinda rolled her eyes at the other two girls.

"Hi, Autumn. Done with your final?" Jeneen greeted. This was the last week of the first semester. Everyone was strapped with final tests before the three-week break for the holidays.

"Yeah," her tired tone and dragging step was not the usual Autumn.

"Tough test?" Jeneen was all concern.

"Oh, the usual. I'm sure I did all right." Autumn mustered some false courage. She might be kidding them, but she wasn't fooling herself. Her final tests were a bear. It would take an act of God to send her through. Her friends didn't need to know.

Steph crawled off the bed. "I'd better get packing. After Malinda and I take our English test tomorrow, we're headed out."

"Yipee! It's home for the holidays for us!" Malinda had the Christmas spirit. "If I don't see you two tomorrow, Merry Christmas!"

Jeneen and Autumn echoed the exchange. Jeneen was headed home on Thursday as well, but Autumn was hanging around an extra day.

"Autumn, I'm going to jog on over to the library and do some reviewing for my last final. You can study here if you like. It will be quiet," Jeneen offered.

"Thanks, I'll do that." Autumn made a pretense of digging her books out of her bag. When the door closed after Jeneen, she slipped her cell phone out of her pocket instead. She desperately had to talk to Luke. They had discussed this issue before, but now, it was serious. She was failing her first semester of college.

Pressing the phone to her ear, she waited for him to answer. "Luke? I have to get out of here. I'm not going to make it."

"I'm sorry, babe."

"Ah, it's okay. I'm not much into books. Did you talk to your dad?" She fingered the zipper tab on her hooded sweatshirt.

"Yeah. He's not too excited about you moving in. He says it's hard enough to scratch together enough money for the two of us to make out."

"Did you tell him I'll get a job and help with the expenses?"

"I did, but he wasn't convinced. Winter's not a good time to go job hunting."

"You want me to come, don't you, Luke?" She felt like she was begging.

"Sure I do. It's just my dad…" His voice trailed off.

Autumn wished she could see his expression. Did he want this as much as she did? "I have to be out of the dorm by Friday. Everything is being shut down for the Christmas break."

"I don't know what to say, Autumn. It's a money thing. We can't afford a place of our own, and Dad thinks you'll be a sponge."

Almost hugging the phone, Autumn implored, "Until I get a job, I'll keep house for the two of you—cleaning, cooking. Your dad will love me."

"He thinks of you as another mouth to feed."

An idea had been forming in Autumn's mind for the last two days. She decided to share it with Luke. "How much money do I need to convince your dad I'm not a freeloader?"

"More than you have. Listen, A.J., let's slow down. You go home for Christmas, and we'll talk about it more during your vacation."

Go home? There was no way she was going back to Prairie City. Having left Luke behind over the extended Thanksgiving weekend, she had experienced the most lonesome days of her life. Having tasted love, she was hanging on for all it was worth.

No, she was emphatic. She was not going home for Christmas. Jacob would force her to take part in all the traditions—chopping down and decorating the tree, baking cookies, caroling, the Christmas Eve service. It wasn't her thing. Luke was.

"Tell me how much I need, Luke. I can get it—$5,000, $10,000, $15,000?"

He could tell she wasn't going to give up. "Whatever you can," he finally relented.

Heaving a sigh of relief, Autumn signed off and then immediately sent a text message to her mom.

"Mom, need to pay tuition and room and board for second semester before break. Please deposit the money in my account immediately. See you soon. Love, Autumn"

And Jasmine did, not realizing it would be almost five years before she'd again peer into the face of her green-eyed princess with the ringlets of golden hair.

Chapter 23

Four Years Later

November in North Dakota was as changeable as a woman's hair color. Some years, old man winter would stoutly shake his fist, whirling in mountains of snow into the state as an austere Halloween prank and then dropping the mercury line in the thermometer to ensure it would stay until spring.

This year, he was benevolent, allowing the Indian summer days of fall to linger past their expiration date. Leafless trees and brown lawns seemed out of place in the unusually mild weather the residents were experiencing. It was a day to hang the laundry on the line, to string Christmas lights along the roof, to wash the outdoor windows, giving them one last shine before the water froze in the bucket.

But the crowd congregated on the russet grounds of Joel Linton's farmyard wasn't here in preparation for the cold season. Lawn tables loaded with food and chairs dotted the porch, spilling onto the dry grass in front of the two-story house. Bright yellow swatches of ribbon danced in the breeze, decorating the railings, the corral fencing, and even the machinery parked by the barns.

Jasmine, along with Joel's neighbors and friends, was here for a surprise celebratory picnic—a jubilant commemoration of Joel adopting his seven-year-old foster son, Carson. Joel's four-wheel-drive pickup truck leisurely rolled along the curved driveway past the slough and into the yard, two sets of eyes stared out of the front windshield at the cheering crowd waving magnolia-colored pennants, as if Joel and Carson were soldiers returning home from the battlefield.

Joel read the words on the banner fluttering from the porch roof. "Welcome home, Carson."

"Why does it say that?" the towheaded youngster was astounded by the scene before them.

"I think our friends are welcoming you into the Linton family. This is your permanent home now, Carson." The new father drew the mite to his side. "That's what the judge said at the courthouse. Your name is now Carson Linton."

"Just like yours?" The blue eyes sought the gray ones above him.

"Just like mine."

When the father and son disembarked from the truck, the crowd surged in, surrounding the pair, smothering them in congratulatory hugs and kisses. Carson smirked at Joel. "This is gonna be some party!"

Jasmine held back, observing the jovial frenzy from the platform of the porch, a smile resting on her lips. Joel was a quiet, gentle-mannered man. No doubt he found this boisterous unexpected reception in his and Carson's honor somewhat disconcerting. He was not one to seek the limelight.

When Carson could scramble out from the clutches of women squeezing the air out of him, he dove between the maze of legs, gesturing to his second grade classmates in attendance. He would show them his baby calves. The cluster of kids ran pell-mell for the corral enclosures.

Jasmine's gaze rested gently on Joel, who had his farmer's cap firmly in place, only allowing his gray-tinged hair to peek out around his ears and the back of his neck. Jasmine's life had changed greatly in the past few years.

After experiencing a second tough winter after Evert's death, she had taken Cynthia's advice, selling her home in Prairie City and moving to Elton, eliminating the treacherous drives between the two towns. The family home had lost its sentimental hold on her when she became its sole occupant. With her friendships in Prairie City growing lukewarm, she was no longer held to the smaller of the two towns. On the other hand, Elton, besides being her place of employment, boasted a hospital and an adequate display of businesses on Main Street to accommodate most of her needs.

Her bluish-gray one-story bungalow was within walking distance of her job. Its back porch and fenced in backyard had been the selling points, allowing her to have room for a vegetable garden and an old-fashioned flower bed. It had a guest room and a futon in the office, in case Autumn's and Jacob's visits coincided. So far that hadn't happened.

Initially, Jasmine had met Joel Linton when he brought his foster son, Carson, to her first grade classroom. She had been impressed by the endearing relationship the adult and the child had built in the short months they had lived together. Joel had a natural affinity beholding him to the child. Parenting was his gift.

It took months into Carson's first grade year before his teacher realized Joel Linton had lost his wife to cancer two years prior. Jasmine was appalled, not in finding he was a widower, but rather in his decision to step into the role of a single parent. Having dealt with Autumn by herself after Evert had died, Jasmine knew beyond a thread of doubt that single parenting was the toughest job she had ever been forced to handle. Voluntarily becoming a single foster parent was beyond her reasoning capacity.

Why would Joel do it? Months later, he had confided in her the answer to her question. His empty farmhouse had driven him crazy; he could hardly stand the intense quietness. Jasmine could relate. She had turned to writing when her solitary confinement drove her up the walls.

Joel and his wife, Melissa, had done foster parenting years prior to her sickness. It was nothing new to him. His main struggle in returning to foster care had been in his belief that a child needed a mother and a father. Carson was being shortchanged.

Watching him today, it was obvious he had worked through the issue. Carson was a lucky boy. Joel's exceptional ability to parent made Jasmine feel even more inept with Autumn.

Once his friends had all patted him on the back, the assemblage moved to the buffet tables, carrying plates laden with homemade delectable entrees.

Jasmine hadn't moved from her sentry's post on the porch. His gray eyes now sought hers, a baffled expression on his face. He mounted the porch stairs, purposefully directing his steps toward her. "Tell me, Mrs. Kirmis, did Carson's first grade teacher have anything to do with the day's festivities?"

Crow's feet crinkling at her temples gave away her attempt at keeping an amused grimace at bay. "Mr. Linton, being the overqualified father that you are, you certainly are aware that Carson moved on to second grade this past fall."

"Ah, dodging the question. I find you guilty." His John Denver smile warmed her heart. What was it about this man that drew her to him? In some ways, he reminded her of Evert, although certainly not in appearance. Her husband had been taller, broader, a Scandinavian coloring to his skin and hair. Joel was smaller in stature, a dark farmer's tan giving him an earthy coloring synonymous with his occupation of farming. Joel was also quieter than Evert, as if his words were mulled over repeatedly before he spit them out. Yet the two of them were both gentle in their mannerisms, courteous; they had a perceptual sensitivity about them that made them adept at feeling out the inner makeup of someone else.

"I'd say it was a joint adventure. You have a lot of friends who think highly of you." Jasmine felt a bit giddy; it had been some time since she had been in his presence.

"Can't understand why. You all really blew us away when we drove onto the yard. Actually, it started with the mailbox. Do you know who switched the nameplate from Joel Linton to Joel and Carson Linton?" He watched the changing scenes on her face.

"My lips are sealed." She gestured zipping her mouth shut. "It's not easy to carry out a surprise, but I think this one was successful."

"They got me all right." Joel nodded.

Glancing at the kids balanced on the side of the corral fencing, Jasmine remarked, "I see you've brought your cattle home from summer grazing in the pasture."

"I just did it. The forecast for the coming week predicts a shift in weather patterns. I didn't want a snowstorm to catch them away from home. It's time to start feeding the hay." His eyes followed hers.

"Carson is sure entertaining his classmates."

"I'll do the same for you if you are able to linger after the rest of the folks pack up." He looked at her uncertainly, wondering if she'd oblige.

"Sure," was all she gave back. "You'd best fill a plate since you're a person of honor."

"I shall." Joel moved off to descend the porch steps. "My cows and I are holding you to it." He sauntered over to the picnic tables.

Much later, when dusk had settled, erasing the last rays of the pink sunset, neighbors began packing up. Carson and Joel waved as their friends moved down the driveway in succession. Only the mustard-colored blotches of ribbons and the banner festooning the yard remained, and Jasmine.

Joel and Carson walked hand in hand back to where Jasmine waited. "Carson, Mrs. Kirmis hasn't seen our bossies since last winter. I think she should meet the new calves."

Carson's eyes lit up. "I'll show them to her." Then faltering, he tilted his head up to his dad. "The calves aren't babies anymore. They're more like teenagers."

Hearing the exchange, Jasmine smirked. "Guess I've missed out on a lot."

Carson let go of Joel's hand and ran to grasp the hand of his previous teacher. "Come on, teacher. You are gonna be really surprised."

Expectantly, the threesome sauntered across the open space to the corral fences. The night air had cooled considerably, coaxing them into heavier jackets. Resting their arms on the top railing, they sought to distinguish the dark shadows from the black Angus cows and their young. Warily, the mothers' heads went up, their eyes holding vigil on the visitors as the matured calves pushed against their mothers, some still wanting to pull on a full udder.

"Are you gonna help us sell them again?" Carson asked, hopping off the railing to scoop up the calico cat named Vicious who had silently followed them.

A giggle rose from Jasmine's throat. Last winter, while gathering research for a second novel, she had spent a day at the Livestock Auction Barn in Bismarck, taking notes on the procedure ranchers and buyers go through in transferring ownership of cattle. It happened to be the very day that Joel was selling some of his critters. Carson had reversed roles with his teacher, instructing her on the basics of a cattle auction. Unintentionally, she had bid on six open Angus cows for slaughter and ended up being the butt of laughter reeling through the barn.

"I think I'd do more damage than good."

Unaware of what she was referring to, Carson objected, "Oh, no, we'd like having you go with us, wouldn't we, Dad?"

Jasmine was thankful for the cover of the darkness when Joel made it unanimous, "Couldn't think of any better company." Heat rose to her cheeks.

Retracing their steps back to the front of the house, Joel suggested, "Care for a short walk?"

"If you can guarantee we won't run into a skunk or some other creature of the night," Jasmine rejoined.

"Vicious doesn't want to go, Dad. I'll stay on the porch and play with her," Carson insisted.

"Okay, buddy. We won't go far." Together, they turned their footprints toward the graveled driveway. An overhead yard light illumined a wide circle stretching their shadows in front of them. Past its circumference, the road disappeared into blackness.

"You have the most unique names for your pets. Vicious?" Jasmine shook her head.

"You like the name, huh? Vicious is a terrific hunter. She drags birds, mice, rats, squirrels, gophers—you name it, to our front door. She's rather proud of her marksmanship."

For a few seconds, they walked, listening to the night sounds of the country—an occasional bird call, the breeze fluttering through the dry grasses.

"So I heard you have a second novel coming out. You had quite a message in your first book. What are you trying to convey in this one?" Joel picked up the conversation.

"I wouldn't want to spoil the suspense. You'll just have to read it and find out." Although she couldn't see his face in the dimness, she envisioned it held amusement.

"I'll look forward to it."

Changing the subject, she asked a question she truly wanted him to answer. "How is it that parenting comes so natural to you, so easy? The bond you have with Carson is clearly visible."

"I can't take any credit. Carson is just a great kid. He likes me, and I like him."

Jasmine wouldn't let him off. "You're such a good parent, and I'm such a crummy one."

"Still no communication with Autumn?" he asked softly, knowing the topic was a minefield.

Shuffling her shoes against the pebbles underfoot, her head sank lower. "At Thanksgiving, it will be four years since I've seen her."

"Long time," he acknowledged.

"I feel like the worst parent ever to walk upon this earth. What did I do to make her hate me? To not ever have a homesick quiver within her breast to draw her homeward? It isn't normal, is it?"

"You're too hard on yourself," Joel objected. "Parenting evaluations aren't exactly black or white."

Jasmine wasn't about to be mollified. "Even though I may exhibit the warm nurturing traits characteristic of a teacher within my classroom, they somehow didn't always travel home in my bookbag at day's end. I was impatient with Autumn's moodiness, her lackadaisical attitude. I could have earned a graduate credit in nagging for the number of hours I clocked goading her into action. We butt heads like two goats in a farmyard."

As was his nature, Joel gave an unhurried response, letting their steps eat up the road. "We've both taken in children we did not sire. We share no genetics, no family idiosyncrasies, or mannerisms with these kids. We're only going on love. But love doesn't always come with a lot of guarantees. I'm just a beginner at this parenting. Melissa and I cared for a handful of foster kids in the past, so my window is pretty small. There's lots of books out there on parenting, yet to be truthful, I haven't read any of them—except the Good Book."

"Like I said, you're a natural."

"Hardly. I guess I try to treat Carson the way I'd have wanted to be treated at his age." Joel was a humble man.

"The golden rule—do onto others as you'd have them do onto you," Jasmine quoted.

"Kind of like that—only, I'm the adult, and he is the child. That gives me the greater responsibility." A coyote set up a mournful howl in the distance.

"At a workshop once, the speaker stressed accepting children as they are. Maybe I wasn't understanding the direction he was going, but it sounded more like putting a stamp of approval on everything the child did." Jasmine stuck her hands in her jacket pockets.

Joel mused, "Maybe a better way to put it would be to love them in spite of their behavior. My best parenting tool is to teach by example, whether it is showing Carson how to set a gopher trap or how to control his outburst when he is angry. My dad taught me a lifetime of worthy lessons, mostly by modeling them."

"It's amazing what a child learns by watching both the positive and the negative behavior. It's difficult to be consistent." The coyote's continuing lament was eerie.

"I believe the greatest gift we can give our kids is to introduce them to our faith. Kids need hope. It is a scary world out there. Without hope, it will be extremely hard for them to prevail."

"In education, we instill a lot of knowledge, but you're right. Wisdom comes from the Lord. They need godly wisdom to direct them." Jasmine's thoughts troubled her. "I tried being a godly parent, but I can't say I was always successful."

"Your heart was in the right place. That counts."

"Joel, I have two adopted children. Why does one accept me and the other push me away?" Their pace had slowed to a snail's stride.

"Each child has a different makeup. Autumn probably couldn't even answer your question. It's her choice, but in my estimation, she is missing out. Proverbs says—"

Interrupting, Jasmine recited the verse for him, "Lead a child in the way he should go, and when he is old he will not turn from it" (Proverbs 22:6, NIV).

Inwardly, she battled with herself. How much should she confide in this man? Did she want to bear her soul? What if he listened to her words and then threw them down and stomped on them?

Although they had been thrown together a number of times in the past, mainly because of Carson being her student, their relationship had been one of a parent and teacher.

Yes, she had spent the day with them at the cattle auction and again on Carson's birthday when Joel had given him permission to invite two friends to his party. One of them had been her.

Back in May, Joel had asked her to accompany him on the four-hour trip to Fargo to retrieve Carson after a weekend visit with a potential adoptive couple. After witnessing how distraught the youngster was at their separation, Joel had then made the decision to adopt Carson himself. It was at this point that Jasmine found herself shying away from allowing their relationship to grow into something more intimate. The comparison between Joel's parenting skills and her own was horribly incongruous. She would only ruin the closely woven composition of the family unit Joel and Carson were constructing. They would be better with out her.

And now, here the two of them were, on a country road too black to distinguish each other's features, she about to spill her guts to him. Taking a deep breath, she let it slide over the still way.

"The first Christmas Autumn didn't come home, the hurt was deeper than Evert's death. He hadn't intentionally left me, but she had. Maria Philips, on her way home from NDSU for the holidays, stopped at my house. Autumn had sent a box of empty canning jars with her, plus a gift for Jacob and another for me. Maria said Autumn was spending Christmas with a friend.

"After Maria left, I lost it. I tried calling, texting, e-mailing Autumn. Of course, she wouldn't answer. I bawled to Jacob over the phone. He promised he'd stop at the dorm on his way through from Minneapolis on Christmas Eve. The college was completely shut down by then. It was the absolute worst Christmas ever. I feel bad about that now. I should have tried to cover my anguish for Jacob's sake. He had driven so far just to spend a few days with me before having to head back to his job.

"Over the holidays, a letter addressed to Autumn came to her home address in Prairie City. Of course, being the good parent I am according to you, I opened it. It informed Autumn her GPA for the first semester was below their standard of performance, and she would not be welcome to return for the next semester. If she so liked, she could register again in the fall. It shouldn't have been such a shock. She'd only graduated from high school out of the merciful grace of her teachers. Why would she suddenly turn into an overachiever in college? But she had used me. Right before she was due home for the Christmas break, she text messaged me asking for enough money to pay her tuition and board and room for the next semester. I dropped it in her account. She left Fargo financially secure, thanks to her ignorant mother."

Joel remained quiet, aware of how hard this was for Jasmine.

"In January, I did everything to hunt her down. Called her old roommate, got a name and number to her boyfriend in Minneapolis. Jacob contacted him, but she was no longer there. Every so often, an acquaintance would drop a remark about something Autumn had written on Facebook. Get this, I even signed up for Facebook, figuring if I could glean some information through the social networking, it was worth it. Should have known she wouldn't accept me as one of her social friends—nor Jacob either.

"I was a basket case. I prayed and prayed, but nothing happened. The only thing keeping me sane was my writing. Maybe I was using it to escape from my present life. I don't know. About a year later, a postcard came in the mail from Louisiana. Cheery, as if nothing had transpired between us. It said she was touring the country. From someone else, I found out she'd gotten picked up by a cross-country trucker. Then she faded away again. Her e-mail message box filled years ago. The cell phone number I have is no longer in service.

"By chance, Jacob ran into her at a car wash in Minneapolis where she was working. He tried to talk to her, but she got angry and said she didn't need him in her life. Feeling he wasn't accomplishing anything, he left. Another day, he returned, but she had quit.

"I don't know what else to do."

Their footsteps had come to a halt. Even though they were face-to-face, they could hardly tell because of the billowy blackness.

"Good." Joel had uttered the single syllable.

"Good?" Jasmine questioned.

"God works best when we run out of ideas. Maybe it is time to give her to the Lord."

"How can a parent give her daughter away?"

"Has holding on to her worked?" She didn't even have to respond. The answer was blatant.

"Did you write the book of Samuel?" she asked dismally.

"Excuse me?" Joel was confused.

"Hannah in the book of Samuel pleaded with the Lord to remove her years of barrenness and give her a child. He did. He gave her a beautiful baby boy she named Samuel. And when he was still but a young lad, she took him to the temple and gave him back to the Lord in utmost gratitude. I've often wondered how she had the strength to do it."

"Could be it takes more energy to do it on our own," Joel quietly interceded.

The discussion had moved into notably tender territory for Jasmine. She'd have to do some high stepping to mull through it all. "You've certainly given me a lot to think about. Should we head back?' Twisting her head back in the direction they had come, she noted, "Your yard light reminds me of the star of the east beckoning us homeward."

Tucking her hand in his bent elbow, he agreed. "I like the comparison."

"Now, Joel, I discover you're not only a good parent, but also a good counselor. Haven't you ever messed up?"

"Ah, too many times to count. My greatest regret was in refusing to honor my wife's request. Like Hannah, my wife struggled with our inability to conceive. We went the round of doctors and possibilities, but it just didn't happen. She was heartbroken. Then we went to a Christian retreat. There was a couple who had adopted three children from three different nationalities. They were cuter than a bug's ear. Melissa took it as a sign that we should adopt a child. I don't know what was wrong with me. I thought I couldn't love a baby that wasn't my own. I pierced her dream." The grating of their footsteps against the graveled surface provided background to their individual thoughts.

"The one thing she really wanted, I refused her."

Jasmine pressed his arm in empathy.

"She's gone. I can't make it up to her. I was unbelievably selfish. And the hardest part is discovering I was absolutely irrefutably mistaken. Carson is the proof. I don't think it is possible to love a child more than I love him. Sometimes, when I look up into the sky on a particularly starry night, I like to fathom Melissa peering down at us—me and Carson—and smiling, knowing she'd been right all along. Crazy, huh?"

Jasmine smiled. With all the obstacles thrown into her life, she was happy to be right where she was at this moment. "They say life isn't for the fainthearted."

When their shadows penetrated the symmetrical wheel of light staked by the overhead electric bulb, Joel let go of her arm. Huddled on the porch steps was Carson, patiently stroking Vicious, the cat lying limp in his arms, her motor purring softly. The two were a perfect picture.

"He sure loves the farm," Joel murmured as they drew closer.

"He loves you more," Jasmine returned. After saying good night to the two Lintons, she retreated to her car, carrying a trunk full of thoughts to browse.

Chapter 24

Curled in a fetal position on the lumpy mattress reeking of embedded pee from past usage, Autumn wiggled her nose from under the layers of blankets. It moved without cracking, a good sign it wasn't frozen. Magnolia lay hidden under her own pile of coverings, her hollow cheeks and one thin arm visible amongst the folds.

Light from the dirty window validated it was morning, a creaking, ice-chilling winter daybreak. As much as she desired to stay in the warmest spot in the dilapidated trailer house, Autumn forced herself to sit up, her backside immediately complaining about the sharp contrast in temperature and her stomach lamenting a nauseousness which translated to her head as dizziness. A fog of stale smoke trapped within the confines of the trailer left the burnt smell of cigarette butts and marijuana joints on everything it touched. If anything was good about the start of this day, it was, having gone to bed fully dressed, she'd only have to run a comb through her blond tangles to be set for job hunting.

The girls had tugged and grunted, squeezing the queen-size mattress through the narrow bedroom door to deposit on the kitchen floor. Pooling their money, they'd squeaked out enough to pay the atrocious rent charged on the trailer, although it wasn't worth even half the amount. Yesterday, after all the warmth had been sucked from their tin can hovel, they discovered the furnace's fuel tank had bottomed out. Their ancient furnace was one of the few in the city not fueled by natural gas. Groveling for survival, they left the electric stove's oven door open as their only remaining heat source.

Two weeks prior, Autumn had been fired from her last job, the boss saying she overfraternized with the other employees, thereby accomplishing squat. Her last paycheck had run out before it was even in her hand.

Flopping over backward onto the mattress in dejection, Autumn succumbed to her body's cry for a few additional minutes of snuggling under the quilts. Maybe her flu symptoms would subside if she lay still. Anyway she needed to formulate a plan for the day. Scanning the walls and meager cast-off furniture and the accumulation of litter that always seemed to follow her—beer cans, clothes, wrappers, empty boxes—she sneered, *What a dump!* What was even more depressing was the fact she was living in the dump. It was better than the street, but only by a hair's breadth.

How had she ended up living on skid road? Her dream to marry prince charming and live wealthy had fizzled with Luke. It was painful to even backtrack to the Christmas she'd left NDSU.

Luke had been grumpy, forced to take a half day off of work to retrieve her belongings, too numerous to fit in her already crammed car. Sandwiched between the pleas of a damsel in distress and his kingly father's harsh language at admitting a vixen into their humble abode, Luke's cork had blown, targeting Autumn. Using her femininity, Autumn had sweetened him up with promises of the night; however, his dad was another case. He glared at Autumn from her first appearance and every day thereafter until he kicked her out after a two-week notice. Their two-bedroom house had been cramped. Though she attempted to make good on her vow to be a first-rate housekeeper, her skills and motivation were definitely lacking. She preferred being catered to, admired, and petted, none of which Ted Boyle dispersed.

Seeing his girlfriend through his father's derogatory critique, Luke's former idolization waned after he had spent her college money on an upgraded four-wheel-drive pickup. How stupid of her to think he'd be indebted to her for life when she had generously spent *her* money on their truck. Constantly, he pushed her to get a job, and when she had one, to work more hours.

In his rush to be rid of her, Ted Boyle found her an efficiency apartment in a crummy part of the city, one step up from the rat hole she was in now, and even paid the first month's rent. Acting as a moving company a second time within a two-month span, Luke had loaded up her possessions and dumped them on the cracked sidewalk outside her new residence. Absentmindedly, he slid his hand into the side pocket of his jeans. "Forgot to give you this. Catch. I found it when I cleaned out the old truck." As a reflex movement, she put her hand into the air and caught the object. His new four-by-four burned rubber as it sped away down the narrow littered street. "I love you too," she had yelled sarcastically after his chauvinistic display. Sticking out her tongue, she'd stomped her foot angrily on the weed-infested cement. For all she'd given him, and then to be treated like gutter trash, was grievously offensive. Her teeth had grated as she flung abuse at the tailgate of the disappearing machine. Clenching her fist, the object he had thrown at her bit into her palm. Her fingers had opened on their own accord, revealing the opal ring. Luke had taken much more than her mother's money from her.

After hauling all the disorganized boxes and totes inside, she'd jumped in her Toyota and driven until she found the main fairways through the city. From her former experience back in Prairie City, she'd banked on snagging a job at a truck stop, and she had.

Every truck driver who came through her till gawked at the long-legged blond beauty, and the lucky ones got more than just a ten-second showing. After letting her apartment go, she'd spent almost an entire year traveling the United States, viewing the mountains, the plains, the ocean beaches, the big cities, and the forests from a high seat in a semitruck, and the nights in the sleeper behind the cab. Celebrating her first Mardi Gras in New Orleans, she'd had a twinge of benevolence and had scribbled off a postcard to her mom. When one driver tired of her, there was always another to give her a lift to the next port.

Eventually, traveling the highways back to Minneapolis, she was peeved to find her Toyota locked behind a chain-linked fence of the city. A friend had allowed her to park the car, stuffed with all the worldly belongings it could hold, on the street alongside his basement hangout. In her absence, he had up and moved. The police department had the abandoned vehicle moved. To get it out of hawk, she'd have to pay the towing charge. With a mere twenty dollars to her name, the car stayed impounded indefinitely. Her clothing consisted of the knapsack she'd carried from one truck to the next.

Reduced to poverty, she'd hoofed it to a city park for her first night in the open air. Although the weather had been cordial, the temperature in the fifties, she'd found sleeping under the roof of a picnic shelter frightening. A man with beady eyes peering out over a straggly beard and a paper bag fastened to his hand had joined her under the overhang. Hastily, she had picked up her knapsack and moved on. Four times, she'd relocated before the light of the dawn filtered through the tree tops. Exhausted from precious little sleep, she'd slumbered on a cement bench adjacent to a water fountain, soaking in the warm sunshine. The second night she'd wandered through stores whose doors stayed open twenty-four hours. Once, she'd wearily sunk down in a chair by the shoe department; however, a store employee had shooed her on.

Frugally stretching her sparse funds, she'd spent one dollar on a loaf of bread; another, on a two-liter bottle of pop. Temporarily camping out on a rectangle planter dotted with geraniums, she ate her slices of bread sparingly. It was at low moments like this, she'd let her mind wander to where she usually reined it in from galloping—home.

She thought of the mauve-colored Bible story book her mom had read to her at bedtime when she was in elementary school. Back then, the story of the prodigal son had seemed absurd. What father in his right mind would hand over a wad of money to his son and watch him leave home set on blowing it on riotous living? The father should have had more sense. When the ungrateful son found himself eating with the hogs, he had lowered himself to that of a beggar and returned to his childhood home. His father saw him coming, and instead of giving him the whipping he deserved, ran to meet him, throwing a hug and a new set of clothes around his shoulder. Her mom had explained the spiritual message of the parable. Whenever God sees one of his wayward children turn his steps back to his heavenly Father, heaven throws a party. She wondered if her mom would roast a festive ham, decorate a chocolate cake, and fill the goblets she stored on the top shelf of the china cabinet if her daughter sauntered up the driveway unannounced.

Heck, why did she do this to herself? She wasn't ever going home, so there was no reason to fantasize about a homecoming. She might be down on her luck, but she loved her independence. No way would she trade it in for a bunch of rules and wagging fingers.

Her eyelids closed briefly. Shivering, she drew the blankets tighter, wishing she'd never have to face the raw winter air both inside or outside of their shack. But procrastinating wasn't going to get her a job. Without a job, there would be no fuel for the furnace. The women's shelter had been better than this.

A tip from a friendly cop had pointed her in the direction of the shelter on a night when the lows had dipped into the forties.

Her lips had been numb, extended across her chattering teeth, her hands pressed between her thighs. Without even giving the kindly officer a thank-you, she'd shouldered her backpack and jogged the entire way to the shelter. Afterward, she felt bad about not showing the policeman any appreciation. His information had given her a roof over her head, a furnace blowing hot air, a cot with a blanket and pillow, a warm meal, safety, and very best of all, Magnolia.

Curls like black corkscrews swarmed across her pillow, her face a smooth umber, peaceful in rest. Her cot was parallel to the one assigned to Autumn. In the dim light, Autumn had crawled beneath her blanket, listening to the ruffled sound of people breathing in their sleep, someone's snore reminded her of a freight train in the distance. In minutes, she too had drifted off, savoring the sanctuary of a safe haven and unbroken sleep.

It wasn't until she awoke to the stirrings of movement— women talking among themselves, clinks of silverware against dishes, the spray of water emanating from a shower, a baby's cry—that she actually met the ginger-colored Magnolia.

Orienting herself to the new surroundings, Autumn had propped herself up on one elbow, flipping her yellow mass of stringy hair back over her head. It had been almost a week since she'd had the luxury of a shower.

"Hiya." At the musical tone of the two syllables, Autumn had rotated her neck to the opposite side of her cot. There, sitting cross-legged on top of her own bed, Magnolia rested her elbows on her upper legs, watching the newest resident of the women's shelter. The velvety brown eyes sprayed glitter at her, reminding Autumn of a fawn playing not far from its watchful mother.

"Hi, yourself." Autumn yawned. "Something smells good."

"Ya. Cocoa Wheats. You musta come in sometime between ten and four. At ten, I went to bed, and at four, I had a potty break." The deer's eyes smiled along with a display of white teeth.

Magnolia appeared to be about fourteen, yet later, Autumn would discover the petite woman had two years on herself.

"What's a pretty thing like you doing in a homeless shelter?" Autumn sat up, smelling a rank odor on her own skin and hair. She needed to take advantage of bathing facilities.

"It's as good a place as any, I guess. Wanted a classy hotel for a few winks." Her grin was contagious.

"You have the most beautiful skin coloring. What nationality are you?" Autumn admired her full auburn cheeks and arms.

"Don't reckon I know for sure. I think my mama stirred the pot when she had me. What about you? What you's doin' here? Some man sure would want to tie his hands up in your hair."

"Lots of fish swimming out there, but can't find one like my daddy," Autumn joked, narrowly missing the truth.

"Wouldn't want one like my daddy," Magnolia returned. "Mama said he was a real jerk. She met him in an alley."

"For real?" Autumn figured most parents were like hers—law-abiding, middle-class, working nine to five, boring.

"Where'd you grow up?" Magnolia was fascinated by the light skin and hair of this chick who didn't seem to connect much with her world.

"Small-town America: house with a two-door garage, picket fence, and flower pots on the patio." Scorn colored Autumn's words.

"Really?" Magnolia acted as if she had never heard of such glorious surroundings. "Did you's have one of those billowy bedspreads with pictures of cartoon characters on it?"

"Yah, when I was young, it was pink with butterflies. When I got to the teen years, it was covered with stars. They matched the stars my mom painted on the ceiling."

"No way. You one of those rich kids I see on TV?" Her fawn eyes widened into two dark pools. "No mom I ever heard of painted pictures on the walls of their kids' room." Then as if a thought from the outside world struck her, she added, "You not fakin' you're homeless just to see what's it like and then plannin' to write some documentary on it, are ya?"

Autumn laughed out loud at the preposterous notion. "No way. I guarantee this knapsack holds the sum total of all my earthly belongings presently available to me. I'm flat broke. Can't even pay my cell phone bill, so the company cut me off. That and my birth control prescription."

Magnolia's eyes seesawed in bliss. "Then it's a good thing you be sleepin' here and not at the Ritz with some guy swirlin' your hair."

"Must be good in every situation, even a homeless shelter," Autumn agreed, liking her new friend immensely. She hadn't had many girlfriends in her years.

Autumn and Magnolia were inseparable the next days, comparing notes on their backgrounds, reciting stories of their experiences. They liked being taken care of, instead of worrying about the next meal or bed.

"All good things come to an end," Magnolia announced one morning. "My time to get out of here. Can't live here forever. They"—she gestured with her head toward the two women clearing off the breakfast makings—"don't let us put our feet under their table forever. I gots to go and prove I can get myself a moneymaking job. You's time must be about up too."

Magnolia walked over to Autumn and wrapped her arms around her back, her head barely reaching Autumn's chin. "Sure nice meetin' up with you. Maybe we'll run into each other again. Hopefully, not in a shelter. Maybe in a palace like where you's from." Autumn hugged her back. She wished they'd met back in high school and had grown up as bosom buddies.

Then maybe she wouldn't have felt the desire to travel so far from home to find a friend.

Chapter 25

In first grade, every holiday warrants an art project. Thanksgiving was no exception. Having mounted a six-foot ladder, Jasmine was systematically stapling a parading line of feathered turkeys across the top of the white marker board at the front of her classroom. In a mere two days, the school would be closed for a four-day weekend to celebrate the holiday first commemorated by the pilgrims and Native Americans.

Humming as she worked, the words exchanged with Joel earlier in the month kept trickling through her conscience. Was she ready to turn Autumn over to the Lord and accept whatever He had for her? Joel was certainly right; struggling to solve the mayhem herself had yielded no resolution.

After Hannah delivered Samuel to the tabernacle, she only saw him once a year. Could she be content with an annual visit? Shaking her head, she chided herself. Thanksgiving marked the four-year anniversary since Autumn's last trip home. Once a year would seem like a gala event!

"Knock, knock," a hushed voice at the door brought Jasmine out of her revelry.

"Katie! And Justin!" Quickly dismounting the stepladder, Jasmine rushed to enfold her visitors in a group hug. Bending down on one knee to Justin's eye level, she appraised the youngster. "My, Justin, you have gotten so big! How many fingers old are you?"

"Feee," Justin readily supplied, holding up three fingers.

"Almost four," Katie interjected. "His birthday is coming up soon."

"Wow! I remember the day you were born. It was the first snowfall of the season, and your Nana Cindy was there to welcome her grandbaby."

Not much for talking, Justin saw the clothes hamper bulging with classroom toys. "Can I play?" he asked.

"You bet." Jasmine regained her stance and helped him dump the basketful of toys onto the floor.

"Didn't mom stay after school today? Her door is already locked." Katie asked, a hint of anxiety in her voice.

"Ah, she had a substitute for her classes. I presume she is sick, but I haven't taken a minute to give her a call. Shall I?" Jasmine moved away from Justin.

"No. She's not at home." Katie's voice cracked, raising Jasmine's antennae. Unshed tears shone in Katie's eyes.

In alarm, Jasmine grasped one of Katie's arms, pulling her down to sit on a student's desktop. Jasmine did the same across the narrow aisle. "What's wrong, Kate?"

With her head tilted back, her eyes sought strength in the ceiling, blinking furiously to control the tears. Unsuccessful, she brushed them away with her fingertips. Finally, in a high pitch, the words squeaked past her lips. "Mom moved to an apartment on Saturday. Didn't she tell you?"

The weight of the words turned Jasmine's stomach to lead; her shoulders fell. In disbelief, she sought clarification. "Your mom moved out on your dad?"

Tears were streaming faster than Katie could wipe them away. The dark cloud of a thunderstorm hung above them. Drawing a wad of Kleenex from her coat pocket, she nodded, unable to speak.

"Oh, Katie, she never breathed a word to me. I had no idea they were having trouble." Gingerly, she drew Katie into her arms and cried with her. As close as she was to Cynthia, she was amazed her friend had never confided in her.

After the tears subsided somewhat, Jasmine asked, "How is your dad doing with all of this?"

Hiccupping and then answering, Katie confided, "He's angry and hurt. He never saw it coming."

Hesitant to put it into words, Jasmine proceeded slowly. "Is Cynthia…is your mom…seeing someone?"

Hanging her head, the response was sluggish. "She met someone online—someone named Roger. I don't think they've actually met in person, but evidently, they talk and Skype frequently. Dad caught her." Twisting her fingers, she swallowed, fighting to keep a fresh set of tears at bay.

"Where would she be today?" Jasmine was speaking her thoughts out loud. "You don't think she's with this man, do you?"

Shaking her head, Katie moaned, "I don't think so, but I don't really know. She gave Dad the impression he's from out of state. Since she was still in town on Saturday, I wouldn't think she'd just up and leave with her job and all."

"Do you want me to talk to her?" Inwardly, Jasmine couldn't fathom what she'd say. Nothing she'd said to Autumn had changed her course of action.

"Please do. Talk some sense into her," she pleaded.

"I can't promise she'll listen to me. She must feel pretty strongly about this guy if she'd take this drastic of a step."

Kate's head nodded dejectedly. "I know."

After she persuaded her son to leave the toys, Katie had one parting plea, "I want Justin to grow up going to Grandpa's and Grandma's *house*, not *houses*."

Jasmine understood, pledging to be in contact.

In the solitude of her room, Jasmine seethed. *How could Cynthia do this to Kevin and Katie?*

She grabbed her cell phone and typed out a short message to Cynthia. "Missed you in school today. What bug have you succumbed to?" Two minutes passed, but there was no answering chirp.

First Autumn, and now Cynthia. Neither had a plausible excuse for their behavior. Maybe Autumn could claim immaturity; however, Cynthia was a middle-aged woman, a wife, a mother, a teacher, a grandmother—no, a nana.

Then a strange thought hit Jasmine. Was Cynthia going through a midlife crisis? First, she deemed herself too young to be a grandparent, and now an affair?

Gritting her teeth, Jasmine growled.

As lost items are returned to their owners, Cynthia Burns returned to her students on Tuesday morning, all of whom had missed their beloved teacher sorely. They had stories to tell her from yesterday, and more for today. Beseeched by kids surrounding her desk, Jasmine had no opportunity to catch Mrs. Burns alone. After school, the principal called an all staff meeting, delaying the confrontation even longer.

Finally, when Mr. Peterson had covered his last point on the agenda, the teachers dispersed in clusters like passengers at Grand Central Station, moving down the various hallways to lock their doors and call it a day. Cynthia, Jasmine, and the two kindergarten teachers did likewise in their corridor, except when Cynthia made a ninety-degree turn into her classroom, Jasmine followed her, closing the door behind them.

"Gotta minute?" Jasmine inquired of her friend's back.

Having gone directly to her closet and lifted her purse from an overhead shelf in preparation for departure, Cynthia toyed with creating an excuse, thought better of it, and instead, stepped out and struck her usual pose on the edge of her desk, careful not to dislodge the bouquet of fall flowers, a mixture of chrysanthemums, Chinese bell flowers, and asters. As always, the reliable grapevine filtering through the staff named the benefactor as Roger. "Sure."

"Did you have the flu bug yesterday?" Jasmine asked nonchalantly, claiming a student-sized worktable to settle upon.

Cynthia looked her full in the face. "Kate stopped to see you after school, so let's not play games."

"Okay, I won't, but are you?" Jasmine had held rehearsals in every room of her house into the late evening, deciding how to best approach Cynthia with this matter. She had decided it would be best to keep her cool rather than blasting in with two pistols drawn.

"I didn't tell you about Roger because you would have gotten upset and told me I was acting like a teenager."

Interesting. Her friend was casting the blame on her. "Cynthia, it doesn't matter an iota what I think. What matters is what you think and what Kevin and Katie think."

Pulling in a noisy breath, Cynthia began, "Jasmine, you've always had a great marriage. You and Evert shared everything. You went everywhere together. If anyone's marriage was made in heaven, it was yours. Kevin and I do not have that kind of relationship. If he gets home from work at a decent hour, we share a meal at the kitchen table. More commonly, he eats a warmed up plate. Then he retreats to his chair, turns on the TV, and promptly falls asleep. When he stumbles to bed hours later, it is not because he is looking for me."

"Have you talked to him about how you feel?"

"Jasmine, you can't talk to a dead man." Jasmine knew that only too well. But Kevin was still breathing.

"How about marriage counseling?"

"Can you see Kevin getting off work early to go to a counseling session? Do rocks talk? I don't think so." Her last words were delivered in a singsong chant.

"Maybe if he realizes his marriage is evaporating before his very eyes, and he has to cap the leak, he will," Jasmine suggested, vexation nipping at her.

Studying the toes of her turquoise pumps, a charged silence ensued. The classroom clock ticked brazenly, as if refereeing the opponents from above.

"It might be that I do not want my marriage revived." Cynthia could not bring herself to meet Jasmine's startled stare.

"Cynthia, we vowed on our wedding days—for richer, for poorer, in sickness and in health, till death do us part."

"Yeah, back in the days when we thought true love was wearing his class ring and dragging Main in an old Chevy. How juvenile were we? A quarter of a century later, a grunt in passing in the morning doesn't cut it." Agitated, Cynthia slid off the desk and rummaged in her purse for her car keys.

"If you are willing to cast your family aside, does your faith go too?"

Almost talking down to her, patronizing her small mind, Cynthia quirked, "If God forgives sin, He'll forgive this one too."

Getting provoked, Jasmine's voice moved up a decibel. "What kind of legacy are you leaving for Justin? You are the torchbearer for the next generation. Are you going to cast it aside?"

With an exasperated sigh, Cynthia moved to the closet to retrieve her winter coat. "You are becoming melodramatic, Jasmine. The truth is, I am meeting Roger in Las Vegas over Thanksgiving weekend. That's why I took a personal day yesterday—clothes shopping. It may be wrong, but I am doing it. I deserve a life beyond first grade."

Jasmine's eyes widened at Cynthia's confession. "Please don't do this, Cynthia. You have so much at stake. Don't risk the family you have for a passing fancy. Honor the marriage God has given you."

After shrugging her arms into her long wool coat, Cynthia lifted her hair out of the offending collar and fastened the buttons.

Without looking again at her friend, she picked up her purse and marched out of the room. Over her shoulder she called, "When you leave, hit the lights and swing the door shut."

The echo of her footsteps pinged on the polished tiled flooring of the corridor until they reached the outer metal door, which banged a termination. Staring at the floral arrangement on her friend's desk, a single tear trailed down Jasmine's cheek, eventually dripping off her chin. The array of flowers was too symmetrical, too tight, overly balanced. More fitting for a casket spray. Jasmine wanted to throw up.

Her words had scratched no dent in Cynthia's selfishly laid plans. A failed marriage was about to become another tally mark in the statistics of divorce. And Kevin, Katie, and Justin would be left to fit the puzzle back together minus a crucial piece.

Life was unbearably choked with thorn bushes. A second tear followed the first. Every direction Jasmine turned, a brier was piercing her soul.

A tiny voice inside of her spoke in a whisper, *Another thing to give to me.*

And there in the empty borrowed classroom, Jasmine let it go; she gave it all. Opening her hands, she relinquished Autumn to her heavenly Maker, whatever that meant for her daughter's future. As her mother, she was tired of wrangling with her to change. God said He loved Autumn even more than her mother did. She would be safe with Him. Daily, she'd pray for Autumn's heart to soften, letting God have His way with her.

Likewise, she placed the burden of Cynthia's actions into God's hands. Only He could change her heart and straighten the road she was determined to bulldoze.

"Cast all your anxiety on Him because He cares for you" (1 Peter 5:7, NIV).

Closing her eyes tightly, the millstones chained about her neck broke and dropped. Freed from their weight, her chest lifted, and her eyes opened in gratitude. The season of Thanksgiving was upon her. She had many blessings to count.

❧❦❧

Totally ignoring her copartner, Cynthia kept to her room on Wednesday. When her first graders were in the gym or music room, she closed her door, a firm declaration she was not available for visitors. Coming out of her own room en route to the office to Xerox a worksheet, Jasmine saw the barricade and sighed. She had spoken her piece yesterday; rehashing the issue wasn't going to change Cynthia's set determination.

Through the glass window of the office, a royal bouquet of deep red roses interspersed with baby's breath could be seen setting on the counter. It was breathtaking. Jasmine stopped to inhale its fragrance before moving to the copy machine. Her eye caught the small envelope nestled into the flowers; its recipient's name written in the florist's flowing cursive—Cynthia Burns. Her stomach did a belly dive.

Over the top of the roses, June Max, the secretary, observed the landslide expression surfing on Jasmine's face. "Aren't they about the ugliest roses you ever set your eyes on?" June's eyebrows crested, her lips pulled to the side of her face.

"Hideous," Jasmine agreed. Her insides rolled. "Excuse me." She dashed through the women's restroom door. This time, she did puke.

Chapter 26

A car wash in the winter? Really? That was hitting low. Job openings within walking distance of the trailer were virtually nonexistent; Autumn had been desperate. Magnolia spent hours folding clothes at the laundry mat, yet her paycheck wasn't enough to buy them a tank of fuel oil, and Merl wouldn't be back for a week, maybe two.

His *business* trips were not the usual corporate board meetings. He didn't tell the girls his destination, length of stay, or the purpose of the trip. Nor did he wear a suit and tie. More like ripped jeans, a stretched out T-shirt, greasy hair, and BO instead of cologne.

Technically, Merl Myrhe was Magnolia's boyfriend, but Autumn shared.

After their initial acquaintance at the homeless shelter, Magnolia and Autumn had parted ways for almost a year. Magnolia had found Autumn again, sitting against a lamppost peeling an orange. Had Magnolia not made the overture, Autumn would not have recognized her friend. The girl with the umber skin had been thin before, now her skin was merely stretched over her bones, like a Halloween skeleton. Dark loops hung below her eyes. Her hair had lost its midnight blackness, a dull variegated gray replaced the shiny slate. Yet her smile remained, the dazzling white teeth reaching up to light candles in her mahogany eyes.

"Hiya."

Before she even looked up, Autumn recognized the greeting, but her return grin froze at the transformation in Magnolia.

"What's you doin' out here on the street by yourself?" the sweet voice teased.

"Waitin' for you to come by and share my orange." Autumn held out a section of the citrus fruit a passerby had dropped into her open palm. Magnolia accepted the token gift.

"Where's you plantin' your feet these days?"

"This spot is about as good as any," Autumn lazily returned.

"Then you goin' come and share my castle." Magnolia twittered a high giggle. Autumn rubbed the juice onto her pants, scraped herself off the cement sidewalk, and followed her friend home.

And that's how they became castlemates, as Magnolia chose to dub them.

When Autumn set her knapsack in the spare bedroom, Merl was off on one of his business adventures. Upon his return, he had no problem renting space to a paying customer, especially one with a body like a willow branch drenched with golden sunshine. He saw himself as the king of Magnolia's palace with two concubines in his harem.

Merl ruled with an iron arm, requiring anyone setting up in his premises to contribute to the coffer. After the car wash, Autumn landed a job at McDonald's. For the first time in four years, having accumulated a long resume of jobs, Autumn loved going to work. It didn't matter if she was taking orders at the till, bagging french fries, or mopping the floor. And because she found the work worthy, she put her heart and soul into it. Her boss, Ned Alman, nodded his approval, even rewarding her with a dime raise.

But the real reason Autumn had no qualms about hiking the mile to the Golden Arches was because of the middle-aged fellow employee, Marlene Modder. Slightly plump, chopped off mousy brown hair, a round wholesome face, and a heart too big to stay within the confines of her ribcage. She'd worked at the fast-food joint for years, providing room in her nest for every new young fledgling under her motherly wing.

After the noon rush had faded, Marlene, carrying a Filet-O-Fish sandwich and a cup of coffee, waved Autumn over to a table. Autumn tailgated her, balancing a soft drink and a Caesar salad. "Always nice to see the crowds come, and it's always nice to see them go again." Marlene stirred her coffee as Autumn removed the plastic lid from her salad. "Seems like you're an old hand at this job already, and you've only been sporting a McDonald's cap for a couple of weeks. Ned is pleased."

Autumn shrugged. "I actually prefer to be busy. The day sweeps by." She forked a mouthful of lettuce greens.

"I like meeting the people, the grumps, the grandpas, the busy moms, the businessman—all of them. Gives me a chance to send each off with a morsel of encouragement." Marlene sipped the hot liquid carefully.

"Yeah, you're good at that. You could have been a counselor instead of working fast food," Autumn chirped, chasing a miniature tomato around the bowl. During breaks such as this one, she had pretty much given Marlene her version of her entire life history.

"Actually, I'm a secretary by profession but a burger flipper by choice. Secretaries only get to see their stuffy boss all day. I'd rather stuff chicken wraps for some little nipper than order flowers for an executive's girlfriend."

"Hmmm. Good way to look at it." Autumn's napkin caught a dribble of salad dressing freelancing a mural on her chin.

"Have you decided what you're going to do about your mom yet?" Marlene had a way of discarding the chitchat and getting to the main menu.

"Which one?" Marlene knew Autumn was adopted.

"Either."

"Well, I did call the adoption agency. Found out it charges a fee to open up past files. Not sure I want to spend my limited funds on a gamble. Since my birth mom gave me up, she probably doesn't want me poking my nose into her life after all these years."

Marlene considered. "There is that risk."

"She's where I belong though. I'm not a true Kirmis. Actually, I don't have any idea what I am since I don't even have my mother's name."

"Hard to understand why she turned you over to social services. Could have been anything—too young, no support, in a compromising situation…" Marlene trailed off. Then she picked up her thoughts again. "But it may have been the right thing. You've seen kids on the street right outside our window. Seems like some don't have much parenting or even a chance in this old world. Maybe by giving you up, she gave you an opportunity she never had."

Autumn stuck a straw into her drink and took a long slurp. "Adoption isn't as cool as having the parents you are born to. I don't resemble my adoptive parents, nor act like them, nor did I inherit any of their talents. We were strangers living in the same house."

"Do you even remember your birth mom?"

"Nah, I wasn't even a year old when I got swiped from her arms and given to Evert and Jasmine Kirmis." She pulled a vacant chair next to hers and propped her legs upon it. "I had no say in the matter."

"Did any of us get to express our opinion as to what family we'd prefer to be born into?" Marlene questioned. "Seems like you might have gotten the cream of the crop in your adoptive home by what you've told me."

"Marlene, you can't possibly understand having never had to leave your birth family. I feel like an orphan."

It was quiet for a moment, Marlene carefully picking up each bread crumb on the table with the tip of her finger, shaking it into the paper wrapper.

Finally, Marlene broke the interlude. "I have. I grew up being carted from one foster home to the next with in-between stops back at my mom's until she'd mess up again, and I'd be plopped back into social services. That is, until I turned twelve. I got my dream family then, the best foster family of all. I told my social worker that if she forced me to go back to my mom one more time, I would run away where nobody could find me. She didn't. I stayed with the Jensens until I graduated from high school. Then they helped get me set up in business school."

Autumn's stare cemented itself to Marlene's experienced countenance. Marlene could see she had all of Autumn's attention.

"You may not have had a choice to whom you were born, but your adoptive parents did have a choice. They chose you and your brother. They chose to give you their name, their spare bedroom, their attention, their love. You could have been one of the little kids we see running the streets, instead you were in a safe haven, well cared for by two adults who wanted to be parents. More than anything else, they wanted to be your parents."

No one had been this blunt with Autumn before. She had always recited her way of thinking to acquaintances, painting a grotesque picture of her own adoption. She wasn't sure if she liked Marlene's ability to read through the lines and cut through the emotions Autumn had sealed up tightly within her.

A Caucasian couple came through the glass door, with three children in tow—one white, one dark with curly knotted hair, and a third with slanted eyes. "Mommy, can we eat in Playplace?" the child's voice pleaded, pointing to the children's area sealed off on the left side of the restaurant.

Crushing the paper cup, Autumn stood up. "It's back to work."

Chapter 27

Propped up in bed with her journal in her lap, Jasmine bit on the end of her pen, attempting to put her thoughts into words reliving the four-day weekend. Jacob, with his job, hadn't been able to make the long trip home for Thanksgiving, having been scheduled to work the Friday after the holiday. Jasmine had internally prepared for her first holiday without family, but even then, it hit hard. She had fought to keep her voice at an even tone, clenching her eyes shut to seal the floodgates as his voice came through the airwaves. "Sorry, Mom, but I'll be sure to get home for a few days at Christmas."

She continued to attend the weekly grief support sessions, maybe not as faithfully as at first, but enough to help her through new curves in the grieving process. One of the last sessions had been on family-centered holidays. How did loved ones left behind live through them? Chet Martin, with his dry sense of humor, confided, "You know, I could handle Ground Hog Day, St. Patrick's Day, and even Columbus Day on my own. But then, the big dogs would show up, Thanksgiving and Christmas. I, a grown man, diminished to the size of a Russian toy puppy, diving under my bed, to circle three times before hiding in the corner and counting the ticks on the clock until the day was over." His challenge was to forgo the pity party and instead orchestrate a symphony of one's own—a maestro with a personal baton.

Jasmine followed his advice. Cooking all the trimmings for a Thanksgiving feast, she filled the table with widows and widowers from the church in Elton, she again attended. The youngest guest had two decades on her, but they were a lively bunch, reminiscing, repeating old jokes, joshing each other. And they too added to the bounteous blessings of the day. Myrtle brought a jar of her home-pickled okra, and Sadie baked a German peach kuchen, a pastry Jasmine had never quite conquered. Ed unwrapped a woodworking project he had made in his shop, a Chinese checkerboard. He said he was mass-producing them so he could deal them out to his grandkids for Christmas. "Then they won't have a reason to be antisocial, pressing buttons on their handheld gadgets when they come to invade my food pantry." Everyone laughed and surmised what they could come up with for children of the latest generation. Karen and Ralph surprised the group by carting along their accordions and entertaining the guests by pumping out polka music and the old-fashioned hymns.

Before everyone departed in the late afternoon, Ruth had everyone sit down once more while she read the poem she'd written for the occasion. In a high shaking intonation, she shared her lines of rhyme.

> It took a lot of testing
> In my days of pain
> To teach me God sends rainbows
> To chase away the rain.
>
> Warmth is bound to follow frost
> As sunshine follows rain,
> There'll always be a healing
> After days of pain.
>
> If I will just kneel down in faith
> And seek the Lord above,

I know that God will heal me,
Because the rainbow proves His love.

Always after trying days
Comes the sweet refrain:
God will send His rainbows
And I'll be well again.

By: Ruth Buchholz

In her quiet mannerism, her blue eyes peered out from her crinkled skin, resting lovingly on each of them. "I'd like to thank you mightily, Jasmine, and all the rest of you, for giving me another rainbow to cherish. This day has been heavenly."

And Jasmine could say *amen* as well. A case of the blues had not ambushed the day by not having Evert, Jacob, or Autumn present. Nor had she shed tears stored up for self-commiseration.

Smiling to herself, she took that back. She had soaked a tissue at the punch line to one of Ed's jokes, one of those unstoppable belly whoppers where the tears fill buckets and the peals of laughter continue to convulse until everyone is in the same condition. A chuckle escaped as she recaptured the elderly man's witticism.

Jasmine had given to these kindly people by spending hours in the kitchen prior to their arrival, but in the end, they had bequeathed her with far more. Each, like her, had lost a spouse, but had moved on, not forgetting their beloved sweetheart and living a fulfilling life regardless, with their memories to pull out of their hearts and enjoy whenever they pleased.

Ding-dong, ding-dong. The two-tone doorbell cut through the gentle thoughts airborne above the white comforter of her bed. She jolted, dropping the notebook. It slid to the floor with a *thunk*. "Who in the world would come calling at this hour?"

Ding-dong, ding-dong. Flooding the front step with light, Jasmine peered out the side window. She was shocked to see the bundled up form of Cynthia Burns stomping her feet lightly.

"Is something wrong?" were the first words from Jasmine's mouth when she removed the obstruction between them, reaching her arms out to draw her friend into the warm room.

"Yes, no, everything. I'm sorry for coming this late, but I had to talk to you before we were surrounded by a cornfield of ears." Cynthia appeared to be bone-tired and terribly distraught.

"Come, sit with me," Jasmine invited. "Can I take your coat?" Jasmine didn't know what had happened, but a least Cynthia had returned from Las Vegas and alluded to being at school tomorrow. Both positive.

Shaking her head, Cynthia literally sagged onto the cushions, her shoulders slumped, her lips pulled down. "I have been incredibly stupid. An outrageous, selfish half-wit!" Her hands flew to her face, covering her eyes; her fingertips massaged her forehead then slunk to her cheekbones.

Finally, seeking Jasmine's eye contact, Cynthia slowly shook her head in bewilderment. "I have hurt my family incredibly and myself along with them. They may not ever talk to me again. What an embarrassment I have become." Cynthia was not out of control in bemoaning her actions. She'd had a plane ride back to North Dakota to think everything through. She was simply stating the facts.

Jasmine couldn't stop herself from asking, "Did Roger hurt you, Cynthia?"

Once more, she shook her head, but her eyes fell. "It was wonderful at first. We met for supper at the Paris Hotel and Casino. I'd never seen anything like it, rich and extravagant. We took a glass elevator to the top. Can you imagine?" She turned to Jasmine with eyes wide. "The doors opened onto an exquisite kitchen, all out in the open. In the dining area, the windows extended from floor to ceiling. Roger had reserved choice seats by the windows. Outside, our view overlooked the Bellagio fountains. Every fifteen minutes, the water show was repeated. It was ecstatic. For this Dakota lady, used to a hamburger joint, my mouth hung askew. That must have been Roger's first clue at how unsophisticated I was."

Jasmine didn't have to ask questions. Cynthia was unloading her heart one chip after the next, the way Jasmine had done with Joel. Cynthia essentially needed her to listen, not to act as a judge. "Roger was a perfect gentleman, catering to me like I was the queen of England—his hand at my elbow, pulling out the chair, acting as a tour guide, explaining the menu, the sites, listening to every word I said as if it was so profound, he wanted it etched into his memory."

"I was blown away by it all—the atmosphere, the meal, the handsome man. I was a goner, Jasmine. Afterward, we attended a show on the Strip, and then dancing. I'm not much to whistle at on the dance floor, but Roger held me and moved me in twirls and then back to his cheek. It was the most romantic night of my entire life."

She paused, as if debating whether to continue. "We went back to the motel. I knew before I stepped on the plane, that the motel room would be part of the adventure. And I went prepared, nightie and all." She swallowed. "But when he put his hand to my back, guiding me down the hallway, I got all flustered and couldn't continue. I apologized and said I wasn't ready. I felt like a pimple-faced schoolgirl on her first date. He was so nice about it, understanding, agreeing we had just met. He backtracked to the desk and rented me a separate room."

Fidgeting, Cynthia wriggled off the couch and paced the floor. "The following day was another page out of a fairy-tale book. Although Roger has been to Las Vegas a zillion times, he was excited about showing a first-time visitor the city. We took in a couple of shows, ate seafood at Emeril's New Orleans Fish House, explored the casinos, and walked the Strip. Dusk was settling on the city, although it was hard to tell with its billions of lights. We were strolling down the Strip, my hand meshed into his, falling in love, when his cell phone rang. It wasn't the first phone call he'd taken in my presence. Roger's a broker for a large financial company. But this call was different. Listening in on one side of the conversation, it was obvious it was family on the other end. He finished the call with, "I love you. Give my love to the kids." Abruptly, her pacing ended in front of Autumn.

Her voice became grim. "Autumn, he never told me he was married and had a family at home. In all the exchange we did online, he never once alluded to a wife. And he lied to his wife through the whole phone conversation. He wasn't attending any business meetings. He hadn't met with any stockbrokers, nor had he worked into the night on Thanksgiving like he led her to believe. Anyway, what company would ever schedule a conference on a holiday?

"When I asked him if it was his wife, he readily admitted it, and in the next breath, was telling me he couldn't wait to show me his favorite nightclub. Like it was no big deal. He was actually taken back when I nailed him about his honesty. He said I was married too, so we were even. How could I shoot bullets at him for the same offense I was committing? And I was, but at least I told him up-front." Listening to her own words, Cynthia amended her defense. "I was as guilty as he was."

"It suddenly all seemed morbidly disgraceful, playing with somebody else's spouse. I felt absolutely filthy. I can't even put it into words, like bugs crawling under my skin sucking up my blood. When I said I thought I should return home, he didn't argue. He left me standing on the sidewalk. I spent Saturday crying in the motel room, and today, I flew back into Fargo. Just got into town."

Having reached the end of her story, she collapsed on the couch, her head flung back on the cushion. "What must God think of me? Or Katie? Or ever faithful Kevin?" Even as tough as Cynthia was, her eyes glistened, wishing she could sprinkle some dust to make the past month vanish.

Figuring the story had come to a completion, Jasmine stepped in. "I'd say you created quite a stir in heaven."

"Yah, I'm sure. God's probably sharpening up His arrows to strike me dead." Cynthia closed her eyes.

"Reread the parable about the lost lamb. It says there is more rejoicing in heaven over the repentance of one sinner than in ninety-nine righteous people who do not need to ask for forgiveness."

"Really." Cynthia didn't ask it as a question. "Sounds like I'll be spending what's left of the night on my knees."

Sliding over to embrace her friend, Jasmine too was rejoicing with all the angels singing above to have her friend back in the sheepfold. They were quiet for a full minute, letting the threads of their estranged friendship weave themselves back into a strong tapestry.

"Kevin. What about Kevin? Do you think he'll take me back?" Cynthia rolled her head toward Jasmine.

"He's a good man. He's hurting gravely," Jasmine murmured. "So is Katie."

"And it's all my fault." She moaned.

"Get things right with God first. Then I have a hunch He'll go with you to right the next blunder." Jasmine patted her hand.

"Jasmine, this is changing the subject, but your daughter is insane for blackballing you. You are the first person I thought of when I got back into town, the only one who'd listen to me even after what I did." She gave Jasmine one more fierce hug then struggled upright. "I'll be seeing you first thing tomorrow. Love you, my friend." And she was gone.

The transformation from Thanksgiving to Christmas on the school calendar begins immediately on the Monday following the Thanksgiving feasts. Paper turkeys, black-hatted pilgrims, and feathered Native Americans are pulled off the bulletin boards and hallway walls, making room for the tinsel and sparkle of evergreen trees, wreaths, and colored lights. An air of excitement, of expectation, floods the learning environment for children of all ages, for even though they may not be acquainted with the birth of Jesus, they all do know about presents.

Jasmine was among them. This would be her fifth holiday season since Evert died. There was still a hollowness within her, but she had overcome the initial onslaught of grief. With the success of the Thanksgiving Day celebration, she meant to carry it over to Christ's birthday, now and for every succeeding year to come.

Cynthia and Jasmine were erecting an artificial tree in the corridor between their two rooms. "Wanna give me a hand with these strings of lights?" Cynthia asked her partner. "They certainly seem to have tangled with each other since we packed them away so methodically last January."

"Some elves must have gotten into the box," Jasmine surmised, going to work.

"I'm going over to see Kevin after supper tonight," Cynthia confided, pulling a string through a loop.

Jasmine looked up. "Good. I'm praying for you both."

"It's funny. I'm more anxious about this meeting than the one I went all the way to Las Vegas to keep."

Jasmine continued to work with her hands.

"Guess maybe because this one is more important, more resting on it—like twenty-eight years of marriage," Cynthia validated quietly. "I don't want to live without Kevin."

After giving the string one more twist, the lights lay out in a lengthy rope. Beginning at the top, Jasmine started wrapping it around the tree.

"I text messaged Katie at noon. We're going to go out to Naomi's Diner tomorrow after school. I feel like she's become the parent and I'm the repentant child."

"Humility doesn't seem to come naturally for any of us," Jasmine vouched. "Healing begins with repentance and then forgiveness." The lights continued to bring life to the manufactured tree as each ring of lights circled the branches until it reached the bottom.

Standing back, Cynthia commented, "It's beautiful, even without adding any other decorations."

"Where's the ornament for the top?" Jasmine asked. "It needs the star,"

"It must still be in the packing box on my desk. I need the star more than the tree does—to find my way back." Cynthia was in a contemplating mood.

"I'll get it," Jasmine volunteered, hopping up from her knees. Walking through the maze of miniature desks pulled into pods of three, Jasmine's eyes were drawn to the teacher's desk. She noted the fall arrangement of flowers was gone, but the red roses remained, drooping, yet still a vibrant crimson. Some of the fragile petals had fallen to the desktop as if strewn by a flower girl in anticipation of a bride fitting her hand into the fingers of her beloved groom. Jasmine ruefully wondered how Cynthia could stomach looking at the arrangement after the fiasco with Roger. She would have gained satisfaction from stuffing them in the garbage bag fastened to the janitor's cleaning cart.

Having reached the desk, Jasmine dug into the storage box for the jeweled star, glancing once more at the roses fading silently beside it. Her eyes landed on the card clipped to the plastic holder amongst the wilted flowers. Unsheathed from its envelope, the words were clearly visible to any observer. "I will always love you. Kevin." They were written in Kevin's uneven scrawl.

Suddenly, the dying blossoms took on a delicate elegance of heavenly origin, heralding young love weathering the tumults of life.

Later, when the decorations had all been hung, taped, and pinned in place, and Cynthia had gone to her apartment to harness her nerves before facing Kevin, Jasmine sat down at her computer. There was no one waiting at her front steps; she could finish up here first. She had the daily student grades to enter into PowerSchool and some parental e-mails to send out on individual students.

Her fingers flew across the keys, making short work of the updates. Scanning her list of contacts for the final parent's e-mail address, she skimmed past Joel Linton's URL, still in the listing from when Carson had been on her roster. A few seconds later, however, she found herself scrolling back to it again.

On impulse, she hit New Message and tapped in his e-mail address. They hadn't visited since the adoption celebration almost a month ago, but their discussion on the dark roadway had hung on the edges of her thoughts continually. It was his counsel that had enabled her to sever the last chord holding her back from releasing her daughter to God. Her heart had been noticeably lighter ever since.

> Joel,
>
> I did it.
>
> > Jasmine

An inner assurance told her he would understand exactly what she had done.

Deliberately, Carson dunked the bloated marshmallows below the foamy surface of the sea of hot chocolate with a teaspoon. He, Joel, and Jasmine took up three sides of a square table at Naomi's Diner, enjoying hot chocolate after the annual school Christmas concert.

Besides singing the traditional carols with the rest of the students mounted on the semicircle of tiered risers, Carson's debut onto Broadway had consisted of wearing a headband of antlers and a bright cherry nose as he led the other eight reindeer prancing through the aisle of chairs set up on the gymnasium floor pulling Santa's sleigh. His forty-five second public premiere didn't seem to have inflated his ego.

When the crowd had lifted to its feet in steady applause after the grand finale, the rows of performers had filed out of the gym to their homerooms, where their parents could readily retrieve them. After claiming Carson, Joel took him by the hand, leading him through the packed hallways to Jasmine's classroom.

It had been with great pleasure he had read Jasmine's short e-mail after Thanksgiving, but other than replying with a few congratulatory words, they had not spoken. Tonight, he had decided to purposefully attempt to change that. Last spring, he had asked her twice to accompany him on an outing, but on both occasions, she had very politely, yet firmly declined. He wasn't sure where he stood with her. If he again received the soft kick of her toed heels in the rear, he'd accept defeat.

She was standing outside her classroom door, always a picture of loveliness, attired in a wine-colored dress, her chestnut hair curled to lay on her shoulders. Parents and children streamed in and out of the room. Unconsciously, Joel felt himself grip Carson's hand tighter. The boy winced and tugged his hand loose of his father's grip. "I'm not going anywhere, Dad."

Realizing what he'd done, Joel smirked, roughing up the blond head of hair at his elbow. "Sorry, buddy."

"Hey, there's Mrs. Kirmis!" Carson squirmed forward. Joel could always depend on Carson to break the ice for him.

Jasmine had seen him coming and welcomed the hearty hug, forcing her to take a step backward to maintain her balance. "If it isn't Rudolph!" she exclaimed. Then looking up at Joel two steps behind him, she added, "and Santa Claus!"

"He's not Santa, Mrs. Kirmis. He's my dad." Carson exclaimed as if Jasmine had forgotten the man with the gray eyes and gentle grin.

"You're right, Carson, and he's way better than any fat old man in a red suit." She met Joel's look above the straw-headed child. During the performance, she had tried to inconspicuously scan the bleachers on each side of the gym to pinpoint Joel's seat. As if by some magnetic force, she had found him, only to discover his gaze locked on hers. Quickly lowering her seemingly daring gawk, she kept her attention on the music director at the front of the room for the duration of the concert.

Joel fumbled with the words of an off-the-cuff invitation for Mrs. Kirmis to join them for ice cream or coffee or something, wanting it to sound nonchalant, nothing heavy or imposing, like he'd just thought of it. His mind went blank. He was willing to risk walking the plank and being decapitated by a shark; however, it would be nice to have something to say.

"Dad, can we get some hot chocolate before we go home and take Mrs. Kirmis too?" Carson's blue eyes pleaded. Unknowingly, the rascal had done the deed for the relieved farmer.

"Sure, that's a great idea—if she wants to be seen with likes of us." Joel winked first at Carson and then at Jasmine.

"Of course you do, don't you, Mrs. Kirmis?" When she nodded in merriment, he added, "See, Dad, I knew she liked us." The laughter stripped away the nervous timidity of the adults.

Now they relaxed at the diner, sharing conversation and chocolate. Carson continued to drop the marshmallows the waitress had supplied into his diminishing liquid. With the bottom of his mug tipped toward the ceiling, his tongue hooked the last melting lumps. Setting down the cup, he noticed a classmate with a grandparent sitting at another table across the room. "Can I go say hi to Brady?" Joel nodded in approval; the boy skipped away.

"What a whirlwind!" Jasmine teased. The lad was already moving in on the table of his friend.

"Yeah, no dust settles in our house. He creates a constant draft of up currents. And it suits me just fine." Joel's eyes rested on the thin boy, love radiating from his irises.

"You two are something all right," Jasmine approved. She raised her mug for another sweet swallow.

"How was your Thanksgiving? Was Jacob home?" Joel knew better than to ask about Autumn.

Shaking her head no, but at the same time verbalizing the opposite, she burst out, "It was heavenly, just what I needed." And she described the elderly people who had composed her guest list and how each one had given her a gift of the heart.

His eyes softened as he listened to her narration of the food they'd eaten, the jokes they'd cracked, and the camaraderie they'd shared in losing a mate.

"I never thought I'd feel as whole again as I did enfolded in their love for the past, with their lives equally fulfilled in the present." She was quiet for a moment and then realized she was monopolizing the exchange. "How did you and Carson spend the day?"

"Ed and Arlene Bautz are neighbors of ours. Maybe you met them at the adoption party. Arlene has been a godsend in taking care of Carson whenever my farming habits interfere with child rearing. They included us at their spread." Joel filled her in on the details.

"And next is Christmas." Joel no longer worried about the holidays. He had made peace with them. Although Jasmine had survived Thanksgiving, he wondered if she was ready for the next one.

"Yup, Chet Martin from my grief support group calls these two holidays the big dogs in the calendar of family events. I've prayed about this and have already come up with my Yuletide plan."

"You have?" Joel asked, a bit surprised. "Care to expound?" The waitress intervened, refilling their cocoa cups.

"I'm going to create an anonymous Christmas for two needy families who have children in our school. One is a two-parent family with five kids, and the other, a single gal with three youngsters. Both in need financially, and in my estimation, spiritually."

"So exactly how are you going to bring this about?" She had hooked Joel's interest.

"For starters, I'm going shopping. I have a pretty good estimation of what sizes they all would wear, parents included. Plus kids deserve some fun things, games toys, movies. And then I want to put together a box of canned and frozen goods for the makings of a Christmas meal. I'll add a big tin of an assortment of my own homemade cookies and candies. That'll take care of the physical needs, but I'd like to ensure the real story of Jesus our Savior coming down to earth as a baby would also be a part of the package."

Joel guessed, "So you're putting in a video of the nativity story."

"Hmmmm. You know, that's not a bad idea. Maybe I will. But I also thought I would stop at each of the five churches in Elton and ask for a program flier of their upcoming Christmas pageant. Usually, they have them on Christmas Eve or the Sunday prior to the actual date, and I'd stick them in the box along with all the other goodies, hoping they might be obliged to attend one of the performances. What do you think?" Jasmine clasped her hands together on the tabletop, pressing her thumbs against each other.

"I like it. Especially the church program part. Every child deserves the chance to hear the real message of Christmas, the message of hope." Joel was intrigued by her shining eyes. "You are a remarkable woman. How can I help?"

"There is one detail I'm not sure how to complete. How do I make this anonymous and at the same time not make the family feel like they're a charity case being signaled out for a write-up in the newspaper? I can hardly deposit the boxes on their step, ring the doorbell, and make a fast getaway." Her eyebrows lowered in contemplation.

Lost in thought for a moment, Joel released his idea. "Maybe I could use my truck and act as a delivery service. You know, clipboard and pen, a uniform of sorts. Something like the UPS man or the postal service."

"You'd do that?" Her eyebrows bounced up to her hairline. "I have a box of hats in my classroom I use with the kids when we study careers. There's one that is flat on top with a hard brim, like a cop wore in the old movies."

"Ah, a Barney Fife off the old Andy Griffin Show. He was rather an inept deputy. I could easily play the part of an inept delivery boy."

Jasmine convulsed into a burst of chortles at the image Joel painted. "Better yet, you could be a pizza deliveryman. Everyone likes to see the pizza boy come."

Chuckles eased up Joel's throat as well. "I think I'll stick with Barney. We'd have more in common. Besides being losers, we're both old."

Jasmine's hands clapped together at the preposterous scene, laughter continuing to well up within her. "Stop, stop," she choked out. Finally letting the bubbles fade, they faced each other, pleased to be partners in a Christmas scheme.

"It isn't that long until Christmas. You' better get hopping," Joel reminded her. "And I have the solution."

"You do, huh?" Jasmine eyed him with amusement.

"Yup. This Saturday, you accept my offer to go shopping in Norbert. We'll pack the carts with everything you deem necessary for this Christmas extravaganza. After which, we will dine at a restaurant of your choice and then take in the Singing Christmas Tree performance done by one of the churches." He had begun his proposal by holding her green eyes in his. But as his invitation lengthened, he found himself glancing away, fearful she might again refuse his gesture of friendship.

"You'd do all of this for me?" she asked softly, bringing his gaze back into hers.

"I would be utterly honored to spend the day in your company." He wasn't smiling. He was dead serious as he waited for her answer. His heart stopped in midtick, waiting with him.

"Thank you. I would like that very much."

"You would?" It was almost as if he couldn't believe his ears.

"I would."

A grin stretched across his clean-shaven face at her affirmation. And it was still there, after he and Carson drove the twenty miles home.

Chapter 28

If ever a day had been packed to the brim, it was that Saturday. After feeding hay and ground grain to his herd of cattle and then dropping Carson off at the Bautz farm, Joel picked up Jasmine at noon. Norbert was an hour's distance away. Although the landscape was hidden under a blanket of snow, the roads were clear and free of ice.

Jasmine knew time would be of essence if they wished to accomplish everything Joel had outlined. Therefore, she wrote up an exact listing of their shopping needs and divided the items into a second list of the stores where they might most readily be purchased.

It had been an exhilarating, hilarious race from store to store, piling the carts high and then trying to pack it all carefully into the confines of the locked utility box on the back of Joel's pickup truck. They had purchased everything from a baby's onesies to a teenager's pajama pants, a crib's musical mobile to girl's ice skates, mittens and caps, snow pants and frilly dresses, socks galore, games and toys, frozen turkeys and canned goods. And a whole lot more. The conniving elves pushed buttons, cranked windups, pulled strings, licked taste testers, listened through earphones, snapped, buttoned, and zippered as they chose the right toy, size, and style for each person on their mystery list. Who would have guessed it would be such a blast to give, never expecting the receiver to give in return?

They were thrilled to be in each other's company on a joint mission. Over a tender beefsteak and salad, they rechecked their lists, reassured they hadn't left anything out.

"You could be a contestant on one of those game shows where the contender has to see how much she can throw into a shopping cart in a set number of minutes. You'd be a whiz," Joel teased the green-eyed lady.

"Once, when I saw that show, they were in a grocery store. I yelled at the lady through the screen to head to the high-priced meat and cheese department first, but she wasted her time in the pasta aisle," Jasmine admitted.

"Maybe she was Italian," Joel quipped.

"Maybe, but it would still be nice to have some meat sauce on those noodles," Jasmine returned, slicing a piece off her steak. "At that time, Autumn was a baby. Next, I would have streaked to the formula and diaper shelves. Those are rather untouchable without a coupon."

"Never had the chance to buy any of those," Joel regaled.

"Oh, I'm sorry," Jasmine was immediately contrite. "I forget you became a father to a six-year-old."

"It's okay. The thought of changing smelly diapers doesn't exactly thrill me."

Jasmine smiled. "Yes, well, they do eventually grow out of that stage."

Refilling his water glass from the pitcher on the table, Joel reflected, "Do you realize we have to unload all of the stuff packed with such precision in my truck when we get back to your house?"

"And then, once it is wrapped in Christmas paper and sorted out between the two families, it all has to be loaded up again for delivery! It's not easy working at the North Pole," Jasmine grinned.

"That will be next weekend's job. We want the boxes delivered before Sunday night in case one of the local Christmas programs is scheduled for that night." Joel reminded her.

"I'll get the cookies baked after school this week."

"Do you want help with the wrapping and sorting?" Joel asked, not sure if she still wanted him in on this lark.

"You better believe you're going to help. And Carson too."

They finished up the meal and then progressed to the Singing Christmas Tree concert. Heavenly carols, sung by a group of carolers on the front sidewalk, met them out in the parking lot. The smell of evergreen was heavy as they were ushered into their seats. On the front platform, a huge wooden tree had been constructed consisting of eight tapering tiers. A staircase connected the levels. Evergreen boughs festooned the railings of each row, giving the structure the appearance of a Christmas tree.

Spectators waited quietly for the performance to begin, humming to the piped-in music during the intervening minutes. Jasmine whispered to Joel in hushed tones, not wanting to break the sacred mood. He strained to hear her soft words but missed them. Laying his arm on the back of the pew around her shoulders, he leaned his ear closer to her lips.

"Isn't this a lovely setting?" she repeated.

He nodded and left his arm about her. She nestled in closer to his side.

The members of the choir entered from the back of the auditorium, filing down the three aisles to the front platform singing,

> It came upon the midnight clear,
> That glorious song of old,
> From angels bending near the earth,
> To touch their harps of gold.

Verse after verse rolled off their lips. Jasmine felt as if she was surrounded by angels lifting her up to the heavenly throne.

When the first carol drew to a close, the strains of "O Little Town of Bethlehem" took over. The choir members continued to harmonize as they mounted the stairway, filing into each tier of the Christmas tree and then facing forward. Each wore a large battery lit star as a headband over the forehead. When the last member took his spot at the very peak of the tree, his star being much larger than the others, the combination of stars and greenery truly envisioned a twinkling tree.

A deep male voice vibrated through the sanctuary, narrating the story of Jesus's birth, interspersed with melodies from the choir. Jasmine was spellbound as the Bible story unfolded. The account ended with the refrains of "Joy to the World" pealing across the spacious room as the choir members descended from the tree and took up positions in the aisles, along the walls, and in front of the audience. With one last song of quiet appeal, "Let There Be Peace on Earth" filled the hearts of the listeners.

But the performance hadn't ended. On a side stage, a drama unfolded as the singers departed. Against a completely white backdrop, a disheveled man attired in shades of gray, with ragged clothing, wild hair, and an unshaven face, bent over double as he dragged himself to the center spotlight. Attached to his right ankle was an iron cuff welded to a linked chain and an oppressive iron ball. Black wary eyes, too large for the woeful man's scrawny face, scrutinized those in attendance with distrust. Each step he took, he bent his back against the weight of the cumbersome ball and chain painfully hauling them with him.

The contrast of gray against the filmy white background was enhanced by oversized black boxes sitting here and there on the stage floor. They resembled bulky presents, except for their drab coloring, and the wires and ropes tied about them in place of decorative ribbons. Winded by the exertion of patrolling himself even a few steps, the man collapsed upon one of the receptacles, resting his arms on his legs, his head bent downward.

Suddenly, an exquisite angel in a gown of shimmering white swept in carrying a glittering box wrapped in all the colors of the rainbow, a rich bow festooned to the top. She offered the gift to the disheartened man, but he shook his head in rejection. She lifted the lid, and love permeated the air above the open container. Colorful swatches of lights swarmed below the ceiling. Again, she held the fancy case out to the man. Once more, he shook his head, pivoting his body away from the heavenly being. After pantomiming the act of snatching back the colored light rays of love she had poured out, the angel set the lid on the box and fluttered away.

A second, third, and fourth angel followed in succession, each bearing a shimmering treasure to offer the man. As he had done with love, the man rejected hope, joy, and peace. A destitute man too blind to see he was in the midst of God's genuine gifts.

When the angelic figures deserted the man, leaving him to his misery, he cumbersomely opened each of the bleak ugly boxes surrounding him. The opened lids released failure, Godlessness, hatred, and guilt. He caressed each character trait, languishing in its familiarity. It was all he knew.

Oblivious to those sitting near her, Jasmine's attention was immersed in the pitiful example of mankind before her. When guilt escaped the confines of the wooden enclosure, a tightening occurred within her, shrinking her insides away from her ribcage. Guilt kept company with her also, like a ball and chain holding her back from freedom.

Although she had released Autumn to the Lord's will, she had still chosen to shroud herself in guilt for the parenting job she had performed. Had she been a better mother, she and her daughter would have had a closer relationship, one which wouldn't have become severed by the storms of the teenage season.

And then Jasmine hadn't been able to shake the consuming blame too, first initiated by Autumn and then nursed by herself as being a key player in Evert's death. Frequently, she wished she could redo the decision she had made against attending the construction show and instead say, "Yes, yes, Evert. I would love to go to the show with you." But she hadn't. Guilt.

Her attention drawn back to the stage, she witnessed the man slumping to the floor, the weighted pressure of his burdens overpowering him. In hopeless distress, he was unaware of the man in white's approach. In fact, it took a second for Jasmine to notice the spotless figure, as he blended in with the stage setting, only his dark hair and beard were a contrast to the white background, and his gentle smile. He carried a gift swathed in white.

Gesturing to the man at his feet, he made it known he wanted the man to open the gift. At first, the outcast refused, fervently shaking his head. Patiently, the man in white waited until finally, a gray arm reached up and pulled the white ribbon loose. The gift tumbled open, pouring out a red film covering the man's head and gray clothing. In awe, the man recognized Jesus, his Savior.

Almost magically, stagehands whisked the black boxes off the stage and helped the forgiven man peel the dark clothing off his body, revealing snow-bleached attire underneath. The four previous angels returned, dumping their gifts of love, hope, joy, and peace while the technician at the electrical box flipped the switch for the rainbow of colors to once more glitter the stage. It was breathtaking—its message of redemption complete.

There, in the straight-backed church pew, with Joel's arm holding her safely against his side, and the strains of "Amazing Grace" whispering through the church, Jasmine closed her eyes and silently thanked God again for sending His Son to wash away her sins and for lifting the burdens she insisted on clinging to, namely guilt. He reached out of heaven, sweeping out the debilitating transgressions from within her. Jasmine's insides relaxed, meshing back against her ribs.

Looking up at Joel, he saw her misted eyes and perceived God had somehow moved within her, bestowing His unfathomable intimate touch. Drawing this woman of faith tighter against him,

Joel's lips brushed the side of her forehead, exceedingly grateful to his great and loving God for allowing them to experience this night together.

∽∂᠖∾

"Yes, the red-and-white Santa hat is loads better than the Barney Fife reincarnation." Jasmine grinned at the sheepish man before her switching hats back and forth for her to get the effect. "Anyway, it's the holiday season in Elton, not *Mayberry R.F.D.*

"My sentiments exactly," Joel responded, tossing the sheriff's hat onto her sofa.

"Why can't you wear your farmer's elevator cap?" Carson asked from his vantage point propped up on stool at the kitchen counter. "It looks more like you."

"That's the problem. I'm supposed to be going incognito." Joel winked at his son.

Carson shrugged. "Whatever that means. Can I go too?" A burst of anticipation lit his blue eyes.

"Sorry, buster. Everyone knows you from school. Me? I'm just an ordinary old man." Joel pointed at himself. "Anyway, you and Mrs. Kirmis have to stay right here and pray I don't mess up my first job as a delivery man."

Jasmine reached for Carson's slim shoulders, "More importantly, we have to warm the apple cider and prepare the sandwiches for his return."

With a clipboard and pen in hand, Joel made his exit, boisterously imparting a final "Merry Christmas to all, and to all, a good night." They watched from the window as he tramped to his pickup truck and got in.

Shaking her head, Jasmine smiled, wondering whether he regretted getting hooked into her brainstorm. It sure had been fun though. The three of them had spent most of the afternoon wrapping and labeling presents and sorting gifts and food items into the appropriate boxes. Carson had taken it upon himself to wrap a miniature motorcycle for a boy on the list. At one point, Joel had to run Carson over to the church they attended in Elton for a final practice for his pageant on Sunday night. Carson's role was that of a shepherd. It was his job to keep two wee preschool lambs in place by the manger. Upon his return, he reported, "I just gave up. They wanted to baaa all over the place." She and Joel had a good chuckle.

When the sounds of his truck returned, both Jasmine and Carson were excited to hear his report. Carson got to the door first, flinging it open before Joel had a chance to turn the knob. "Did the little boy like the toy motorcycle?"

Joel didn't answer. There was almost a tender glow about his face. He leaned against the wall, fighting for the right words.

"Didn't he like it, Dad? I thought it was cool," Carson insisted. He pulled on Joel's coat sleeve. Mechanically, Joel removed his Santa hat and placed it on his son's head, tugging it down over his ears.

Not sure what Joel's quiet demeanor meant, Jasmine sensed something had gone wrong. Maybe the people were offended and refused to take the gifts. Or maybe they were rude to Joel, or possibly, they didn't embrace the tradition of exchanging gifts.

Meeting Joel's eyes, she couldn't define what it was they held. It was like he had witnessed a catastrophic event they had missed.

Finally, his voice came, low and wondrous. "I am sorry I agreed to act as the middleman for you."

Jasmine rushed to take the blame. "You're right, Joel. It was my whimsical notion to give some families a Christmas they may not otherwise have had. I shouldn't have snagged you into my idiotic scheme and then, of all things, forced you to act as the dispatcher for Mrs. Goody Two-shoes. I—"

Joel held up a hand to stop her and then reached for her hand and Carson's, enfolding both of them into his loose embrace.

"Let me finish. I'm sorry the two of you didn't get to experience what I did. The astonishment on the faces of the recipients was unbelievably real. They couldn't believe anyone would have sent them such abundance. The man said I must have the wrong address, but when I asked him if he lived at 227 Wild Oak Lane, he admitted it was the place. His wife's face was wet. At the single mom's apartment, she asked who her benefactor was. I told her my job was only in the delivery department and she would have to contact my superior for such information. Fortunately, she didn't ask for a name.

"I've never seen such unabashed gratitude from people before. They realized their children had little, and now it was like I had brought them the miracle they hadn't dared to hope for. They thanked me over and over again, wishing me a merry Christmas. And I was just the delivery boy."

His forehead met Jasmine's forehead. "I wish you could have seen the joy you brought to these people for yourself." Jasmine's heart swelled. God had used them to brighten someone's holiday. She hoped the two families would bring their children to at least one of the nativity programs to hear the real message God brought at Christmas.

Her head found his shoulder, and her arm encircled his waist, the other drawing Carson in tighter against them both.

"And my second wish is," his words dropping quietly into her ear, "that I had another delivery to make."

Leaning back to look up at him, Jasmine smiled. "I wonder if God felt this way on Christmas morning after sending His Son to earth as a gift for all mankind."

An expectant contemplation fell upon them until it was broken by Carson's unanswered question. "You didn't tell me, did the boy like the motorcycle or not?"

Chapter 29

It was to Marlene that Autumn dissolved her deep dark secret. Well, not exactly deep. In a few weeks, anyone who so much as looked at her would see the obvious. Had Autumn had a choice, she would have chosen sweet Magnolia as the first confidant of her tale. But being that Merl was, in a manner of speaking, Magnolia's boyfriend first, she could hardly confide in her by saying, "By the way, Merl and I are expecting a baby."

That left Marlene, who had once referred to Autumn's life as a soap opera serial, as the initial recipient.

"Ah, the plot thickens." Marlene squirted ketchup on her burger, replaced the top of the bun, and bit into America's sandwich of choice.

"Yeah, I'm a real heroine." Autumn took a swig of milk and then recapped the individual-sized jug.

"How are you doing?" Marlene eyed her closely. "Are you okay with this pregnancy?"

Contemplating the question, Autumn's face softened. "Yeah, I'm okay."

"When's the baby due?"

"August." Autumn rubbed an apple on her thigh until it shone, unconsciously allowing her other hand to rest on her stomach.

"You've been holding out on me." Marlene set the hamburger down and reached for a french fry. "That would make you about three months along. You'll be showing soon."

"I had to get used to the idea myself first. Whether I could do this or not. I've never been a mama before." Her voice lowered. "It's kind of scary." Her front teeth gnawed a white spot into the apple peeling.

"Any morning sickness?"

"The first six weeks were horrible. I thought I had the flu, only it didn't go away. I felt different on the inside too. Made me suspect I was in the motherly way. The pregnancy test confirmed it."

"You hid it right well." Marlene picked up the burger again.

Autumn smiled wryly. "Actually, I was afraid you'd catch on by all the trips I made to the restroom. It's better now. But I resolved, when the test strip showed positive, that I would be the best mother ever from that day forward."

"I take it the milk and apple are part of your resolution?" Marlene struck a face at the greasy french fries she was inhaling.

"You bet. No caffeine or alcohol. Lots of fruits, vegetables, lean meats, and milk. And I'll have you know, I haven't puffed on a marijuana joint in three months."

"Bravo, young lady. You are taking this seriously."

"Guess I learned a few things in school." Autumn gave her a saucy grin then sobered. "I may have done a lot wrong in my life, however, this I want to do right."

"I'll coach you through the trimesters. I've done the motherhood gamut twice. Should count for something." Pushing the french fries aside, she boasted, "You might even be an influence on my diet!"

Having Marlene's backing, Autumn's confidence was bolstered.

"We can do this," she whispered to the tiny infant growing within her.

❧❦❧

Back when Magnolia and Autumn had met up after a year's parting, the physical deterioration of Magnolia's body was a decisive indicator she was hooked on something. Something bad. More than likely, something illegal. Having had more of her mom brush off on her than she'd like, Autumn's first response had been to *fix* her friend.

Contentedly propped on the trailer's seedy couch, which was missing its middle cushion, Magnolia and Autumn shared a half dozen open bottles of nail polish sitting in the depression between them. Reminiscent of two junior high girls at a slumber party, they had traded girl talk while stroking neon hues onto their toenails, tittering at the gaudy patterns bespeckling their toes. Moving to the fingernails, each painted the other's. "It's a whole lot easier than tryin' to put that polish on with my's left hand," Magnolia declared. "Lemme do yours first." Her tongue darted from her mouth to wet her dry lips, a perpetual habit she'd acquired of late. That and facial ticks.

Compliantly, Autumn held out her right hand. Using a turquoise polish on the thumb, Magnolia dipped the brush into the bottle and whisked nice even strokes over the nail. *How nice it was to have a friend to do silly things with*, Autumn thought. She studied Magnolia, who was curled over her hand to perform her best manicurist workmanship.

Magnolia's dusty hair, once such a shiny curly black mass, resembled an aged lady in a nursing home—thin, drab, without body. The rich skin of youth had shrunk to a web of unhealthy wrinkles, as if her body covering was too massive for her tiny frame. Even the dark hollows under her eyes had the semblance of a raccoon's mask, rather than a comely woman in her twenties.

"You's too quiet," Magnolia scolded. "You's have to talk while I paint." Holding up the applicator, she paused in her work. "I's know. Let's play To Tell the Truth. I ask you's a question and you's have to tell the truth. Then you's ask me one, and I'll tell you what you's want to know. Fair?"

Autumn nodded. "Sure, sounds fun."

Resuming her painting, Magnolia asked, "My first question is, if you's could have picked your own first name, what woulds it be instead of Autumn?"

"Gee, I hadn't expected a question like that." She leaned back into the flat cushion behind her to give it some thought. "I would have chosen Hannah."

"Hannah? You's don't look like no Hannah, maybe a Wanita or a Tiffany. How'd you pick that one?" She stuck the tip of her brush into the bottle of jack-o'-lantern orange.

"Hannah is a name from the Bible. My mom used to tell me this story about a woman who couldn't get pregnant. She begged God to give her a child. Finally, God granted her prayer, and she gave birth to a baby boy. But mom didn't like this Hannah much. I think it was because God answered her prayer, but not my mom's."

"So why's you want to be Hannah?"

"Just to exasperate my mom. A living reminder of her imperfection."

Magnolia shrugged, not quite understanding her friend's reasoning. "Okay, your turn."

Autumn was ready. "All right, little lady. Do you think Merl is handsome?" When Magnolia looked up at her with one eye squished shut, she laughed. "You have to tell the truth, Magnolia!"

"Okay. Handsome is not the correct word for him. He no wear fancy clothes or sweet-smellin' cologne. He's maybe not what some would call a hunk. Maybe *character* would be a good word. He maybe not so handsome, but he a good character in bed. Comprendo?" Her high-pitched giggles hit the stained ceiling.

Quieting down, she said, "My turn. What's the best job you ever had?" Magnolia reached for Autumn's left hand.

"Easy question. The one I have right now, McDonald's." Autumn didn't even have to think.

"What makes it so good?" On this hand, she started with hot pink.

"There's one older lady there that kind of fills in for my mom."

"I's thought you didn't like your mom. What'd you want another one for?" Magnolia shook her head, a grin sliding across her cheeks.

"Yeah, well. Sometimes, they come in handy. I'm next. Why won't Merl allow us to go in that locked door at the back of the trailer. What's he do in there?"

The lights in Magnolia's eyes were immediately extinguished. The iridescent bulbs burned out. "You's don't ask about that. It's none of our business." A layer of perspiration erupted on her gray forehead, giving off a subtle unpleasant odor.

"Hey, come on, fair is fair. You have to tell the truth." Autumn tried to cajole the information out of her, but the tiny lady was firm.

"Nope. You's want to see me skinned alive? I'd be dead." She jerked her chin downward in a "that's final" gesture.

"Okay, I take that one back. Here's a new one. Are you high on something?"

After sticking the brushes all back in the bottles of polish, Magnolia twisted them tightly. In a huff, she stood up, almost tripping over the debris at her feet. "You's too nosy. You's don't ask questions like that." Jerkily, she walked to the bedroom she shared with Merl and shut the door behind her. She'd shut down faster than a factory whose workers were on strike.

Magnolia's reaction only heightened Autumn's suspicions. Although the word *meth* had never been breathed within the four walls of this junk box, on the street, others had made reference to the drug and Merl in the same sentence. Whatever Magnolia was taking, it was done behind closed doors. Autumn wouldn't be surprised if there was a home methamphetamine lab operating right at the end of the hallway, but only hobby-sized. Merl's real infiltration was done in the world beyond their trailer house, filtered in from Washington, Denver, and Mexico. Autumn wondered if Magnolia was entrusted with any inside information. She strongly doubted it.

So much for helping Magnolia with a drug problem.

Autumn's traitorous body would eventually betray her condition. Baggy sweatshirts and jogging pants couldn't contain the concealed evidence much longer. Her secret had been hidden for over four months, but each day, she was twenty-four hours closer to being discovered.

Her long walks to work each day provided the exercise necessary to keep her growing body strong and in shape. During these lengthy jaunts, she would hold long-winded conversations with the little one forming inside her womb, divulging how much the wee one was already loved. She'd give glowing descriptions of the baby's father, how he would also be enamored by the precious infant as soon as he knew of its existence.

Sometimes, a church bell would peal from its high tower, licking the sky, resonating the rolling report across the cerulean heavens. Once, Autumn had detoured to find the building with its echoing gong. And she'd found it—a stately white clapboard church supporting a tall steeple reaching to the heavens.

Unlike the modern church architecture, with its sprawling buildings in every shape and color, this one reminded her of the country church her grandpa and grandma had attended called Goshen. Built in the land of plenty, similar to the Israelites living in Egypt, it was the focus of a farming community. Her mom and dad had been married there, the bell had sent its congratulatory strains across the countryside. When her grandparents had died, the bell had tolled once for each year of their long lives.

"Baby, this just might be our Goshen. Instead of it being surrounded by acres of emerald grass and fields of harvest, it will be our personal oasis in the middle of this vast city of pavement and traffic." Even though Autumn had not attended a church service since seeing North Dakota reflected in her rearview mirror, the thought made Minneapolis feel a bit more like home.

A creak of weight on the dilapidated wooden steps, a scrape of metal siding where the screen door fit unevenly, the dull thud on the torn linoleum floor when something heavy was dropped, followed by the raspy cough of a smoker—these were all signs Merl had entered the premises. Had there been a grandfather's clock to mark the hour, it would have chimed once or twice. Merl never returned before midnight. His "business" usually took him into the wee hours of the morning, if he came in at all.

After Magnolia's downward mood spiral, Autumn had finished painting her own nails, drunk a glass of milk, added the empty glass to the brimming sink of dirty dishes, and trudged to her own room. She was scheduled to work the 7:00 a.m. shift. After disentangling her bed covers, she crawled in and fell into a fitful sleep, dreaming her water had broken, yet Merl refused to drive her to the hospital. Her wrist slapping against the crate she used as a bedside table woke her. Her breath was ragged, her heart pounding against her sternum.

The flush of a toilet, the gargled clearing of a throat, a blob of spit hitting its target were all strangely comforting. Merl hadn't refused her request. It was just another nightmare.

Lying still, she waited. Would he enter her room tonight, or head to the one he shared with Magnolia? It was ironic. If ever the three occupied the kitchen dining area simultaneously, Merl never made any overture to her, no look with a hidden agenda, no stolen kisses, or taboo touching. He was Magnolia's man to all outward appearances, walking the straight and narrow.

In the dead of the night, the rules changed. Under the cover of the shifting shadows, he'd steal into Autumn's room, slide under her covers, and have his way with her. In her twisted soap opera mentality, Autumn believed Merl loved her more, but Magnolia was the most needy, the most fragile.

Did Merl and Autumn really believe Magnolia was ignorant of their habitual midnight rendezvous? Not for one second. But what happened under the blanket of darkness was not intermixed with the light of the day. Similar to Merl's business or Magnolia's habit, it was simply not a topic for discussion.

Thus Autumn waited for his intentions this night to take form. His tread advanced toward her door. An audible expletive cut the air when his toe stumbled against the box of cleansers and cold tablets he was forever collecting. She smiled to herself, feigning sleep, her posture curled into an L shape, facing away from the door.

The knob squeaked a high note from lack of lubrication; the door hinges added a run of tones in a minor key. Smug on her mattress, Autumn inwardly chanted a victory cheer; Merl was all hers for a few hours.

Hear him, wee one? Daddy's coming.

Clumsily, he felt his way across the cluttered floor, his knee bumping the mattress. Lifting the blankets, he stole in beside her, molding his body to her feminine curves, his hot breath on her neck. He ran his fingers up the length of her leg onto her smooth thigh. She gloried in his touch, allowing her back to melt into his chest, waiting for his caresses to bring her to the only kind of ecstasy she craved—love from Merl.

Maybe tonight she would tell him of the addition coming to their family, of the life sprouting from their own bodies—a new tiny being with traits of them both. He would cradle her in his arms in the fashion of a royal prince taking the hand of an enchanted princess, like the man her father said she deserved.

A wet kiss soaked her collarbone while his hand moved across her belly, igniting a fire within her. His hand hesitated then froze.

Giving a mighty roar, his arm whipped the blankets back from the bed, his feet hit the floor, and his fingers the light switch.

Autumn blinked in the blinding difference even a sixty-watt bulb can exude when not expected.

Merl's face had contorted into a grotesque sneer, his extended arm pointing at Autumn's midsection. "You're pregnant, you fool!" he shouted, not caring if his angry words carried beyond the thin walls. "What stupid broad wouldn't use protection?" Rage colored his face, the vein in his neck sticking out like the Nile River on a three-dimensional map.

"Nobody makes a daddy out of me. You get rid of that kid tomorrow! Do you hear me?"

Pulling the covers up over her nightie, Autumn said nothing, picking at the folds in the sheet.

"I said, 'Do you hear me?'" He took a step closer. Autumn cowered.

"Answer me!" he yelled, his face lowered to hers.

Softly, she mouthed the words, "I can't."

He drew back, almost in astonishment that she had refused what he had ordered.

His voice became lower, more menacing. "You try to get one penny of child support out of me, and I will kill you and the brat." Hatred in his eyes scorched her skin. The parting threat still dripping from his curled lips, he tore out of her room, slamming the door with such force, the trailer walls rattled in fright.

Merl's reaction to parenthood unnerved Autumn and marked an atmospheric change in the hovel the three adults tagged as home. The brunt of the altercation weighed on Autumn. After his verbal onslaught, Merl never passed over the doorsill of her bedroom again. If by chance, the two occupied the same living space elsewhere in the trailer for mere minutes, he never said a word to her unless it was absolutely necessary. In his estimation, she and her protruding belly had become invisible.

With the tension compressing the air, Autumn contemplated moving out, but where would she move? It was hard enough to scrape together the rent payment on the trailer with three of them contributing. How would she do it alone, and in a few months, support her child as well? Keeping the boat floating at an even keel was her best chance of survival. Thus, on the first of every month, without fail, she had her portion of the rent payment lying in plain sight on the kitchen table. She wasn't about to give Merl any excuse to throw her out.

Magnolia, having heard the outburst that night, tread softly as a middle person, careful not to let her allegiance swerve into Autumn's court. She had gained importance in her own eyes. No longer did she have to share her lover with a roommate.

Yet Magnolia was rapidly deteriorating physically, enough to alarm Autumn in her own shunned condition. Even though the girl was her competitor for Merl's affection, she still was indebted to her for sharing her humble living quarters, as bad as they might be.

Once, when Magnolia had come down from a high, and Merl had disappeared for a week, the thin girl became violently paranoid, screaming at the bats she insisted had invaded the trailer. Autumn hunted thoroughly for the bird-like mammal; however, she could not even unearth one of the vampires Magnolia screamed was sucking the blood right out of her. Her hallucinations grew in size, becoming hideous masks looming on the walls and ceiling, shrieking insults at the petrified girl curled in a ball on the floor, infused by the constant ammonia odor clinging to her skin.

Unable to take the pitiful sight any longer, Autumn took action, declaring she was hauling Magnolia to the emergency room even if it meant carrying her. Without a vehicle, that could have become a reality. Adrenalin kicked in, Magnolia fought her tooth and nail. In her expectant state, Autumn backed off, helplessly witnessing the bizarre facial expressions and exotic flailing Magnolia continued to exhibit.

Merl's sudden appearance was a relief, although his solution would be only to give her another fix. Scooping her off the floor, he carried her into her bedroom, knocking the door shut with the back of his heel. Feeling her own limbs shaking, Autumn wobbled to her own room and huddled under the covers. Was their no cure for Magnolia? Would this monster of addiction forever fasten itself to her back?

Not surprisingly, Magnolia was fired from her job the following week. Her work productivity had slacked off to the point her boss couldn't warrant issuing her a paycheck. Merl treated the forlorn nymph as a heirloom china doll sitting on a shelf. He soothed her with soft words and caresses, like a small child sobbing over skinned knees. Again, he lifted her and transported her petite, weightless form to her room, the two not emerging for the rest of the evening. For all his evil ways, Merl could be a gentle kitten when he tended to Magnolia. Autumn's heart stirred wishing he would see her and their child in a similar fashion.

All was quiet the next morning. Hopefully, Merl was gone, and Magnolia would sleep the day away. Her crazed mind seemed to be a perpetual windmill, ever turning, never pausing for rest.

Cautiously, Autumn opened her bedroom door a sliver, peeked out, and when she thought she was alone, ventured out. Rounding the hallway corner to the kitchen-living room area, she abruptly came face-to-face with Merl's unshaven face and oily hair. In his hand, he wielded a coffee cup, draining the last of the granules from the bottom down his throat. A sneer met her appearance. Then purposely setting his eyes on the grimy window beyond Autumn's bloated silhouette, Merl informed her in a low grating tone, "Your rent has gone up a hundred bucks." To refrain from asking where the heck she was supposed to dig up any more cash, she purposely bit her tongue. His mocking eyes fell on her heated face. His lips curled in contempt, he spouted one last threat before exiting, "Pay up or get out."

Slumping on top of the clothes discarded on the couch, she hugged her swollen tummy. A hopeless desolation invaded her spirits. She knew she shouldn't give up. She had to be a fighter, to keep putting one foot in front of the other—the way her mom had done when her dad died. Her mom hadn't caved in, she hadn't crawled under the covers, quitting her job, her role as mother, or her life.

But the strength to do so had seeped from Autumn's muscle tissue, one sinew after another had been clipped and disabled. Her backbone had folded, one vertebra buckling on top of the one below it until all that remained was a pile of useless human matter, ready to admit defeat. Another pile lay beyond the wall of Magnolia's room.

Movement within her belly went unnoticed initially as she wallowed in remorse over the manure heap her life had become. Then, as if perturbed by the lack of attention its kicks and punches were receiving, the unborn little gymnast within her womb went into full performance for Mommy, even throwing in a chain of hiccups. Wriggles, flips, and acrobatic tumbles staged a workout within the womb. Autumn ran her hands over her tummy, reveling in the miracle within. "I feel you little one. You display more fortitude than your mother." Continuing to rub her belly, she murmured sweet refrains to her baby, singing songs of love and ending with "Jesus Loves Me."

Pushing herself off the lumpy couch, a fresh vitality invaded her, reconstructing her backbone and mending her wretched muscles. She couldn't give up; she had a child worth fighting for. Merl may have thrown a roadblock in her path, but it was temporary. She'd climb it or detour it or do whatever it took, for she was not letting it deter her.

Autumn would plead for a few hours of overtime. Ned didn't like giving anyone more than a forty-hour week; however, she'd been a faithful employee. Hopefully, he'd relent and be moved by the predicament she was in. Merl would relish kicking her into the gutter and throwing her hodgepodge of possessions after her. For her unborn baby's sake, she swallowed the vile bitterness poisoning her taste buds and began to plan.

Chapter 30

"Twist, twist, twist, let go," Joel instructed. "Here, I'll show you again. Bend the wire in half around the intersection of two rebar lengths. Use the hook to grab the end loops then twist, twist, twist, let go." Joel was the teacher, Jasmine and Carson the novice students. He was setting up cement forms to provide a foundation for the three hopper bins he had purchased and would soon be moving onto the farmstead to provide storage for the fall harvest of soybeans, corn, or sunflowers.

He had spent days leveling the site, hauling in gravel as fill, and then pounding stakes into the hardpacked ground in a fifty-five-by-eighteen-foot rectangular shape, bracing them with two-by-twelve and two-by-four-inch boards. Before pouring the wet cement, he was laying two levels of long lengths of iron rebar inside the enclosure to strengthen the finished product. To prevent the rebar from shifting out of place during the cementing process, Carson and Jasmine were to tie the bars together at each intersection with a tool designed especially for the job.

"Got it?" Joel asked.

"Got it, boss," Jasmine returned with a glimmer in her eye. "You too, Carson?"

The young boy nodded, grabbed a handful of wires from the cardboard box, and took off for the far end. "I'll start down here, teacher, and we can meet in the middle."

"Sounds like he can handle the job," Joel noted. His eyes easily slid over Jasmine, admiring the fitted blue jeans and T-shirt, her hair clamped back in a clip to prevent it from being snarled in the breeze. "Think you're up for this?"

"Aye, aye, Captain." She saluted, accepting the tool from his hand.

He clipped her chin lightly with his knuckle. "I sure do fancy the farmhands I've acquired."

"Hey, don't fraternize with the hired help. I gotta keep up with that rascal." She dipped her head toward Carson. "I don't want to be coming up short." She bent down on one knee to start wiring the rebar.

As he walked back to his tractor, Joel called, "If your back gets sore, take a break."

Jasmine was loving the change of pace she experienced whenever she was out visiting on Joel's acreage. Even though she'd lived in the country as a young girl, she had spent the last two and a half decades being a town girl. Yet she still considered herself a rural resident of North Dakota, living in small towns like Prairie City and Elton.

The wide-open view sweeping across the flat fields to the horizon and capped by blue skies was broken only by a shelterbelt of trees at a section line or a windbreak hugging the boundaries of a farmstead. No neighborhood houses blocked the spectacular sunset God provided, tucking the sun into bed or rolling in the storm clouds billowing across the prairie. It was a panoramic view of creation at its best, a thrilling freedom of the spirit.

Even now, the meadowlarks sung their trills to each other, the gophers raced fifty-meter dashes to their holes, and an occasional long-legged white-tailed deer gracefully loped a pasture fence. Joel assumed she was out here to lighten his workload and to share his companionship. Undoubtedly, he was correct. Their shared hours accumulated more readily if they could use the workday instead of being limited to a few evening hours or an occasional Saturday or Sunday afternoon. But in retrospect, she also enjoyed the boundless spaces, the emancipation from being enclosed within the four walls of a classroom or the privacy fence of a backyard or the boundaries defining city limits.

Jasmine Kirmis was not only falling for the kindhearted Joel Linton, but also for the country style of living he was enamored with—close to the land and to his Maker.

School was closed for the summer months. The manuscript for her third novel had been edited and submitted. Schedules had evaporated and paperwork completed, allowing her vacation days to be infiltrated by a new curriculum with Joel, the acting instructor. He had taught Jasmine to run his John Deere tractor. It been a hilarious experience, the only tractor she'd ever driven before being a lawn mower. He had been patient as she practiced releasing a clutch slowly, deciphering which hydraulic lever raised or lowered a trailing implement and which one put it into gear. She had helped him sort cattle—accidentally letting a calf get by her when she was supposed to cut it off—and she'd hauled mineral tubs and salt blocks to the pastures for summer grazing.

Looking up, she checked to see how Carson was doing tying wires. "Why you little bugger," she scolded. "You're already progressed to my half!" Carson grinned in delight.

The following morning, when the sun was still low in the eastern sky, Jasmine again drove out from Elton to the farm. Today, the cement trucks would roll in. She intended to catch the day on her digital camera if her physical assistance was not required. Aromas from the Crock-Pot and baked goods filling her backseat would tantalize the hungry cementing crew at noon. Besides himself, Joel had hired three additional men to help with the labor-intensive project.

By 8:00 a.m., the first cement truck, with a drum mixer rotating on its back, lumbered down the driveway. The driver skillfully backed the machine close to the cement forms. Like thick pudding, the concrete mud poured down a chute extending from the mixer to the forms. Two of the men, wearing tall rubber boots and wielding long-handled spades, were ready to guide the concrete to the far corners covering the rebar while the second set of hired hands placed a board on its side to screed the thick liquid into an even surface.

The truck had barely finished dumping its load when the second truck came peeling in, following the same procedure. Jasmine would have a slide show for Joel to view later. Carson was not to be left out. Using a small hand trowel, he smoothed the edges of the concrete.

In all, five truckloads of cement were required to fill the concrete foundation for the grain bins that would be moved in a week later. There was no downtime for the men pulling and pushing the heavy mixture into place. When the entire rectangle had been screeded, Joel began working with a long-handled bull float, sliding it back and forth across the top, giving the surface a sleek coating.

By twelve thirty, Joel was satisfied with their workmanship, giving the crew the nod to break for lunch. On the end gate of his pickup truck, Jasmine set out the barbecued-beef-filled buns, potato salad, chips, chocolate brownies, and soft drinks. Carson was too busy to slow down for a sandwich. In his estimation, Joel had manifested him with the best job of all. Using a water hose, he sprayed the wet concrete off the spades, trowels, and bull float to prevent it from permanently hardening onto the tools in the July heat.

Teasingly, the workers joshed him, "Hey, Carson, you missed a spade." Dutifully, he sprayed the tool they pointed out. "Over there, Carson, is another trowel." Again, he obeyed their directions. After a fourth directive, he got wind of their shenanigans. With a smug look on his face and a devilish look in his blue eyes, he turned the hose on the spectators, sending them scrambling for cover. One of the younger guys dashed through the impromptu rain shower to apprehend the human fire hydrant. Grasping Carson around the waist and lifting him off his feet, he wrestled the hose from his grasp. The man set Carson down and did an about-face, turning the full blast of the water on the boy. Carson screamed in delight, the onlookers applauding.

The friendly banter and conversation continued until one by one, the men cleaned off their muddy boots and drove off. Joel moved the food containers back from the edge of the end gate, giving the three of them remaining a place to sit.

Viewing the glistening cement pad, Joel was pleased. "It is only missing one detail." After lifting Carson off the end gate, Joel dug in his pocket for a nail. Side by side, the two knelt at the edge of the cement. "Use the nail to write your name in the wet cement. I'll add the date," Joel explained.

Surprised, but only too willing to comply, Carson painstakingly scratched each letter into the soft surface in his best manuscript printing.

"This hunk of cement is now forever yours." Joel grinned at his son.

"Wow!" Carson was impressed.

Returning to where Jasmine sat on the end gate, Carson asked, "Are we just going to sit here and talk?"

"Boring, huh?" Jasmine interpreted, her legs dangling above the ground.

"Yeah. Can I ride my bike and see if I can ramp that mountain of dirt?" His finger indicated a small pile of gravel leftover from leveling the bin site.

"Sure," Joel agreed. "But don't go on the wet cement."

The youngster took off like lightening.

"So you're boring." Joel gave Jasmine a funny look.

"Me? No, he was talking about you." She nudged him with her knee.

They watched Carson circle his bicycle to a distant location. Then standing up to push on the pedals as hard as he could, he spun straight for the dirt pile, only to get his front tire stuck in the soft gravel. Joel chuckled. "At least he's not bored." Rummaging behind him, he attacked another brownie. "I've been thinking," he began.

"That's a good thing to do." Jasmine liked ribbing the quiet farmer.

Readjusting his cap, he parried back, "You gonna be a smart aleck?"

"No way. Just agreeing with you." Her lips were a straight line, yet her eyes danced.

Those deep jade irises were his undoing. If Carson hadn't been a stone's throw away, he would have taken her into his arms and kissed her soundly. Instead, he continued, "There's a family camp scheduled for the last week end in July at Crystal Springs, about an hour and a half drive from here. I was thinking maybe Carson and I should take it in. Thought maybe you'd like to join us?"

"Really?" Her eyes widened.

"Is it so astounding that we would want the pleasure of your company?"

Breaking out in a burst of laughter, she clarified, "What I meant was, 'Really? Crystal Springs?' Jacob and Autumn used to attend that camp when they were kids."

"Really?" he mimicked, getting an elbow in the ribs. "So is it a yes or a no?"

"Of course, I'll go!" She flashed him a winning smile.

Forget Carson. He pulled her into his arms and smacked her loudly on the mouth. Farming sure was fun when she was in attendance.

Crackling flames from the campfire rose heavenward, licking the dry wood at its base, sending forth a cozy ring of light and warmth to the campers singing old choruses to the strum of a guitar.

"Kumbaya, my Lord, kumbaya. Oh, Lord, kumbaya."

Snuggled close to Joel's side, Jasmine blended her soprano voice with his deep bass. Carson had wriggled out of their tight huddle, preferring to roast marshmallows with the new friends he had met. Joel weaved his fingers into Jasmine's; her head found a comfortable spot against his shoulder. The first two days of the family setting at Crystal Springs campground had been incredible. Many of the families sharing the weekend had made this camp an annual event. They welcomed the newcomers, pulling them into their close-knit circles, warming their hearts with stories of how God's still small voice was working in their daily lives—sometimes in the form of a miraculous answer to prayer, and others, through lessons learned in tragedy.

During the morning breakout session, the adults and children had been divided into separate classes. The adult speaker focused his talks on the blended family. Whether it be by death, divorce, remarriage, adoption, foster care, or single parenting, a large percentage of families across America were no longer comprised of the traditional family grouping of father, mother, and offspring. Using scriptural backing, he gave them ideas on how to have a Christ-centered family, no matter which geometric shape one's personal family resembled. Family dynamics may have changed, yet the goal remained the same.

"But as for me and my household, we will serve the Lord" (Joshua 24:15, NIV).

Jasmine thought of the ways her immediate family had shifted, bulging and shrinking through the passage of years. First, there was her and Evert—a young married couple—then becoming parents to a pair of adopted children. And now, she, a widow alone in an empty nest—still with two children—except one was estranged. Joel's family dimensions had altered too.

Carson had drifted back to his dad when his stomach was full of the sweet chocolate and melted marshmallows sandwiched between honey crackers. Rubbing his hand over his son's back, Joel gestured for them to call it a night and head for their bunks. Immediately, Carson objected.

"There's another day of camp activities tomorrow. You need some rest so you can keep up." Joel firmly set him on his feet.

"Can I go tubing again tomorrow? And climb the waterslide? Will you take me for another paddleboat ride?" Carson's questions bumped into each other, not giving his dad space to answer.

"Yes, yes, and yes."

Covering a yawn, Jasmine added one of her own. "Are you men going to help a lady find her cabin through the pitch blackness?"

Carson was the first to respond, jumping to her side. "Yes!" Holding hands, the three walked through the dewy grass under the star-studded firmament. Shadows of their cabins loomed out of the darkness. At her door, they said their good nights before Joel and Carson continued onto their cabin.

Alone in a cottage meant to provide room for a family, Jasmine lay in bed staring at the underside of the bunk above her. Her thoughts became prayers, remembering Jacob and his job, a single man in the business world. She prayed he'd remain true to his faith when pressured by superiors. She prayed for Autumn, for God to place godly people in her life at strategic locations. Carson was next. He was being given a second chance having been adopted by Joel. And then there was her growing friendship with Joel. *Lord, let your will be done.* and she drifted off to sleep.

Chapter 31

Apprehension prickled on Autumn's upper lip, tiny sweat beads forming. Should she, or shouldn't she?

Her work schedule at McDonald's gave her every other Sunday off. Usually, she used the day to sleep in or to cart a load of clothes to the Laundromat, but this Sunday, she'd felt an overwhelming yearning within her chest—a longing to honor a Kirmis tradition. She wished she could again hear her dad calling, "Wake up, sleepyhead. Church day." Even without his encouragement, today, she had followed the summons beckoning within her.

Autumn now stood on the sidewalk outside the white clapboard church, the sun beating on her brow. According to the sign, the weekly service had barely begun.

Wetting her lips, she hesitated. *To enter* or *not to enter?* Finally shaking her wavy train of hair, she scolded herself, *This is silly. Going to a church service is no big deal.*

Resolutely, she marched up the exterior cement steps and pulled the heavy door open. Strains of the old hymn "How Great Thou Art" were boisterously being sung by the parishioners; a lady pumped out the tune on a gigantic organ. Autumn decided to be as inconspicuous as possible and slipped into an empty back pew. Once the song ended, the congregation sat down, the aged benches creaking a well-worn tune of their own. A pastor stood behind a bulky pulpit, opening his Bible. Autumn wasn't here to mingle with the faithful church attenders. Her soul sought someone more significant.

At the front of the room, mounted high on the wall, was an enormous wooden cross, not sanded and varnished to resemble a decorative piece of furniture, rather ribbed and coarse, similar to a rough timber torn from an old barn. A beam that had stood the test of time, stalwart and aged.

Mesmerized by the symbol, Autumn hunched down in her seat, envisioning Jesus dying on a cross comparable to this one, His bare back sliding against its uneven ridges, thick splinters piercing the torn skin, spikes penetrating His hands, driven there by a mallet from the hand of a Roman soldier. For the first time, it seemed dreadfully real to Autumn, like she was one of the bystanders at the foot of the cross watching the Son of God being torn and bloodied for her.

Everything surrounding her was wiped away—the fellow worshipers, the pastor, the furnishings. It was Autumn and the cross, it was Autumn coming face-to-face with the Savior. Like a prearranged appointment, she was here to meet her Maker, to confess the errors she had made in navigating her own course, for selfishly lusting after her own desires, not caring how they affected others, nor her Lord. Foregoing the preliminaries, the two got right down to business.

Tears coursed down Autumn's cheeks unto her neck, wetting the neckline of her shirt. For lack of a tissue, she swiped at them with her sleeve and the back of her hand, never lifting her eyes from the image of the cross. It was as if she could see His sad eyes regarding her with unabashed love, His arms held out for her to come. Her lips forming the words, *I'm so sorry. Please forgive me.*

Sobbing silently, she bent over, letting the moisture wet the tight knit top stretched over the belly of her unborn child. She hugged the baby still safe in her womb.

Unexpectedly, the story of the Biblical Hannah revisited her again. How Hannah had prayed for a baby and then given the child back to the Lord. Autumn hadn't done either of those. She hadn't prayed to become pregnant; it was one of those consequences her parents used to talk about. Truth was, she hadn't prayed at all.

However, her birth mother had at least done a comparable deed. She'd had a baby girl, named her Autumn, and had given her away.

Now that Autumn was just days away from becoming a mother herself, it struck her how difficult and unselfish that act must have been for her biological parent.

Autumn couldn't imagine not holding the living urchin she was carrying. The very idea was agonizing. Yet what chance would her baby have of living a wholesome life in the slum conditions Autumn existed in? The filthy trailer was no place to raise a child—a possible drug lab in the spare bedroom and three individuals satisfying their own ungodly cravings outside of marriage, yet not wanting the responsibilities a relationship enlisted.

Had her birth mom had these same thoughts only eleven months after she had been born? Had it been an act of love for her to give Autumn to Evert and Jasmine Kirmis, the ones Autumn now thought of as her *real* parents, the ones who had chosen to love her, the ones who had chosen to raise her, the ones who had chosen to stick by her, even when she rejected them?

What a mixed-up world. The rejected being accepted. The accepted choosing to reject.

Lifting her head again to embrace the cross, Autumn poured out her failures to her Savior. In turn, He poured out His love upon her. It had been there all the time, but that too she had rejected. With her eyes closed, she reveled in this new sensation of a cleansed repentant heart.

Oblivious to Autumn, the church choir rose to sing the anthem by John Newton, yet the words penetrated her conscience.

> Amazing grace, how sweet the sound
> That saved a wretch like me.
> I once was lost, but now am found,
> Was blind, but now I see.

A soft kick within her abdomen brought her hand back to her baby. She'd never given birth before, but she knew it was a painful procedure.

Autumn was scared. Although she would love to have Merl at the delivery, she knew it was highly unlikely. Who would be there to coach her, to encourage her to keep pushing?

Mom?

Yes, she wished her adoptive mom would be at her side, her calming mannerisms quieting her inner turmoil, not flinching when Autumn would dig her fingernails into her hands while the contractions raged on within her guts, assuring her daughter she could do it, reminding her of the end reward.

Mom would come, but Autumn wouldn't ask her. She was ashamed of how she had treated the woman who had given her a home and given her a second chance.

Oh, God, please help me. Be with me in the delivery room. Give me the strength to bear my child.

And He would.

During the pastor's closing prayer, Autumn crept from her secluded bench into the bright July heat sizzling outside the door. As she skipped down the stairs, her step was lighter, her heart buoyed by the load removed. A child who had returned home.

The angels in heaven were shining the silverware and suspending the helium balloons for another celestial party.

And thus, it was Marlene who witnessed the entrance of the Kirmis baby into the world in the evening hours of August 5.

Autumn had felt the slight tremor of a contraction before heading off to McDonald's. She didn't feel she possessed the energy to put in her eight hours of shift work; however, who would have assisted her had she stayed home? Magnolia, roller coasting from one high to the next? Merl, his erratic schedule thundering an appearance at odd hours of the day or night?

No, she'd be safer at work, surrounded by fellow employees and her boss. By the time the golden arches loomed ahead, she was spent. Marlene and Ned hobbled her to the employees' lounge in the back of the restaurant, scolding her for setting out on the extended walk in her condition. There, she passed the day, doing crossword puzzles and sipping ice water between contractions.

Seven hours later, Marlene deemed it was no longer wise to wait. Nature was known to be unpredictable. Among well wishes and cheers, Autumn was escorted to Marlene's Subaru and whisked away to the hospital.

Close to midnight, Autumn, wet with perspiration and sore from the delivery process, totally exhausted yet ecstatically happy, cuddled a five-pound-two-ounce baby girl. She had blonde hair and bluish-green eyes. She was beautiful, so small, so perfect.

Marlene admired the child with her mommy. "You did it." Her finger held the tiny hand; each fingernail and knuckle was flawlessly formed. "You did good."

"I couldn't have done it without you, and God too," Autumn admitted. "Thank you for being here."

"Wouldn't have missed it." Marlene brushed Autumn's damp hair off her forehead. "Bringing a baby into the world is quite an ordeal, but now you have her for a lifetime."

"Yup, and I'm going to be the best mom ever."

"You already have been. Remember the healthy diet you've been munching on while I inhale the sodas and deep fat fried foods?"

Autumn smiled lazily. "Hmmm. That was the easy part. Now come the challenges, especially if she's anything like me!" Her grin widened, peering down at the pink face, whose eyelids closed in sleep. Fine eyelashes brushed her cheeks. "Mom researched this thing called reactive attachment disorder. Something about how important it is to hold a baby and answer its cries of stress. A bonding takes place that will follow the child right up through her adulthood. Seems unfathomable, doesn't it? Love shown to an infant makes her a more secure woman?" A fingertip followed the contours of the cheekbones and chin, the tiny nose. "You better get used to me, little one, 'cause we're going to be inseparable."

"You did a lot of yelling when you were on the delivery table. Do you recall who you were screaming for?" Marlene asked, warmed by the sight of Autumn as a mother.

Shaking her head, Autumn questioned, "Merl?"

Marlene's facial expression refuted the guess.

"You?"

"No. I was right here with you. You didn't have to call for me!" Marlene teased. "You screamed for your mom and dad, and some guy named Jacob."

Autumn's green eyes misted. "I hope someday I can share my baby with my mom and brother. Dad missed out."

"Have you thought of a name?" Marlene ventured.

"I'd planned to name the child after my dad had it been a boy, but I didn't pick out a girl's name. It will take some mulling. For now, let's just call her Tootsie." Kissing the baby's forehead, she murmured, "You fooled me. For some reason, I was sure I was carrying a boy."

Rousing herself, Marlene bent over to plant a kiss on Autumn's head. "I best be moving out of here, so you can get some rest. Don't suppose you'll be trekking into work tomorrow?" She grinned and was gone.

In seconds, Autumn would join her daughter in repose. This was her first day as a mom, as a single mom. She so wished there would be a father in her little one's life. *Please, Lord, let Merl be moved when he sees the precious daughter you have given us. You changed water into wine. Can't you change a drug pusher into a father?*

Slumber drifted her into a running series of pleasant dreams.

Why was she crying all the time?

Not the baby, but Autumn. It seemed as if she'd lost control of her emotions. The slightest infringement, a moment of uncertainty, thoughts of the future, her daughter's angelic face—almost anything brought on a weeping spell that threatened to dissolve her determination to become a model parent.

What did she know about taking care of a baby? Other than the articles in parent magazines, sporadic information gleaned from other mothers, and Marlene's helpful nurturing, she was a basket case. The baby didn't talk. Did her whimpers mean she was hungry? Yet she wouldn't suck. Was her diaper soaked? No, it was dry. Did she have gas? Autumn walked the bundle back and forth in the short space allotted from the dresser to the bed, patting her back. When the kittenish cries diminished, Autumn would fall into an exhausted sleep, the child lying inches away. Two hours later, the circuit would commence again.

After two nights in the hospital, faithful Marlene had been there to transport the little family to the trailer house. Mess and dirt had met them at the curb and accompanied them inside. Autumn had managed to straighten her bedroom the week prior to the birthing, reasoning she didn't want her child's first impression of her mother to be that of a rotten housekeeper. She had considered taking on the rest of the trailer; however, the sight had been too daunting, her stamina at nine months pregnant, too feeble.

Marlene never showed any annoyance outwardly at the state of affairs in the baby's new home. Once Autumn and her daughter were settled in the bedroom, Marlene had firmly closed the bedroom door and gone to work—sweeping, scrubbing, sorting, and throwing until the discolored linoleum was unearthed, the tabletop cleared, the sinks empty, and the windows washed.

Magnolia had stared long and hard at the newborn infant, partially envious of Autumn for having Merl's child. She'd even tentatively stretched out her skinny fingers and softly trailed a line across the round rosy cheek. Then as if being caught licking frosting off a double-layered cake under the sneeze guard at the bakery, she jerked it back, then dashed to the bathroom and rinsed her hand under a spray of water, washing any contamination down the drain.

Her daughter was five days old when her papa came home to the cleaned up trailer. Autumn had been nursing the child in the corner seat of the couch. She had envisioned this moment for months—Merl meeting his daughter for the first time. In her naivety, she pictured him stopping in midstep to cautiously peer into the swarm of pastel-colored blankets. His expression would soften, his heart melt. He would ever so gently stoop to gather his own flesh and blood into his arms, cooing to the infant and then turning to smile benevolently down at her mother, the one who had bestowed such a treasure of life upon him. And it would be the beginning of a complete family.

Merl pushed the door open ahead of him to cart in a toolbox, jug, and an additional sealed tote. A surprised expression crossed his face, almost as if he thought he had entered the wrong trailer, unaccustomed to the orderliness that met him. He dumped his load on the floor and then spied Autumn. For a minute, he stared.

Autumn willed him to come forward, to say something kindly, to show an interest in his child.

His Adam's apple bobbed up and down like a duck struggling to free a kernel caught in its throat. A naked look betrayed him as a man from a previous age who had once had scruples and valued the simple sentiments of life. It was brief, as if it had prowled out before he could snap the lid back on. But the passing flicker gave Autumn hope, hope of a man who could be a father if he allowed himself to reach out. She chanced a slight upward curve to her lips.

In reply, he sneered, "What's this? Suzy Homemaker wet mopping the floor with a snot-nosed kid hanging from her? This ain't no nursery school. You get that kid out of my sight and keep it there, or you'll wish you had." His eyes burned black with hatred, forfeiting all chances to be someone of significance in his child's upbringing.

Autumn could feel her cheeks blazing scarlet in his denunciation of the two of them. She had seen the rawness displayed in his fleeting expression. If he'd listen to his heart, he'd open up his arms and let them in.

And yet, at the same time, she was scared of his anger. Scared enough to clench her teeth together, hugging her daughter more closely to her breast. Merl was volatile. Too much was at stake to chance an explosion.

Seething, he slammed into Magnolia's room, leaving a trail of cuss words to scorch the air they breathed.

Trembling under her blankets, Autumn lay awake, her daughter fretfully sleeping on top of her stomach, lulled by the beating of her mommy's heart. Autumn listened to the soft miracle of her breath. Tonight, more than the previous nights, she would have to be vigilant at rocking and attending to her daughter. Not that she hadn't been, but the baby's fussiness had unnerved her those first two days at home. Merl was on the other side of the wall. He wouldn't tolerate an infant's cry.

Would he really hurt such a tiny one? Or was it an empty threat meant to terrorize her mother instead? She should move out. But where? The only possibility wasn't even one. Marlene's daughter had moved back in with her after a relationship had soured, with two grandchildren in tow.

Jacob lived somewhere in this vast metropolitan area. By chance, they had bumped into each other when he had brought his vehicle into the car wash where she had previously been employed. The sight so unnerved her that she had flown off the handle instantly, telling him in no uncertain terms to get out of her life. He had left. Soon afterward, she had gotten fired.

Did she dare show up on her brother's doorstep? She was sure he'd take her in; however, she'd have to be willing to listen to his lectures and live by his standards. As low and scared as she was right now, his place would be paradise.

But then, Jacob didn't keep secrets from Mom. He'd tell all, and Mom would come to Minneapolis for a visit.

Yes, she wanted to straighten things out with her mother, but she wasn't ready yet. She was too busy getting acquainted with her own daughter and learning how to juggle everything the title of motherhood brought with it.

At Thanksgiving, it would be five years since she had last seen or talked to her mom. How did she span those intervening years after having purposefully shut her mom out, doing whatever it took to be difficult and to humiliate her? Actually, the preceding high school years hadn't exactly been an angel food dessert either. Mom had put up with a lot.

Autumn would bridge the gap, but not yet.

Having sorted through her limited list of options, it was evident she was stuck here for the duration. And yet, maybe this was where God wanted her. Wasn't there still a chance Merl would come around? He just needed more time to get used to the idea of being a daddy. She couldn't rush him. Patience was a godly trait. She would pray harder.

God would want the three of them united—a family that was meant to be.

Chapter 32

"What the world?" Pink helium balloons floated above each cashier's till, a giant one emblazoned with the words, "It's a Girl!" Another tooted, "Mommy's Little Girl." All the employees were decked out in pink party hats, tiny bibs tied about their necks, and all wore toothy grins. A pile of colorful gifts set on the counter beside a cake swathed in pink swirls of icing.

Autumn's jaw dropped, her eyes widened at the excited squeals of "Congratulations," as she entered her place of employment toting her daughter's car seat. Marlene followed with the diaper bag. Immediately, everyone clustered about them, wanting a peek at the baby who delighted them with a small yawn.

"Oh, what a darling."

"Autumn, she has your hair and eyes."

"I bet you looked just like her at this age." She had. Back home, tucked into a photo album, was a newborn snapshot the adoption agency had given her parents. A nurse had stuck a tiny pink bow on her golden head for the photo shoot.

"Why in the world would you want to come back to pushing fries and milkshakes instead of singing lullabies to this sweet one?" another employee demanded, helping to free the wee one from the constraints of the car seat.

Most mothers, after being granted extended maternity leaves, still bemoaned the day they had to return to the work force. Yet here was Autumn, outfitted in her McDonald's cap and shirt, celebrating her baby's one-week birthday at her job site.

A handful of answers pushed to the forefront, all drastically important to Autumn. The confines of the fast-food restaurant provided a safe haven for the mother and child. Merl never came in to order a hamburger or shake. Here, she did not have to worry about his temper igniting to the point of inflicting harm on their innocent baby. At least for eight hours each day, she wouldn't be pressured to muffle her daughter's cries against her own body or under a blanket.

Besides Marlene, two of the other workers were mothers. Autumn yearned for their maternal advice. They'd be able to counsel her on the correct procedures for caring for a tiny infant, to douse her worries, to bolster her confidence. Her boss was an angel, letting her bring her baby to work with her, setting up a corner of the employees' lounge as a makeshift nursery. She wouldn't even let her mind entertain the question of what she would do about day care, once her child had grown beyond the infant stage.

And then there was the age-old problem of money. Before having a child, she'd had only herself to provide food and lodging for, now it was doubled. Formula and diapers were expensive. She'd nurse from her own breasts as long as it was feasibly possible; in the not too distant future, the grocery bill would expand beyond formula. She kept one container of it at home and one in her diaper bag for emergencies.

This, of course, was all in addition to the trailer rent. Autumn had slept on the street before, but she wasn't going to risk her baby's health by setting up housekeeping on a park bench. Her rent would be paid on time, even if she herself had to go hungry.

Yup, right here at work, was where she would be the most content.

"It's my turn to hold her." Her fellow workers passed the baby from one set of arms to the next. Autumn was delighted by their enthusiasm and acceptance of a single mom.

Even with the baby shower in full swing, the restaurant had to operate. The employees worked and partied simultaneously, flipping burgers, rolling wraps, waiting on customers, and eating cake. Technically, Autumn was on the day's payroll, but she was kept busy opening gifts and tending to her daughter's needs. She was overwhelmed by the generous mound of baby necessities her friends had given her, some new, some used, all appreciated.

One customer ordering the breakfast special asked what all the fuss was about. When told they were celebrating Autumn's initiation into motherhood, he poked a fifty-dollar bill into her diaper bag. All morning, Autumn's eyes had gleamed with unshed tears; at the stranger's generosity, they spilled over.

At the end of her shift, she hugged each of her fellow workers, too emotional for words. Marlene helped her pack up the assortment of gifts, and of course, the most precious gift of all—her baby daughter. Tomorrow, a more regular routine would begin.

For two weeks, Ned benevolently scheduled Marlene and Autumn for the same shifts. That way, Marlene could act as a taxi service for Autumn and the baby at the start and end of each day. It was sacrificial giving, for Marlene drove a good distance out of the way to accommodate the service. Autumn was only too aware of the extra minutes she was adding to her friend's day.

At the beginning of her third week back at work, Autumn insisted her daughter was old enough to ride in the stroller she'd been given, to traverse their route to the McDonald's restaurant. Marlene immediately objected. "What about the weather?"

"These warm August days are certainly conducive for a baby. We'll take you up on a ride if it rains." Autumn was firm. With the encouragement she received at work, Autumn was becoming more secure in her new role. She had to learn to stand on her own two feet. Parenthood was an extended commitment; Autumn was firm in sticking it out for the long haul.

Even with her noble vows of dedicated devotion, Autumn chewed her nails and twisted the ends of her hair in consternation. That the future was approaching rapidly was evident in her daughter's growth; her wee voice and appetite were thriving. How long would she be content in a bassinet or playpen in the employees' lounge? Autumn's paycheck wouldn't stretch to handle day care. And sure, the warm temperatures were balmy now, but in two months, winter was due. Autumn didn't have the funds to buy a car, even an old beater. Transportation problems would reoccur.

And then there was Merl. He hadn't made any paternal overtures. Admittedly, he frequented the trailer more, not because of the baby, but due to Magnolia's depleting connection with the world. For some reason, he was honoring his role as her caretaker.

Rarely did Autumn have her daughter out of the bedroom. The very sight of the innocent child seemed to increase Magnolia's paranoiac agitation. It didn't go unnoticed by Merl either. Two nights ago, he had banged on her bedroom wall, a warning to get the *kid* to stop bawling. Autumn's door was always locked; however, that was a minor obstruction for Merl's anger to break through. Autumn's only trump card was her rent payment. She was worth that much to him.

As usual, Marlene and Autumn shared a sandwich during their break. Since the baby's appearance, their private dialogues had moved from the front dining area to the lounge in the rear, for privacy while she nursed.

Autumn didn't always agree with Marlene, yet she asked for her advice anyway concerning her pending predicaments.

"You've put off the obvious long enough. Don't you think it's about time you buckled?" Marlene had pondered the days ahead for the young mother as well.

Kissing the golden curls of her child as she suckled, Autumn thought of feigning ignorance. Marlene wouldn't let the matter rest, best to face it head on.

"My mother?"

"She's alone, and you need assistance. Who would be better than her?" The older woman was always matter-of-fact.

After propping her baby on her shoulder, her hand patted the miniature back, coaxing out a burp.

"It will break my mom's heart to find out I had a child out of wedlock. My parents taught my brother and I well about the Biblical order of kids in a relationship."

Marlene dismissed the excuse with a wave of her hand. "You don't think her heart isn't already packaged in a jigsaw puzzle box? You said you've not spoken to her in almost five years now. I think we're past the fragile state. It's busted."

Immersed in thought, Autumn continued to cuddle her baby.

"Here, hand that little papoose over to me for awhile so you can eat." Marlene reached for the youngster.

Releasing her, Autumn readjusted her own shirt before biting into her sandwich. "After all these years, it would be difficult to even know what to say."

"How about, 'Hello, Mom, this is your daughter Autumn.'" Her body swayed in rhythm for the baby.

"That's the easy part. Then what do I say? Anyway, I couldn't do it over the phone. That's too off the cuff. Knowing her, she'll ask me something I don't want to answer." She set the bun down. Her stomach was feeling queasy.

"Postal service still delivers mail."

Lightly, Autumn replied, "You don't give up, do you?"

"Nope. I can give you two good reasons, and they're both in this room."

For five nights in succession, Autumn struggled to put words on a paper. For four nights, she wadded the paper into a ball and aimed for the wastebasket. Tonight, she came to the conclusion it didn't matter how she said it, what excuses she made, or how nicely she asked for assistance. The facts remained the same. She hadn't spoken to her mom in almost five years, she'd quit college without notifying her, she'd spent the college money deceitfully, she'd lived a life contrary to her parents' values, and she had given birth to a daughter.

Resolutely, Jasmine turned to a clean page in her spiral notebook. With determination, the ink began to flow.

> October 16
>
> Dear Mom,
>
> It has been a long time, too long. I'm sorry about that. Life seems to get in the way of what should be done.
> I want you to know I'm doing okay. I have a job and two roommates here in Minneapolis. Rent is high.
> There's two things I want to share with you—hopefully, both will excite you.

She paused, her pen hovering over the sheet of paper. Autumn then closed her eyes and imagined the clapboard church; she wanted to capture it perfectly for her mother, its resemblance to the one of her youth. The words came; the pen scrawled filling the lines of the paper.

Then she faltered. How could she tell her mom about the baby? The depth of love she felt for her daughter? The new knowledge of what her parents must have felt when they'd held her for the first time.

Taking a deep breath, Autumn plunged on before she lost her nerve, letting her thoughts bump into each other as they collided into a jumbled message, willing her mom to understand.

Not bothering to reread her efforts in fear she'd again send it sailing to the trash can, she quickly brought the letter to a close.

In this final draft, she decided not to ask her mom for help. She figured it would come regardless.

> As I've said, I'm sorting things out. I'm not ready to come for a visit yet, but maybe soon. I want to introduce my daughter to her grandmother and good old North Dakota.
> I do love you. Forgive me for being such a pain.
>
> A.J.

Luke used to call her A.J., and Merl, too. She'd liked it and used it almost exclusively when she'd first moved to Minneapolis. Made her sound more sophisticated.

On second thought, she'd always been Autumn to her family. Crossing out the initials, she signed her given name—Autumn.

The next morning, Autumn second guessed herself and reread her letter. As an afterthought, she added a postscript on the bottom then folded it and stuffed it into an envelope. In her half print and half cursive scroll, she addressed it to her mom, omitting the return address. She didn't want her mom or Jacob to appear on her doorstep and see how she had been living. Pushing the child's stroller on her way to work the eleven to seven shift, she dropped the envelope into a curbside postal receptacle.

There, she'd done it. *Out of my hands and into yours, Lord.*

Just maybe, she'd be back home before the first snowflakes of winter wet the ground.

Marlene greeted the duo while another worker whisked the baby stroller to the backroom for some playful cuddling before getting back to her station. Having worked the breakfast shift, Marlene would be off at two. A respite ensued before the lunch crowd would dribble in.

"How's our resident mother hen and her chick doing today?" Marlene was busily refilling the napkin dispenser. Autumn joined her, grabbing the ketchup and mustard jugs from below the counter to replenish their containers.

"Good. Merl wasn't home at all, so I didn't have to worry about keeping Tootsie quiet. I'm concerned about Magnolia though. She used to be such a giggly, smiley gal. Now, it's as if her merry soul is buried deeper than the underground water pipes. Hardly a word escapes her lips, unless she's coming down from a high. And then you don't want to be near her. Mostly, she just stares, particularly at my baby. Almost the way a customer would scrutinize a worm in our Southwest Salad. It gives me the creeps."

"Jealousy," Marlene labeled the description. Using a wet cloth, she wiped up the smears on the condiment bar.

"Maybe," Autumn affirmed. "Whenever she's like that, I whisk Tootsie out of the room faster than you can hand out an order on the drive-through."

Giving Autumn a tight expression, Marlene warned, "You'd better watch her. In her state of mind, she's liable to harm the child."

"Yeah, I've thought of that." The jingle of the door interrupted their discussion. The first business people on lunch break had arrived. Autumn took up her position behind the center till. "Good day, sir. How can I help you today?" She rang up his order, gave him his change, and his tray. Another customer waited behind him.

The next minutes flew as all the cashiers were swamped taking noon orders. Engrossed in her steady flow of customers, Autumn didn't notice Merl's entrance into the establishment. Looking rumpled in his faded T-shirt and stained jeans, he planted himself at the rear of Autumn's line, trailing a mother with two small children. When the cashier next to Autumn opened up, the gal congenially called out, "Sir, I can take your order over here."

Merl shook his head, pretending to focus his concentration on the overhead menu display, obviously preferring the line he was in. The cashier shrugged; soon, another customer moved up to her till.

It wasn't until Autumn asked the two children whether they preferred milk or apple juice with their Happy Meals that she recognized the greased-back hair, the aristocratic nose, and the suggestive rake of Merl's bold inspection. A hint of a smirk indented his lips.

Autumn's stomach flipped. Righting itself, she converged her attention back on the young mother. "Pardon me, did they say chocolate milk?"

"Andy wants the milk, and Lou said apple juice." Placing the items on the tray, Autumn started pushing numbers on the computerized till. "Will that be all, ma'am?" Autumn glanced up, but it was Merl's burning eyes she inadvertently landed on, rather than the lady. He licked his lips, indulging in her discomfort. Her heart quickened. This was the Merl she was attracted to, the one who could turn her insides to Jell-O just by a stance of sexy lewdness.

"That's all," the mother replied. She paid the bill then carefully picked up the tray, with the two children pulling on her arms.

"Thank you, ma'am. Have a nice lunch." Autumn steeled herself to be strong.

"Hello, Merl, what will it be for you today?" She kept her voice even, no hidden innuendos, a regular customer. *What is he doing here? Why is he here acting like nothing has transpired between us? Or more like everything is fantastic between us?*

"Do I have a choice?" His eyes held hers, commanding her not to dart away.

"Of course you do. Check the menu." She felt breathless.

"What I want isn't on the menu, A.J." His voice was suggestive, hypnotizing. Speaking barely above a whisper, his utterances were for her ears alone. "I was thinking about a little family adventure—you and me, and the baby. Just the three of us. A romantic picnic. You bring the food, and I've got the blanket. I have a weakness for blonde hair and long legs." The familiar smell of his clothes and body rushed over her.

He wasn't making sense. Previously, his disgust of her pregnant state had been terrifying. Was he playing her along? If so, she wasn't falling for it.

"You haven't exactly been a chivalrous suitor, nor a doting father." She tried to appear hard and unmoving.

Merl leaned over the counter. "Hey, A.J., that was for Magnolia's welfare. She falls apart easily. We won't go to the trailer. We'll find a secluded picnic setting out in the country. It's about time I got acquainted with our little princess."

Princess. That was one of her father's pet names for her when she was young. *Was Merl for real? Was God answering her prayers?*

"I'm surprised you even know the baby's a girl."

"Dressed in pink? Of course, she's a girl. And she looks like her mommy." His eyes softly caressed her without a touch.

"I don't think it would be a good idea. Are you placing a lunch order?" Autumn took a step back from the counter, fighting to regain the upper hand.

"Give me a chance," he cajoled. "Just this once. And then, if you don't think I can be a family man, I'll back away." His gaze pleaded. Her resolve fractured.

"I have to work until seven," Autumn conceded.

"I'll be here. You pack us a lunch, and I'll take care of everything else. I promise it will be a memorable night."

Their eyes held until another person waiting in line objected. "Are you going to order or not?"

Obligingly, Merl backed away, saluting Autumn with two fingers, sealing the date. In a daze, Autumn went through the motions of taking and filling orders, but her mind had already fast-forwarded to seven. *It's happening! My prayers are coming true! My guts always told me Merl wanted me, and now Tootsie, too. Thank you, God!*

She had mailed the letter too soon. She could have spared her mom the ugly details and simply gone home for a visit...as a family.

When only a smattering of diners still remained in the enclosed eating area, Marlene wearily shuffled her footsteps to the employee's lounge to collect her belongings and kiss Tootsie good-bye. She'd been on her legs since before 7:00 a.m. having been scheduled for the early shift. It would be a welcome relief to put her feet up on her own hassock.

Seeing her friend's back disappearing down the hallway, Autumn hastened to follow her. Behind the privacy of the closed door, she burst out the news to Marlene. "Guess what!" Not giving her friend a chance to answer, she continued on. "Merl is taking Tootsie and me on an outing after my shift, just the three of us! It's what I've been praying for!" She hugged her motherly confidant, rocking the solid form from side to side.

"Hump!" Marlene didn't share her exuberance. Stepping out of the embrace, she continued, "I saw you conversing with him, and I had my suspicions. I wouldn't trust that man any farther than my nose for the way he has treated you. Have you forgotten how you were trembling under the bedsheets, fearful he'd hurt this precious wee one?" Bending over, Marlene carefully lifted the younglin' from the bassinet. She clucked to her in a motherly fashion, rubbing her nose against the rosy cheek. "No, siree. He doesn't get near you," she assured the youngster.

"He said it was a facade in order not to arouse Magnolia's suspicions," Autumn explained, disconcerted by Marlene's comeback.

"And you're going to believe that toad face? The only decent thing he ever did was to give you this child. It doesn't seem too likely he is suddenly going to become father of the year." Marlene was dogmatic. Her loyalty was to Autumn and her daughter. Merl would have to bulldoze her over to get to them.

Her friend's adversity baffled Autumn. Was she right? Was Merl about to blackmail her holding their child aloft as the bartered goods? But Autumn had prayed about this. This was exactly what she'd petitioned—a husband for herself and a father for their child. What could be wrong? It had to be right.

"So you don't think we should go?" Autumn implored, dropping into a folding chair, the excitement ebbing from her.

"No, I do not. He isn't to be trusted." Marlene continued to oscillate with the baby in her arms.

Autumn pondered Marlene's indictments. "If I don't accept his solicitation, he will for sure kick us out of the trailer, and probably tonight." Autumn was dejected. "What if you're wrong, Marlene? What if he is truly sincere?"

"Then he'd hardly send you packing tonight, would he? He'd put on the old charm, he'd be understanding, admitting his faults, becoming the man you think he is."

Indecision seesawed with the young mother's emotions, her dream falling victim to doubt. Slumped at the table, she ran her fingers through her blonde tendrils, finally grasping two handfuls of the hair, she gritted her teeth. "Grrrr, why does everything in my life have to be hard? Where is my prince charming? Am I forever going to be a Rapunzel shut away in a tower without a prince?"

Sympathetically, Marlene bumped her artillery down a notch. "Maybe my calculations are faulty. I'm just an old woman who doesn't want to see you get hurt anymore than you already have been. How about a compromise?" She lifted the baby's car seat up on the table from its corner storage spot. Rarely was it utilized, since Autumn used the stroller on their jaunts to McDonald's.

"If you're going to volunteer to be a chaperone, I don't think Merl will go for it." Autumn stuck out her tongue.

"Not at all." Marlene slipped the baby under the shoulder straps of the safety seat. "Tootsie spends the night with me, and you and Merl get reacquainted on your own. Deal?"

Autumn's head pricked up. Her chest lifted at the wisdom of the offer. If anything happened to her precious daughter, she would blame herself. However, if Merl desired to have both of them like he said, then he shouldn't object to a romantic picnic with her alone. It could be fun. Let them iron out the wrinkles in their relationship before pushing the baby carriage together.

Her excitement returned, an expectant fluttering within her tummy. Happily, she flew out of the chair, enfolding Marlene into a bear hug for the second time. "You are the best! Thank you, thank you." Then she peered down at her daughter's carefree slumbering face. Softly, she planted a tender kiss on her tiny nose. "I love you, peanut. You be good for Marley."

After helping Marlene with the car seat and diaper bag, Autumn blew kisses until they were lost in the flow of traffic.

Humming a nervous tune, there was an extra spring in her step as she went about her duties of wiping off tables, refilling the condiments, tidying up PlayPlace, and waiting on occasional afternoon customers. Tonight was her chance to show Merl what the two of them could be if united—the Evert and Jasmine Kirmis of Minneapolis. She chuckled out loud at the image.

There'd be no powdering up or sorting through a closet full of outfits, even if she had one; this date would be strictly off-the-cuff. As the clock's hands crawled stiffly to seven o'clock, an electrifying sensitivity had her wound tight. She wondered if Merl was as elated as she was over the prospective rendezvous. A little romantic dazzle would be sweet, but she doubted Merl was the type.

Five minutes before the appointed hour, Merl reentered the establishment, appearing every bit the same as he had six hours earlier, except for the wider circles of sweat ringing his T-shirt armpits. A veil of disappointment dampened Autumn's spirits, who'd been unconsciously hoping he'd come with a bouquet of flowers or a teddy bear for his daughter. When their eyes met, a smile widened his face. Her heart melted; he was elated to see her, and he hadn't kept her waiting, or worse yet, stood her up.

An unaccustomed shyness enveloped her radiant face, her long lashes casting a gentility to her cheeks.

"Hey," he said softly. "Are my girls ready?"

Removing her McDonald's baseball cap, the full length of her naturally blond hair cascaded to her shoulders and below. Merl sucked in his breath at the sight. "You are one seductive lady."

Smiling shyly, her eyes glowed. "I packed us a lunch." She tapped the bags ready to go on the counter.

"Then let's move." He hastily confiscated the paper bags, gesturing with his head for Autumn to precede him.

"I'll get my stuff from the backroom and clock out," she clipped hurriedly.

"Good," he replied. "I'll meet the two of you at the truck."

Fairly flying to the rear lounge, Autumn nervously viewed herself in a small wall mirror, readjusted some hair strands, pinched her cheeks, and flew on. After sliding her card into the machine, she tarried as it punched her out.

Not wanting to keep Merl waiting, aware that patience was not one of his virtues, she ran.

Merl's pickup truck was parked by the front door, the motor idling. Tugging the door open, she couldn't keep her expression from lighting up like a neon sign.

"You forgot the kid." Merl's accusation brought her up short. A look of panic dulled her radiance. She faltered frozen to the sidewalk.

"She's not here. A friend's babysitting. Anyway, the fall evenings are cool. A picnic would be t-too chilly for her," Autumn stammered.

A look of frustration crossed the uneven planes of Merl's face.

"Next time?" Autumn offered timidly, tucking a strand of her golden hair behind her ear.

Merl swallowed and gave in. "Yeah, next time."

When Autumn got in, he reached out an arm, grabbed her around the middle, and slid her forcefully next to his hard side, kissing her fiercely full on the mouth. After releasing her, he shifted the gear stick on the steering column and roared off.

Autumn's knees sat high on the middle hump of the floorboards. Merl looped an arm around her left leg, massaging the muscle below it.

"Let's make this a monumental night," he uttered huskily.

Attached to his side, totally enraptured by her boyfriend's masculinity, Autumn eagerly willed the miles to disappear and transport them to Merl's secluded hideaway in the country. The night was young; their agenda, lengthy.

Not quite, but almost, Autumn could hear the faint notes of Mendelssohn's Wedding March echoing through the candlelit sanctuary of the little white church.

Chapter 33

S ipping a cup of tea on her back porch, Jasmine relished the crisp morning air of autumn warming slowly to an Indian summer day, like a pheasant roasting on a campfire spit. The once-green lawn was camouflaged by the gold and red leaves having relinquished their hold to the branches above. Soon, it would require a rake and a wheelbarrow to tidy up the yard, but for now, she would just enjoy the autumn scene. Above her, the maple and birch canopy was still too full; yardwork would be premature.

A flock of geese soared low over the quiet town, honking a final farewell to the residents. She basked in the sight of flight and the lingering chorus of the wild.

Jasmine was finally at peace with Evert's abrupt departure. Unlike the predictable flight of the birds veering south to their winter homes, he'd left with no warning, no good-bye. She had adjusted to his absence, as hard as it been. She mused at the thought of someday pulling a similar stunt on him when she'd appear in heaven unannounced.

Love was tenderly plucking the strings of her heart anew, creating a fresh enraptured melody within her soul. For months, she had fought the budding feelings within her for Joel Linton and his son, Carson, starving them off, wallowing in her own unworthiness as a parent. On their own, those strings were composing a melodious ballad, coaxing her to love again. God was gifting her with a second chance.

The vibration of her cell phone in an inside pocket brought her out of her reverie.

Jacob.

He always made his Saturday morning calls without fail.

"Hi, honey," Jasmine greeted.

"Hello, Mom, what are you up to?" A controlled stiffness warped Jacob's usual upbeat tone, but Jasmine missed the tightness.

"I'm out on the porch breathing in the fall season. I can almost smell the burnt odor of leaves smoldering and pumpkin pie baking in the oven. I wish you were here. I'd talk you into helping me clean the dried plants out of the garden."

"Save it for another day, and I will." Uneasiness made his words stilted.

"The colors of fall always make me think of Autumn and her scenic name." Jasmine set her empty mug down on the porch floor.

"Actually, Mom, that's why I'm calling."

Jasmine's back went ramrod straight. "You've seen Autumn?"

"Not exactly." He paused, searching for the right words. "Mom, I had a call from the police department this morning."

"What? Has she been arrested?" Suddenly, the vivid fall colors faded to a muted gray.

"No, Mom." Her senses picked up his struggle to convey the message.

"Jacob, is she okay?" Restless, Jasmine stood up and began pacing the length of the small porch. A guttural cry escaped from Jacob's throat. "Jacob, is she hospitalized or...?" She couldn't verbalize the last word of her thought, in case it became factual. Her steps halted, waiting for a response, trepidation banging at her sternum.

An anguished, "Mom," came through the line. Then his voice broke. Jasmine knew the answer before he affirmed it. "Mom, she was found dead." Then her ear was filled with the convulsions of Jacob's weeping.

Dead? Autumn dead? Was the nightmare premiering a second time? She'd already lived through a family member's death. Her dues were paid. Leaning against the pole adjacent to the steps, she felt the familiar enemy of grief settle once more upon her chest, like a smoker's cough—hacking determined to do its damage.

Jasmine had to know the details. "Was it an overdose?" She grasped the cell phone with both hands, pressing it to her ear.

Gaining some control, Jacob relayed the scant information he'd been given. "Her body was found in the early morning hours by a search team, out in the tall grass of an abandoned farmstead." Jacob broke down again and then collected himself. "I was asked to come in and identify her body. I prayed all the way it wouldn't be her…but, Mom…it was."

A gut-wrenching sob overtook Jasmine. Hearing his mother cry, Jacob broke a second time. It was some minutes before her next words reached his ears. "How, Jacob? Tell me what happened. Don't coddle me."

Sniffles preceded his answer, then quietly, he answered, "Strangulation."

Jasmine's back slid down the pole, her jeans hitting the ice-cold step, yet the freezing temperature did not penetrate her senses. Her chest tightened like a jar lid, locking the air from her lungs.

Jacob continued, "She was seen leaving her job at a fast-food restaurant with a man on Thursday. When she didn't show up for work on Friday, her boss first thought she'd overslept. By midmorning, one of the employees went to check her living quarters. It was empty. The police were then notified."

Although they were separated by hundreds of miles, mother and son wept as one, united in pain.

"Mom, there'll be an autopsy. I gave the authorities the name of the Elton funeral home, so they'll handle that. I wanted to tell you in person, but I was afraid the news would beat me home. Just as soon as I hang up, I'm going to arrange to be gone from work for a week, and then I'll hit the road."

Jasmine moaned, yet something inside of her reminded her she was the parent. Jacob had a long solitary drive. He needed to stay focused, not to be worrying about her. Through her swollen throat, she pushed out the words, "Thanks, Jacob. We'll work this out after you get here. You don't have to rush. What's done has been done."

"I know, Mom." He blew his nose. "Mom, you have to promise me something."

"Of course, honey." Her head lay on her arms in her lap, her tears soaking into her sleeves.

"As soon as we disconnect, I want you to call someone to come and be with you. I don't want you to be alone. Will you do that, or do you want me to contact a friend for you?"

That was her Jacob, always thinking of her. "I promise I'll call someone. You take care of you. Get here safely." She gulped. "I love you," the words coming out in a wail.

"I love you, too, Mom." The line went dead.

At first, Jasmine could not move, an iron-cased numbness welding her hostage. A slide show of memories flashed through her conscience depicting Autumn at every stage of her short life. All Jasmine had left was a mental treasure box full of video clips and a stack of photo albums to prove she'd existed. Folding her arms across her chest, she yearned for a different ending.

When she had finally become a Hannah and given Autumn back to the Lord, Jasmine hadn't expected her daughter's life to be terminated by a murderer's hand. Somehow, Jasmine reasoned that because of her unselfish act, Autumn would come back to God and fulfill the glorious plan He had for her. Like Samuel, Autumn would become a servant of the Lord and bring joy to her mother's heart, as her name *Autumn Joy* insinuated. Jasmine had thought redemption, healing, and reunion would be God's road map for her daughter, and for herself.

However, there was no joy in this mother's heart. The ballad she had minutes earlier entertained, was silent. What good had it done to be a Hannah?

Remembering her promise to her son, her finger touched Joel's name on her contact list. He was the friend she'd enlist. Listening to the shrill ring, in her mind, it transformed to the ambulance and police sirens rushing to Autumn's limp body.

Joel's phone vibrated against his chest, underneath his Carhartt jacket. High in the cab of his combine, harvesting his corn crop, Joel's eyes concentrated on the cobs being stripped from their tall standing stalks and falling into the machine. To a farmer, the planting season in the spring and the harvest season in the fall were the two most critical periods of the year. Harvest was the annual paycheck, the crop he worked all year to bring in.

Earlier, he had left Carson off at Ed and Arlene Bautz's farmstead, his retired neighbors. They often helped him out with child care when he was working in his fields. Joel intended to run his machine all day and deep into the night, filling his semitrucks and new grain bins with the yellow kernels. A North Dakotan farmer was always caught in the narrow margin between fair weather and the onslaught of winter, which buried his hard-earned living in a snowbank.

After quickly unzipping his jacket, his hand felt for the phone in his shirt pocket. Jasmine's name lit up. He smiled. Like Glen Campbell's country western song, Jasmine was always gentle on his mind.

"Hello there, sunshine. Are you just crawling out of bed?" he teased, continuing to monitor the harvester as it devoured the stalks before him.

He heard a muffled sob from the other end of the line. Then her request came out high and skinny, in the fewest words possible, yet it conveyed the message. "Joel, I need you. Can you come?" His heart dropped, yet when he spoke, he did so as calmly as possible—for her.

"I'm on my way."

With an urgency, Joel brought the combine to a halt, turned off the key, and ran in great strides toward his semitruck. He'd drive the truck to his yard, switch to his pickup, and tear up the twenty-mile stretch to Elton, not bothering to change out of his field clothes.

A rattle had wavered in Jasmine's feeble murmur. He'd heard it once before and recognized it as the rattle of death.

His corn crop could wait.

For six hours, Joel simply sat holding Jasmine on her living room couch, letting his presence be the only comfort he could offer. He had no words for her. He had never met Autumn, but in his heart, he knew if anything happened to Carson, it would be his undoing. To have suffered the agony of loss once, Joel couldn't stomach the unfathomable thought of being stripped twice. Yet Jasmine had.

Intermittently, Jasmine talked and cried. Sometimes, she seemed content to have Joel's arms instilling strength into her shaking body, and at others, she wriggled free to tread lines in the carpet. They did not call anyone to pass on the news, for Jasmine wasn't emotionally prepared to have her house flooded with the sympathetic eyes of friends mouthing well-meaning but empty phrases of consolation.

Only once did the phone trill. It was Jacob reporting he was on the road. He'd be there by early evening. "And, Mom, a suspect has been arrested and is being held in custody." It made no difference to her. Autumn was already gone.

At Jacob's arrival, Joel backed away. He had met her son last Christmas and again at a gathering over the summer. But Joel was not family. His presence would be uncomfortable for Jacob. After retrieving some items for them at the grocery store and urging them to call if he could be of any more help, Joel pointed his pickup truck back to the farm, holding up the Kirmises in prayer.

Everything that could be done was done. The funeral was scheduled for Wednesday. Grandma Emily and Evert's siblings and families would arrive the day before. Jasmine was off from school indefinitely; Cynthia was updating the substitute teacher. Food and paper articles arrived at their door hourly. Kindhearted neighbors raked and bagged the leaves in the backyard while Jasmine and Jacob were at the funeral home making arrangements and ordering flowers for the casket. Pastor Harke met with them to formulate the service.

Jacob and Jasmine now lingered in the interval of *waiting*, the space in time where life comes to a standstill. There was no going ahead, and the past was unreachable. Waiting was all there was left to do, to watch the hour hand procrastinate its pitiful progression. Nights and days blended into one sleepless marathon.

On Monday, Jacob came in from emptying the mailbox attached to the front of the house, a thick bundle of cards in his hands. Using a letter opener, Jasmine sliced open two of them, but the kind handwritten notes inside only brought a fresh deluge of tears to her already swollen face. Jacob suggested they put the cards away until a later date. She agreed.

In contrast to the preceding days, the actual day of the funeral sped into double time. The house was full of relatives staying overnight, the church was packed with community support. A steady stream of kisses and hugs kept Jasmine occupied, her tears at bay.

Autumn's body was laid to rest in the plot to the left of Evert's in the country cemetery west of Prairie City. An abundance of colored leaves continued to float a spiral descent during the burial, adorning the grave of their namesake.

The house emptied again on Thursday, leaving Jasmine and Jacob in solitude. They took meandering walks together, reminiscing and grieving all mixed into one.

More details from the murder had filtered in. The man in custody was Merlin Myrhe, a suspected drug dealer. Autumn had been living with him for almost a year, but the autopsy had not detected any drugs in her system. Another female roommate wasn't listed as an accomplice to the crime. A Minneapolis newspaper stated that a fellow McDonald's employee had tried to persuade Autumn not to leave with Merlin on the fated night. It seemed the suspect and Autumn had an intimate relationship. The homicide may have been a result of a domestic violence incident.

Jasmine cringed at the reports broadcast on the news and printed in the papers, reckoning everyone in the two adjoining states was supplied with as much information as they had about Autumn's death. Nothing was private. Similar to the public viewing, her life was laid out in the open for all to fabricate an opinion on. Jasmine shuddered.

In some respects, the manner in which Autumn died bothered Jasmine more than her actual death, for Autumn had left her mother long before her lifeless body was discovered. Five years ago, Autumn had purposefully excommunicated herself from her mother and brother by moving unannounced to Minneapolis. Yet, even prior to her disappearance, she had stepped out of the family circle, maybe not physically, yet willfully staying outside of her mother's reach.

Jasmine's grief for her husband and daughter had begun simultaneously. She grieved for the adult relationship she would never have with Autumn.

Both mother and son were dreading their last farewell when on Sunday, Jacob would have to head back to his job. It would be a reenactment of the days following his father's death, except then, there had been three family members to share adieus.

Unbeknownst to Jasmine, Joel had contacted Jacob earlier, arranging a departure hour. As soon as Jacob and Jasmine had said their good-byes, Joel would be there to take over, not wanting Jasmine to be left crying on the sidewalk alone.

Neither mother or son could keep up a front as they stood outside his loaded car. Wrapped in each others arms, the tears splashed on the floor of their hearts, hating to be severed from each other. "Mom, if I never thanked you and Dad for choosing me to be a part of your family, I'm doing it now. I love you with all my heart." Then not lingering, he jumped into his vehicle. Backing out of the driveway, he blew her kisses, promising to keep in touch. As he straightened the steering wheel out on the street, Joel's pickup truck pulled up along side of his. Lowering the electric window, Joel stuck out an arm. Jacob did the same, grasping the hand of his mom's friend.

"You take care, Jacob. You have made your mom very proud," Joel spoke sincerely, his eyes steady on Jacob's misted pupils.

Swallowing, Jacob tightened his hold on the older man's strong handshake. "Will you take care of her for me? I know she's crazy about you."

Joel nodded. "I'll do that son. I'm crazy about her too."

Jacob pressed his top lip over the bottom one to keep from bawling.

"If you ever need a man to talk to, Jacob, I'd be proud to be that man." Joel gave the hand one last squeeze and let go. Jacob raised a hand and rolled past.

Jasmine viewed the scene from the walkway in front of her house. She didn't hear the words; however, she witnessed the handshake. She wasn't alone, she had two good men, and the Lord, standing by her.

Joel's truck parked in the driveway vacated by Jacob. "Ma'am," he said through the open window, "would you give me the pleasure of accompanying me on a country drive?"

Her eyes glistened from the wetness, yet her smile glistened from the solace the sight of her friend brought her.

"Only if it is a very, very long drive," she replied, her green eyes mesmerized by the sunlight in his gray ones.

"I think I can oblige." Smiling warmly, he opened the door and let her slide in beside him.

Chapter 34

Eyeing the wicker basket, which was stuffed to the brim with condolence cards, Jasmine contemplated, *Should I?*

Determination set her jaw. *Yes, I can do this.*

After pulling a hooded sweatshirt over her head, she took up the basket and found sanctuary on the couch of the back porch. Although the leaves had been raked off of the frost-pricked grass tops once, a fresh layering of the multicolored blanket had sifted down, spreading autumn's touch everywhere. Jasmine set the basket on a side table and ventured out into the dry rustling leaves, a sound she had always loved.

Scarlet maple leaves laced with serrated edges lay at her feet, symmetrical shapes of beauty. Sinking to her haunches, she reached out to retrieve a handful of the season's jewels, which were free for the taking. She smoothed them out on her bent thigh. As an idea took shape within her, she reached for the golden paper birch leaves of nature's storehouse as well. She would dry the leaves between pages of a book and then frame them into a collage, forever remembering the wonder of her Autumn.

Caught up in the venture, she soon had collected a few dozen specimens. Retracing her steps to the kitchen, she found some dated magazines. Carefully, she filed the red and yellow leaves between the magazine pages, adding books to provide more weight upon the top. Satisfied with her preliminary workmanship, she once more resolved to read the notes sent to her by sympathetic friends.

Crossing a leg underneath her, she sank back into the cushions of the porch lounger. Gingerly, she selected a card, tore open the envelope, and read the contents. Then another, and another. Delightful anecdotes of Autumn paraded before her; friends and acquaintance recalled incidents of the young gal with the golden hair—the time she brought a salamander for show-and-tell in second grade, Autumn showing off her artistic talents in the chalk pictures drawn on the neighborhood sidewalks, the piano solo she played at the nursing home, the window she'd broken trying to prove she could hit a baseball. Sometimes, Jasmine found herself laughing; over other cards, she cried, tugging tissues from a box at her elbow. Some of the stories she remembered, others were brand-new.

The shadows across the backyard mural of leaves shortened as the midday sun rose high into the sky and then lengthened as it began its downhill descent.

Only a handful of letters remained in the basket when she selected the long narrow envelope. Its elongated shape resembled a business letter more than a sympathy card. Something about the penmanship seemed familiar, but the absence of a return address gave no clue. She held the envelope up closer for inspection. The postmark was smeared, maybe an "MN." Slipping a fingernail under the flap, she slid her nail along the full length of the letter. Her fingers pulled out an ordinary piece of folded notebook paper, its fringed edge a telltale sign that it had been ripped from a spiral notebook.

Curiously, she unfolded the sheet then sucked in her breath, her spine stiffening, In panic, she stared at the lines of script, which was a combination of printing and cursive. She now recognized the penmanship as Autumn's. She let the paper fall through her fingers, as if it was hot to the touch, lightly floating to the pile of envelopes spilling off the couch.

How?

Why?

This couldn't be possible. Her heart thudded loudly. Painstakingly, she reached out, snagging the paper back into her lap. A letter from the dead? Unfathomable.

Seeking to understand, she read the date at the top—October 16, the day before Autumn had died. After all these years, could Autumn have actually decided to write her mother on the eve of her death? Jasmine's gaze sought the branches overhead, now barren and skeletal.

Closing her eyes, she prayed. *Lord, should I read it, or will its words cut too deep?* The banging in her chest dulled, a peace prevailed.

Holding the letter up, she began to read.

Dear Mom,

It has been a long time, too long. I'm sorry about that. Life seems to get in the way of what should be done.

I want you to know I'm doing okay. I have a job and two roommates here in Minneapolis. Rent is high.

There's two things I want to share with you—hopefully, both will excite you.

On my way to work, there is a church replica of Grandpa and Grandma's country church, white siding and even a steeple. It has been a daily reminder of home, especially when the bell peals.

One Sunday morning, I felt compelled to go inside. It was a vivid flashback of my past, of what I took for granted: you and Dad, Jacob, too, the faith you exemplified, the love you put into action. Hey, you took me in, right? I wasn't an easy kid to raise. I feel bad about that and for blaming you for Dad's accident. I've always known it wasn't your fault, I just wanted someone to blame. But it didn't stop the hurting.

Anyway, at the Sunday service, I rededicated my life to the Lord. I hadn't planned on doing it, but when I hit that bench, He got a hold of me. I've kind of messed up things on my own. I have a long ways to go, but my focal point is turning. Thank you for pointing me in the right direction when I was just a snot nosed kid.

There's some things I still have to work through. It's hard to give it all up at once. Pray for me.

Jasmine looked up from the letter, back to the blue sky distinguishable between the naked branches of the tree limbs. The Lord had had His eye on Autumn all along. Who would have thought He would plant an old-fashioned wooden church in the center of the big city to draw her back to Himself? Who would have thought He would direct her to finally communicate with her mom, unknowingly giving a last farewell? Sitting here on the back porch, Jasmine felt so small, so insignificant in the vast universe—and yet God saw fit to send her one last message from her precious daughter. Her eyes closed in repentance for striking out at the Lord, for second guessing His ways.

Refocusing on the letter through blurred vision, she found her place and continued to read.

The second item is kind of hard to write in black and white. You will be disappointed, yet hopefully at the same time, happy.

You are a grandma to a baby girl born August 5th, a beautiful baby. You will probably say she looks like me when I was a baby—golden hair and green eyes. Healthy.

I love her so much. I've never felt like this before. I think you'd say I'm a good mom—eating right, holding and cuddling her, bathing and feeding her.

A baby. Jasmine cherished the first day she and Evert had held Autumn—the golden ringlets, the jade eyes. How her heart within had soared. Yes, Autumn, I experienced that same happiness when I was given you.

> I'm living with her father—hopefully we'll soon be married, maybe in the little white church. I want our daughter to have the sort of parents you and Dad were to me and Jacob.
>
> As I've said, I'm sorting things out. I'm not ready to come for a visit yet, but maybe soon. I want to introduce my daughter to her grandmother and good old North Dakota.
>
> I do love you. Forgive me for being such a pain.
>
> A.J.
> Autumn

Oh, Autumn, I forgive you. Forgive me because I too was such a *pain.* Tiny teardrops fringed her eyelashes.

A.J.?

You will always be Autumn to me.

PS: Your granddaughter's name is Hannah Joy.

Hannah Joy? She tried the name, letting it roll off her tongue—Hannah Joy. This time in utter unabashed rapture, the rain clouds of heaven opened, sending a torrential downpour cascading over the fullness of her cheeks, splashing on the floor of her grandmother's heart, gurgling in the sweet sounds made from a baby's tiny tongue. How could there be joy amidst so much pain?

When the tumult subsided and the raging rivers were once again within the boundaries of the banks, Jasmine's thoughts scrambled to set in motion the legalities of finding Hannah and bringing her home. Somewhere out there, her granddaughter was waiting—waiting for the arms of her grandmother.

Carefully, she freed herself from the mass of cards and envelopes covering her lap and slipped inside. Googling Minnesota social services would be a starting point. She fished a pencil and pad of paper from the desk drawer below her office computer and went in search of Hannah Joy.

Rrrring. Rrrring.

Biting on a wooden pencil as she typed, Jasmine was frustrated by the interruption of the reverberating phone on her kitchen wall.

Rrrring. Rrrring. Jacob invariably called her cell phone, so it wouldn't be him checking in on her. She was tempted to ignore its summons, but what if it was Joel?

Quickly, she pushed the chair backward and hopped up, trotting down the hallway to the kitchen.

"Hello."

An unfamiliar voice spoke into her ear. "Hello, this is Sadie Robins with the Minnesota Department of Human Services. I am looking for Jasmine Kirmis."

"This is she." The call was unexpected.

"Jasmine, a baby has been brought to our offices. We believe she is the biological child of your daughter, Autumn Kirmis. Does this sound reasonable?"

"Yes." Realizing what this call meant, Jasmine was more forceful. "Yes!" Her eyes widened as she listened.

"My condolences to you on the passing of your daughter, ma'am. A few days ago, the child was brought to our attention by a friend of your daughter's and has been placed in a temporary foster home. Since our reports show that the birth father is being held as a possible suspect in a legal case, he is denied guardianship at this time. If a suitable and willing relative can be found, the child can be released to the relative's care. We are asking your help in determining if there is such a home available."

Jasmine couldn't believe this was happening. "Yes—yes, I want my granddaughter! Tell me what to do to get her."

"That is wonderful. There is extensive paperwork to do to bring this to completion. Would you like me to drop the forms in the mail, or would fax or e-mail be better?

"Oh, please e-mail them, and I will fill them out immediately." Fireworks were exploding inside of her.

"You should have them at your fingertips in minutes. I'll be in touch as soon as you have sent them back to me."

"Ms. Robins?"

"Yes?"

"My granddaughter's name is Hannah Joy."

Jasmine had been *a* Hannah, and now she would receive Autumn's Hannah. It was miraculous. It was a God thing.

Autumn's sweet eleven-month baby face smiled out of the photographer's frame sitting on the dresser of what was now Hannah's nursery. Rocking her granddaughter, Jasmine stared at the photo and then at Hannah, who was nestled into the crook of her arm, comparing the mother's baby picture with her daughter. The resemblance was remarkably distinct. Besides the hair and eye coloring, Hannah shared her mother's heart-shaped face, the faint cleft in the chin, and the pursed upper lip. Almost like twins—separated by over two decades.

An ivory crib stood next to her rocker, reminiscent of those used for Autumn. Joel had helped her dismantle the full-size bed and replace it with the baby furniture. With Hannah's expectant arrival, Jasmine had first considered repainting the walls of the spare bedroom into hues that are more baby-friendly, but Hannah had arrived more quickly than her paint and brushes could do the transformation.

Hannah gurgled in her sleep, stretched her mouth into an elongated yawn, then settled back into a deep slumber.

She'd had a big trip. Two social workers had driven from Minneapolis to Elton, arriving in the early afternoon to deposit their fragile cargo. After getting the granddaughter situated in her grandmother's home and completing some final paperwork, they had left. Jasmine felt like a new mom, learning all over again how to mix formula, to burp after every few ounces, and to apply salve to the baby's bottom before changing into a fresh diaper.

However, Hannah fit perfectly into the space hollowed out by her bent elbow. Jasmine was content to sit and rock for hours if Hannah concurred.

Leaning her head back to rest on the high back of the rocker, her eyes lost themselves in the star-spangled firmament overlaying the ceiling; it was the one remodeling adjustment she'd given the room, only these were white stick-on fluorescent stars she'd found at the local Ben Franklin store. She thought Autumn would approve.

Jasmine wished she'd be able to roll back the years and regain the close mother-and-daughter link they'd had when Autumn first became theirs. Staring into Hannah's bitty face, it was as if she was observing Autumn's flushed cheeks and button nose.

The social workers told her about Autumn's friend, Marlene Modder, who had kept the baby overnight on the last day of Autumn's life and for a few succeeding nights. Had she not intervened, it was highly likely Hannah would have died with her mother. Jasmine shuddered and closed her eyes in utmost gratitude.

Marlene had sent a manila envelope of photos she'd taken of Hannah and Autumn together and had written Jasmine a letter describing the devotion Autumn demonstrated toward her child. The letter further explained the baby's chosen name. *Hannah* was in honor of her biological mother who had given her up as a baby. *Joy* was for the happiness she had brought into the home of her real parents, Evert and Jasmine.

Jasmine felt a kinship with the birth mom, for she too had relinquished Autumn, not as a baby, but as a twenty-two-year-old.

After Autumn's death, Jasmine had been silently critical of God. Although she had not vehemently railed against Him, she hadn't expected her daughter to die such a horrible death. Why hadn't He intervened? Yet when all the pieces were fitted into the puzzle, she could see God's presence had always been there, wooing Autumn unto Himself.

Back as a freshman in college, the Lord had given her Jeneen Andrews for a roommate. She'd been a gem of a gal, a girl after His own heart; she had accepted Autumn's rough edges without complaining. After taking off for Minneapolis, God had always provided a shelter for her physical needs. And remarkably, He'd set a little white church in the neighborhood a half century before Autumn moved there, preparing in advance for her rededication to Him. This very minute, she and her dad could be conversing in heaven. And then there was Marlene, an angel attired in a McDonald's shirt, who swooped in and saved baby Hannah at the last hour.

Jasmine was humbled by the way God's hand had worked behind the scenes. He'd always been there, waiting. Ultimately, it was Autumn who made her own choices—some correct, others off course.

This was Jasmine's second chance, maybe not with Autumn, but with her daughter, Hannah. Yet the thought of parenting this little one by herself caused a ripple of apprehension, a nervous twitter in her stomach. Could she do it?

There was a light tap on the outside door, which she identified as Joel's. She had told him if she didn't answer, to let himself in, for she might be occupied with her new granddaughter.

His shape filled the nursery door; he gazed upon the woman he loved, holding the baby girl she'd been gifted through tragedy. Never had she appeared more radiant, the crease lines gone from her forehead, her eyes glowing with affection.

Joel pulled up a chair close enough for his knees to touch hers, letting his heart be filled until it spilled over, inhaling the sight of God's miraculous plan for this innocent baby.

Raising his head, he stared into Jasmine's deep green eyes, drinking in her profound gratitude at having been blessed so unconditionally. He pronounced the same benediction. Life took away and then bequeathed back again. It had happened to him also.

Jasmine's lips moved, her eyes wistful. "Joel, I don't know if I can be a single mom again. I struggled with Autumn." A mist dropped a veil over her eyes.

He lifted his hand to cover hers, resting lightly on the baby. "Then let me help you. I thought when Melissa died, my heart had shut its doors forever, but then Carson came, and I found love I never thought I had.

"And then I met you. I chanced to consider whether I had any love left in this old heart. I've found that when God created love, He made the heart profoundly deep. Love never runs out.

"I love you, Jasmine Kirmis. Please say you'll be my wife, along with being Hannah and Carson's mother. We're a package deal."

His chest ached waiting for her answer. He watched the shifting shades move across her face.

Tears dug furrows down Jasmine's cheeks. "I've also discovered there's no end to tears." She smiled through the glistening shower. "But these are happy tears. I love you, Joel, and I am ready to become your wife."

Their lips met in an arch over baby Hannah who slept on, totally oblivious of the promises of love enfolding her on every side.

Epilogue

The Christmas holidays were a mingle of sorrow and happiness, of tears and smiles—maybe the way God felt when He sent his holy infant Son down to an imperfect earth. Late sympathy cards intermixed with the early yuletide greeting cards in Jasmine's mailbox. The "red princess" philodendron plant given to the family as a memorial for Autumn vied for attention with the miniature tabletop evergreen tree shimmering with white lights. Brushing wayward droplets off her cheeks, Jasmine's lips tenderly curved upward as she reached for her granddaughter in the crib. Love and grief had somehow developed a companionable friendship.

Joel and Jasmine were united in marriage during a small simple ceremony held amongst the pine boughs and poinsettias adorning the church.

Cynthia Burns and baby Hannah stood up for Jasmine, Cynthia carrying the pink bundle to their designated spot on the side of the platform. Kevin sat in the second row holding their grandson Justin; Katie and Stephen were next to him.

Proudly, Jacob walked his mother down the aisle as Joel and Carson waited at the front of the church. Releasing his mom's arm to Joel, Jacob took up his place beside Carson, the two about to become brothers. Feeling left out of the family circle so far removed in Minneapolis, Jacob put in for a transfer to a sister bank in Bismarck, moving him hours closer to the Linton farm, where Jasmine and Hannah would now reside. Joel and Carson intended to teach Jacob everything he needed to know in order to be a weekend farmer.

Jasmine resigned from her teaching position to become a stay-at-home mother to Hannah and Carson, and of course, to Jacob on weekends. The Linton home had emptied but was now being filled up; all the bedrooms were occupied. Just maybe, Jasmine would have some spare minutes to pen another novel, but her first obligation was to Joel.

"To love and to cherish from this day forward until death do us part."

It was Jacob who later made the connection as he reread the letter Autumn had written to their mother. "Autumn wanted Hannah to have the sort of parents she had. Her wish has come true."

Jasmine and Joel have lived long enough to know there are no promises to a happily-ever-after future. The road of life is filled with potholes, roadkill, dips, icy spots, slush, and road construction. Taking Jasmine's hand and squeezing gently, Joel quietly assured her, "When those roadblocks pop up, we'll remind each other *to be a Hannah*, and give it to the Lord."